The Titanic's Mummy

By

David J H Smith

Happy Birthday Morten

David Smith

FIRST EDITION

iii

Paige Croft Publishing, Yeovil, Somerset

David J H Smith asserts the moral right to be identified as the author of this work

A catalogue record for this book is available from the British Library

Cover art 'The Mummy's Descent' by Dom Richards

First Edition – 2011

Published by Paige Croft Publishing

ISBN – 978-0-9568305-0-0

www.thetitanicsmummy.com

Printed and bound in England by
CPI Antony Rowe, Chippenham and Eastbourne

The Titanic's Mummy

About the author

David J H Smith was originally from Slough, Berkshire but is now living in Somerset.

He graduated from Thames Valley University with an Honours Degree in History & Geography before going on to study History at Post Graduate level at Westminster University.

Although working in various jobs such as Immigration Officer, Retail Manager, Facilities Officer and IT, his overriding passion is for writing and the publication of this book sees fulfilment of a lifelong dream to see his work in print.

CHAPTER 1

Professor Charles Montacute impatiently paced up and down the guest room. He glanced across at his travel clock, carefully positioned on the bedside table, by the still perfectly made bed, which indicated it was a fraction before midnight. He nodded to himself, happy at the thought that by now, all the staff, the rest of the guests, along with Rainsbury Hall's owners, Thomas and Jennifer, would most likely be asleep, while Jazmine would be in position waiting for him. The weekend party had been arranged by Thomas himself to celebrate Easter. He, along with eight other guests, had been invited up for a relaxing weekend of country walks, shooting, fishing and fine dining.

This fitted in perfectly with his plans.

He stopped and caught himself in the full length mirror that was in one corner of the room. His image always surprised him. He seemed to forget that he was approaching his mid fifties. He felt no different to when he was thirty or for that matter when he was twenty. He was just under six foot, dressed in brown shoes, tweed casual trousers, a white collarless shirt, with the sleeves rolled up to the elbow and braces partially covered by a tweed waistcoat. His full head of hair was white, matching his neatly trimmed beard, and he wore metal framed glasses. Despite his age he was fit and athletic, not quite as athletic as he had once been, but he seemed happy with his present state, especially considering the punishment his body had taken over the years. For some being a historian was a peaceful experience: lectures, seminars, endless study in the library, the writing of papers, and book contributions. Charles Montacute, however, took a different viewpoint. He saw the need to take historical knowledge and act practically upon it, to improve the present and set right ills of the past. It was a philosophy which had caused him to travel the world and had led to a number of strange and terrifying adventures.

Moving away from the mirror he turned his attention to the travel chess board that he had placed on the table earlier. Five pieces stood on the board: three white; King, Rook and Knight, opposing two black; the King and Queen. This was not a game, but a set puzzle. White to mate in two moves, he looked at the board, then shook his head and moved away. The puzzle would not normally elude him for long, but tonight was different, for tonight his mind was preoccupied with other things.

Again he looked at the clock.

12.01 am.

Moving over to the bed, he picked up a pair of thin brown leather gloves and put them on before making his way over to the door, which he opened, and stepped out onto the landing.

All was quiet; there was no sign of life. Cautiously he moved towards the main staircase where he silently descended. This was going to be a difficult undertaking. Above all he must not be caught. He was a friend of the Rainsburys, he had been so for years, and being found stealing from them would instantly end their friendship, as well as cause a scandal, which would no doubt end his career and could even result in a prison sentence. Even with his silver tongue he would not be able to talk his way out of being caught with his hands in the safe. But then again, there were some risks that just had to be taken.

Reaching the ground floor he made his way over to the study door. He was about to try the handle when he thought he heard movement from within. Carefully he placed his ear against the wooden panel and listened. There was a crash, a smash, someone was inside!

2

He slowly turned the handle. It was locked. Bending down to look through the keyhole his vision was blocked by the key. Whoever was inside had not removed it after locking themselves in; a fortuitous error. Standing up he looked around. On a hall side table nearby there was a discarded newspaper. He took it and, opening it out, slid the sheets underneath the door. Then from his waistcoat he took out his pocket knife, opened it and placed the blade into the keyhole. After a few moments of movement there was the sound of the key landing on the paper the other side.

He paused and waited, as he put the knife away. Had whoever was in the study heard it? No, nothing. Except the occasional clunking and muffled crashing sound of a clandestine search. Slowly he pulled the newspaper towards him and the key came along with it under the door. Grabbing it he stood up, returned the paper to the table and then placed the key in the lock, turning it until there was a satisfying sound of the lock being released. He slowly turned the handle and opened the door slightly.

Peering through the gap, he could see inside Thomas Rainsbury's private study and library, which was partially illuminated by the night's full moon streaming in through the window. The first thing that caught his attention was straight ahead of him over on the far wall. An entire section of the large bookcase had been moved outward into the room like a door; beyond it was an open gap. Whoever was here had managed to gain access via a secret passage. The next thing he noticed was the state of the room itself, papers were strewn everywhere, books lay all over the floor, there was an upturned table and many Egyptian artefacts scattered around. Thomas Rainsbury had one of the best private collections in the country. It was a wonder that a robbery had not taken place long before. However, he had a feeling that the cause of this raid was one particular object; a black scarab beetle on a gold chain; the object that he too had set out to acquire by whatever means.

Carefully the Professor looked around further into the room. On the far right, hidden by the open door was a figure, with his back towards him. By the figure, discarded on the floor, there was a framed papyrus covered in Egyptian Hieroglyphs. Charles knew this was used to cover the safe. The thief was six foot tall, broad, wearing a long brown coat which went down to the floor and a matching wide brimmed hat. Slung over his shoulder was a leather satchel, filled with bulges which Charles presumed was some of Thomas's collection.

The Professor stared for a moment, he knew who this person was all too well and had encountered him before; he knew that what was to come would not be pleasant.

Still half hidden by the open door, he turned to his immediate left and to the wall display which was adorned with edged and blunt weapons of all descriptions from down the ages. He selected a Samurai Katana sword that was mounted unsheathed on a stand although he knew that it would not afford him much protection. Carefully the Professor edged into the room so he was directly behind the intruder who was totally unaware that he was here, absorbed by his efforts to open the safe.

"Of course, you would find it a lot easier if you had the combination. Perhaps try using a stick of dynamite?"

The thief swung around instantly.

Even though Professor Montacute was expecting the sight that greeted him, he still instinctively stepped back at what he was faced with, for underneath the open coat and hat, the figure was wrapped head to toe in old yellowing bandages with two eyes glowing red.

The Mummy let out a low moan and started to advance.

Changing his strategy slightly, the Professor quickly stooped down and picked up a fallen statue and hurled it at the Mummy, who dodged it with surprising speed and dexterity for a creature so long dead.

The creature then extended his right arm. From it a stream of bandage flew out and wrapped itself around the Professor's hand that was holding the Katana. The Mummy then tried to pull the Professor off balance, but the old man was quicker and turned the sword downwards cutting through the bond. Before the ancient creature had time to react, the old man rushed forward and thrust the sword as hard as he could into the Mummy's chest, but the creature remained standing and unharmed. For a moment the Professor was able to stare directly into the creature's brilliant red glowing eyes, almost totally obscured by the ancient wrappings. Then the Mummy struck, picking him up by the throat and throwing him backwards across the room. He landed badly, hitting his head on the corner of the large desk on his way to the floor. He yelled out in pain and fought to stay conscious. The Mummy, totally unharmed, pulled the sword free and held it up while the Professor, dazed, scrambled backwards away as far and as fast as he could trying to put as much distance between himself and the advancing creature. His hand brushed upon a discarded book, and instantly an idea came to him. From his pocket he produced a book of matches, struck three and set the pages alight. He stood up and thrust it out at the Mummy, who, despite having the sword, instantly started to retreat. The creature then seemingly decided not to chance being turned into a fireball, lifted the sword with both hands and threw it forward, but the Professor seeing the intended attack was able to move, and the sword sailed past him missing his head by inches. The Mummy, his attack and his attempt on the safe thwarted, let out another roar before heading back towards the secret passage.

The Professor dropped the book and stamped on the flames to put them out, so as not to set the whole room ablaze; then, still confused, he stumbled over to the safe. He had memorised the combination, acquired through devious means, and armed with this information started to turn the dial.

Forty five – left.

Sixty three – right.

Thirty eight – left.

Sixty seven – right.

He turned the handle.

Nothing.

He tried again, his head still spinning and eyes not fully focused on his task.

Again nothing, the handle stayed firmly in place.

Shaking his head, he abandoned the attempt, heading over to the passageway. Logic dictated that he should persist opening the safe, retrieve the scarab and go, but there was an overwhelming, almost insane urge to continue after the Mummy. So he ran over to the open bookcase and ventured into the passageway.

CHAPTER 2

Richard Mallory sat in the busy, and possibly one of the roughest of public houses in the East End of London, The Three Crowns, trying his utmost to look inconspicuous. He sat hunched over what passed for beer, doing his very best not to look up and catch anyone's eye. However, he was becoming acutely aware of the number of glances that were being directed his way. Strangers stood out like a sore thumb here and were not welcome. Pretending to take a sip of the warm brown liquid, he cursed Alfie for choosing such a place to meet. Why couldn't he have chosen a park, a coffee house, or even just a well picked spot in the street? Mallory was dressed in old clothes, which hid his athletic build. His normally well combed hair was ruffled and he wore a five o'clock shadow around his face. He was trying to pass himself off as a labourer. He thought that he had done a good job too, but the locals seemed to see right through his disguise. He prayed they did not think that he was a constable and decide to confront him; otherwise things would turn very nasty. Without warning Alfie appeared from nowhere and sat at the empty seat opposite him. Mallory looked the man over. He was a short, almost rat like figure, and was very nervous. Hardly surprising, he was out of his league in this impending transaction. Alfie was a very small fish, trying to make a big deal in a large pond.

"Alfie, you have kept me waiting for nearly an hour."

"I'm sorry. I had some trouble getting away."

Mallory ignored the excuse; he wanted to get this over with and out of here as soon as possible. "Have you got it?"

Alfie smiled and reached into his pocket and pulled out a handkerchief, which he opened to reveal a diamond necklace within. Mallory recognised it instantly from the picture he had seen some days before. It was the necklace that had been stolen six months earlier in a robbery at a jeweller's in Kensington. Alfie then quickly wrapped it up and returned it to his pocket, checking that no one had seen him.

"No good," said Mallory, "I need to look at it properly. I'm not handing over any money before I know that it is real and not some……"

Suddenly, Mallory found himself being hauled backwards out of his chair by two rough looking men; one on each of his arms. Two more men appeared and grabbed a startled Alfie.

"Get your hands off me!" Mallory yelled as he struggled against his two captors, but it was no good, their grip was too strong and there was no way he was going to get free.

"Fat chance!" growled one of the thugs in a broad London accent. "You are coming with us, matey. A very serious word is required!"

Mallory tried to lash out with his elbows, but all he found was thin air. In front of him there was a frantic scream as Alfie was being dragged off in the opposite direction.

"Let me go," cried Mallory, "or I'll…."

"Or you'll what, sonny?" snarled one of the thugs, releasing his grip enough to dispense a subduing punch to the stomach. Mallory yelled out, winded, and caught a glimpse of the pub's patrons, staring at him and smiling. Something told him that there was not going to be a bystander jumping to his defence, nor anyone going to summon a constable.

The two thugs dragged Mallory round the bar to a door which took them to a small narrow staircase. He was manhandled up these, before being thrust through another door into the private sitting room of the pub, where he then found himself being deposited on a wooden chair and was quickly and efficiently searched. The thugs remained by his side, holding him firmly down as he tried to stand, but they were too strong, even for him, and he found himself being pushed down into the wooden seat. "Sit still! We can do this the easy way or the hard way!"

Mallory, realising there was nothing he could do, stopped his efforts, the thugs loosened their grip.

"So what are we waiting for?"

"Christmas!" barked one of the thugs. "Now, shut up! Another word and I'll wallop you again."

Mallory did as he was told; he wanted to see where this was going. It was clear that he was wanted alive otherwise he would already be dead. He noted that across the room was a window. If he got desperate, really desperate, he could use it as a means of escape.

8

Without warning the door to the room opened and in walked a well dressed man in his forties. "Captain Richard Mallory!" said the man as he moved to stand in front of Mallory.

"It's just Richard Mallory now. My army days are over."

The man shook his head. "Once an army man always an army man. You may think that you can shed that yolk but you cannot. I bet that you still wake in the early hours, are meticulously neat and tidy and of course still have your service revolver."

Mallory ignored the comments, even though they were all true. "Do I know you from somewhere?"

The man laughed. "Fortunately for you, no, for if you did you would already be dead. No all we had in common was our late mutual acquaintance, Alfred Roberts."

"Late?" asked Mallory worriedly.

"Yes, it seemed that the knife between his ribs disagreed with him." This made the two thugs laugh. "No doubt the Thames will eventually give up his body. He won't be missed. I doubt he will even be identified."

Mallory looked over at the window - it was seemingly becoming his best option. "This is all very cosy, but is there a point to all this? You obviously want something or you would not have gone to the trouble of bringing me up here."

The man looked at Mallory, and then from his pocket he produced the handkerchief containing the diamond necklace. Mallory noticed that the white cloth was now stained with fresh blood. The man took the necklace and held it up. "Richard, let me be frank with you. I am in a position where I need funds urgently and my usual sources are no longer willing to oblige." The man nodded and the two thugs released their grip. "I understand that there is still a reward outstanding for the recovery of this item and that you might be in a position to make a deal."

Mallory shook his head. "That's not how it works. You cannot steal something then expect to sell it back."

"Ah, but that is the beauty of the situation," said the mysterious man smiling. "We did not carry out the original robbery."

Mallory shook his head. "Are you going to try and blame Alfie for the theft?"

The man shook his head. "No, not at all! My people managed to," he paused trying to find the right words, *"recover it*, from a certain East End family. Our friend Alfie then stole it from me, well you know the rest."

Mallory nodded. 'An East End family.' That narrowed it down to three possibilities. "You knew that he was going to try and sell it to me, so you followed and disposed of him and now you want to make the deal yourself."

The man smiled. "Something like that, yes." He then threw Richard the necklace. He caught it and looked it over. It was one of the most beautiful pieces that he had ever seen.

"Well, do we have a deal?"

Mallory looked up and nodded, he then threw the necklace back at the stranger. He knew full well that he would not be allowed to take it with him. "I will have to speak with my people to make the necessary arrangements, they should agree, but there is a chance that they won't. In cases such as this we normally meet for a formal exchange. Four days time, ten o'clock in St Ethelbert's?"

The man nodded, happy with the arrangement.

Mallory stood. "I have to reiterate sometimes the company I work for decides that they will not pay. There is no rhyme or reason for it and it is a decision that is out of my hands. That is the chance you have to take."

Again the man nodded. "I am sure that you will do your best. My colleagues will show you out. I have had a word with the proprietor of this establishment. There is a fresh drink waiting for you, to show that there are no hard feelings and to make up for your earlier rough treatment."

Mallory looked to his left and right at the thugs who were now giving him a friendly smile. One even patted him on the shoulder as though he were a life long friend. Mallory ignored this. He was angry, but also secretly relieved that he was going to leave intact by the front door rather than by having to throw himself out of the window. The two thugs escorted him down to the pub. As they entered the bar area the patrons fell into silence and looked at them. On the bar, as promised, was a fresh drink. The barman nodded towards it to indicate that it was his for the taking, but Mallory ignored it, and instead headed directly for the main door, still flanked by the two thugs. At the door one of his captors opened it for him, while the other, the one who had punched him, held out his hand. "No 'ard feelings mate eh? Shake."

Mallory looked at the outstretched hand, then with his left hand parried it away, while with the right, punched the thug in the stomach. The man fell to his knees, winded. Mallory looked over at the other thug at the door half expecting a response, but there was none. Gasping for air the first thug looked up at Mallory and nodded. "Guess I deserved that didn't I?"

Mallory nodded curtly and turned, then walked calmly out of the public house into the street. He looked back in time to see the door being closed behind him. Breathing a sigh of relief he turned and walked briskly into the night, he wanted to get away from this place as quickly as possible.

CHAPTER 3

The secret passage itself was dimly lit by what appeared to be some form of glowing green mould which cast an eerie shadow on the wall, which was made from large blocks of

11

stone. Slowly the Professor edged his way forward. As he did so, the old story sprang to mind of how over a hundred years ago the Prince of Wales had had a secret, and serious, affair with one of Lord Rainsbury's descendants. Could this passage have been the way the Prince entered the house unseen?

Unexpectedly as he rounded a corner, two bandaged hands reached out and grabbed him firmly by the throat. He then found himself being turned and slammed against the passage wall. Instinctively he reached up to grab at the hands that were trying to choke him.

"Kkkkiiiillll !"

The Professor gasped, partly through being strangled and partly through surprise, it sounded as though the creature was talking, of sorts.

"Kkkkiiiiillllll !"

He let go of the Mummy with his left hand and then swiftly moved his entire forearm between himself and the Mummy at eyelevel, breaking eye contact. Then with his right arm he slammed down against the Mummy's elbows, which buckled, causing the grip to be released. It was a basic self defence move that the Professor had picked up, but one that (nearly) always worked. With the Mummy slightly off guard, Charles took the initiative and pushed the creature away. He then punched him hard, twice in the head. No point in aiming at the chest, the Professor reasoned as the creatures internal organs had long been removed in the embalming process thousands of years ago.   The creature staggered back before regaining its balance and reaching down to its leg, where he produced a long knife that was literally hidden in the bandages.

The Mummy held up the blade menacingly. "Kiiillll," it wailed as it moved forward.

"Interesting," mused the Professor, slowly stepping back.

"Now why didn't you think of bringing out the blade earlier? Let me guess, *thinking* is not one of your strong points eh? "

"Kiiilll Yooou!"

The creature lunged forward, but the Professor was quicker, dodging the blade, grabbing the creature by the arm then guiding the weapon hard into the wall. The tip broke off and then the Professor, in a wide arc, pushed it against the wall and back towards the Mummy, who suddenly found himself showered with sparks. He jumped back and beat at his bandages through fear of them being set alight; then realising that he was in fact unharmed let out a scream before turning and running off into the depths of the tunnel.

The Professor let out a sigh of relief, and realising that with another confrontation he might not be as fortunate, he turned back and headed up the passageway to the study, where the black scarab was waiting for him.

Before he got back to the entrance he heard a noise, someone moving in the study. Slowly he edged his way forward from the darkness and peered into the room.

There was someone there alright, dressed in a dark suit; it was one of the household staff, possibly alerted by the earlier commotion. The Professor swore to himself. He must not be discovered, but the events that had just happened had underlined the vital importance of getting the scarab. From the shadows of the passageway he continued to watch the figure. He would have to act soon, for all he knew the servant could have already raised the alarm and the place could soon be swarming with other staff, weekend guests, and worst of all the police.

The figure in the study turned and bent down again to retrieve some of the fallen books. The Professor saw his opportunity, running forward and making a fist, hit the unfortunate servant as hard as he could on the back of the head. The man fell to the floor unconscious. He would wake up soon with a tremendous headache, but most importantly of all, he would be unable to identify his attacker.

The Professor then made his way back over to the safe, to again try to open it.

Forty five – left.

Sixty three – right.

Thirty eight – left.

Sixty seven – right.

This time the handle turned! He must not have moved the dials properly on his last attempt, allowing the internal tumblers to fall correctly into place.

Opening the safe he was confronted with piles of bank notes, legal papers and boxes of jewellery; it was these that he was interested in. One by one he opened the boxes and seeing it was not what he wanted discarded it.

Gold rings.

A string of pearls.

A gold pocket watch.

A diamond broach.

A sapphire necklace.

Then, reaching into the very back of the safe he found a small blue box. Inside was the scarab. It was jet black, the size of the top of a man's thumb, with the details of the beetle carved carefully on the top. The underside was flat, and covered with tiny intricately etched hieroglyphics, which were almost impossible to make out with the naked eye. At the top the two antennae were slightly extended and linked, allowing a length of gold chain to be attached. The chain itself looked new, modern. He briefly wondered what had happened to the original, but no matter, it was the scarab itself which he was after.

This was it! This was the sacred black scarab that he had been desperate to acquire for so long. He had almost gained

14

it on three separate occasions, but fate had conspired against him. But no more, the priceless artefact was now his!

"What on earth!" a male voice cried out.

The Professor spun around; the study door was now wide open, but fortunately it separated him from whoever was on the other side, but he knew that it would be a matter of moments before the person ventured in and he would be discovered.

Gripping the scarab firmly in his hand, he launched himself at the door, hitting it with the full force of his weight. The door started to slam shut, and the unfortunate newcomer was caught between the edge of the door and the frame. Grabbing the side of the door, the Professor quickly opened it and closed it three more times in quick succession until the figure on the other side crumpled to the floor unconscious.

Quickly the Professor replaced the scarab into the box, stopped for a moment to pick up the fallen Katana and put it back in its place, and then opened the door again, peered out to ensure that there was no one else around, before venturing back out into the hallway and up the main staircase.

Safely back in his room, he closed the door behind him. He put the little blue box on the chess board, along with his gloves, then deciding that there was not time to change properly he quickly took off his shoes and socks and rolled his trousers up over the knee. Lastly he attended to the remains of the bandage still attached to his wrist, ripping it off and dumping it under the bed. Then, from underneath his pillow, he grabbed his long nightshirt and put it on over the rest of his clothes. Back at the chess table he picked up the blue box, only stopping momentarily to move the Rook down the board to threaten the King, before heading over to the large sash window which he opened.

"Jazmine! Jazmine! Are you there?" he called out.

From the shadows below a young woman appeared.

15

"Yes, I'm here father. Your forehead!"

He instinctively moved his hand to the spot his daughter was referring to.

There were traces of blood.

He reached under the nightshirt and retrieved a cotton handkerchief. "It's nothing," he said as he wiped at the wound.

"Did you get it?" called the girl expectantly.

He threw her the little blue box. "Yes I got it alright, in more ways than one, the Mummy was there."

Jazmine let out a small cry of surprise.

"It escaped down a secret passageway," continued the Professor, "and I was nearly discovered and had to knock out two of the house staff."

"Oh dear, you have been busy," said Jazmine, unsurprised about the turn of events, while stealing a peek at the scarab. Her father rarely did things straightforwardly.

"The point is though, the Mummy is still on the loose and soon the house is going to be a hive of activity. You need to get away as quickly as possible," clarified the Professor.

"Understood," she replied. "But will you be alright?"

He nodded. "No doubt the police will be called and I will end up being questioned, but as far as anyone is concerned I was here in my room all night, but the important thing is we have what we came for." He wiped his forehead again.

"Get back to the university and keep the scarab safe. I'll catch up with you as soon as I can."

"What about the Mummy?" Jazmine asked.

The Professor smiled. "We have a good idea where the Von Brauns are taking it. We follow them and make our move when we can. Have you made the necessary arrangements?"

"Yes, Father. The booking was confirmed yesterday afternoon."

"Good girl, now you had better get going and be careful!"

With that Jazmine turned and disappeared into the night, clutching the small blue box in her hand, while the Professor closed the window and made his way over to the bed which he climbed on, again dabbed the wound on his head, and waited.

Less than a few seconds more passed before the expected knock on the door came. Smiling to himself he got off the bed and went to the door which he opened to find one of the house maids.

"Sorry to disturb you Professor……" She stopped in mid sentence. He realised that she was looking at his injury. He smiled. "Knocked my head on a shelf," he explained. "My own fault, I should have been more careful."

"Oh," said the girl. "Um, I'm sorry to disturb you, but there has been a robbery."

"Really?" he said trying to sound surprised. "When?"

"A short while ago it seems. I've been asked to check on the guests, to see that they are alright and to find out if they heard anything."

The Professor shook his head. "Sorry, I was sound asleep until a few moments ago."

The girl nodded. "Right, um, er, the Constable has been called and they might want to speak with you."

The Professor nodded, he assumed that the police would want to speak with everyone in the house; fortunately there would be nothing to connect him with the events which had taken place in the study.

The maid nodded politely and then left while the Professor closed the door and made his way back to the bed.

A smile crossed his lips. The black scarab was at last his and he had survived a direct encounter with the Mummy; there were many who had not been so lucky. The one thing that bothered him though was the maid's attitude. She seemed

17

unduly hesitant, unsure. Something more than the shock of a robbery, it was almost as though she did not believe him. Could it be that she saw him returning to the room? Then suddenly all his exuberance and cheerfulness was drained from him as the answer leapt out at him. His eyes rested on the perfectly made bed, which he had clearly not been asleep in as he just stated.

CHAPTER 4

Richard Mallory reached forward over the breakfast table for another piece of buttered toast. He was now freshly washed, shaved, dressed in his normal clothes and feeling a lot better after last night's ordeal, partly due to the safety and familiarity of his home. The irony of his address and that of his now chosen occupation seldom went unnoticed. After leaving the British army he decided to setup a small, independent, private investigations bureau. A suitable property became available in London's Baker Street which he took advantage of. Work was steady, partly due to the fact he had let the occupants of number 221 know of his existence. It amazed him how much work he gained from this, with people being redirected to him when they found out that Mr Holmes 'doesn't actually live here'. For the past eight months another source of regular work presented itself in the shape of Oldfield & Harper Insurers, who specialised in antiques and jewellery claims. They would contact him regarding a claim which he would investigate, ideally trying to recover the goods before the claim had to be settled. Mallory had a high degree of success with the cases given to him, to the point where he was even given the task of trying to recover stolen items from already settled claims. Once found, the insurers would approach the owner to return the goods and, with skilful negotiation would either claim any past reward offered or strike an arrangement to either keep the item or have the client return some of the claim money; again, Mallory's successes in this were also exceptional.

Mallory pondered the events that took place last night, thinking particularly of poor Alfie. He himself had a lucky escape. If it was not for the fact that he was needed, he too could easily have ended up dragged into the alley and disposed of. A shudder went through him, the words of the mysterious felon running through his mind. *'No doubt the Thames will eventually give up his body. He won't be missed. I doubt he will even be identified.'*

Mallory reached over to pour himself another cup of coffee when the bell at the door rang. He got up, and made his way into the hall and opened the door.

"Morning Captain!"

Mallory glared at his visitor, Michael Collier, a representative from Oldfield & Harper and personal friend. "I wish people would stop calling me that! Come on in." He turned and headed back to his breakfast, Michael followed, closing the door behind him. In the dining room, both men took a seat at the table. Michael seeing the laid out breakfast immediately started to help himself, with Mallory looking on with some amusement. "I suppose you want to know how I got on last night."

Michael took a big bite of toast. "Partly, but something else has come up and you are needed for that, top priority."

Mallory nodded.

"So go on then," Michael urged. "Did you find the necklace?"

Mallory nodded. "Not only found it but I held it in my hands, for a few moments anyway."

"And?"

"It's a fake," Mallory confirmed. "A very good one, but a fake never the less."

19

A genuine look of surprise spread across Michael's face.

"I think that we need to take a closer look at the jeweller's themselves," continued Mallory. "My hunch is that when the copy was stolen they decided to pass it off as the real one, which is no doubt hidden somewhere."

Collier nodded; Jewellers making flawless copies of original items was a common practice. It allowed the replica to be worn in public without fear of damage or theft while the real one could be kept safe elsewhere. "We are not going to be able to stop the claim unless we have firm proof, can you get hold of the copy?"

Mallory shuffled awkwardly in his seat. "I've arranged a meeting with the 'current owners', but there is a problem."

"Isn't there always?"

"This one is pretty big. After the original theft, the necklace was stolen again, by my informant, who himself was murdered last night. It's his murderers who want to make a deal with us, they think it's real."

Michael winced. "That's going to get messy. Have you been to the police?"

Mallory nodded. "Straight after my encounter with them. I was pretty vague on some of the finer details though. We need to find the real necklace and fast. I arranged a meeting for a few days time for a formal exchange. If we can prove the jewellers are at the bottom of this and can recover the real necklace we can go to the press. That way the people I dealt with last night will know the case is solved and any potential deal is off."

Michael nodded. "Quite, we are not going to pay out for a fake, especially when the original is recovered."

"And then I can go to the police and give them the full details of the murder, not that it will do much good though. I've a feeling that these people are very good at what they do," added Mallory.

"Well, it's worth a try anyway," said Michael. He paused and took another piece of toast. "We will have to deal with that later, as I said, an urgent case has presented itself and the powers that be have decided you are the man for the job."

"Ahhh," said Mallory. "This will be the 'something else' you mentioned."

Michael nodded. "Have you ever heard of Thomas Rainsbury?"

Mallory shook his head. "I've come across the odd article about his travels and large charity donations, other than that, nothing."

"Well he has one of the most notable antiquities collections outside the British Museum. He is very wealthy and well connected. Anyway, late last night or in the early hours of this morning there was a robbery at his house."

"Was much taken?"

"Not as much as there could have been. It seems that the robber was disturbed during the raid by staff, both of whom got a crack over the head for their efforts." Michael reached into his jacket pocket and produced a piece of paper which he passed over to Mallory. "That is a list of what we know to be taken so far."

"How on earth did you get it so quickly, the robbery only happened a few hours ago?"

Michael smiled. "We have our sources, but it is only a preliminary list. There will no doubt be more items to add. The item that we are most concerned with though is the black scarab beetle.

"How much is it worth?"

"We insured it for ten thousand pounds, but it is suspected that it is worth a lot more."

Mallory winced at the amount. It was a lot of money. "I'm presuming that it was kept in a safe?"

Michael nodded. "A concealed Chubb wall safe, an unusual model as there is no key required, just a dial. It was found with the door wide open."

"If they got into the safe it could point to an inside job."

"Unlikely," replied Michael, "most of the staff have been with the Rainsbury family for years, and those that have not have been through strict vetting beforehand." He paused. "There was a group of guests staying at the house though, invited up for Easter."

"It could be one of them."

"Again unlikely, all are professionals and pillars of society; doctors, Judges, Lords, a Professor."

"What else was kept in the safe?" asked Mallory, suddenly looking at the list.

Michael smiled. Mallory had spotted what he was about to point out. "All the usual stuff you would expect; money, jewels, deeds, private papers,"

"And yet none was taken? That is very odd, I know you said he was disturbed, but you would have thought that he would have been able to grab some of the other items too."

Michael nodded. "That's what we thought too. Even though the items taken seem to be Egyptian in origin, you would have thought that with an open safe crammed full of jewels and banknotes, they would have taken advantage of the situation. There are some more items on the reverse."

Mallory turned the paper over. "A head rest?"

"Yes, when an Egyptian Mummy was placed in the coffin, the head was put on a head rest. This one was solid gold. Fortunately for us though, it was a new acquisition and not yet insured."

"I'm not sure Thomas Rainsbury will share that view."

Michael laughed. "Yes, you're right. Still hopefully with your detection skills, you will be able to recover *all* the stolen items to him safe and sound. Find one and find all!"

Mallory smiled. "Which also means the claim he will no doubt be putting in shortly will not need to be paid out."

Michael sat upright on his chair, put his thumbs in his waistcoat pocket and tried to look noble. "It is our duty to do our best for our clients and in most cases that is to ensure that they are reunited with the items that they hold so dear!" He paused to smile, then took a more relaxing pose. "Anyway, there was another item taken too that's not on the list. It was a manuscript. Rainsbury was working on a book, something about the true role of High Priests in Egyptian society and how they were the true wielders of power rather than the Pharaohs."

"Why would someone want to take that?"

Michael shrugged. "At this stage I'm not totally sure. I'm hoping that it could be for blackmail. You know, 'give us money or we burn your book.' That way there will be direct contact with the thieves and that usually leads to a chance to catch them. Anyway, I have not got to the best bit yet."

"Which is?"

"They gained access to the house via a secret passage."

"What!" said Mallory, genuinely surprised.

"They got into the house via a secret passage," repeated Michael almost excitedly. "It opens up straight into the study itself."

"Who knew about the passage?"

Michael smiled. "This is what we are going to find out. Grab your hat and coat; we are going to Rainsbury Hall straight away. Well, just as soon as I finish the rest of your toast!"

23

CHAPTER 5

Richard Mallory and Michael Collier walked up the long gravelled drive to Rainsbury Hall.

Both could not help but stop and look in awe at this magnificent building, which had belonged to the Rainsburys since the 1600s.

At the door Michael rang the bell and, after a few moments, it was opened by a tall, elderly butler, who eyed the two with a certain air of indignation. "Yes?"

Michael stepped forward. "Um, we are here in connection with the robbery which took place last night."

"More police?"

"Um no, we are here on behalf of Oldfield & Harper Insurers."

"Do you have a card?"

Michael fished out his business card from an inside pocket and passed it to the butler who took it, before abruptly closing the door on them.

"A friendly chap!" commented Mallory.

Michael shrugged. "You know what it's like. Robberies of this kind tend to make people defensive. It attracts all sorts of attention, and the Rainsburys are notorious for keeping private. I suspect he thought we were from the papers, sniffing around for a story."

The door suddenly opened and the Butler stood to one side. "You may come in. Lord Rainsbury will see you shortly."

Inside the main hallway it was a hive of activity with uniformed constables and well dressed people, presumably the house guests, all milling around. The butler pointed to a long sofa in the hallway. "If you two gentlemen would be kind enough to wait there, Lord Rainsbury will be with you shortly." The butler then turned and walked off without waiting for a response. Michael smiled and totally ignoring the request to wait, went up to the nearest constable. "Excuse me, we are from Oldfield & Harper Insurers, can you direct me to Detective Inspector Wilder?"

The constable pointed to a large suited man just emerging from the study door who was talking to another officer. As Richard and Michael approached, Wilder looked and quickly dismissed his colleague who disappeared back into the study, closing the door behind him.

"So what can I do for you?" asked Wilder eyeing them carefully.

"Oh I'm sure you can guess," replied Michael. "By the way, how is that lovely wife of yours?"

Wilder smiled. "Your sister is fine, blooming, and will hopefully be providing me with another son in a few weeks time."

Mallory looked over at Michael. He had no idea of the family connection. It certainly explained how Michael got so much accurate information in such a short time period. Wilder turned to look at Mallory.

"Oh, sorry, I forgot that you have not met," said Michael. "Benjamin, this is my colleague Richard Mallory; Richard, this is one of Scotland Yard's finest, Benjamin Wilder."

The two men shook hands and greeted each other.

"So, Ben," asked Michael, "what else are you able to tell me? Can we take a look around the study?"

Wilder shook his head. "Not yet, I think that you have more than enough information already."

"Which I am most grateful for as always," said Michael with a smile. It was a discreet and somewhat unorthodox arrangement that the two men had between them, but one that seemed to reap rewards, as more often than not this co-operation would produce both an arrest and the recovery of goods.

"There will be a copy of my report ready for you by the end of today," said Wilder. "In the meantime I am sure that you will want to talk with Lord Rainsbury himself, and start your paperwork, as well as talk with some of the remaining guests, although I do not think that they will be able to help much."

"Oh come on," pressed Michael, "what about a quick peek at the crime scene? I am dying to take a look at that passage. Do you know where it leads?"

"I hope that passageway is not going to be a problem with any claim," said a new voice behind them.

Michael and Mallory turned to find Lord Rainsbury himself standing in front of them. "My man Hughes said you were from Oldfield and Harper."

"That's correct Sir. I am Michael Collier and this is my colleague Richard Mallory."

Lord Rainsbury regarded the two men politely. He was a tall man, dressed in a tweed suit, with a slightly worried look on his face. "Well, will the passage affect any claim that is made?"

"That is one of the reasons I am here," replied Michael honestly. "After all, as you appreciate, there has been no forced entry and of course the safe was opened rather than forced."

"I have paid your company a lot of money over the years to be protected from just such a situation. I did not expect that you would try to wriggle your way out of it on the basis of some blasted technicality," replied Rainsbury with a distinct note of anger in his voice.

"Sir, I can assure you that we are not. I am merely here in a capacity to initially assess what has happened, and give any support that is possible. In fact Richard Mallory here, a former Captain of the British army, is our chosen private

26

detective who will be assigned exclusively to this case. He has had particular success in recovering lost items."

"So a military man eh?" said Lord Rainsbury. "Where did you serve?"

"India mainly, but I also spent some time in Afghanistan," replied Mallory, not wanting to go into too much detail of his time in the army.

Lord Rainsbury smiled, seemingly impressed. "Afghanistan eh? So you're a participant in The Great Game then?"

"Not so 'great' I'm afraid, Sir. They kept changing the rules on me."

Lord Rainsbury laughed and nodded. "Well I suppose that you will want to take a closer look at my study, and the passage in particular."

"Yes very much," said Michael, quickly looking over at Wilder who shook his head but then opened the door for them. "Alright, you can take a look, but do not disturb anything."

So Mallory and Michael stepped over the threshold into the study. Michael took a deep intake of breath at the room before him.

"Yes, impressive eh?" said Lord Rainsbury following. "I have been collecting for years."

As well as normal bookcases, filled with books, there were specially made display cases with items relating to ancient Egypt, each set into its own little alcove. All were original items that had been acquired over the years by legal methods. However, it was the collection of swords behind the door which adorned one wall which caught Mallory's attention.

"Yes, that is my other passion," explained Lord Rainsbury. "Look up there, top right, a British Cavalry sword used at Waterloo, and next to it, its French counterpart. Of course the British blade was far superior."

Mallory moved closer. "I'm more interested in that Samurai Katana sword actually."

"Ah, you have taste."

"Thank you, but I think that it has been moved. It looks crooked in its display cradle."

Lord Rainsbury took a closer look. "By Jove you are right! It has been disturbed! Well done man! Wilder, what do you make of that?"

Wilder shook his head, neither he nor his men had noticed the sword had been touched. Just then they were disturbed by movement from the open bookcase as two police constables appeared in the roughly cut door.

"You took your time," chided Wilder. "So where does it lead to?"

"The chapel Sir," replied one of the constables.

"What, my private chapel in the grounds?!" gasped Lord Rainsbury in astonishment.

The constable nodded. "A hatchway opened up in the middle of the chancel. The door to the chapel had been forced open."

Lord Rainsbury looked over at Michael, concerned how this would affect any claim. "Well?"

"I will have to have a word with my superiors, but as a forced entry has taken place on the grounds, which resulted in direct access to the house, albeit via an unconventional route, I do not think that there will be a problem with any claim, providing of course the passageway is just that, a secret, and not publicly known about."

Lord Rainsbury looked visibly relieved.

"Of course," added Michael, "we will do all we can ourselves to recover the items, which is where Mr Mallory comes in."

Lord Rainsbury looked over at Mallory again and nodded, seemingly happy at the arrangement. "In that case, if there is any help I can extend to you, please feel free to ask."

"Sir." Lord Rainsbury turned. It was the butler who had spoken. "I am sorry to interrupt, but there is a telephone call for you."

Lord Rainsbury nodded. "Gentlemen, if you would excuse me." And with that he turned and left the room.

"Right then," said Mallory to Wilder, "if you have no objections I would like to look around. What of the guests?"

"A few are still here," confirmed Wilder. "Most have already left though, but I can give you a list of their names and where they can be contacted."

"I'd like to take a look at the passageway and chapel if that's alright."

Wilder nodded.

"Well Richard, if you are going to be stumbling around hidden passageways," said Michael, "I think that is my cue to find myself a nice cup of something hot to drink and start some boring paperwork."

Mallory found nothing in the passageway or the chapel to help with his investigation, although he was surprised about the amount of damage to the wooden chapel door itself. Whoever had kicked it down certainly had great strength. Back in the study he again found nothing of any significance which could help him. The desk drawer containing the manuscript, like the chapel door, had appeared to be forced by brute strength rather than by the use of some implement. The safe held no clues for him either, so instead he decided to try to question some of the remaining guests. After hearing the same story of 'I was asleep and heard nothing', followed by their own individual theory on the case; he was about to give up, when he happened to notice one of the house maids looking over at him intently. Making sure that no one else was looking she beckoned to him to follow her, then moved away down the long corridor. Seizing the opportunity, Mallory followed and found her waiting for him nervously.

"You are not with the police are you?"

"No, I am employed by an insurance agency," replied Mallory.

The young woman nodded. "Good, Lord Rainsbury said that we were not to speak to the police, but as you are not with the police......" Her voice trailed off, it was clear to Mallory that she was very apprehensive. "I might have some information for you regarding the robbery."

"What is it?"

The woman looked down nervously, almost expectant. Mallory had played this game before. He reached into his jacket pocket and pulled out his wallet. From it he produced a banknote. The woman reached for it and he snatched it back out of her grasp. "In my experience information sold for cash usually is not accurate, sometimes even made up. How do I know for sure that yours is different, after all you are prepared to go behind your employer's back?"

The maid looked nervous, almost as though she was about to burst into tears. "The money's not for me. It's for my Father. He's sick, been so since the winter. The Doctor is so expensive and then there is the cost of the medicine."

Mallory, realising that she was genuine, handed her the note and she took it quickly. "When it was discovered that a robbery had taken place I was instructed to check on the guests. Well when I went to the Professor's room...."

"Professor?" broke in Mallory.

"Yes, Professor Charles Montacute," said the maid. "Well he said that he was sleeping and that I had woken him, but he was wide awake and more than that, his bed had not been slept in. He also had a fresh cut on his head as though he had

30

been in a fight. Now it might be nothing, but he does have a reputation."

"For what?"

"Grave robbing, supplying these items to museums, and he has a shifty look about him too."

Just then Michael appeared, the maid seeing him, quickly excused herself and left.

"My! She is a pretty one," said Michael cheekily, "you arranging yourself a date?"

"No, better than that," replied Mallory, "I think we have a possible suspect. Now what do you know about a one Professor Charles Montacute?"

CHAPTER 6

Lord Rainsbury sat in the waiting area outside Ahmed Hawass's office in the Egyptian Embassy, trying his best to decipher some hieroglyphs, which hung on the wall, to pass the time. He had been kept waiting for nearly half an hour by the Egyptian official. The only reason he had not tried to barge his way into the office was that he did not want to antagonise the man who claimed he had direct information regarding the whereabouts of the stolen items. In particular, the manuscript for his book, which he was hoping to send to his publisher in the coming months. Lord Rainsbury had been summoned to London by the phone call he had received yesterday when he was showing the police and Insurers around his study. The instructions had been perfectly clear. If he wanted to see his manuscript and the other items that were taken from the robbery, he was to turn up at the Egyptian Embassy not telling anyone of the visit, and most important of all, bring the black scarab beetle that he owned with him. This was of course a mystery in itself for

Rainsbury, for surely whoever had taken the manuscript and other items also already had the beetle in their possession. Still, this was a chance that Lord Rainsbury was not going to pass up. Perhaps after this meeting he would have a clue as to who really had the black scarab which he had searched for, for so long.

The door to the office opened and a middle aged woman, no doubt Hawass's secretary, appeared. "Sorry to keep you waiting for so long. An urgent matter came up, but Mr Hawass will see you now."

Rainsbury rose from his seat following the woman into the office. Inside, he was invited to sit down in front of the large desk where Ahmed Hawass was seated waiting for him. The secretary then collected some papers before leaving via the door they had come in from.

Lord Rainsbury turned with a start as he heard the lock of the door turning.

Ahmed smiled. "Just to ensure that we are not disturbed in any way. You don't mind do you?"

Lord Rainsbury did mind, but he could not let it show. "No, no of course that's fine," he replied turning back round.

Ahmed nodded. He was in his fifties and had been attached on this London assignment for the past two years, but he yearned for his beloved homeland. His only comfort was the task that he had been given; not the task of running the Embassy, but the *other* task that he had taken on, the one which gave glory back to his beloved Egypt.

"I trust that you told no one of your visit here?"

Lord Rainsbury shook his head. "No, I just said that I was going into town on business, although I did not expand on what type, and then on to my club."

"That is good, very good." Ahmed paused looking expectantly. "Do you have the black scarab with you?"

32

Lord Rainsbury shook his head. "No. It was taken in the robbery."

A look of surprise crossed Ahmed's face. "Are you sure?"

"Yes, the safe had been opened and the scarab was gone."

Ahmed stared at Rainsbury, his expression becoming very serious. "Are you *really* sure?" he repeated. His tone became more hostile.

Lord Rainsbury nodded.

"I think that you are lying Lord Rainsbury," said Ahmed coolly.

"What?!"

"I think that you still have the sacred scarab and want to keep it for yourself. I doubt that you know its true value or significance, but I think it is an item that you still have."

Lord Rainsbury stood up. "Why, how dare you! Are you calling me a liar?"

Ahmed too stood up. "I shall go much further than that. You yourself are no better than a thief, a robber. You acquire artefacts stolen from those in eternal sleep treating them like prizes, displaying them like trophies!"

"I object sir!" retorted Lord Rainsbury. "I am a collector and Egyptologist. I hold your culture in the highest of regard. I have funded many digs that have recovered hundreds of items which may be used to learn and even glorify your heritage. I have pumped thousands of pounds directly into your country. I have even written a book which sheds enlightenment on the importance of those who ruled!"

Ahmed opened the drawer to his desk, pulled out the hand written manuscript that Rainsbury had spent so many years working on, casually dropping it on the desk. "You mean this, your book which tries to reveal the true secrets of our culture to the western infidels?"

Lord Rainsbury stared at his beloved manuscript for a moment, and then a flicker of understanding swept over him.

"It was you wasn't it? No, wait, I doubt you would have the boldness to carry out the robbery with your own hand, but you were behind it weren't you?"

Ahmed smiled, and nodded. It did not matter that Lord Rainsbury knew the truth; his life could be measured in minutes. "Yes, I was behind the robbery and I advise you to reveal the location of the black scarab."

Lord Rainsbury paused for a moment then quickly reached over the desk grabbing his precious manuscript before making a bolt for the door. Ahmed did nothing to stop him, and when Lord Rainsbury tried the handle he realised why, for the door was of course locked from the outside. He turned to face his captor.

"Lord Rainsbury, I advise you not to try anything rash. Your situation is one of great peril and I implore you not to try to prolong your agony."

Lord Rainsbury turned back to the door and frantically yanked at the handle, yelling for help that was never going to come. Realising that there was no escape from this route he turned and looked around the room for another means of escape. In the wall on the right there was another door, one that probably led to a connecting office, and ultimately out to freedom. He ran over to it, his manuscript still clutched tightly in his hand. Grabbing the handle he quickly turned and pulled the door open towards him then stopped in surprise at the sight which greeted him.

A six foot tall Egyptian Mummy, just standing blocking his way.

"What on earth?" he exclaimed.

The Mummy's head drops slightly and Rainsbury finds himself looking into the creature's glowing red eyes just visible through the yellowing linen.

The manuscript landed on the floor, its pages spilling everywhere, but Lord Rainsbury barely registered that he was no longer holding it. Instead, somehow, he managed to take three faltering steps backwards; he turned to look at Ahmed, still standing at the desk calmly, without any emotion. Ahmed nodded to the Mummy, who launched himself forward.

The next thing Lord Rainsbury was aware of he was on the floor with the Mummy's bandaged hands tightly around his throat with the feeling that Ahmed was standing somewhere nearby.

"Help me! Let me go!" gasped Rainsbury.

Ahmed sneered. He had no intention of letting Lord Rainsbury go. He had been after him for a long time. "I would introduce you to my ancient friend here, but as yet I am not entirely sure of his name. I strongly suspect that he is a High Priest, but only time and research will tell. Of course you will never actually find out."

"But, it, it, it's alive!" gasped Lord Rainsbury, trying to make sense of what he was seeing before his eyes.

"Yes, that's right. Through ancient, forbidden magic and the modern wonders of science I was able to reanimate the Mummy. He acts on my words or through those that I have entrusted to carry out my work."

"His eyes!" wheezed Rainsbury as the Mummy tightened his grip slightly.

"Yes," said Ahmed excitedly, he was proud of his accomplishment, but was never normally in a position to boast about it. "Well as you know, as part of the mummification process the vital organs, as well as the eyes are all removed. In order for my friend here to 'live' I was forced to find a new brain and eyes. For some reason, that I have yet to discover, the new eyes have this reddish glow to them. Now where is the black scarab?"

"I don't know! Please, I have connections. I can give you money."

35

"I want the scarab and for you to pay for your crimes against my people."

"It was the Mummy that carried out the robbery wasn't it?"

Ahmed nodded. "Yes that is right. He got all of the items he was requested to retrieve, apart from the scarab which you claim to be missing. I think that you, on realising the robbery had occurred, decided to take advantage of it by taking it and hiding it."

"You are mad! I tell you that it was stolen, perhaps if you were to ask your friend here, perhaps *he* decided to keep it for himself!"

Ahmed let out a deep laugh. "Impossible, he has no need for material possessions and acts strictly on the orders given. Now I give you one last chance – Where is the sacred black Scarab?"

"Go to hell!"

Ahmed shook his head realising that he would not get the answers he sought. "I fear that you will be there long before me. Lord Thomas Rainsbury, for the crimes against the Egyptian people I sentence you to death. Your mortal body shall be taken from this place and turned into a contemporary Mummy, which shall be sold as an ancient relic, the money gained from this being returned to the people of Egypt."

The Mummy looked up at its master who nodded; the creature then tightened his grip around Lord Rainsbury's throat. Ahmed turned and went to retrieve the scattered pages of the manuscript, the sound of Rainsbury's death throws ringing in his ears. By the time the manuscript had been gathered, the Mummy was standing over the lifeless body of his latest victim.

"Well done," said Ahmed as he placed the manuscript back in the desk drawer. Then from another drawer he took out a large brown envelope and moved to face the Mummy. "You are to take the body to the lower floor where it will be prepared. Then don your disguise, you are to go to your given master and mistress, and present them with this." He handed the Mummy the envelope. "Inside is a list of tasks that must be carried out, along with the appropriate travel documents. As always you will be under their instruction. You must obey them as you would me."

The Mummy let out a moan indicating that he understood.

"Now hurry, there is little time."

Again the Mummy let out a moan and went to Lord Rainsbury's body, which he scooped up in his bandaged arms. Ahmed returned to his desk where a smile spread across his face. Over the next few days many wrongs committed against the Egyptian people would be set right.

CHAPTER 7

Richard Mallory walked through the grand wood panelled entrance hall of King's College, pausing briefly as he went, to take in the grandeur of his surroundings. Yesterday, after hearing Michael Colliers brief biography of Professor Montacute's life, he decided to do some more in-depth research into what seemed the most likely suspect of the case. What he found convinced him that Charles Montacute was indeed responsible for the robbery at Rainsbury Hall. The Professor was a sometime lecturer at the University, frequently allowed 'extended paid leave of absence' which he used for research assignments and the acquisition of historical items, all of which were funded by the University, who also shared in any financial benefit from the Professor's work. There were however, some questions raised by the Professor's methods. Some saw him as one of the greatest Historians and Archaeologists of all time, while others regarded him as nothing more than a maverick, a glorified thief, re-writing some aspects of history for his own glorification. The thing that particularly interested Mallory was that Charles Montacute had recently returned from a six month visit to Egypt where he had advised and overseen two separate digs, as well as extensive research into an alleged 'Pharaoh curse' attached to a recently discovered tomb which he promptly and very publicly debunked, declaring it nothing more than a hoax; possibly government propaganda to scare people away. After this he was promptly asked to leave the country by the Egyptian authorities, but at the port of Alexandria, just as he was about to board a ship, he was stopped, searched, and was found to be in possession of a number of items stolen from the digs that he had attended. In fact, there were several similar incidences throughout the Professor's career where he was accused of stealing artefacts, then trying to smuggle them out of the country.

The Professor's dubious practices, his connection with Egypt, and the house maid's observations from the night of the robbery all led Mallory to one conclusion – Professor Charles Montacute was directly involved in the robbery at Rainsbury Hall. So, armed with that information, he set out to track down the scholar to question him about the events which had taken place.

Despite the University officially being closed for Easter, it was there that the Professor had told the police he would be found, as he was in the middle of researching his latest paper, and needed access to the University's extensive library. Mallory's efforts the day before had proven fruitless. The Professor's office was locked with a sign on the door saying that due to unforeseen circumstances his office hours had changed and would not be available in the holiday after all. Mallory suspected something more sinister though. He believed that the Professor was deliberately making himself scarce in case he was wanted for questioning. So Mallory adopted a different approach. He had left a note, slid under the office door, giving his details, and saying that he would not be available for the next few days and he would try again then. But now, just one day later, he had returned, hoping to catch his quarry out, and having walked up three flights of steps, Mallory congratulated himself for his cunning, for as he approached Professor Montacute's office he could see the outline of a figure moving behind the frosted glass.

"Come in," called out a female voice in response to the knocking on the door. Mallory opened the door and entered looking round the small and crowded office in the hope that the Professor was here, but he was not. Instead a young dark haired woman in her late twenties stood by a desk swamped with books and papers.

"Can I help?" she asked. "Are you with the British Museum?"

"Um, no," replied Mallory handing the woman his card. "I work on behalf of Oldfield and Harper Insurance." As he did so he took the opportunity to take a closer look at the woman. She was of medium height, wearing a long grey dress which hid her figure. Her hair was dark, shoulder length, but held up with a number of hair clips. Her light brown eyes were set in a rounded, pleasant face, not stunningly beautiful, but never the less pretty.

She passed the card straight back to him. "I'm sorry but my father is out at the moment."

"Father?" said Mallory in surprise.

"Yes, that's right, Professor Montacute is my Father. I work here at the University as his assistant." She looked Mallory up and down. "I'm afraid that you have missed him, he will be gone for a while."

"It's alright, I can wait," replied Mallory looking around for a chair in which to seat himself.

"I'm afraid that is not possible. Anyway, didn't you put a note under the door saying you would come back the day after tomorrow?"

Mallory nodded. "My plans changed, so I thought that I would try my chances."

"Well I am afraid that you have had another wasted journey."

"Perhaps you can help? Um I did not get your name."

"Miss Montacute will be just fine," Jazmine replied frostily.

"Um, of course. I was wondering ...." He stopped in mid sentence, realising of course that it would be unlikely he would get anything useful from the girl. "Um, er, no matter, I really need to speak with your father, but can you at least make a formal appointment for me?" His eyes travelled down to the desk where there was a large black appointment diary.

Jazmine picked up the diary and opened it flicking through the pages before picking up a pencil and scribbling inside. She then slammed the diary shut placing it back on the desk. "There. Wednesday 10th April, two o'clock."

"Thank you." Mallory paused, with a formal appointment made there was no reason to prolong the visit, but at the same time he felt that he was being dismissed, and that in leaving this office and this girl he was also going to lose his immediate chance to make contact with the Professor.

"This is an amazing office. I don't think that I have ever seen so many books crammed into such a small place." Mallory continued looking at the overcrowded shelves that adorned every wall.

"Well in that case, I suggest you take a tour of the University Library," replied Jazmine quickly.

Mallory looked suitably embarrassed, and cursed himself for such a stupid statement "Er, I meant that, um…"

Behind him he heard movement at the door, he turned to see a figure outside. Jazmine seeing the figure too, responded immediately, moving round the desk and over to it. For a moment Mallory thought that it was the Professor, he presumed Jazmine did too, hence her haste to get to the door first, but hearing the conversation that was going on it was clear that it was a student. Mallory turned back to the desk, his eyes fell upon the appointment diary; checking that Jazmine was still busy he quickly leaned over and opened it. The appointment that Miss Montacute had supposedly written down for him was not there; instead the only appointment for that day read 'Waterloo 9.45 am Platform 12'. He turned the page to see that the following week was blanked out entirely, then fearing he would be discovered, quickly closed the diary turning back round, just as Jazmine had finished dealing with the student, who had left. "Will there be anything else Mr Mallory? I am very busy" She opened the door wide inviting him to leave.

"No, that's fine," he said as he moved towards the door.

"Um, the library is where?" He smiled slightly, trying to make light of his earlier comment.

"Ground floor, past reception, straight down to the left," she replied with a dead pan face. "It's closed at the moment though." And with that she closed the door on him abruptly.

Mallory shook his head and started to walk down the long corridor. 'Waterloo 9.45 am platform 12' he thought to himself, so the Professor was planning a trip and, from the way his daughter was reacting it was clear that she was involved too. He contemplated returning to the office to wait for Jazmine and to follow her, when a voice ahead called out, "Professor Montacute!" It was the student who had just been to the office. He had seen the Professor emerge from a side room and had tried to attract his attention.

Along the corridor Mallory saw the Professor look up, first to the student and then to him, a flicker of understanding went across the old man's face and Mallory realised he knew who he was.

The Professor then quickly turned and walked away in the opposite direction.

"Professor!" called out the student again somewhat confused as to why he was being ignored, just as Mallory sped past him.

The Professor's pace increased and soon he and Mallory were running. The Professor soon reached the stairwell where he started to descend the three floors until he was at the main reception. He then turned back on himself and headed down another corridor. From Jazmine's flippant comments Mallory realised that they were heading towards the library, which was closed. However, at the large library doors, Montacute stopped and from his waistcoat took out a key which he used to open it.

Just as Mallory got to the door, the Professor was locking it shut behind him. Safe inside he held up the key to show Mallory through the thick glass panel of the door and then placed it back in his pocket.

"I know that you committed the robbery at Rainsbury Hall," called out Mallory grabbing at the handle and pulling at it in the hope the door would open.

The Professor laughed. "Then you know very little my friend!"

"Why did you steal the artefacts? Where is the black scarab? I shall go to the Police!"

"And say what exactly? Where is your proof?"

Mallory knew that the Professor was right; all he had was unfounded suspicions that could easily be explained away.

"Open this door!"

"Or what?"

Mallory reached inside his jacket and produced his army service revolver pointing it at the lock. "Or I will blow it open."

Without a flicker of emotion or fear, the Professor reached into his own jacket, quickly producing a firearm of his own and aimed it through the glass at Mallory himself.

"I would not do that if I were you."

"What kind of Professor carries a gun?" exclaimed Mallory in surprise.

"One who does not like people having the upper hand. Now as my gun is pointing directly at you, and yours is pointed at the lock, I think that I have the advantage."

"You would not dare!"

"Try me! After all I am a fiendish robber, so what other levels would I stoop to?" The sentence was spoken with an air of sarcasm. "Now drop the gun."

Mallory paused, he briefly thought about turning the gun upward and firing, but decided against it, so instead he dropped the gun to the floor.

"Very well done, now kick it away down the corridor."

Mallory did as he was told.

"Now take your left shoe off."

"What?"

"I said take your left shoe off and throw it down the corridor in the opposite direction to the gun."

Again Mallory did as he was told realising the Professor's intentions. Without his shoe it would be harder to run and fetching the shoe and putting it on would delay him. Even stopping to take off the right would allow the Professor to gain valuable seconds to get away and that was without any further delays in retrieving the gun.

Slowly the Professor started to back away down the library, the gun still pointing at Mallory until he ducked down behind a bookcase out of sight. Mallory grabbed at the door and shook at it again in frustration. There was no way now that he would catch the Professor and he knew that by the time he got back to the office, Jazmine would be long gone. They had out manoeuvred him, of sorts; for he knew that tomorrow morning they would be catching a train.

CHAPTER 8

Richard Mallory arrived at Waterloo station much earlier than he needed to. He hoped to find the Professor and confront him before he had a chance to board the train, but taking no chances, he decided to buy a ticket just in case he had to travel himself. He was genuinely surprised when he found out that the train that he wanted was a boat train, bound for Southampton docks, and the passengers onboard were destined to connect to the new 'unsinkable' ship the RMS Titanic, bound for New York. He had of course read reports about the ship in the press, the papers were full of it, but had failed to make the connection. He had found out that this was the second train to leave today for the Titanic, the first was already on its way containing second and third class passengers, while the 9.45 am would be filled with the great and the good of first class.

After walking up and down the platform to check that the Professor was not already there waiting, he positioned himself at the platform gate so he could observe the passengers as they filed past in the hope of spotting Professor Montacute, although he was not actually sure how he would proceed. After all, this was a dangerous and violent man who had already pulled a gun on him without hesitation. Suddenly he wished that he had followed the advice of his friend Michael Collier, who he had gone to, to report events after his encounter at the University.

"He pulled a gun on you?!" Collier had gasped in surprise.

"Well actually I pulled my gun first, but that was only at the lock."

"Right, we need to get the Police involved."

"No, there is no actual proof the Professor was responsible for the robbery. I want to find him again and confront him."

"You are mad!"

"Probably."

"At least take Hawkinson and Adams with you, they can act as back up, this man sounds unhinged."

"No, I'll be fine. In this type of situation I work better alone."

Mallory looked back at the platform; it was getting crowded with people milling about waiting for the train. A large crate was being unloaded from a trolley and being placed with care on the platform. Mallory shivered, for the crate was the size and shape of a coffin. He hoped that this was not an omen of things to come.

Mallory turned back to look at the concourse and then suddenly his attention was caught by a familiar face walking towards him. It was Jazmine Montacute in a long dark purple dress with a small suitcase. Mallory ducked back, not wanting to be seen. Then from the left, another figure appeared dressed in a tweed suit carrying a medium sized carpet bag in one hand and a walking cane in the other. It was the Professor.

Then from behind, there was a whistle, which made Mallory turn. It was the boat train, slowly reversing into the station, ready to take on the passengers. Mallory turned back, only to find to his horror that the Professor and Jazmine had disappeared. He looked around the concourse and at the passengers who were about to file past but could not see them. Blast! He thought they must have seen him. Still as long as he stayed put, they would eventually have to come back this way or miss their train. Reluctantly he moved back

45

deeper into the station to try and get a better view, mindful not to go far just in case he was being lured out so they could slip by him. Then in the distance, Mallory spotted them. The Professor was talking to a police constable, who turned and looked straight at him. It seemed that the Professor had just handed the constable something which he was looking at, before turning and purposefully marching towards him. In the background the Professor smiled and waved to him, before he and Jazmine again disappeared into the throng.

Mallory cursed, he had no idea what tale the constable had been spun, but from the look on the officer's face he was not happy. With no other option he moved towards the officer hoping that he could talk his way out of whatever situation he had been put into.

"Hello Sir," said the constable sternly.

"Um, hello officer," replied Mallory quickly. "My name is Richard Mallory, I work with ...."

"Is this yours sir?" interrupted the constable holding up a worn brown leather wallet.

"Um no," replied Mallory in surprise, he had not expected this.

"Are you sure? Only I was told that it belonged to you, it was seen falling out of your pocket."

"No, it's not mine," said Mallory, trying to look beyond the constable to see where Jazmine and the Professor were.

"But you have not even looked at it Sir."

Realising that the only way to get out of this was to play along, he took out his own wallet from his jacket pocket and showed the officer. "See, this one is mine."

"Oh, alright then sir, I'll take it to lost property," said the constable satisfied that he was not the owner. "Sorry to have bothered you." With that he touched his helmet in a half salute and turned and walked away smartly.

Mallory frantically began to look around the station to see if he could see where the Professor was. He was sure though that they had not slipped past him. He glanced up at the hanging clock which now read 9.34am, then back towards the people milling about. With no sign of them he was about to return back to platform 12 to see if he could find them, when out of the corner of his eye he spotted them.

They were rushing towards platform 1.

Mallory's mind jumped back to the diary he had seen the day before, could he have got it wrong? Was it platform 1 and not 12? Or could it be that they had seen him and decided to change their plans?

Either way, the Professor and his daughter had disappeared through the gate, towards the waiting train, so with little choice Mallory ran after them as fast as he could. As he sped towards the gate he realised that he did not have a ticket valid for that train, or even a platform ticket, however, luck was on his side as a large man was having a disagreement with the gate inspector. Moving past, Mallory held his Southampton ticket in the air and the harassed inspector, distracted, waved him through. Then breathing a sigh of relief he boarded the train finding himself in the first class carriage.

Quickly he made his way down the train's corridor, looking in each compartment hoping to see the Professor or his daughter, but they were not there.

At the end of the last carriage, he opened the door and jumped out onto the platform, aiming to re-board the train at the next carriage along to continue the search.

It was then that a though hit him.

They were not on this train at all!

He was being duped, he had been lured away from platform 12, quite convincingly, by a spur of the moment deception, and they had probably already double backed past him and were heading back to the Southampton boat train!

Mallory broke into a run back down the platform and burst his way through the gate, much to the surprise of the ticket inspector. Pausing for a moment he looked down the concourse; to his left he could see the figure of Jazmine in her purple coat, just disappearing through the gate of platform 12.

He looked up at the hanging clock which now read 9.42am, before breaking back into a run. A woman suddenly stepped backwards blocking his way, Mallory tried to dodge her, but in doing so he ended up ploughing into a city gent resulting in the both of them falling to the floor. Quickly Mallory got up and helped the man to his feet before then continuing on his desperate run with tuts and comments from those who had seen the incident.

At the platform gate the inspector stood across the entrance like a ceremonial guard. "Ticket please, Sir."

"But you have already seen my ticket! I left the platform a short while ago."

"Maybe so Sir, but I still need to see a valid ticket before I can let you onto the platform."

Mallory put his hand in his pocket, but the ticket was not there. Frantically he searched his other pockets but he could not find it.

"Um, I cannot find it!" he said to the inspector.

"Then I am sorry Sir, but I cannot allow you to pass, regulations you understand. You must have a valid platform ticket or a ticket of travel to be allowed access onto the platform."

Mallory looked up at the stern faced inspector and briefly considered physically trying to barge to the train, but realised that this would be classed as assault, and he could easily end up being arrested, so instead, he again went through his pockets hoping that he had missed the ticket, but the ticket was not there. What had he done with it? Where had he put it? He had had it when he used it to bluff his way onto platform 1, but had no recollection of putting it away afterwards. Then he realised, he had not put it anywhere, he had kept it in his hand the whole time and was holding it right up until...... Quickly he ran back to the spot where he had crashed into the city gent and desperately scanned the concourse floor.

The fallen green ticket caught his eye, lying where it had dropped a short while before, as people walked round it. Mallory lunged at the small piece of paper, scooping it up in his hand before again returning to the gate at platform 12 where he held it up triumphantly. The inspector looked at the ticket, then ushered Mallory through. Gratefully, Mallory moved onto the platform and ran down it, aiming to make his way as far forward down the train as he could. From somewhere behind he heard a whistle from the guard, who also held up a green flag to signal the driver to leave. Very slowly the train started to pull away. Mallory deciding not to push his luck any further grabbed the handle of the nearest carriage, opened it and as the train started to gain speed, jumped aboard, slamming the door shut behind him.

Exhausted by his efforts and wanting some thinking time to try to work out what to do next, he opened the nearest compartment door, entered and flopped down on the empty seat, took a deep breath and then looked up into the eyes of one of the most beautiful women he had ever seen.

CHAPTER 9

"I'm afraid that this is a private compartment."

Mallory sat up straight in his seat, looking at the woman who had spoken. Even though she was sitting down it was clear that she was tall, possibly nearing six foot. She was wearing an expensive long blue dress with equally expensive looking black leather boots. Mallory estimated she was in her late thirties and her olive complexion, dark brown eyes, along with her long dark hair pinned up, gave the impression that she was of foreign origin although she spoke with a middle-class English accent.

"Um, sorry, I almost missed the train. I had problems with my ticket."

The woman just looked at him, and Mallory, realising that he had outstayed his welcome, stood to find another carriage. At the door he turned. "Um Miss, I don't suppose you happened to see an elderly man with a trimmed beard dressed in a tweed suit with a pretty dark haired girl in a dark purple dress board the train?"

The woman looked at him curiously. "Why?"

"Um, I'm looking for them."

"Are they friends of yours?"

Mallory shook his head. "No far from it! I'm sorry. I'll leave you in peace."

"No wait!" said the woman quickly. "You have me intrigued. Please tell me more, or at least stay a while until you have your breath back."

She indicated back towards the seat and Mallory sat down. "My name is Richard Mallory."

"I am the Countess Elisabeth Von Braun," she replied.

Mallory looked suitably impressed, if not a little surprised.

Elisabeth smiled. "I was born in Oxford, but married an Austrian Count in case you were wondering; people often do."

"The thought never crossed my mind," he lied with a sly smile.

"Now tell me Richard, who are these people you are looking for and is there an interesting tale attached?"

Mallory knew from experience that it was unwise to reveal too much about his work, so instead he opted for a sanitised

50

version. "Um, I work for an insurance company. I need to speak to the Professor regarding a robbery that took place a couple of days ago. He might have some valuable information that could help in solving the crime, and does not even know it."

"A Professor?" replied Elisabeth in surprise. "How exciting, a Professor of what?"

Richard shrugged, realising that he was not exactly sure.

"Um, History. Do you think that you have seen him?"

The Countess sat back in her seat looking thoughtful.

"I'm not too sure about the Professor," Elisabeth replied, "but I think that I may have seen the woman you mentioned."

"Jazmine," said Mallory.

"Yes, Jazmine," replied Elisabeth, "I think that I saw her. I remember thinking that the dress was similar to one I had made in Vienna."

"Do you travel a lot?" enquired Mallory.

"Yes, we mainly live between London and Vienna, but we also travel extensively whenever the chance arises. My husband is travelling separately at the moment, but we shall meet up on board Titanic. I am so looking forward to seeing New York, are you?"

Mallory nodded, although his plans only involved getting as far as Southampton docks. "Um, the girl, Jazmine, did you see where she went?"

Elisabeth paused trying to think. "No, not exactly, I just saw her board the train, I think that she was heading towards the front. I'm sure it won't be too difficult to track her down."

Mallory stood up. "Well in that case Countess, I had better resume my search. Thank you for your time."

"No, thank you Mr Mallory, it was a pleasure meeting you. I wish you good luck in your hunt."

With that, Mallory opened the compartment door and returned to the carriage passageway. Having entered the train towards the back, he decided that he would move forward along the carriages in his search, then, if he could not find them he could double back on himself. Slowly he moved forward, checking the compartments as he went, noting the ones that had their blinds pulled across. He would have to return to those later, finding an excuse to knock on the door and try to gain entry if he could not find the Professor and Jazmine straight away. Still time was on his side thought Mallory, the train journey he had been told when his purchased his ticket, would be an hour and three quarters arriving at 11.30. The fact that this was a non-stop journey, would also go some way in his favour, meaning that the Professor could not leave the train at an earlier stop and continue the trip by other means.

At the first compartment in the seventh carriage Mallory found what he was looking for. Jazmine Montacute was sitting alone, gazing out of the window as the view rolled by. He opened the door, quickly stepped inside, seating himself in front of the woman, who sat up in surprise staring back at him.

"We meet again Miss Montacute," said Mallory, inwardly cringing at his own mellow dramatic statement.

"Yes, it appears that we do," replied Jazmine coolly. "I thought that we had left you back at platform 1."

"You very nearly did."

She smiled. "Quite a good plan don't you think considering it was hatched at a moment's notice? Get a constable to delay you while we buy a platform ticket and then ensure you see us heading away."

"And then when I am on the wrong train you double back to the train you were going to catch all along, leaving me high and dry," continued Mallory.

Jazmine just smiled back at him innocently.

"So where is he, your Father, the Professor?"

"Around, he went to stretch his legs. He should be back shortly."

"I'm quite happy waiting."

Jazmine just looked at him, it was clear from the expression on her face that she was not.

"Look," said Mallory, trying a new tack, "I know that your Father, and possibly you, are directly involved in the Rainsbury Hall robbery."

"That's quite a statement to make Mr Mallory. I hope you have the suitable evidence to back it up; defamation of character is quite a serious offence."

Mallory sat up straight, trying to look as official as possible. "I do, more than enough."

"So why aren't the police here instead of you?" she asked.

"I'm here to make a deal," replied Mallory trying to side step the glaring observation that he was actually lying. "The most important thing here is the recovery of the stolen items, the manuscript and the other artefacts. If that happens, Lord Rainsbury will be happy, the company I work for will be happy and the police will be happy - to a point. Of course they will want to find who carried out the crime, but with everything returned it will drop down their list of priorities. The case will effectively be closed, especially as I cannot see Lord Rainsbury wanting to pursue the matter any further. Now please, co-operate with me, I am trying to help you."

Jazmine leant forward slightly. "Mr Mallory, you seem a reasonable sort of man, so, please let me save you a world of pain. You have stumbled into something big, something that goes far beyond the robbery you seem so intent on solving. So, I implore you, leave this compartment, forget all that you think you know, which, I hasten to add, is far wide of the mark. Go make out a report saying that you are unable to solve this case and move on with your life."

"I cannot, and will not do that. Where is the manuscript and artefacts?"

Jazmine shook her head almost sadly. "Mr Mallory, you are dealing with forces here that you cannot possibly comprehend. I implore you one last time. My Father and I are not to be trifled with, let alone the powers we are fighting."

Mallory stared at the woman, unsure if she was mad or was genuinely concerned with his well-being. "I don't understand. 'Powers you are fighting?' What is this? Look, please just tell me where the artefacts are."

Jazmine stood up. "I am sorry Mr Mallory, you have been warned." She then moved towards the compartment door, but Mallory was faster, on his feet in a flash and quickly standing in front of her blocking her way. "I'm sorry Miss, but I..........."

His words were abruptly stopped by Jazmine throwing herself at him. A second passed before it fully registered that she was kissing him firmly on the lips, then her arms were round his body, he tried to pull back; but then found himself being turned round and then pushed roughly to the floor, with Jazmine standing over him now smiling.

"What the....." was all a stunned Mallory could splutter.

Jazmine, who now had her back to the compartment door, turned to look behind her and through the door's glass down the coach's corridor beyond. "Oh dear, Mr Mallory!" she said looking back to him. "You have gotten yourself into a mess haven't you?"

"What?" asked Mallory, totally stunned at the turn of events. "What do you mean mess?"

Jazmine Montacute held up a small green piece of paper in her hand. "Tickets please!"

54

Mallory reached into his waistcoat pocket where he had placed his ticket, but of course it was not there. Instinctively he tried his other pockets, but of course his search was in vain. "Give me that ticket!" cried Mallory, well aware of the trouble he would find himself in.

Before Mallory could get up, Jazmine opened the compartment door and stepped out into the carriage's narrow corridor. Mallory jumped to his feet following, but by the time he had joined her it was too late. She had opened the window opposite, and had flung out the ticket.

"Jazmine?"

Mallory turned. In the narrow corridor, just outside the next compartment, heading their way was Professor Montacute, but, more worryingly than that just behind him, was the ticket inspector.

CHAPTER 10

For a moment Mallory just froze, waiting to be approached for his ticket, but instead, the inspector suddenly turned and rapped on the door of the carriage next to the one he had found Jazmine in. "Tickets please!" He then opened the door and disappeared inside.

"So you found us Mr Mallory," said the Professor.

"My ticket!" cried Mallory turning to Jazmine, ignoring him.

"What?" said the Professor confused.

"Let me explain Father. Mr Mallory here has lost his ticket."

"I didn't lose it," said Mallory hotly. "You picked my pocket then threw it out of the window!"

"Oh, well done Jazmine!" cried the Professor, visibly proud of his daughter's actions.

Just then the ticket inspector opened the neighbouring compartment's door, having ensured that all tickets were present. Realising the awkward situation he was about to find himself in Mallory had no other option, but to turn and run back down the carriage, away from the inspector and the Montacutes.

Two carriages down, Mallory stopped and caught his breath. He had been totally outfoxed by Jazmine, although he did allow himself to smile at the thought of her kiss, but that aside he realised that he was in trouble. Boarding a train, particularly a first class train, without a ticket was a criminal offence, and worse still in his present situation he could find himself locked in the guards van or the train could be stopped at a station, and he would be forcibly ejected. Either of those situations would see the Montacutes get clean away from him along with all hope of solving the Rainsbury robbery.

He briefly thought of heading back to the Countess Von Braun, and asking her for help, but then a better idea came to him. Quickly he made his way down the carriageway until he came upon two doors off to the side. The lock on the right door had been turned showing the word ENGAGED in black capital letters.

"Tickets please!" called out Mallory in a deep voice as he knocked on the toilet door.

"What the devil?" came the reply from within.

Mallory took a deep breath. "I'm sorry Sir, but I need to see your ticket."

"Damn it man! I'm in the lavatory!"

"Sorry sir, but I have to check, some people hide in the facilities to avoid paying."

"But ruddy hell man, this is first class! Things like that don't happen in first class!"

Mallory smiled. "I'm very sorry Sir, but I have to check all tickets. Just slide it under the door for me if you would."

There was mumbling of discontent, and then from the bottom of the door a first class train ticket appeared. Mallory stooped down to pick it up, then with his new ticket in hand turned and headed back to the Montacutes compartment.

"Tickets please!"

Mallory came upon the ticket inspector as soon as he re-entered the next carriage. Smiling, Mallory handed him the stolen ticket, which was checked, stamped and returned to him. Breathing a sigh of relief he continued his way back to the Montacutes compartment, but he arrived there only to find the compartment empty. The professor, his daughter and their luggage were gone.

With no other option Mallory resumed his search of the train, carriage by carriage. However, this time, aware that the Montacutes knew he would be looking for them, and may have taken to a new carriage, drawing all the blinds to hide themselves, he took the dangerous step of knocking on all the compartment doors, even the ones where the screens had been drawn. The response to those innocent passengers concerned was as to be expected and combined indignation at being disturbed to near anger, despite his cover story of being lost and trying to find his own compartment.

Taking a deep breath, Mallory rapped on the door of another compartment marked 'PRIVATE.' "Darling it's me!" and with that he opened the door before there could be any objections.

A hand grabbed him firmly by the collar and Mallory found himself being dragged inside, his legs promptly being kicked away from him, sending him crashing to the floor.

He turned to get up, but found himself being pushed down again, looking up he found himself staring at a now familiar sight, the barrel of Charles Montacute's gun with the Professor behind it and beyond him Jazmine, who had shut the door firmly behind her.

"Mr Mallory, this is becoming an annoying habit."

"Then give me what I want and then I can leave you in peace!"

"I'm sorry, but that is not possible. Anyway, how did you get past the ticket inspector without a ticket?"

Mallory smiled defiantly. "Give me what you stole and I will tell you."

The Professor pulled back the hammer of the gun, Mallory winced, realising that there was no time for him to reach for his own weapon, but the Professor's weapon remained silent.

"Jazmine told me that you think it was me who carried out the robbery."

"That's what the evidence so far looks like."

"Well the evidence is wrong – sort of. Mr Mallory, there are things going on here that you cannot understand…."

"Let me guess," interrupted Mallory. "You are going to give me the same strange powers speech your daughter did? Hardly convincing."

The Professor's expression changed. "I can see Mr Mallory that you are the type of person that cannot be dealt with in a normal manner." His words were stern and threatening.

Mallory tried to get up but the Professor kicked at his legs sending him back down to the floor with a bump.

"Father!" cried Jazmine in partial protest.

With his free hand the Professor dipped his hand into his pocket and pulled something out and held it up in the air.

Mallory found himself gasping. It was a gold chain, on the end of which was a small black stone in the shape of a scarab beetle.

"I don't believe in beating around the bush Mallory," said the Professor sternly. "Yes, it was me. I took the scarab, but despite what you think I was not responsible for the other items being stolen. That was not my doing!"

"Father!" cried Jazmine again, clearly concerned that he was giving away too much.

"If that's the case give me the scarab," said Mallory. "That will go some way to appeasing Lord Rainsbury."

The Professor shook his head. "You have no idea do you? Lord Rainsbury did not return from a trip to London yesterday."

A look of horror crossed Mallory's face.

"No, it's not what you think. After our encounter at the University I went to Rainsbury Hall to speak with him, to try and smooth things over as much as I dared about the robbery, but he was not there. I was told he was going to London on business and then onto the Reform Club. I waited for him at the club for hours but he did not show up."

"That means nothing," replied Mallory. "He could have changed his plans or decided to head home later."

"I doubt that very much," replied the Professor. "I fear that something sinister has happened to him. I doubt very much he is still alive."

"If what you say is true, that is all the more reason to co-operate with me. At the moment you are certainly in the frame for theft, but if what you say is true and the police make the same connection that I have, you could be looking at a murder charge and that means the death penalty!"

"Or you could leave me alone and let me carry out my plan, which would solve this whole ruddy mess."

Mallory shook his head. "All I see here is smoke and mirrors, you both hint at a fanciful tale, a wild claim that Lord Rainsbury is missing or dead, you protesting the robbery was really down to someone else, but the fact is that it is you with a gun, holding the stolen scarab. If what you say is true and someone else was involved, tell me, give me a name and let us go to the police."

The Professor shook his head. "I'm sorry; it's far too late for that."

"Which can only mean that I was right all along; you are the thief and are trying to escape to America."

"Oh think what you ruddy well like………"

Then without warning, the compartment was plunged into darkness as the train sped into a tunnel. Mallory blindly kicked his foot upward, hoping to knock the gun out of the Professor's hand. Simultaneously four sounds erupted into the air; the Professor yelling as his hand was kicked upwards, the gun going off and the bullet slamming into the carriage roof, Jazmine screamed and the sound of the train's whistle almost drowned out the other three.

Mallory scrambled to his feet and dived to where he presumed the Professor would be, while at the same time, the Professor slammed his arm downwards, hoping to hit Mallory. The two men smashed into each other, but the momentum of Richard's dive sent them both crashing backwards straight into Jazmine who tumbled over the both of them. The tangled bodies tried to disengage themselves and get to their feet as quickly as possible. Then the carriage was again filled with daylight as the train emerged from the tunnel. The Professor stooped down to the floor to try and pick up his gun which he had dropped in the struggle. Mallory, seeing this, kicked out his foot and the gun was sent spinning across the floor away from the old man, who then moved his elbow up sharply, hitting Mallory hard in the face, sending him sprawling back across the compartment, almost breaking his nose. In response, Mallory reached for his own gun and pulled it from his jacket. "Get back, I'll shoot!" The words were barely spoken when he found his arm being wrenched sideways and slammed into the seat, causing him to drop the weapon. Jazmine, out of his line of sight, had dived forward and had managed to disarm him. Surprised, Mallory looked up to see Professor Montacute looming towards him, gun in hand and raging anger in his elderly eyes.

CHAPTER 11

Richard Mallory was woken by the gentle and constant movement of the train as it continued its journey to the Southampton docks.

The first thing that he became aware of was the throbbing of his head, from a particular spot where there was now a bump the size of a small egg, caused as he had been hit hard with the butt of the Professor's gun. He then became aware that his hands were now above his head, tied firmly together and attached to the overhead luggage rack. His legs too were bound at the ankles, and his mouth gagged with a handkerchief.

Looking around he could see that he was alone and that the blinds shielding the compartment from the narrow passageway were drawn shut.

Mallory struggled against his bonds but they were too tight, expertly tied. He tried to yell out for help, but his muffled callings went unheard. Trying an old trick he had to employ in his army days, he slowly started to try and push the gag out of his mouth bit by bit with his tongue.

Suddenly there was a frantic banging on the window and a woman's voice called out, "Richard Mallory! Are you in there? Richard? Richard?"

Mallory could not immediately place the voice, although it did sound familiar. He tried to call out but realising that he still could not be understood, opted to bang his feet on the floor in response. There was silence from outside, followed by a call. "Oh thank goodness I've found you! It can only be you in there!"

"Who's there?" called Mallory getting the last bit of gag out of his mouth.

"It's me, Elisabeth Von Braun."

Mallory smiled, it was the Countess, but more importantly, help. "Countess, can you open the door?"

"No, it's jammed."

Mallory cursed under his breath. No doubt the Montacutes had sabotaged the lock in some way.

"Richard, I saw Professor Montacute and his daughter, he had a gun. He tried to hide it but I saw it, I came to find you. Oh Richard! I'm starting to get scared, the look in his eyes!"

"You did the right thing coming to find me."

"Shall I go and call a guard to open the door?"

"No," replied Mallory quickly, "I don't want anyone else involved just yet."

With all his strength he pulled down with his arms and the bar that his hands were tied to gave way. Then, with some difficulty, from his jacket pocket he managed to retrieve his pocket knife, and noted as he did so that his revolver was gone, the slightly open carriage window gave him a clue as to where it had ended up. With some difficulty he managed to open the knife, and cut through the ropes tying his hands and then those around his feet. Now free, he went to the compartment door but it would not open, so instead he pulled on the blind, which snapped upwards and found himself staring at the beautiful face of Elisabeth Von Braun through the glass.

"Richard! Are you alright? What's going on here?"

"The Professor is a thief," confessed Mallory. "The robbery that I told you about, he and is daughter were the perpetrators. They took a number of valuable items including a black scarab worth a fortune. I'm trying to get them back."

The Countess looked visibly shocked.

Mallory tried the door again but it refused to budge, being completely jammed, sabotaged by the Professor. He then tried the sliding window on the door itself, and the two side windows as well but they too did not budge, all three, like the door, stuck in place. "Stand back!"

Elisabeth did as she was told, then Mallory pushed as hard at the door as he dared, but it remained firmly shut.

"We could break the glass!" suggested Elisabeth.

Mallory shook his head. "That would bring too much attention, and besides, the glass is reinforced." He looked around and his eyes focused upon the window opposite with the English countryside rolling past.

"I've an idea. The next carriage is occupied, but the one after that is empty, go there, open the window and wait for me."

"Wait for you?" asked Elizabeth, confused. "Oh my goodness, you are not going to do what I think you are?"

Mallory nodded. "I'm going to have to climb outside."

"But you will be killed!"

Mallory shook his head. "It's alright, I had to do something similar once in India."

The Countess's face switched from horror to one of surprise.

"All part of being a Captain in the British army," replied Mallory with a smile, remembering the incident. "At least this time no one will be shooting at me! Now go!"

With that the Countess turned and disappeared out of view. Mallory then headed over to the carriage door, which would in normal circumstances only be opened to allow passengers to get on and off the train at a station. As he did so he stopped to pick up the broken bar from the luggage rack which he looked over before then tucking it into his shirt. He would need to have some kind of weapon and this small rod of metal was better than nothing.

Mallory first opened the window, checked that there were no trains coming, then leant out as far as he could to try and work out the best way of climbing down the carriage. He concluded that there was only one real option. Once outside with his feet on the runner which stretched the length of the carriage, he would have to edge his way along using a combination of the window edges and door handles, until he reached the Countess, where she would open the door and he could climb back into the empty carriage.

Taking a few deep breaths to steady his nerves he reached backwards out of the window, placed his fingers of one hand, then the other, on the roof's lip and pulled himself up slightly so he ended up sitting on the bottom frame of the window, with his back totally outside of the train. Again he paused, then in one fluid movement he pulled himself upwards and manoeuvred his legs completely out of the train before lowering them until they were firmly on the carriage runner, before moving his hands back down to grip the open window.

The feeling of speed as the train hurtled along was far greater than Mallory had expected, as was the force of the wind against him which not only threatened to knock him off altogether, but made breathing itself difficult. He turned his head back down the train to allow himself to take in a few deep breaths, then turning back he slowly but carefully started moved along the train.

At the next compartment, he peeked round. Inside there was an elderly gentleman and his wife. Then at that very moment, the man stood up, said something to the woman, and then left the compartment. The woman then reached for her bag and pulled out her embroidery, and turned her back slightly against the window. Taking this opportunity, Mallory moved past as fast as he dared.

He had just made it past the compartment window, near to where the Countess would be waiting for him, and to safety, when disaster struck. Struggling against the wind, his right foot slipped off the runner; pitching him forward, and causing his remaining foot to buckle, and then also slide off the ledge. The sudden burden of weight on Mallory's hands almost caused him to let go totally, but somehow he managed to cling on to the window frame, his legs flaying around wildly near the spinning wheels as he desperately tried to regain his footing. He then managed to bring his foot up and rest it back on the runner, allowing him to relieve the strain on his hands, before then hauling himself up once more. Mallory paused to compose himself, and then carefully moved down until he reached the next compartment.

Once there he peered inside, but the Countess was nowhere to be seen. Undeterred, he tried to open the door from the outside only to find that it was locked, he then tried the window, but that would not budge either, so carefully he moved along the runner to the next compartment which he found to be occupied by a family, forcing him to return to where he expected the missing Countess to be.

Again he tried the door and window in vain, then looking up he saw movement. In the narrow passage beyond the compartment two well dressed men walked past. Mallory held his breath realising that if they turned, he would be seen, but the two walked past oblivious to the fact that a man was hanging from the train a few metres away, immersed in their conversation. Then straight behind them a woman walked into view, a small child, a little boy wearing what looked like a sailor's suit, followed behind her. He turned suddenly and stared straight at Mallory who froze, aware that he was now discovered. The child raised his right hand and waved excitedly at him. Mallory found himself smiling back, nodding his head in acknowledgement. Satisfied, and as though it was perfectly normal to see someone clinging to the outside of a carriage, the boy turned back and continued to follow the woman. As they moved out of his field of vision, Mallory's eyes rested upon an open window on the opposite side of the carriage and he realised that that was the way he would have to re-enter the train.

With his muscles aching, Mallory hauled himself upwards. His fingers grabbed the top lip of the carriage and his feet found purchase, first on the panelling of the door and then on the very handle itself, then with one supreme effort he dragged himself up onto the train's roof, where he rolled on his back, laying flat, exhausted by his exertions.

CHAPTER 12

Mallory lay motionless on the top of the carriage for several minutes. It was a strange feeling with the wind rushing over him and the continual juddering as the train's wheels passed over the joins in the track, almost surreally calm. He wondered what had happened to the Countess. Why wasn't she at the compartment? Had she decided to abandon him or had something more sinister happened to her? The other thought that crossed his mind was how on earth was he going to deal with this mad Professor and his equally deranged daughter? They were not going to hand over the black scarab without a fight, but he must find a way to retrieve it somehow.

Slowly and carefully Mallory rolled onto his stomach, then onto his knees. Keeping his weight as far back as he could he edged his way forward to the roof's edge and peered over the side, trying to work out where exactly the open window was that would allow him to gain access to the train's narrow corridor.

It was then that he heard the train's whistle.

Looking around he could see the front of the train disappear into a tunnel. Sheer horror gripped him, for he

66

could clearly see that there was little room between the top of the train and the tunnel roof, certainly not enough room to accommodate him, even if he were to lay flat on the roof. If he did not act soon, he would be knocked clean off the train. He looked back down at the side of the train, considering his original plan, but ruled it out, it was a difficult manoeuvre and he was not sure if there was enough time. So instead, with little other choice, he jumped to his feet and started to run as fast as he could down the carriage away from the tunnel mouth, towards the rear of the train.

Despite being still physically fit from his army training, Mallory found himself making little progress running against the speeding train. In fact, he soon found himself actually drifting backwards towards the tunnel mouth.

A break in the carriages came up and he leapt over it, but on landing lost his footing, and ended up falling forward landing on his knees. By the time he managed to scramble to his feet he had been pulled back even farther towards the tunnel mouth.

Looking ahead, Mallory could see that there were only two carriages left. Pushing himself harder, he tried to increase his speed. His only chance would be to drop off the last carriage and grip onto the roof.

The next gap came up, this time he jumped over it successfully, even made up some ground. Onward he pushed, his leg muscles now aching as much as his arms.

With the final carriage looming, he jumped the final gap, then with the remainder of his strength ran as fast as he could, his foot nearly slipped, but somehow he managed to regain his footing, then with one final effort he reached the end of the train.

Quickly he sat down with his legs dangling over the back of the carriage, and then turned his entire body round, his legs still hanging in mid air so he was facing the tunnel mouth.

Mallory gasped in surprise to see that the tunnel was almost upon him. Instantly he allowed his body to drop, gripping the edge of the carriage for dear life. His head missed crashing into the stone roof by a matter of mere inches and he found himself plunged into total darkness.

The carriage emerged from the other side of the tunnel with Mallory still clinging to the back. It had taken less than twenty seconds to pass through, but to Mallory it had seemed a lifetime. Realising that he was still alive and unharmed, he started to climb his way round the train, the passageway side, to find a way back into the train.

Luck was on his side. Not only was the passageway empty, but a window had been left open by someone, allowing him to climb back inside the train with relative ease.

Mallory collapsed to the floor, partly through shock, partly through exhaustion of the supreme physical effort he had just put his body through. He closed his eyes, and took in a few deep breaths to steady himself.

"Richard! Oh thank God you are alright! They came after me!"

The figure suddenly kneeling beside him and grabbing his arm was The Countess Von Braun, her beautiful face etched with worry.

"After you?" was all Mallory could say.

"Yes," replied Elisabeth, "Charles Montacute and his wretched daughter. I had to run and hide. I went back for you, but could not find you. Richard, they went to my compartment and ransacked my belongings!"

"That sounds like the Professor all right. Did he take anything of value?"

Elisabeth nodded. "An eye of Horus on an Amulet. It is an Egyptian symbol of healing. My husband got it for me after a visit to Egypt last year."

Mallory rose to his feet. "So, he's up to his old tricks. Come on, he cannot have gotten far."

With that, Mallory headed down the train to find the Professor, pausing to look into the Countess's ransacked compartment.

As the two continued down the train they had to negotiate a rather portly gentleman in a heated conversation with a guard; as Mallory heard the contents of the argument he sped up, realising he was the cause of the disagreement.

"But I tell you I gave my ticket to the inspector already!"

"No you did not Sir!" replied the ticket inspector.

"But I did! I pushed it under the door of the lavatory when I was asked for it, and when I got out the chap was gone........."

As he entered the next carriage Mallory saw them, heading down the narrow passage. With his anger rising, he broke into a run.

"Montacute!"

They turned round to face him.

"I thought we left you nicely tied up and out of harm's way," groaned the Professor. He then looked at Mallory's dirty smoke covered clothes. "You look a state. Oh my goodness! You didn't climb out of the train did you?! Well you have got more guts than I gave you credit for!"

"You are a thief!"

"Not this one again."

"This time you have overstepped the line and I am going to make sure you are brought to justice for all of your crimes! I know you stole the eye of Horus on an amulet from the Countess Von Braun."

The Professor's face suddenly changed. "You know the Countess?"

"Yes, I met her when I boarded the train."

"I warn you Mr Mallory, the Countess is not all she seems, by a long chalk, and we never took any amulet from her."

"Like I can believe that!" scoffed Mallory. "Enough's enough, I'm going to call the guard and have you detained! You are in possession of two, possibly more, stolen items."

"You can try you blithering idiot!" replied the Professor menacingly, as he reached for his stick, pulling the handle slightly to reveal the top of a blade.

"It's all right Father I'll deal with this," said Jazmine, pushing her way past to get to Mallory, "I'm so sorry about this Richard, but it's for your own good, really it is."

"What are you - oooopmh!"

Mallory doubled over in agony as Jazmine's knee connected with his groin. He gasped for air and tried to speak, but all that came from his lips was a low whine. He then found himself being pushed to the floor.

"Father, your hip flask."

The Professor responded as he was bid, and Jazmine unscrewed the top, and then moved in for the second part of her plan. Mallory then found his jaw being forced open and (good quality) brandy being poured into his mouth. It hit the back of his throat causing him to splutter and cough, he tried to spit the liquid out, but Jazmine held his mouth shut, even grabbing his nose forcing him to swallow the alcohol.
The rest of the flask was hastily emptied over him.

Jazmine stood up and looked down at her victim. "Again, I am so sorry."

Looking up Mallory caught a look of genuine regret in her eyes before, to his astonishment, she grabbed at the shoulder of her dress and ripped it. She then screamed at the top of her voice, "Help me! He attacked me! He attacked me! Oh please somebody help me!"

A look of sheer horror spread across Mallory's face as he realised that he was being set up in the cruellest way possible.

He tried to get up, but again Jazmine kicked him in his already injured groin, causing him to collapse back down to the floor.

Numerous compartment doors began to open and other passengers came out to see what was going on. A tall young man was first on the scene, emerging from the door right by them. Jazmine, the 'helpless damsel in distress' threw herself at him sobbing. "Oh please, he attacked me."

"He did what?" exclaimed the man looking angrily at Mallory on the floor.

"Yes, he has been pestering me and my dear Father this entire trip. I tried to spurn his advances, but he suddenly went berserk and attacked me. It was horrible!" She then buried her face on the stranger's chest pretending to sob bitterly.

By now there was a small crowd gathered around looking on.

"Is she alright?"

"She is now."

"What happened?"

"I don't know. I heard a scream."

"That excuse for a man attacked her! The one writhing around on the floor like a dog!"

"What! The blaggard!"

"Disgraceful!"

"Looks as though she gave him what for though!"

"Good for her!"

"Call the guard!"

"Never mind that, call a constable!"

"I would not waste my time, throw him off the train!"

"Can you smell that? He reeks of alcohol!"

"Like a regular brewery, what a disgrace!"

"Look at the state of him too!"

"He looks as though he has been riding on the roof!"

"Blasted cad, keep your unchristian urges to yourself!"

71

"I did not attack her!" gasped Mallory. "This is not what you think!"

"Oh it is! I saw you try to kiss her!" said the Professor, quickly trying to fan the flames of hate towards Mallory.

"Excuse me! Excuse me!" It was the guard, a huge man with a stature more befitting a boxer, pushed his way through. "Hello, what is going on here?"

"That man," cried Jazmine pointing. "He attacked me!"

The guard took one look at her ripped dress and her tear stained face and drew his own conclusion. "Right you little unmentionable, you are coming with me!" The man grabbed Mallory by the scruff of the jacket hauling him to his feet, then pulled back slightly as the odour of alcohol hit him.

"What the…? I'm innocent," protested Mallory. "Where are you taking me?"

The guard looked him squarely in the eye. "I'm taking you to the guard van where you will spend the rest of the journey incarcerated. Then when we get to Southampton I am turning you over to the police!"

CHAPTER 13

"Let me go!" protested Richard Mallory, as the guard marched him along the narrow passageway towards the front of the train where the guard van was located. "You have got this all wrong."

"Save it. I know what went on."

"But that's just it you don't. Arrrgggghhh!" Mallory yelled in pain as the grip on his arm tightened.

"Oh I'm sorry," said the guard sarcastically, "did I hurt you?"

Mallory turned to glare at him, but realising that there was nothing more he could do, allowed himself to be taken through the train. At the end of the final carriage the guard opened the door, took out his key, and then opened the entrance to the guard van itself. He then roughly pushed Mallory through, following close behind.

"I'm taking no chances with you," said the guard as he propelled Mallory towards a security cage built into the carriage itself. With one hand the door was opened and despite Mallory's protests he was pushed inside, the door slammed shut and locked behind him. The guard stared at him through the grating with contempt, and then took a quick look at his pocket watch. "We get into Southampton in a little over half an hour. I'll be back for you shortly after that." With that he turned and left the van.

With the guard gone, Mallory took the opportunity to acquaint himself with his new surroundings. The cage was constructed of wire grills that appeared to be welded into the train itself. The presence of a small safe in the corner, and the sturdy construction of the cage door seemed to indicate that this was in fact a temporary strong room. The rest of the van was filled with assorted mail bags and boxes, all bound for Titanic. But the item that caught Mallory's attention the most was that of a large wooden coffin like crate. He distantly remembered seeing it when he first arrived on platform 12 at Waterloo in what seemed like an age ago.

Suddenly he heard a scratching and scraping sound at the door to the guard van. A few moments later the door was flung open and in came none other than Professor Montacute, followed by Jazmine.

"I'm guessing that you are not here to rescue me. Let me guess, more plunder here for you to steal?"

"No, Mr Mallory," replied the Professor. "The reason we are here is to do what we were aiming to do all along. Use the black scarab to stop an Egyptian Mummy."

Mallory just stared at the two, registering the seriousness in their faces. "You are mad; both of you; totally insane!"

73

"I know it sounds fantastic Richard, but it is true," said Jazmine. "The black scarab is the only thing that can stop the creature." She stepped forward towards the cage, but Mallory, bitten twice before, instinctively took a pace back, despite the protection of the cage door.

The Professor pointed over to the large coffin shaped box. "In there is an Egyptian Mummy, raised from the dead then used to carry out thefts and murders. I've been on the trail of it and those who control it for the past two years. The black scarab will stop it. Look, I don't expect you to understand. Let us do our work and I will guarantee that I will smooth things over with the authorities in Southampton. I may even be able to find a replacement scarab for you."

"Oh Father, he does not believe you."

"He will when he sees the Mummy! Come on Jazmine, let's get this over with."

For the first time Mallory noticed that Jazmine was carrying a small black doctor's bag. She passed it to the Professor, who placed it on the floor, opened it and produced a hammer and a sturdy looking screwdriver. He then went over to the oblong crate and using the tools, proceeded to lever the top open, which was then placed on the floor.

Mallory gasped at what was inside.

It was an Egyptian Mummy case, the top of which depicted a man with folded arms.

"I would not get too excited Mr Mallory," said the Professor seeing the reaction. "This is only an inner case, it was normally placed inside a larger one that was decorated and coated with gold. Jazmine, grab the feet of the lid."

With that she moved to the foot of the sarcophagus while her father moved to the top. The Professor then made a count of three, and they lifted the lid together, lowering it to the floor before standing back up staring inside the crate.

"What in the world!" cried the Professor in pure dismay at the sight that greeted him.

"Oh come now Charles, you did not really think that I would be travelling with the Mummy did you?"

All eyes turned to the newcomer's voice.

It was the Countess Elisabeth Von Braun, standing in the doorway of the guard's van, pointing a small revolver at the Professor.

"Countess! Over here!" called Mallory.

"Oh shut up you fool!" she replied.

Mallory's heart almost skipped a beat. It seemed that she was not here to help him after all. She turned her attention back to the Professor. "Now, I know you are armed. Drop your gun on the floor and kick it away."

The Professor paused trying to work out if he could draw his weapon and shoot in time. The Countess seemed to know what he was thinking and so moved the gun to point at Jazmine. "Do as you are told!"

Reluctantly, the Professor took the gun out from his jacket, dropping it on the floor before kicking it away. The Countess stooped to pick up the weapon and swapped it for her own, placing her small revolver into her pocket. She then moved over to the cage where Mallory was staring at her through the grating, her expression cold and merciless.

"Richard, I want to thank you for your selfless sacrifice on behalf of the Egyptian people."

She then fired the gun.

Mallory felt the bullet hit him at point blank range causing him to fall backwards. He hit the back of the carriage wall before doubling over, collapsing forward on the floor, and ending up curled over almost in the foetal position facing the cage door. From somewhere in front of him there was a scream, Jazmine, while the Professor yelled out in protest.

But as he lay there Mallory realised that a miracle had happened. There was no blood, no searing pain or gaping wound, he was winded but otherwise uninjured, for the pipe, part of the luggage rack which he had placed in his shirt earlier and had failed to remove, had taken the bullet.

He saw the Countess move closer to the cage, he closed his eyes, playing dead and praying that she would decide against a final shot to the head to ensure the task was finished, but there was nothing. Slowly opening his eyes a crack, he saw her move away then turn back towards the Professor and Jazmine. "Of course you two will be blamed for his death. I shall make sure of that." She held up the Professor's gun to emphasise the point.

"Oh you are a wicked piece of work!" said the Professor. He then pointed to the empty coffin. "Where is he?"

"The Mummy? He is with Otto of course, Cherbourg to be precise. It was arranged that we would try and tackle some of our targets in France. There is a lot for us to accomplish on this assignment! Now give me the black scarab!"

"I don't know what you are talking about," he lied.

"I know you have it, Mallory told me it's in your possession."

"He was wrong!" put in Jazmine.

"I'm going to count to five!"

"Why bother, you are going to kill us anyway!"

"Because I want to see the look on your faces, I want to watch you squirm, watch the anguish in your eyes."

"You sadistic witch!"

Elisabeth smiled, she had been called a lot worse in her time. "One.......Two........."

With the final realisation as to what was really going on, Mallory rose to his feet. Trapped in the cage he was severely restricted as to what he could do. Only one thing sprang to mind, he just hoped that it would be enough. From his shirt he took the metal rod which had just saved his life and went over to the cage placing one end between the metal gratings, while supporting the shaft in his left hand. Then with his right he hit the end of the rod as hard as he could.

"Three........Four........Arrrggghhhh."

The metal rod flew across the van and hit the Countess hard on the back of the head, she jolted forward. The gun went off, the bullet slamming harmlessly into a bag of mail. Jazmine ran forward to tackle her, knocking the gun out of her hand while the Professor, wanting to safeguard the Scarab at all costs took it from his pocket and hurled it to one safe place totally beyond the Countess's reach. "Mr Mallory, catch!"

Out of the corner of her eye Elisabeth saw a streak of black and gold fly through the air. Pushing Jazmine away she tried to reach out for it, her fingers grazed the gold chain, but the priceless projectile continued on its way, landing safely in the waiting hand of Richard Mallory. He caught it instantly, clenched his fist, retracting it back into the safety of the cage.

The Countess screamed out in despair that her plan had been ruined. Now unarmed, with the scarab unobtainable, she opted to take the only course of action open to her, she ran; ran to the door and out of the guard van.

A stunned silence filled the air. Mallory stood in the cage holding the scarab in his hand while the Professor and his daughter looked on.

Slowly Professor Montacute moved forward to the cage. "I think, Mr Mallory, that we got off to a bit of a bad start don't you? My name is Professor Charles Montacute. This is my daughter, and assistant, Jazmine." She nodded in acknowledgement. "In addition to my lecturing duties at King's College London I also undertake recovery of lost artefacts and the solving of Historical mysteries."

He then held out his hand for Mallory to shake.

Reaching through the wire grating, black scarab still in his fingers, Mallory grabbed the Professor's hand and firmly shook it. "Richard Mallory, former Captain of the British army, turned Private Investigator; currently working for Oldfield and Harper Insurers……Um…..I don't suppose that you can get me out of here?"

CHAPTER 14

Bruce Ismay, the owner of The White Star Line, stood proudly on the grand first class staircase of Titanic. In front of him were a number of reporters from the newspapers, as well as an increasing number of passengers who had seen this small press conference, and had decided to listen in.

Ismay had been talking for a little over five minutes. The contents of the speech had been well rehearsed the night before in his hotel room at the South Western Hotel, Southampton. What effectively was an enthusiastic monologue covered all the important points that the press would want to hear; the importance of transatlantic travel, the conception of Titanic, a brief overview of the build along with a dazzling array of facts and figures about the physical ship and its cargo.

Suddenly an eager young reporter desperately trying to find a different angle for the story shot his hand into the air.

Ismay saw him and smiled politely. "There will be an opportunity to ask questions at the end."

"But I just wanted to quickly ask you your opinion about these new airships that are being developed. Do you think that they will ever rival the ocean liner?"

"No," replied Ismay, a little annoyed that he had been interrupted, and forced to digress. "I seriously doubt that one of those contraptions will be able to transport a fraction of passengers that Titanic will in its lifetime. To me the claims that are being made about them and what they will do for travel in the future sound nothing more than just a lot of hot air!" He paused as there was a ripple of laughter at his joke. The young reporter was about to ask another question, but before Ismay could silence him and return to his own agenda, another journalist piped up.

"There are all sorts of speculations that an attempt on the Blue Riband crossing is going to be attempted, can you confirm or deny this, Sir?"

Ismay paused; the Blue Riband prize was given to the passenger ship which made the fastest Atlantic crossing. Cunard currently held the record with the Mauretania, prior to that it was Cunard's other flag ship the Lusitania, which had not only set the record in 1907, but had managed to break it on three other occasions. The White Star Line had not held the Riband since 1891 with the Teutonic, and they were desperate to reclaim it. But the harsh reality was that Titanic would not be able to retrieve the record. This was a liner built for luxury, not for speed. However, Ismay was certainly not going to admit it publicly.

"All I am prepared to say Gentlemen is that I am confident that the White Star Line will get the Blue Riband, at some point in the very near future. How soon in the future that will be I cannot say! However, please bear in mind that the average cruising speed of Titanic is twenty one knots and it is expected that she can easily accommodate twenty four knots over a prolonged period."

There was a mumbling from the reporters, and a furious scribbling on their notepads, picking up on the implications of what was said. Ismay remained silent, allowing them to draw their own false conclusions. He desperately wanted the prize of the Blue Riband, and was sure that it would be his, not with Titanic, but perhaps the next ship the White Star line was building.

Ismay was about to continue when he was momentarily distracted by what sounded like a heated discussion coming from somewhere nearby. The reporters heard it too and turned to see a well-dressed woman walk into view with, presumably, her husband by her side.

"No, no, no!" said the woman firmly. "I want to get off this ship as soon as possible!"

"But darling! You are making no sense at all!"

The woman turned. "No sense! No sense? This is an unlucky ship and I want us to get off as soon as possible."

"But the tickets; our plans for New York!"

"I don't care! I want to get off this ship!"

The man looked over at the gathered crowd, slightly embarrassed at the scene that was being created, then turned back to his wife and, in a whisper that only she could hear, said, "Emily, it was only a stupid dream, brought on by a late night, too much wine, and the anticipation of the trip. Nothing is going to happen and this ship is certainly not going to sink!"

"Is everything alright?" called out Ismay.

The woman turned, and not realising who she was addressing said loudly, "No it is not, my man, I want to get off this ship."

"Why? Is something wrong?"

The woman, now seeing the gathering crowd, particularly those who were reporters, stopped and checked herself. "I… I… I… have changed my mind about the voyage. I would like to get ashore, as soon as possible."

Ismay was not totally surprised at her behaviour, some people were nervous about travelling by sea, fearing the worst, and did indeed need to be coaxed. More importantly from his point of view it allowed him to move into the realms of safety advances that Titanic had made. "Madam, please let me lay any possible fears you have to rest. This ship has been built to the highest possible standard, with particular attention to safety. Titanic has a system of bulkheads which divide the ship into sixteen compartments. The idea being that in the unlikely event of any collision, the affected area can be sealed off safeguarding the ship, averting disaster."

"Is that system of bulkheads what makes the ship 'unsinkable'?" asked a reporter as he frantically scribbled down what was said.

Ismay turned to him and smiled. "I think you are misquoting there. The ship's builders, Harland and Wolff, have gone on record as saying that this system makes the ship *virtually unsinkable,* let's not tempt fate eh?"

There was another ripple of laughter.

He turned back to the woman who was still looking nervous. "In addition Madam, as well as ensuring that there is a lifejacket for everyone onboard, Titanic also actually *exceeds* the number of lifeboats recommended. We are also using Marconi's wireless technology allowing us to be in constant communication with other ships in the vicinity and able to request assistance should it be needed."

"Thank you, but…I really think that…."

"…and of course," continued Ismay, more for the benefit of the reporters, "Titanic is under the more than capable command of Captain E J Smith, Commodore of the White Star Line and Lieutenant in the Royal Naval Reserve, who saw active service in the Boer War and was decorated with the Transportation Medal which you will see, proudly displayed on his lapel. He is the most capable and professional of Captains, and one with a sound reputation for smooth uneventful voyages!"

The reporters took down the facts hungrily. One raised his hand, about to enquire about Smith's impending retirement when the woman again turned to her husband, evermore alarmed.

"Please, please! I don't want us to travel. Let's spend a few more days here in England. We can go later, please, I beg of you."

The man looked at his wife, and although he did not really understand, he nodded and she gave a big sigh of relief.

Not wanting to let this opportunity slip by to prove how accommodating the White Star Line could be to its passengers, Ismay nodded and then suddenly a White Star official appeared. "Now," said Ismay in a big friendly voice, "two of our passengers here have had to change their travel plans without warning. Please go with them and ensure that their luggage is retrieved and before they leave the ship make sure they are re-issued with another ticket so they can travel aboard Titanic at a later date." Seeing the approving look on all those gathered, apart from the woman herself, who seemed to suddenly go quite pale, he added, "Oh, and ensure that their new ticket includes complementary sessions in the Turkish bath, swimming pool and gymnasium."

The woman stared straight at Ismay, and timidly thanked him. Although it was clear that a new ticket was the last thing on her mind, while her husband made a joke about how the old adage of it being unlucky to have women on ships certainly rang true for him. The couple were then quickly escorted away and the crowd returned to Ismay, who was smiling to himself as he created good press and avoided the possible issue of a full refund. "Now, where were we? Are there any more questions?"

"Yes, what does the White Star line have planned next?" Ismay smiled. "The third vessel in our 'Olympic class' of course, an even larger vessel, able to carry even more people in greater luxury."

"And after that?" pressed another reporter, desperately wanting more.

"After that," said Ismay with a smile, "it will be time for me to call a more formal press conference, to reveal the further expansion into luxury travel for the masses. Now ladies and gentlemen, if that is all, you will have to excuse me, there are a few more matters which I have to attend to before we sail."

From somewhere at the back of the group an elderly woman started to clap and the others joined in.

Ismay looked on smiling, taking in the applause, pleased that despite the talk not going exactly to plan, he had come out of it well.

CHAPTER 15

Richard Mallory sat in the train compartment looking over the black scarab he was holding, with Professor Montacute and Jazmine looking on.

The lock on the security cage had not been a challenge to the Professor, who had managed to open it in seconds using a set of lock picks that he had brought with him. The three then quickly made their way back to the Professor's compartment where the blinds were drawn for privacy. Aware that a search might take place for Mallory when the guard finally returned to the van and found him missing, the Professor kitted him out with some spare clothes from his travel bag. Fortunately they were the same size and the fit was perfect.

With just a few minutes until they were to arrive at Southampton Docks, the Professor was able to fully brief Mallory as to what was really going on. "Jazmine and I have been on the trail of Otto and Elisabeth Von Braun for the past two years. As you have witnessed, she is ruthless and does not let anyone stand in her way."

Mallory nodded, remembering the look in her eye when she shot him. If it was not for the metal pipe in his shirt he would have been killed without question.

"Her Father is Egyptian, and despite being born and brought up here in England, then marrying an Austro-Hungarian, her loyalties firmly lay with Egypt. Shortly after marrying Otto, and taking the title of Countess, she was recruited by the Egyptian government for one purpose; to reclaim items 'stolen' from the Egyptian people and to seek revenge on those who had 'plundered' its treasures, although to the world she and her husband are dealers in antiquities working on behalf of the Egyptian government itself."

"A water tight cover story, and I presume the title of Countess opens many doors," said Mallory.

"Oh quite," said the Professor nodding. "The Von Braun family is known and respected throughout Europe and far beyond. An announcement that they are travelling to a certain country is normally followed by invitations by the great and the good as well as officialdom. That coupled with the fact they are working for an official government means that no area is out of bounds to them. If only people knew their true aims."

"So what is this Otto like?"

"A nasty piece of work," replied the Professor. "He spent a short while in the Austro-Hungarian army, bought his way up to rank of Captain, before being discharged on 'medical grounds'. The reality was much more serious. He was guilty of severely beating a young recruit. The lad survived but the head injuries left him disabled. It also seems there were a number of severe irregularities with the Count's expenses."

"In other words he had his hands in the public purse?" ventured Mallory.

The Professor nodded. "He was claiming for three 'second homes' he did not have, as well as a lavish list of items including a small ornamental house for his ducks! Anyway, in light of all this, the army decided that they were better off without him, and so, to avoid a scandal, pensioned him off.

Afterwards Otto spent his time drinking, gambling and generally spending the family money as fast as possible, until he met and fell in love with Elisabeth, then this new line of work presented itself."

"Alright," said Mallory, "that part of the story I can accept, but a Mummy raised from the dead and used as an assassin?"

The Professor laughed. "It took me a while to get my head round that one too. I first thought it was a man in a costume, but after I put four bullets into him and he kept on coming I had to revise my opinion!"

"But how can it be alive?" pressed Mallory.

"We are not totally sure on the exact details," said Jazmine. "We think that a living human brain was used in conjunction with a variety of forbidden Egyptian magic, to bring the Mummy back to life. The Mummy was then supplied to the Von Brauns to use any way they liked to achieve their given goals."

"A living human brain," pondered Mallory. "So someone was murdered, and their brain transplanted into the Mummy; very Mary Shelley."

"I actually would not go so far as to say 'murdered'. I have a gut feeling that the brain was donated from a willing volunteer, with the promise of immortality and a guaranteed passage into the next life."

"But why go to all that trouble, why not just use ordinary people for the tasks?"

"You have not seen the Mummy!" replied the Professor with a chortle. "As well as being six feet tall with super human strength it is practically immortal; that and the very fear factor of seeing the creature itself puts it at a tremendous advantage."

"But it's a bit conspicuous."

"Yes, but it does have a disguise; of sorts, and it mostly carries out its tasks at night."

"It also fits in nicely with the Von Brauns cover story," added Jazmine. "'Oh we are travelling to Paris, to exhibit the Mummy.'"

"They put it on show in open sight!" gasped Mallory.

"Yes, of course, then it is in a 'sleeping state', awaiting a command from either Elisabeth or Otto to awaken it using, for want of a better phrase, 'a magic word,' and then it will do their bidding."

Mallory held up the scarab amulet. "So how does this fit in with things?"

"Amulets and charms had great power in ancient Egypt," said the Professor. "When someone died they passed onto the afterlife. They would be judged by a jury of gods to see if they were worthy of the gift of eternal life. This was done by weighing their heart against a feather, which was a symbol of truth. If the heart, burdened by earthly deeds, was heavier, the soul was rejected, and thrown to a monster called Ammit, where it would be devoured, but if the feather outweighed the heart they would be given eternal life. Now for this process called 'weighing of the heart,' spells, charms and amulets were often used to 'help' to ensure that the feather would be heavier."

"In other words cheating," said Mallory with a smile.

The Professor nodded. "Yes, cheating. However, sometimes, enemies of the deceased wanting to ensure that they did not achieve eternal life would ensure that 'cursed' or 'negatively charged' items were placed with the body to throw off the whole weighing process; usually achieved by the use of High Priests or those preparing the body. The black scarab that you hold in your hand is one of those items."

Mallory looked at the small black beetle in surprise. "You mean that this can kill the Mummy?"

"No, not kill, for that a red scarab is needed, but it seems that that black scarab, placed directly on the Mummy has the power to slow it to a virtual stop, and if it were to be placed within the body itself it will create the effect of suspended animation."

"Why not use a red scarab and have the Mummy destroyed completely?"

"Well that is the thing," said Jazmine. "We have never actually seen one. Our research indicates that there were a number of them created, but as yet none have actually been located."

"In fact," added the Professor, "as far as we know there are only three of these black scarabs ever found. The one you hold now, another on display in the Cairo museum, a third in the hands of a private collector somewhere in San Francisco."

"Are there any other types of scarabs around?" asked Mallory.

"There is a blue one," replied Jazmine, "which would cause the body to rapidly decay and a purple one which would trap the spirit in the sarcophagus." She paused. "Oh, and a yellow one which is designed to confuse the judging process by summoning other spirits."

"Not that there is any proof that those scarabs exist," said the Professor.

"Quite," replied Jazmine. "The sources explaining about them were hardly reliable, or even recognised by most Egyptologists."

Mallory took another look at the black scarab in his hand.

"Did Lord Rainsbury know its true purpose?"

"No," replied the Professor, "he knew it was rare but he had no concept of the power it held. Information detailing these scarabs and their purpose were kept mainly secret for obvious reasons."

"Now, the robbery at Rainsbury Hall."

"Ah yes Mr Mallory, your favourite subject," said the Professor with a wicked grin. "Well I confess it was me who stole the scarab."

"I'm stunned and shocked at the revelation!" replied Mallory.

"I could not tell Lord Rainsbury the truth, even if he believed me which I very much doubt, he would never have given it up, so the only option was for me to, um, get it myself. The problem was that when I got into the study the Mummy was already there, he had helped himself to a number of items, but the scarab was locked in the safe and he could not get at it. We fought and he got away. I then opened the safe and took the scarab. Now we already knew that the Von Brauns were taking the Mummy to New York via the Titanic, so we booked ourselves tickets in an attempt to catch up with them and stop the creature before it could do any real damage. I thought they would all be travelling by train, but it seems that Otto and the Mummy slipped away to France, and will join the ship at Cherbourg."

"But one thing that puzzles me; if the scarab stops the Mummy, how would he be able to take it from Rainsbury Hall?"

"The scarab only works if it is placed *directly* on the Mummy's chest, it is possible for him to hold it in his hand without the effects working; and in this case the scarab was kept in a box."

Mallory nodded, this real version of events, bearing in mind what he had been told made sense. "My insurance firm has been dealing with a small number of stolen Egyptian artefacts of late; do you think that the Von Brauns are involved?"

The Professor nodded. "Yes undoubtedly, they seem to be increasing their activity lately. I know for certain that when they are in New York they are seeking to murder at least one person. Who knows what they are planning in the meantime? I doubt that they are just using the Titanic as a means of travel."

Mallory paused for a moment. "I am coming with you."

The Professor and Jazmine started in surprise.

"I'm coming with you," repeated Mallory firmly, "from the sounds of things you are going to need a hand and as they are really behind the Rainsbury robbery I am already on the case. In fact from what you have said there are a number of other similar cases that this all ties into. Besides, I'm hoping that there might be a way to stop this Mummy without the scarab so I can return it to Lord Rainsbury……..assuming that he is alive."

"There is one problem though," pointed out Jazmine, "you don't have a ticket for the trip."

"That's alright," replied Mallory, "I can buy one when we get to the docks."

"I doubt that very much," said Jazmine. "The ship will be full to capacity."

"Oh I think that there is a way around that," replied the Professor thoughtfully. "Jazmine, give him your ticket."

"Father!" exclaimed the girl. Mallory shuffled in his seat, visibly uncomfortable that he, a virtual stranger, had been placed above his daughter.

"Oh, don't be disturbed," replied the Professor reading his thoughts. "It will be easier for me to get you onto the Titanic with a wrong ticket than none at all. As for my beloved daughter here, well, she is a woman of infinite resource and charm; she'll find a way onto the ship somehow." The Professor then stood and took down his small bag from the rack overhead. "And speaking of 'infinite resources', if you will give me a few moments, I just need to forge a letter."

CHAPTER 16

Captain Edward Smith sat bolt upright, eyes fixed forward. To his left was first Officer Murdoch and to his right were Chief Officer Henry Wilde and Sixth Officer James Moody. Behind them, standing, were the rest of Titanic's Officers, also in fixed poses, staring forward.

"Are you going to be much longer?" asked Captain Smith. "I do have a ship to run you know."

This raised a smile.

"I'll be as quick as I can," replied the photographer, who was having problems with the plate. "I want to get this right, after all, this photo is going out to the press, and will no doubt be used time and time again due to the significance of the ship and its maiden voyage!"

"Perish the thought!" said Chief Officer Henry Wilde making everyone laugh.

"Five……Four……Three……..Two…….One……and we are done; thank you gentlemen for your time."

Blinking the flash of light out of their eyes, the Officers of the Titanic broke their positions.

Smith had barely taken to his feet before the photographer was upon him. "Captain Smith, if I could just have one of you on your own."

He paused, this was an inconvenience, and he had far more pressing matters to attend to, but seeing the almost pleading look on the photographers face, relented. So he took a standing pose as the photographer got himself ready.

"Five……Four……Three……..Two…….One…….."

The flash went off again, making Smith blink.

"That was great, now if I could……."

"Thank you," broke in Smith, "but if you would excuse me." He then turned, promptly moving away; he had to be somewhere else. He could of course use the ship's internal telephone system for the task, but he wanted to assess the situation with his very own eyes. As he walked he could hardly believe the course of action that he was seriously contemplating. If as Captain he called a halt to the voyage, there would be serious repercussions; aside from the inconvenience to the passengers, and the damaging publicity, he would have to answer to those at the White Star Line personally, and there would of course be the damage to his own reputation. So he wanted to go to the heart of the problem itself, and deal with those with the first hand knowledge, after all it would be their experience that he would in affect be relying on.

From the fireman's passage, Smith entered the tank top deck which housed the two massive reciprocating steam engines, each over thirty foot tall, the largest ever to be made; powered by one hundred and fifty nine separate furnaces set in twenty nine boilers. The heat and the noise hit him immediately; around him firemen frantically shovelled coal into the furnaces, so absorbed in their work that they did not even register that their Captain was there. This subterranean world was so far removed from the opulence and glamour far above. Smith moved his way through boiler room number six and over to two men who were talking intensely. "Gentlemen, I trust things are going well."

"As well as possible under the circumstances," replied the Chief Engineer, Joseph Bell. "Sir, this is Leading Fireman Fredrick Barrett, I'm not sure if you have met."

Barrett held out his hand, but realising that it was covered with soot and oil quickly retracted it. "Um, pleasure to meet you, Sir."

Smith smiled and nodded.

"The boilers are up to pressure and all ready for the off Captain," continued Bell.

"Very good," replied Smith, "but I am sure you are aware of why I am really here; the fire, what news of the fire?"

"It's still going Captain," replied Bell with all seriousness, "and it seems to be getting worse."

The fire had started in Belfast during the final speed trials, and was located in the reserve coal bunker near boiler room number six; despite this fact, the Board of Trade had been happy to officially sign the ship over to the White Star Line ready to sail. Coal bunker fires caused by spontaneous combustion, was not an unusual occurrence, however, left unchecked the consequences could be disastrous and despite efforts to put it out, no headway had been made.

"How is it being dealt with?" asked Smith.

"The coal on top is being constantly dampened with water to stop the flames from coming up through, while at the same time we are trying to empty out the bunker," replied Bell.

"Into the furnaces or to another bunker?" asked Smith

"Straight into the furnaces, Sir," said Barrett. "It seems a wasted effort moving the coal into another bunker when we will only have to pick it up again to put it into a furnace eventually. Besides, if we do that there is a risk, albeit a small one, that we end up spreading the fire."

Smith nodded, the procedure that had been outlined was the normal way fires of this type were dealt with. "How many men are you planning to assign to fight the fire?"

"Twelve men, two stokers from each watch for as long as it takes," replied Barrett. "If we need to we can assign more as we go."

"And how long do you think that it will take to reach the actual fire itself?" pressed Smith, time was of the essence in these situations.

"There are tonnes of coal in the bunker, Sir, as you are well aware," replied Barrett. "It also depends how far down it is, but I think, working on that shift rota, with no other problem, two days, possibly a bit less."

Smith nodded, taking in the time scale, which would put them in the middle of the Atlantic, before they could even reach the burning coals which would then have to be dealt with. "And there we were thinking we would not have enough coal for the trip at all, now we have so much it's causing problems! How much was added to number six here in Southampton?" Smith was referring to the national coal strike which had threatened to halt the journey before it had even begun through a lack of fuel; but the White Star Line, determined that the journey would commence had intervened by cancelling the scheduled sailings of its two other ships The Oceanic and Adriatic. The coal reserves had been transferred to the Titanic along with their passengers and most of their crew.

"I could not say for sure, Sir, how much extra coal went into number six," replied Bell almost sheepishly, "but it was a lot. The coal deliveries just turned up, and were loaded as quickly as possible. It seems that my order not to load number six was lost in the confusion."

"Well that 'confusion' has possibly made a bad situation a whole lot worse, making it even harder for us to reach the problem!" Smith paused, looking at the faces of his two colleagues. "I am considering a postponement; outline the dangers if we sail." Of course the reality was he was all too aware of them, but wanted to hear it from the crew himself.

There was a pause before Bell answered. "Well there of course is the constant risk of explosion by a spark igniting coal dust; the fire itself might not be able to be controlled and grow ever hotter potentially putting unreasonable stress on the hull. When we eventually get to the burning coals and put

93

them into the furnaces it will mean a hotter fire affecting the speed of the ship." Bell paused. "Aside from those physical elements, there is also the risk of panic if the news somehow filters out. These things are as hard to control as the fire itself. Rumours spread among the crew then to the passengers themselves."

"But are those potential dangers enough to warrant postponing the trip?" asked Smith. "Is it safe for us, in your opinion, to proceed?"

Bell took a deep breath, all too aware of how important this journey was. "At the moment I would say yes, we can go ahead, although it's not the most ideal of situations. In a perfect world we would delay and ensure, using the port resources, that the fire was out, or at least that it was totally under control before we left."

"But we are not in a perfect world are we?" replied Smith. "Are you able to give me any good news?"

"Yes, apart from the fire, everything seems to be working as it should, there are a few minor problems here and there, stiff handles, hinges need oiling, that sort of thing, but apart from that, considering the fact it's a new ship, she's doing rather well."

"Well then, it's nice to know that my 'Guarantee Group' will have an easy time of things!"

"I wouldn't say that Andrews," replied Bell to the man who approached. "I'm considering getting you and your men to do a shift of fire-fighting!"

Thomas Andrews smiled. He was the Managing Director of Harland & Wolff, and builder of the ship. He and a group of eight hand picked men were to travel with the ship on the maiden voyage. Their purpose was to ensure the smooth running of the ship and to iron out any problems that arose.

"I have just been given an evaluation of the fire situation," said Smith.

"I heard. Are you really considering a delay?"

Smith paused, thinking over what he had been told, and then slowly shook his head. "No, not any more." He looked over at Bell. "But I want regular appraisals of the situation and I leave it to you to decide on increasing manpower to the fire fighting as you see fit. Do whatever is necessary to put that fire out."

"Aye Sir."

"I also want to keep this between ourselves as much as possible. Few people know about what's happening and I want to keep it that way."

"What about Ismay?" asked Andrews.

"He knows there is a fire, but not how bad. I said that I would keep him informed, but the less he knows the better."

This raised a small laugh from both Bell and Andrews.

Smith then took out his watch, noted the time before closing it.

"Well gentlemen, if you will excuse me I had better be getting back, last minute checks and the like. Keep up the good work." With that Captain Smith turned to leave, wondering if he had made the right choice to gamble upon the fact the fire could be brought under control before disaster struck.

CHAPTER 17

The Titanic's boat train had barely stopped at the Southampton dockside platform before the Professor had opened the door and was stepping out, followed immediately by Mallory and Jazmine.

The platform they stood on was almost directly next to berth no 44, from where the Titanic would depart. Mallory took a few moments to take in his surroundings; the dockside was a hive of activity with hundreds of people milling about,

95

some were here to see off family and friends, while others had come just to see the spectacle of the ship itself. At the bow a crane was in operation, finishing loading cargo into the front holds. At present it was in the process of guiding a dark green Austin car into the hold.

The Titanic itself, of course, dominated the view and Mallory was astounded at its sheer size. The ship was just over eight hundred and eighty eight feet long and over ninety two feet wide. Three of the four funnels projected smoke into the air, the final funnel was a 'dummy'; its only purpose to add to visual balance of the ship. Built in Belfast by Harland and Wolff, it was to be one of three new liners, the first being the Olympic, already in service, with the Gigantic yet to come. The Titanic, which had been built bigger than the Olympic, was the largest ship in the world as well as the pinnacle of style and luxury.

"Keep your head down Mr Mallory," warned the Professor, tapping him on the arm. "Remember you are nicely locked up out of harm's way."

Mallory looked back towards the train and the guard van; already there were a number of porters, no doubt to take the luggage stored there, including the Mummy's coffin to the forward cargo hold of the ship. The fact he was no longer there would soon be realised and a possible search mounted. In response Mallory looked down. "Come on let's get going."

"Yes," said Jazmine hotly. "I suppose then I had better; especially seeing as I no longer have a ticket. I'll see you later."

With that she gave Richard a cursory look then turned, disappearing off into the crowd.

The Professor turned to Mallory and smiled. "Oh, take no notice of her Mr Mallory, she'll calm down in a little while, you wait. Next time we meet she'll be as placid as a kitten."

"Assuming, of course, that she is able to find a way onto the ship."

"Oh, she will, you can count on it!"

Mallory shook his head. "I think you are expecting too much, Professor, no ticket, with barely half an hour before the ship is due to sail."

The Professor smiled. "Trust me. She'll make it! She has the feistiness and charm of her dear Mother."

"So what does she make of this, her Mother I mean; taking on the Von Brauns, and a reanimated, homicidal Egyptian Mummy?"

The Professor suddenly looked sad. "Her mother, my dear Victoria, passed away a few moments after my beloved Jazmine entered into this world."

"I'm so sorry."

"That's alright, how were you to know? But in answer to your question, my dearest Vicky would probably scold me for bringing Jazmine along, then break into an excited smile, and would want to know all about the adventure and if she could help in any way!"

"So you brought Jazmine up yourself?"

"Yes, as best I could. There were of course Nannies and the like. My sister helped where possible, but, yes I raised her. Although I sometimes wonder if I have done her a great disservice."

"How? She seems a wonderful young woman, if a bit, er um......"

"Feisty? Self-reliant? Confident? Capable? Intelligent?" continued the Professor. "And that I think is the problem; what place is there in this world for a woman who can speak Latin, translate Hieroglyphics, has studied far Eastern martial arts, even drives a motor car as well as understands the principles of the combustion engine that powers it? Most women of her age are either married or embark on careers of

97

child care or domestic service. Blast it, she is even talking about joining and becoming an active participant in the suffragette movement!"

Mallory was stuck as to what to say, the Professor's analysis of the role of women was true and he had no idea what chaos a woman like Jazmine would do if she took up the cause for women having the vote. He looked around uncomfortably. "Look Professor, over there!"

Mallory turned catching the sight of a familiar figure, it was the Countess Von Braun. She looked over at the two and glared, before turning then losing herself among the other passengers.

"Come on Mr Mallory," said the Professor, "time for us to get going."

"This way please!" called a large man in a White Star uniform, who had started to usher the arriving train passengers towards the gangways. Behind him a number of porters moved forward to help those leaving the train, especially those carrying any luggage which had not already been sent on ahead.

"Excuse me Sir!"

The White Star official turned, the Professor smiled at him. "Can I help you Sir? Do you need a porter?"

"No, no we are fine, apart from the problem with our tickets." The Professor made an erratic almost theatrical search of his pockets before finding them and holding them out. "There has been a mistake. My name is Professor Charles Montacute, from King's London. My colleague here, Richard Mallory, and I are travelling to New York to give a lecture at New York University. However, there has been a problem with our tickets. My daughter made the reservation, but when they arrived in the post, it seems that they have been made out for myself and her rather than myself and my colleague Mr Mallory."

The official looked at the tickets, noting the hand written name on the top right corner, one for the Professor and one for Miss J Montacute.

The Professor then held out another piece of paper. "Here, this is a letter from the Dean of the New York University confirming the details for myself and Mr Mallory; it was dated last month before the booking was made. The tickets only arrived through the University's internal post two days ago. A telegram was sent to register the mistake, but I did not hear back."

The official looked at the headed paper, the date and the content and nodded, seemingly happy with what he had seen. "I do apologise Sir. Do you have any more carry on luggage with you that you need help with?"

The Professor held up his bag. "No, no. I've just got this." The Official nodded. "Then if you will both come with me."

"I cannot believe this might have worked," whispered Mallory as they followed behind the Official.

"Faith Mr Mallory! Have faith!"

"The letter from the New York University, you wrote that in the train didn't you? How come you had a piece of blank headed paper?"

"I've got several with me actually for different institutions. If there is one thing that helps you move through the corridors of officialdom, it's even more officialdom!"

The White Star Official let them both up the gang plank to the First Class entrance. Just inside there was another White Star Crew member checking off names from a clipboard. The dockside Official explained the situation regarding the 'error' and the clipboard crewman nodded, searched his list, and made two ticks before indicating to the Professor and Mallory to board. The first official handed back the paperwork, wished them a pleasant trip before disappearing back down the gangway, while another porter appeared to lead them directly to the rooms that had been booked.

At the door to the Professor's room the porter left them, happy with the tip that he had been given.

"Come with me, Mr Mallory," said the Professor as he stepped through the door of the first class suite.

Mallory looked round in awe at the room. The walls and ceiling were lined with oak panelling; and thick velvet curtains hung from the cabin window. To one side there was a bed, with a wardrobe next to it and in the centre of the room there was a table and chairs, all made from heavy dark wood.

"Now in case you were wondering, your room is through there," said the Professor pointing to an interconnecting door which led directly to the next cabin. "Well it's yours now; it was of course Jazmine's." The Professor's eyes rested upon a travel trunk that was in his room, placed there hours before by a porter. "That also means that you will find her travel bag there too. Never mind, I always pack more than I need so you will have to borrow from me."

"So Professor, what is our plan of action going to be?"

The Professor paused. "Well, as the Mummy is not coming aboard until France, where no doubt it will be reunited with the sarcophagus, at present there is little more that we can do except find our bearings, and take a look around. After that though, I think that we are going to have to launch a direct assault on the Mummy itself."

Mallory nodded, it seemed logical.

"Now the sarcophagus was going to be loaded into the front cargo hold."

"How do you know that for certain?"

"Didn't you see the label on the crate when you were in the guard van?"

"Oddly enough, no, I was too busy being held captive and being shot at," replied Mallory with more than a hint of sarcasm in his voice.

"Ah!" replied the Professor, missing the gravity of the comment totally. "There was a label on the side of the crate 'Forward cargo – via hatch No 1'. Pretty conclusive! Anyway, we need to act fast so we will make our move tonight."

"But what happens when the Von Brauns try to animate it and it does not respond? Surely they will realise that the scarab has been planted and try to remove it?"

The Professor smiled. "Planting the scarab is only the first phase of the plan Mr Mallory. After the amulet is in place we are going to take the Mummy, weigh it down then throw it over the side of the ship sending it to the bottom of the sea where it can never harm anyone ever again."

CHAPTER 18

Captain Smith looked out of the window of the Bridge's wheelhouse at the crowds which lined the dock, then to his pocket watch.

It was nearly time to depart.

Putting the thoughts of the coal bunker fire out of his mind he turned to look at the man by his side, who was at this moment in time the most important man on the bridge, even superior to himself; 'Uncle' George Bowyer, Southampton's Trinity House Pilot, who would be responsible for guiding the Titanic out into open water, before being dropped off.

It was a strange fact that Captain and Pilot looked so similar; both were about the same height, the same age, both sported a neatly trimmed white beard; even their uniforms, apart from subtle differences, were identical.

"Soon be time," said Bowyer. "I bet that you are excited, eh Smith? What a way to end your career, the maiden voyage of the Titanic."

Smith smiled. "Yes, it will certainly be one to look back on, although rumours of my impending retirement are actually premature."

"Oh?" Bowyer looked surprised.

Smith nodded. "I'm going to keep charge of Titanic, for the time being anyway. White Star is going to make an announcement when we return. They want me to keep my hand in so I can take out their next new liner for the maiden run. *Then*, I get to put my feet up! Keep it under your hat though."

Bowyer nodded, happy that he would get to work with Smith a few more times at least.

The door to the wheelhouse opened and in walked Bruce Ismay and Thomas Andrews, both of whom had requested that they could be on the Bridge for the actual departure from the docks.

"Ah, Bruce, Thomas, I wondered if you had decided not to join us," said Smith.

"No, no, not at all," replied Ismay. "I got side tracked with some reporters, tried to give them a few columns regarding the ship; trouble is I think I gave them enough for a whole page!"

The bridge crew laughed politely.

"Anyway," continued Ismay, "one thing they were all quite keen to know was if we were going to make an attempt on the Blue Riband."

"As I think Mr Andrews will testify," replied Smith, "this is a ship built for luxury rather than speed."

"Oh that's what I told them, of sorts anyway," replied Ismay, "but still a fast run won't do any harm eh? Show the world what White Star is made of, and make Cunard a bit nervous to boot!"

"Well, we will see," replied Smith, thinking that a fast run may be more a reality than Ismay realised, but not for the sake of the Blue Riband. If the bunker fire was not able to be controlled, getting to New York with all haste for help was a real possibility.

"Are we ready for the off?" asked Ismay.

"We are pretty much there," replied Bowyer. "Just a few last minute checks."

"Good, good, good," replied Ismay excitedly, "and I hope that there will not be any incidents; after all I know what you two are like when you get together!"

The attempted joke was met with a collective silence from all those on the Bridge. Seven months earlier, on September 20th 1911, Smith was Captaining the Titanic's sister ship Olympic and, on leaving the Southampton docks, with Bowyer as pilot, the ship crashed into the warship HMS Hawke, causing tremendous damage to both vessels, as well as embarrassment to the White Star Line and had even delayed the building of Titanic, as repairs to Olympic had taken priority.

Neither Captain nor Pilot were happy to be reminded about the incident.

"Um, Mr Murdoch," said Smith, looking away from Ismay, who realising his error, deliberately stepped to the side of the wheelhouse out of the way, "please issue the order for men to report to stations and let me know when the gangways are secured."

"Aye Sir," replied Murdoch, who then went over to the internal telephone system.

Smith looked over at Andrews knowingly. "I trust all is well."

Andrews nodded. "Yes Sir, nothing more to report from me."

Smith nodded then looked over at Murdoch, who had returned. "Are we clear to proceed?"

Murdoch nodded. "We are now. There was a small problem with some fireman who stayed too long in the pub, but they have been turned away. The gangways are all up, and the doors secured."

With a final look at Bowyer, Smith took a deep breath. "Very well, take her out!"

Three long blasts of the Titanic whistle were sounded and, on the dockside, mooring lines which were holding the ship were released, allowing the five small but immensely powerful tugs, under the guidance of Bowyer from the bridge, and signalling to each other by a series if whistles, to ease Titanic away from her berth.

Steadily the tugs pulled Titanic along the River Test, a small stretch of water which would lead out to the open sea.

Upon the signal from Bowyer the five tugs simultaneously dropped their lines moving away. Smith gave the signal and the ship's mighty engines roared fully into life; the Titanic was finally underway.

After a few moments, from somewhere on the portside there came a snapping sound followed by a scream.

"What was that?" asked Smith.

"I'm not sure," replied Murdoch.

"Look to port, to port!" cried Bowyer.

Everyone looked to the left. The Titanic was close to berth number 38 where two ships, the Oceanic and the New York had been berthed side by side, placed out of action through the coal strike. Again there was the sound of something snapping and another mooring line arched into the air and the two moored ships began to move violently.

"It's our displacement!" said Smith out loud. "It's our displacement that has done it!"

Smith was right, the size and the speed of the Titanic had caused a mass of water to crash against the two moored ships, so much so that the mooring of the nearer ship, the New York had snapped.

"The stern's drifting!" observed Murdoch.

With no lines to hold it in place the back end of the New York steadily began to swing outward towards them. A thought suddenly entered Smith's mind, it was to do nothing; to allow the New York to hit his ship. The damage would not be much, but it would be enough to result in the voyage having to be postponed. The Titanic would have to be stopped, the ships separated, damage assessed. A crash such as this would easily delay sailing for twenty four, maybe forty eight hours; time enough to deal with the fire which raged below.

Smith looked over at Bowyer who looked as though he was about to speak, but also seemed to hesitate.

"Look!" cried Murdoch suddenly. "One of the tugs is moving out."

It was true, from their vantage point in the wheelhouse they could see one of the small tugs, the Vulcan, was moving steadily towards the drifting New York, no doubt to try and secure a line to it before it hit Titanic.

"All stop and full reverse!" The order had left Smith's lips before he had even realised that he had said it. Bowyer, who was technically in charge of all such commands at this point, nodded in approval.

"All stop and full reverse!" The order was repeated and was carried out.

Smith and Bowyer moved to the far wheelhouse window where they had a clearer view. The stern of the New York continued to move out towards them, coming ever closer.

Suddenly a blast of a horn was heard, it came from the Vulcan, no doubt indicating that the line was attached. At the same time, those on the bridge could feel the pull of the mighty engines starting to slowly pull Titanic into a reverse path. All the while New York drifted ever closer, pulled in by the continuing buffering of the waves.

"Twenty feet and closing," called Murdoch.

"We are not going to make it," said Bowyer, his voice filled with angst.

"No, we are not are we?" replied Smith, secretly relieved.

"There will be a delay and an investigation into this," said Bowyer solemnly, his mind going back to the aftermath of the Hawke collision, "not to mention the further damage to our reputations."

"Ten feet and closing."

"This was not our fault," replied Smith quietly. "Do not fear about that, I am sure that when........."

"Look!" cried Murdoch pointing at the drifting ship which was now less than six feet away from the hull of Titanic.

Suddenly, the New York seemed to almost stop, the power of the tug now taking the full strain of the drifting ship. Then the New York started to move in reverse, the gap between the ships now widening, not closing.

There was a collective sigh of relief from all those in the wheelhouse realising that disaster had been averted by the narrowest of all margins.

"All stop," ordered Smith trying to keep his voice steady. He then turned to Bowyer. "Mr Bowyer, please convey my thanks to the Captain of the Vulcan for his quick thinking, and can you also contact the port authorities to ensure that all other docked ships we will be passing are secure?" Smith then turned round to Ismay, who smiled and silently nodded in thanks. However, a feeling of dread and impending doom sat in the pit of the Captain's stomach as he wondered if he had taken the right course of action.

"One more thing," he then said addressing the crew of the wheelhouse in general, "if anyone wants to make a joke about '*New York* coming to us instead of us getting to New York' or any other such quip, I would ask them to remove themselves at once!"

This raised a few quiet smiles.

Smith turned to Bowyer. "I believe that the bridge is still yours."

Bowyer nodded, the order to continue would be his; however it was an order that he was determined not to give until he knew for certain that the docked ships were tightly secured.

CHAPTER 19

Richard Mallory and the Professor, who had positioned themselves on the open deck for the departure, witnessed the entire New York incident, only having to move briefly aside to allow a priest, armed with a small camera, to take a picture of the near collision.

"That was very close," said Mallory, as he watched the New York being pulled away. "I hope that is not a sign of things to come!"

"I did not take you for one of those superstitious types," replied the Professor slightly surprised.

"I'm not, well not really." Mallory paused. "I had a few routines of things that I would do before missions, if that counts, mostly checking equipment and men."

"That sounds more like common sense to me."

"Perhaps, but if I did not do it in a certain way I used to get uncomfortable," he paused, "so then, what now?"

The Professor shrugged. "I suppose it would be wise for us to take a nose around and familiarise ourselves with the ship."

"I need to get a message to my employers about the sudden change of events," said Mallory. "They need to know about the scarab and that I may be onto solving other cases."

"The ship's telegraph?" said the Professor.

Mallory nodded.

"Alright, you go and send your message while I take a stroll around. I might find something useful about the Von Brauns on my way."

Mallory wandered along the ship's corridor trying to get to grips with the events of the last few hours. The Rainsbury Hall investigation had gone way beyond what he had ever expected. He was used to danger and conflict in his work, but it seemed that what he was suddenly involved in was far beyond what he was used to - the supernatural.

Then coming towards him he saw a familiar figure. It was Elisabeth Von Braun. She caught sight of Mallory and was visibly shocked to see him. "Mr Mallory! What an unpleasant surprise. I see that you made it on board; most impressive."

Mallory smiled. "Yes, thank you, turns out that I got hold of the wrong end of the stick as to what was really going on."

"How nice of the Professor to put you right!" Quickly she took the telegram that she had just collected and stuffed it in her handbag. Then she moved beside him, quickly took him by the arm, smiling at him innocently. "Mr Mallory, will you walk with me for a few moments?"

"It looks like I don't have much of a choice doesn't it?"

She laughed as she started to move off. Mallory walked with her, captivated by her beauty and more than a little curious as to what she was going to say.

"Professor Charles Montacute, with that whore of a daughter of his, are well known in our circles as nothing more than grave robbers."

"Circles?" asked Mallory with curiosity.

"Yes," replied Elisabeth. "There are a number of us, all over the world dedicated to the preservation and reclamation of the items stolen from Egypt, and of course ready to ensure that appropriate punishments are carried out as required."

"And do these all have their own Mummy to carry out their bidding?"

She paused, trying to decide how much he could be told. "The use of ancient Mummies in our work is more common than you would think. Now, do not think for one minute that there is an army of the living dead on the rampage. The process to create a living Mummy is long and complicated. However, suffice to say, there are enough for the tasks required."

A chill went down Mallory's spine. The thought that there were more creatures of this nature in the world unsettled him.

"Anyway," she continued, "there are several arrest warrants outstanding for your Professor all over the world. There are even some places where if he showed his face he would be killed on sight."

Mallory nodded. This did not surprise him in the least, from what he had seen of the man's Machiavellian methods.

"Richard, I think that we can come to an agreement that would be mutually beneficial to us both."

"Is this where you offer me a bribe?"

For a moment Elisabeth almost looked hurt at the suggestion of such a thing. "No, nothing as vulgar as that, no I was thinking more of some financial remuneration for the trouble and inconvenience that you have suffered so far. I was thinking one thousand pounds. I will even arrange a replacement for the black scarab that you seek. All you have to do is leave the ship at France and then forget all about the last few days."

"I'm sorry Countess," said Mallory shaking his head, "you know that I cannot do that."

"Mr Mallory, this is going to be your one and only chance to come out of this venture unscathed. If you refuse me, you will certainly end up dead, probably in the most unfortunate of ways."

"Well it's an improvement on being shot, left for dead in a guard van."

Elisabeth smiled, appreciating the reference to their last encounter. "I'm sorry about that, but it was necessary."

Mallory found himself nodding, but then checked himself. This woman, no matter how beautiful and demur, had tried to kill him in cold blood a few hours before and now was walking with him, chatting, bordering on flirting as though they were old friends. "Necessary for who?"

"For me," she replied simply.

"I think that I had better be going," said Mallory and he tried to pull away, but Elisabeth had other ideas and gripped his arm tighter.

"And I think that you need to understand the true nature of the danger that you face."

With that she produced what looked like a small stone tablet, no bigger than her hand. She brought it up and pressed it hard against Mallory's cheek before he could react. At the same time she started to chant.

Mallory felt the effects instantly. He suddenly became weak and his legs started to buckle. He lifted his hand, to grab the tablet, but the effort seemed almost too much for him. Then he noticed with horror that the skin on his raised hand, as on the rest of his body, had started to change in colour and texture.

He was rapidly ageing.

"What are you doing to me?" was all he could say as he managed to wrap his fingers around Elisabeth's sleeve. He pulled on it as hard as he could but his strength was virtually gone. The tablet stayed in place and the spell continued to ravage his body.

Elisabeth smiled. "You need to be taught a lesson as to what you are involved with." She then moved away from him totally. He slumped against the nearest wall, gasping for breath. Moving his fingers to his face he ran them over now totally unfamiliar features. He imagined how he must look to others, an ancient old man, probably over the age of a hundred. "You have stolen my youth!" he croaked with the voice of an old man.

Elisabeth looked on smiling, enjoying what she had achieved. She moved closer. "Mr Mallory. The powers that have been unleashed on our quest are not to be dismissed."

"You, you, you...!" Mallory pushed himself forward, Elisabeth caught him and he tried to reach for the tablet she still held, but she pulled it away.

"Is everything alright?"

"No," wheezed Mallory looking at the woman who had appeared, she was dressed in a White Star uniform.

"It will be in a few moments," said Elisabeth quickly. "My dear *grandfather* here has had one of his turns. But they pass."

"Are you sure that you don't want me to get the ship's Doctor?" continued the crew member.

"No, that's quite alright," said Elisabeth. "He will be alright in a few moments."

Mallory was about to gasp a protest, but then stopped himself, after all what could he say? So instead he just nodded and the crew member wished them a good day and headed away.

111

"Now then Mr Mallory are you convinced that you should leave the ship at France?"

"In my present state I think that I will want help to make it to the end of the deck!"

Elisabeth smiled and held up the tablet. "The spell is but a temporary one, but is a taster of what you are involved in and what you could face if you persist in this venture."

"Temporary?" asked Mallory, hope raising within him that he was not doomed to stay this way.

"Yes," she replied almost with a hint of regret, "if I smash the tablet it will be reversed instantly, otherwise the effects will wear off in a few hours. Either way by the time we reach France you will be back to your normal self, which means that you will be able to get off without any problems, and of course if you do leave at France you will be doing so a very rich man."

Although momentarily tempted, Mallory shook his head. "No, you need to be stopped. Professor Montacute is the man to do it and I will give him every assistance possible."

Elisabeth paused, looking almost sad before nodding. "Very noble of you!" A wicked smile passed her lips. "I bet you are sweet on that vixen of a daughter of his."

The image of Jazmine flashed into Mallory's head.

"What would she think of you now *old man*? Still no matter," continued the Countess. She paused. "Mr Mallory I think that you could add a very interesting dimension to this trip. So, on that basis, I give you back your youth." With that she threw the tablet to the deck. It smashed instantly into a hundred pieces before disappearing into dust. Instantly the effects of the curse started to wear off and Mallory started to revert back to his own age. At the same time the Professor appeared. "Mr Mallory!" he called, as he grabbed the very top of his walking stick and drew out the long thin blade. He pointed the swordstick at Elisabeth.

"Oh put that toy away!" she said, unconcerned. "Mr Mallory and I were just having a little chat weren't we?"

Mallory, now restored to his normal self, nodded.

"Now Gentlemen, if you will excuse me, there is nothing more for me here so I shall be on my way. I'm sure our paths will no doubt cross again. I look forward to it!"

With that she calmly walked past the two men, nodding to them politely and headed off.

"Mr Mallory!" said the Professor as he ran up to him. "What happened? Are you alright?"

"I think so," he gasped in reply, as he rose from the deck. "She had this tablet thing with writing on it. She touched me with it and I became old."

"A spell tablet," said the Professor. "On it was written a spell which was activated when it touches the victim. You were very lucky. I've heard of some of those tablets carrying spells that turn the victim to dust or drive them insane. What did she want?"

Mallory smiled. "To warn me off."

"Did it work?"

"No," he said with a smile. "Now is there anywhere on this ship we can get a drink?"

CHAPTER 20

Due to the 'New York incident', the Titanic arrived in Cherbourg nearly two hours later than planned. Because of the ship's vast size Cherbourg's piers were unable to accommodate her at the main dock, so, as previously arranged, Titanic moored off shore, and the task of transferring the arriving and departing cargo and passengers between Titanic to the French shore fell to two White Star tenders, called Traffic and Nomadic.

Count Otto Von Braun stood on the deck of Nomadic, surrounded by fellow first class passengers gazing at Titanic as they slowly approached. His excursion to France had not gone as well as he had hoped. The Mummy had arrived at his London home with a large envelope from Ahmed early yesterday afternoon, with their instructions for the days ahead. Otto was surprised to see that hurried arrangements had been made to get him and the Mummy to France overnight, but then on seeing the target he understood completely the urgency and the importance of investing as much time as possible in completing that particular task. Egyptian intelligence had reason to believe that a red scarab beetle, capable of destroying reanimated mummies had not only been found, but had been bought innocently by rich tourists who would ultimately end up in America. The tourists concerned were the millionaire John Jacob Astor and his much younger, and pregnant, bride Madeleine, who were returning from their honeymoon.

As well as the Astors scarab, there was a number of other 'tasks' outlined in the envelope, all of which would need to be 'attended to' before they arrived at New York, where further orders would be waiting for them via a contact at the Egyptian Museum.

"It is an amazing sight is it not?"

"Yes, it certainly is," replied Otto, turning to look at Lord and Lady Astor.

"And what better way for us to return home than the maiden voyage of Titanic for us to start our new life together?" said Lord Astor proudly gazing at his bride. Madeleine looked down almost blushing. Otto, however, did not even notice her reaction; his eyes were firmly fixed upon the item that she wore around her neck - a small red scarab which hung on a gold chain.

"Otto, I hope that we will be able to dine together one night, I am so looking forward to meeting your lovely wife."

"Oh, you can be sure we will, John," replied Otto quickly. Tracking the Astors down had been more difficult than Otto had hoped. Due to concerns of unwanted press because of the 'scandal' of their relationship, John and Madeleine had maintained a low profile while in France. Newly divorced Lord Astor had made no time in marrying Madeleine, who was twenty eight years his junior, who had quickly fallen pregnant with his child. Otto had only managed to meet up with them as they waited for the tenders. From then however, Otto had managed to weave his charm, and in a short time had won them over.

Madeleine innocently started to play with the scarab around her neck. Otto cursed, the object he sought was within a few feet of him, an item of such rare power lost for thousands of years, now in the hands of this, this mere child! Still, he knew that by the end of the journey it would be in his possession. Getting it would be easy; it was just a matter of time.

Slowly the tender moved into position by the Titanic's open boarding door. A gangway was dropped and the passengers were helped aboard.

Elisabeth Von Braun was waiting for her husband by the entrance. As soon as he was on board she rushed over to him, throwing her arms around him.

"Nice to see that romance can last, eh?" said John Astor as he helped his wife aboard.

"Darling," said Otto turning, "may I introduce Lord and Lady Astor?"

"Charmed," said Elizabeth as Lord Astor took her hand to greet her. Lord Astor then formally introduced his new wife. Elisabeth saw the scarab straight away; her eyes widened in surprise, but managed to regain most of her composure.

"What a lovely necklace you have!" was all she was able to say,

"Do you like it?" asked Madeleine. "John bought it in Egypt for me. It's apparently quite rare. It was either this or a purple one, but I liked this one better. It will match a lot of my other jewellery."

"Women, eh?" broke in Otto. "First thing they do is talk about baubles! Now darling we must go and leave these good people in peace."

The two couples said their farewells and made arrangements to meet later, and with that they headed their separate ways to their respective cabins.

"Otto!" said Elisabeth as she walked with her husband.

"I know," he replied, "I could not believe it either."

"Do you think that it could be genuine?"

"The only way we will know for certain is for us to get hold of it and look at the inscriptions on the back, which we will one way or another," he said menacingly. "How was your trip?"

"Eventful," she replied. "Charles Montacute was on the Waterloo boat train."

"What!"

"I'm afraid he's onto us and he's got help, some insurance investigator he hooked up with. They are both here on the Titanic."

"Damn!"

"It gets worse. They have the black scarab. They tried a raid on the guard van where the empty Mummy case was. Seems they did not know you had taken him."

"Good, but this complicates matters."

Elisabeth smiled. "No, it just makes for an interesting trip."

She looked over at Otto who smiled at her.

In a matter of minutes they had arrived at their first class cabin, booked and paid for, in secret, by the Egyptian government. Inside, Otto looked around approvingly at the décor. He moved over to the table, where in the middle was a welcome hamper filled with fine wines, cheeses and the like, a present from the White Star Line itself.

"Of course," said Otto as he took a closer look at the hamper, "it will be a certainty that Professor Montacute will attempt to stop the Mummy in its dormant state. That is when he is most vulnerable."

"Let him," replied Elisabeth with a wicked smile on her face. "Arrangements have been made."

Otto nodded in approval, whatever his wife had planned it would no doubt be of the most ingenious cunning and would outsmart the Professor. Beside the hamper there was an open telegram, the one which Elisabeth had picked up just before her encounter with Mallory. Otto picked it up and read it. It was a message from their counterpart in New York, confirming the arrangements for their arrival and, more importantly, that the horror writer Fredrick Spencer-Grace had accepted the invitation to the Ambassador's reception, where they would be able to make their move upon him. "I almost feel sorry for Spencer," commented Otto, knowing what lay in store for him.

"I don't," replied Elisabeth almost angrily. "His outputs of cheap, pulp, horror writings have cheapened our Egyptian legacy to the world, reducing it to fourth rate adventure stories!"

Otto smiled. "Yes, especially that story about the Mummy brought back to life by magic then used to kill those who disturbed his tomb, a very original tale, and much truer than he could ever imagine!"

Elisabeth tried to glare at her husband, but instead dissolved into a fit of giggles. "Alright, I'll let you have that one." She paused. "There is much to be done before we arrive in New York isn't there?"

"Yes," he replied, thinking of the contents of Ahmed's letter outlining the tasks set. "The Astors of course will be the main priority, but I want to deal with Henry Blackwell tonight, before he makes any new friends who may report him missing."

"I think the most difficult task is to intercept Douglas's package."

"Yes," replied Otto. The package was from Miles Douglas, an American businessman based in Cairo. The contents of which was a semi-mummified cat, over two thousand years old, which he was trying to smuggle to the United States and had opted to do so simply by using the postal service. The importance of the cat was that the mummification had not been fully completed and it was feared that if the deceased cat was fully analysed in an American laboratory the exact secrets of the embalming procedure, kept secret for thousands of years, would be exposed to the world, and even copied. Douglas himself had been killed the week before, mugged in a side street by thugs who were never going to be caught, and his rooms ransacked with his notes destroyed, but the package still had to be intercepted and dealt with.

"I have been giving that a lot of thought. Getting into the mail room should not be a problem; the issue is finding one parcel amongst the hundreds that are being carried. I think that there is only one option. We will have to set a fire."

Elisabeth's eyes widened in delight. "Otto that's a fantastically evil idea, but it will have to be done with care."

"Agreed, we don't want to endanger the ship. I suggest it's done just before we are to arrive in New York. That way help is near if things get out of hand."

Elisabeth nodded in agreement and was about to mention some of the other tasks on the list when she was interrupted by a knock at the door. She went over and opened it and in

118

came a steward pushing a small silver trolley, on which was a bottle of the finest Champagne in a bucket of ice with two glasses. The steward deposited the trolley, and discreetly left.

"Oh Otto!" cooed Elisabeth as she threw herself into his arms.

Otto Von Braun looked straight into the eyes of his wife and smiled. "That is just a little reminder my darling, that this trip should not all be about killing and destruction. I want us to be able to spend some time together. The same goes for our actual stay in New York."

Elisabeth nodded enthusiastically, this was going to be an assignment that she was determined that they were going to remember for years to come. "Now," said Elisabeth, "let me tell you the whole story of my adventure on the boat train."

CHAPTER 21

The interconnecting door to Mallory's room flew open and a slightly flushed Professor entered. "Here, you are going to need this," he said as he threw a black bundle which was caught by Mallory.

"What's this?" he asked looking over what he had been thrown.

"A White Star overcoat," replied the Professor who had kicked the door shut and was now examining the other coat which was draped over his arm.

"Where on earth did you get them from?" replied Mallory as he opened it out to take a closer look.

The Professor smiled. "Let's just say it's amazing how careless some people can be with their uniforms. Just a pity I was not able to pilfer a hat too."

Mallory put on the coat. It was a surprisingly good fit. "Is this really going to be necessary?"

119

"Very much so," replied the Professor as he dumped his coat on the table before sitting down in the leather tub chair. "The cargo hold is strictly 'off limits' to passengers. This will go some way to help keep a low profile if we are seen."

Mallory looked over at the clock on the mantle which read a quarter to midnight.

"What time are we going to go?"

"Soon, Mr Mallory, soon."

Mallory shuffled nervously, he was not looking forward to the professor's plan. "Any sign of Jazmine?"

The Professor shook his head. "No not yet, but be assured she will make herself known to us when she is able."

"If she made it onto the ship."

"Oh, she made it Mr Mallory, you can be sure of that!"

Then it was the Professor's turn to look over at the mantle clock. "Alright Mr Mallory, I think it's time we made our move. Let's go and destroy a Mummy!"

It did not take Mallory and the Professor long to make their way towards the bow of the ship where they positioned themselves on bridge deck B which overlooked the sunken forward well deck, and the raised forecastle deck beyond.

"This is going to be problematic," said the Professor out loud. "You see that door there?"

"Yes," replied Mallory looking at the white door set into the side of the forecastle.

"Well that door leads into a crew only area, from which the cargo hold, among other things, can be accessed. The problem of course is that it's going to be locked from the inside."

"So what are our options?"

"Well we can wait and hope that someone decides to access it and then make our move talking our way in, which could result in us standing here catching our death until we reach New York, or there is the access hatch directly on the forecastle."

"That's impossible," replied Mallory, "it's overlooked directly by both the bridge and the two lookouts. Any attempt to use it and we will certainly be challenged. There has to be another option."

The Professor looked at the crow's nest attached to the mast set into the forecastle deck. In front of it was the hatch they needed to get to. Mallory was right. They could not fail to be spotted. "Well at the moment I cannot think of any other possibility. I'm afraid it's the hatch or nothing," said the Professor, slightly frustrated.

"I bet the Von Brauns won't be having this difficulty getting to him," said Mallory.

"Oh, you can be sure that they have made the appropriate arrangements."

"Why not try to find a crew member and see if they will take us down to the cargo hold?"

The Professor shook his head. "In the middle of the night? Even if we could find someone willing to help I certainly don't want them hanging around while we 'kill' the Mummy. No this has to be kept just between the two of us."

Just then, from below, two White Star Crew men appeared in the sunken deck and started to head for the forecastle, at the same time the two men high up in the crow's nest started to move towards the ladder.

"The changing of the watch," said the Professor excitedly looking at his watch to see that it was just after midnight. "Right, this is going to be our best chance. Come on."

The Professor, with Mallory not far behind, moved to the steep steps and downwards directly onto the sunken well deck. "Walk with confidence Mr Mallory. Look as though you are supposed to be here!"

"But we're not."

121

"I know – so shut up and play along," replied the wily scholar through gritted teeth.

The Professor and Mallory quickly climbed down the stepladder onto the sunken well deck taking the short walk past the two large hatch covers, and to the right hand side ladder on the other side which would take them up to the forecastle, just as the two lookouts were finishing their watch and descending from their post.

"A cold night eh lads?" said the Professor conversationally.

"Um, not that bad," replied the first lookout as he went past, more concerned with getting to his bed than making small talk with these two other crew members. The second lookout passed them too with a nod, then the Professor and Mallory climbed the steps onto the forecastle itself.

"I don't believe that worked," said Mallory. "They did not challenge us!"

"I know! The confusing time of a shift change. Those finishing want to get away and those starting think that as we are in situ we have permission to be here. Although I don't think that we are totally out of the woods yet."

The two men made their way over to the forward hatch which protruded out of the forecastle. Over the hatch was a large white cover, in which there was a small access flap.

"And of course it's locked and we don't have a key," said Mallory as he tried the flap.

"Keys are rather overrated in my book," replied the Professor as he looked at the lock before reaching inside his jacket for his lock picks.

"So where did you learn how to do that?" asked Mallory as the Professor set to work. "That's not the normal skill I would expect an academic to have."

"I think that you would have realised by now that I am not an ordinary scholar! But since you ask, I have a very unconventional upbringing. I was abandoned as a baby and taken in and raised by three-well- 'Ladies of pre-priced affection' is a polite term. Women with hearts of gold but forced by circumstance into the world's oldest profession. We lived in rooms in the East End of London and the streets were my home. It was a rough area to say the least with some very interesting characters around, one of whom was a thief who happened to teach me his trade. I also learnt a number of other skills which I have put to good use in my career."

Mallory stared at the old man in shock. It was certainly not the background he had expected, but it did however seem to fit with the no nonsense, Machiavellian character which he displayed. "So how did you end up as a Professor of History?"

"My 'Mothers' insisted that I studied. Not only did I have a flare for it but I relished the learning experience. I ended up going to a private school, and then on eventually to University."

"No disrespect, but bearing in mind your childhood, how on earth were you accepted into private school? Those places are notoriously elitist."

"It seemed that my Mothers knew key members of the board of governors in a 'professional capacity', not to mention a good percentage of the teaching staff! When this was realised I was welcomed with open arms. It did turn out well for them though. I consistently was head of my year, and even ended up as a library prefect."

"What about you? What's your background?" asked the Professor suddenly realising that he knew very little about his new friend.

Mallory shrugged. "Not a great deal to tell, joined the army when I was sixteen, worked my way up 'til I became a Captain." He paused. "I then left and became a private investigator"

"Left?" repeated the Professor sensing that there was more to the story.

"Let's just say that there was an incident and it was decided that I should leave."

"Mr Mallory, I am more than a little intrigued! Come come!"

Mallory smiled. "I fought a duel with a senior officer while I was in Afghanistan. He was a nasty piece of work and wanted me and my men to carry out a raid on innocent and helpless villagers. I refused, we argued, one thing led to another. The following morning we fought, I won and he ended up in hospital without any prospect of fathering children."

The Professor winced.

Mallory smiled. "It was the finest shot of my life. Still that sort of thing is not to be condoned, so I was invited to 'leave' with an honourable discharge. Fortunately those on the Court Martial panel realised the true nature of what went on and the Major I fought was one of the most disliked in the British army otherwise I could have ended up in front of a firing squad."

"What's going on here?"

The Professor and Mallory turned. They had been so absorbed in their conversation they had not seen one of the new lookouts climb down the ladder and walk up to them.

"We've been sent to check the hatch," said the Professor quickly, putting on an East End accent. "There is a terrible noise coming from it down in the cargo area. We think there might be a gull trapped in the shaft."

"Couldn't it wait till morning?" asked the lookout.

"That is exactly what I said," replied the Professor sounding slightly indignant, "but no, 'it needs to be sorted now – get to it and stop complaining', you know what it's like, you can't argue can you?"

124

"No, not really," replied the lookout, almost sympathetically. "Well I'll leave you to it then, if you need any help, give us a yell. It gets boring as hell up there."

The Professor nodded and the lookout turned and headed back to the ladder which would take him back up to the crow's nest.

"That was close!" said Mallory.

"Yes," replied the Professor, in his normal voice, "but I think that it was enough to put their mind at rest. Oh blast this lock."

"Do you think that we could talk the lookouts into getting us the key?"

"Ha!" said the Professor excitedly. "No need." And with that he opened the flap of the hatch cover.

Peering down they could see the long shaft which went all the way down to the cargo holds in the orlop deck space. Just by the hatch there was a narrow ladder which disappeared into the darkness.

"Right then Mr Mallory," said the Professor. "After you."

CHAPTER 22

Sir Henry Blackwell poured himself another generous glass of brandy. "Another one Otto?"

Otto Von Braun shook his head and watched Sir Henry place the bottle back on the table before settling back into the leather chair. The first class smoking room was deserted apart from the two lone drinkers, who occupied a table in the far corner.

"Now," Sir Henry continued, "I have to admit, I was actually dreading this trip."

"Why was that?" asked Otto, doing his best to look interested.

"Well apart from the dashed awful business meeting waiting for me in New York, I was travelling on my own. The wife normally comes with me, but she's had to go up to Doncaster to visit a sick Aunt. I've travelled before on my own, and that precisely is how you normally end up for the whole trip, 'on your own' and bored out of your mind." He then took a massive swig of the glass, almost emptying it.

"Well I hope that I have come some way to alleviate that!"

"Oh you have Otto, you have; another top up?"

"Perhaps a bit later," said Otto as he watched Sir Henry help himself to another large drink; he was truly amazed at how much the man had been able to consume, and still only be mildly inebriated. Otto had approached Sir Henry in the Dining Saloon; at the final sitting of the night they had ended up taking a meal with him. The conversation developed and then moved to the Smoking Room where they had been ever since, talking and downing drink after drink.

"So, Sir Henry," said Otto, "I'm very interested to hear more about this finance you provide for these Egyptian digs."

Sir Henry moved forward, as though about to divulge a great secret. "Otto, I tell you that country is ripe, ripe for the picking! I'm making thousands upon thousands and all I do is write out a few cheques now and then. Find a half decent archaeologist, finance them, then sit back and wait for the money to roll in. The place is littered with undiscovered tombs, filled with all manner of artefacts. It's criminal how easy it is and how much money I'm raking in!"

Otto nodded politely; he knew all too well how much money was being 'taken' from Egypt via the removal of their antiquities. It was a fact that was constantly repeated by their contacts over and over again. "Sir Henry, I am interested to know about this new venture you hinted at."

Sir Henry smiled. "Interested in a piece of the action too, eh Otto?"

"Maybe."

Sir Henry sat up straight. "There is an amateur Egyptologist goes by the name of Theodore Davis, an American. Now he claims that there are still tombs to be found in a place called the Valley of the Kings. According to other Egyptologists the whole place has been done to death, as it were. I have found a man who is convinced that he knows the whereabouts of the tomb of a boy Pharaoh by the name of Tutten Kammon or something like that. I don't pay much attention to the history; it's just the return I'm interested in. Well anyway, my man has tried all over to get finance for this dig with no luck. No one would even consider the idea, until he found me!"

"But if the valley is exhausted, surely it is a waste of money?"

Sir Henry shrugged. "I like a bit of a gamble, and besides, this chap is good, better than people give him credit for. If he says that this Tuttn, or whatever his name is, is there, he'll find him."

"And you will take the fruit of any findings."

"I take fifty five per cent of anything as well as the raising of my public profile! Not bad eh? Got him over a barrel, as I say no one else is prepared to put up the cash!"

"A most fortunate position, if he finds anything."

"And he will," Sir Henry said as he picked up the bottle and tried to pour himself another drink. "Oh dash it, all out." He paused, then snapped his fingers pointing to Otto excitedly. "Cards, Otto, cards; how about a quick game of cards to round off the night?"

"Or to start the day?"

Sir Henry smiled. "Yes, well, it is a bit early, but how about it?"

Otto smiled. "Yes, why not?"

"Excellent. I have a deck back in my cabin and a bottle of 'nearly unopened' port as well!"

The two men rose and moved the short distance across the smoking room. It was clear to Otto by the way his companion walked, using the chairs as a guide, that the mass of alcohol that had been drunk was now actually taking effect. At the other side of the room Sir Henry opened the door and out into the hallway. "What the devil…?"

Slightly in front of him, to the left was a small staircase that led up onto the boat deck. Standing on it was a figure, wrapped head to toe in yellowing bandages.

Confused, Sir Henry just stared at the figure for a few moments trying to make sense of it. "Otto! There is a man in costume dressed as an Egyptian Mummy. Hey you there!"

The Mummy slowly walked down the stairs to his victim who just stood there, looking intently.

"Otto, is this some kind of prank? Are you pulling my rope?"

"No not in the least," replied Von Braun, his heart thumping with excitement as to what was to come. "You see Sir Henry, it has been decided that your financing of the plunder of Egypt must stop, especially this new venture you are looking into."

Sir Henry's head snapped round, his mind suddenly clearing as he detected the change in his companion's voice and demeanour. "Otto?"

"It is Von Braun to you." Then before Sir Henry could react, Otto grabbed him by the arm and turned him round so they were face to face before pushing him backwards, where he was caught by the Mummy, who put his bandaged forearm against Sir Henry's throat.

"Otto!" gasped Sir Henry.

"I am an agent from the Egyptian government, and in case you were wondering, my friend here is genuine, dead for thousands of years before being resurrected."

"Help! Help! Someone! Mmmph!"

Sir Henry's cries were silenced by the Mummy clasping his other hand over his mouth. Taking full advantage of the situation, Otto moved forward and then reached inside Sir Henry's jacket, removed the wallet, opened it, took out the banknotes for himself and replaced it. He then took Sir Henry's pocket watch, opened it and seeing there was an inscription, meaning the watch was traceable, put it back. Otto then nodded to the Mummy, who then manoeuvred a struggling Sir Henry to a side door on the left, then out onto the first class promenade deck and over to the guard rail.

"Stop! Stop! Please!" begged Sir Henry as The Mummy moved his hand away from his mouth in order to get a firm grip on his clothes so he could lift him up and place him over the rail. The Mummy then paused, looking at his master for the final order.

"Please! Please! Otto! No! I'm begging you!"

But Otto was not interested, smiling, enjoying every second of this moment. He nodded and in one push, Sir Henry Blackwell was launched over the side of Titanic into the sea.

Otto looked over the rail and in the darkness could just make out the figure of Sir Henry in the water, his arms flaying. At night, with no life jacket, in the freezing water, with no hope of help he would not last more than a matter of minutes. He was in actual fact lucky to have survived the fall into the water. Of course it would be realised at some point that he was missing from the ship, but by then it would be too late, the only conclusion that could be drawn was that he had gone overboard, then eventually the body would be found.

The important thing though, was that without him, and more importantly his money, the planned dig in the Valley of the Kings would not take place, and the tomb of the boy King Tutankhamen, would remain, for the moment, undisturbed.

"Hey, you there, what's going on?"

Otto turned. Standing a few metres away from him on the deck was a man dressed in the uniform of a steward, staring at him and the Mummy in surprise. Otto turned to the Mummy, snapped his fingers and then pointed to the crew member. "Kill him, over the side."

"Kiiiillll," repeated the Mummy as he reached out his right arm. Without warning the right hand detached itself and flew across the deck like a cannon ball discharged from its muzzle. Otto followed the projectile as it flew and caught the startled crewman by the throat. Otto had seen the Mummy's 'party piece' before but it still amazed him. The creature could detach the limb at will and could control it over great distances by the power of his mind. It was a function that had served well in the past, not only allowing access to small places but instilling further terror in its victim.

Somehow the crewman managed to prise the bandaged fingers from his throat and in one desperate move had tried to throw it over the side of the ship. The Mummy however, had other ideas, and through the telepathic connection, guided the hand as it flew through the air to the guard rail, where the fingers caught hold, stopping it from going into oblivion. The Mummy then held out his arm and the hand flew back through the air reattaching itself at the wrist.

The crewman gaped at the sight, then gripped by terror, turned and ran. The Mummy and Otto pursued; the Count praying that no one else saw them.

The three figures ran along the promenade deck, past the first class lounge, the reading & writing room and the wall

130

that was the boiler casing, then back into the ship to the first class reception.

Unwilling to be chased down the stairs, the crewman ran round the back of the staircase to the Titanic's passenger lift opening the metal concertina door before stepping inside and trying to close the door behind him, but the Mummy was upon him, grabbing the door, preventing it from being closed and pushed his way in. By the time Otto arrived, the lift was descending and there were sounds of muffled screams coming up from the shaft. Otto frantically pressed the call button to summon the lift but it continued to move down. After what seemed an age, he could hear the lift stop, then slowly start the journey back up to the promenade deck where it eventually stopped.

Otto grabbed the door handle opening the metal concertina door. The Mummy was standing calmly and at his feet was the body of the crewman, his neck broken.
"I Kiiilll hhimmm!"

"Very good," said Otto looking at the body. "Now let's get rid of this body and ensure that this time we are not seen." With that he knelt down, and started to make an opportunistic search of the still warm corpse, just in case there was anything of value that he could salvage for himself.

CHAPTER 23

Slowly, Mallory and the Professor descended down the shaft into the forward cargo hold. Once at the bottom, Mallory located the electric light switch and turned it on.
The hold was filled with wooden crates of all sizes, tied securely together in batches with heavy cargo netting.

"It should not be too hard to find," said the Professor confidently, looking around. "I'm sure that the Von Brauns will want easy access to it, so look for something either on its own or on top of something else."

The Professor's assessment was correct, for a few minutes later Mallory found the crate that they had encountered in the guard van, placed to one side, covered with brown sacking, which was promptly removed. From a glass covered case on the wall the Professor freed the emergency axe and used it to prise off the crate's lid.

"Well here it is," said the Professor, looking down at the sarcophagus that lay within. "Mr Mallory you are about to meet a real 'live' Egyptian Mummy, albeit in its dormant state. It is a sight that few people ever get to see."

Carefully Mallory and the Professor took hold of the sarcophagus lid and, on the count of three, lifted it up and moved it out of the crate, placing it carefully on the floor.

"Nothing!" cried Mallory as he looked inside the empty sarcophagus. "It's not here!"

"Blast it!" cried the Professor, looking down at the empty space where he had expected the Mummy to be.

"Do you think that…?" Mallory left the words hanging, "that our ancient friend is out and about causing mischief?"

"That could be the case. But I'm wondering if there is an altogether more simple explanation."

"Which is?"

"That our friends the Von Brauns anticipated we would try again to stop the Mummy directly, and had him loaded into another part of the ship. It was a good few hours before we arrived in France, plenty of time for Elisabeth to make arrangements and have them carried out."

"Or it could be both," pointed out Mallory.

"Yes, you could be right," conceded the Professor, stroking his beard thoughtfully.

"Still," said Mallory trying to sound cheerful, "at least we have Jazmine up our sleeve as it were. I'm sure that she could ask around and find out more details for us – well, assuming that she's onboard."

"Mallory look," cried the professor suddenly pointing. At the base of the coffin was a small crack in the stone, from it there was movement. Then very slowly a large dark green locust appeared and scampered into the coffin. It was followed by another, then a third. Then the crack seemed to widen allowing a large number of the creatures to flow out into the sarcophagus floor.

"What in the world…!" exclaimed Mallory with some revulsion.

"The base of the coffin must be false, with the locusts living underneath," explained the Professor.

"But why?"

"It must be some kind of trap. "Locusts have veracious appetites, I can only conclude that the Mummy gets his victim, places them inside, closes the lid then waits for the locusts to eat them alive!"

"That is terrible!"

"We are dealing with terrible things here I am afraid, Mr Mallory."

By now the base of the sarcophagus was covered with a thick layer of locusts, a few flew into the air.

"Come on Mallory, let's put the lid back on and get out of here. I don't really want to be responsible for a mini swarm. These things can cause an immense amount of damage."

So, carefully, the two picked up the heavy sarcophagus lid and dropped it back into position, sealing in the flying and buzzing insects.

"There," said the Professor, relieved that it was in place, "all safe and sound."

THUMP!

The Professor and Mallory jumped back in surprise staring at the lid.

133

THUMP!

"What's going on?" asked Mallory looking over to a slightly bemused Professor.

"I'm not sure."

THUMP! THUMP! THUMP!

The lid of the sarcophagus jumped slightly.

THUMP!

"There can't be anyone inside," said Mallory. "We saw that it was empty."

"Agreed, it must be the locusts. We need to bind this crate up quickly, get the lid."

THUMP!

The lid of the sarcophagus literally flew into the air before crashing to the floor with a clatter. Then from inside the coffin a figure started to rise up and form.

"Dear God help us!" cried Mallory as he stared at the creature that stood before them.

It was humanoid in form, around seven feet tall, with claw like hands, and a large oval head. The monster was made up entirely of locusts.

"Professor!"

"Get back Mallory!" he cried as he stooped down and picked up the fire axe, before taking a swipe at the locust creature.

But the attack did not work.

The blade passed directly through the monster, as though it was not there, leaving it totally unharmed. Quickly the Professor turned the blade and made another sweep, this time aiming for the head. As before, the blade passed through the mass of locusts like an oar through water. The creature then jumped up out of the coffin, making the Professor retreat.

"Professor!" yelled Mallory who had himself moved to a safe distance. "How do we stop it?"

"I've no idea," came the reply.

The locust man roared again and turned, bent down and picked up the sarcophagus lid by the end in its hand like pincer, and swung it round in a wide arc.

The Professor threw himself backwards, with the stone lid whizzing past his head by a matter of inches. Realising that he had missed, the creature swung the lid back again, hoping to hit his enemy on the return, but the Professor anticipated the move, and darted forward and half dived, half rolled forward out of the way.

Meanwhile Mallory had decided to launch his own assault on the creature, and had picked up the discarded sacking used to hide the sarcophagus from view and hurled it at the locust monster like a net. It landed directly over the creature causing it to temporarily stop, making it look almost like a statue waiting to be unveiled. Then the air was filled with a sudden clicking sound and the brown sacking just seemed to dissolve into nothing.

"It's eaten through it!" cried Mallory in shock, realising what this creature could do to a man.

The locust monster turned, and seeing the person who had attacked him, let out a yell, then threw the sarcophagus lid at him. It flew through the air. Mallory jumped to one side as the lid fell with a crash on one end, turned on its own axis then toppled in a different direction. Unprepared for the new way it was falling Mallory was unable to get clear in time and the lid crashed down onto him, pinning him to the floor by his left leg. Mallory realised with relief that the lid had not broken any bones, but then that feeling was replaced with one of horror as he tried to move the heavy lid finding that he could not. He was trapped, and if he could not free himself would be at the mercy of the locust man.

Seeing that one enemy was out of the fight, the creature turned to the Professor and lurched his way forward. Almost backed into a corner between the crates, he decided that he

135

only had one option and with all the speed he could muster he ran forward directly at the creature. For a moment he was totally absorbed by the locust man before emerging out the other side. It was the last thing the creature had expected, so much so that it continued forward, hitting the crates and temporarily losing its form altogether. However, the Professor had not escaped unscathed, as a number of the locusts had attached themselves to him on the way through and had started to bite into him. To combat this he threw himself to the ground rolling as though his clothes were on fire and he were extinguishing the flames.

Meanwhile, the scattered locusts had reformed themselves, but this time had formed two smaller creatures; one making its way towards the professor while the other moved towards the still trapped Mallory.

"Mallory, I've an idea! Take courage!" With that the Professor dived into the open sarcophagus. Almost immediately, one of the creatures lurched and headed after him. The second locust monster glided over towards the still trapped Mallory who was still frantically trying to free his foot. Looking over at the sarcophagus he could see the first monster rear up before diving inside to devour the Professor. Then Mallory felt himself being swamped as the locusts began their attack, the stolen White Star coat seemed to be offering him some protection, but it was not long before he could feel the locusts needle like pincers digging directly into him. He wanted to yell out loud, but stopped himself in case the creatures climbed into his mouth. With his hands he slapped at the creatures, but realised that it was futile. He was going to die here on the Titanic, ending up as nothing more than a meal for a locust monster that should not exist.

Then suddenly, just as he finally managed to pull his foot free, the locusts seemed to cry out as one before then quickly moving off of him. Surprised, Mallory sat up and watched them as they headed off almost in neat straight lines back to the sarcophagus. Then from the stone coffin the Professor appeared, throwing himself over the side landing on a heap on the floor. The locusts filed past ignoring him completely.

The Professor got up and staggered over to Mallory.

"What happened?" asked Mallory as he stared at the old man, his White Star coat no more than rags.

"I suddenly realised that there must be a way to control these creatures. Inside the sarcophagus there is a recall button which calls the locusts back to their secret compartment. Are you alright?"

"I think so," replied Mallory nodding, "my foot feels alright and I don't think that the locusts caused any real damage, but another few minutes and it would have been a different story."

"Good," said the Professor. "Now let's get that lid back on the sarcophagus and get out of here!"

CHAPTER 24

Mallory and Professor Montacute sat in the busy first class Dining Saloon where breakfast was being served. Taking a later sitting, due to sleeping in because of the adventure in the cargo hold the night before, they found themselves on a table that could seat six people, and had been joined by an elderly couple who had seated themselves opposite them. The couple made no attempt at conversation, which suited Mallory and the Professor as they discussed the present situation. However, the two were subject to a number of discreet glances due to the number of bites that were visible on their hands and faces, marks caused by the locusts the night before.

"What about if we just find the Von Brauns and confront them?" said Mallory. "Um, just a little scrambled please." The last comment was directed at the stewardess who had rolled up a serving tray to the table and had started to serve them their cooked breakfast.

The Professor shook his head. "Unwise, they are too dangerous, besides there is the other matter of their, um, 'travelling companion' which we need to deal with. Can I have an extra rasher of bacon please Stewardess?"

"It is a shame that we could not have 'met' with the 'travelling companion' last night." Mallory looked around, aware that the elderly couple and the stewardess, let alone anyone else, could be listening to them.

"Oh don't worry yourself about that Mallory, we'll meet up with him soon enough. It is a reunion that is well over due and a necessary one."

Mallory suddenly yelped in pain as boiling hot coffee was poured onto his hand.

"Oh, I'm terribly sorry, Sir," said the stewardess, "are you alright?"

"Yes, fine," replied Mallory as he grabbed a napkin and started to wipe the liquid from his hand. He then looked up at the stewardess; straight into the eyes of Jazmine Montacute, who had been serving them as they talked.

She moved forward again to fill his cup, before doing the same to her Father. At the same time, she discreetly dropped a piece of paper on the table which the Professor, now realising who was attending to them, hurriedly covered with his hand so nobody else could see it. "Thank you very much my dear."

"My pleasure, Sir," she replied with a hint of sarcasm, before turning, placing the coffee pot on her trolley then moving off to another table. The elderly couple opposite them also stood up, bid farewell and left.

"I told you she would manage to find a way on board!" whispered the Professor triumphantly as he reached for the note.

138

"What does it say?" asked Mallory eagerly.

"Well the first three lines seem to be…….. um …er……obscenities. She also makes a wild accusation about your parentage……um ……… 'been reduced to a serving wench'… 'sharing a tiny cabin with four other women when I should be in first class' …..'working long hours'…. 'all kinds of stupid rules to obey'…. 'hate you both'…. 'staff food is worse than animal fodder'….. 'this is not fair'…. 'will get even with you both for this if it's the last thing I do!' "

Mallory and the Professor looked at each other with dread; the wrath of Jazmine Montacute was not something to be taken lightly. "Professor, I thought you said that the next time we met with her she would be as placid as a kitten?"

"Yes, um, well Mallory it seems that this kitten still has her claws!" He then continued to read the rest of the note. "She goes on to give us the Von Brauns cabin details." He then stopped and chuckled.

"What is it?"

"She says that if we are planning a raid to find the Mummy and disable it while it's in the front cargo hold, not to bother as it's not there. Elisabeth made arrangements for him to be stored elsewhere, although she has not been able to find out where as yet."

"A pity we did not know that last night," said Mallory, as he rubbed one of the locust bites which was starting to itch. "Now that is interesting. It seems that the Mummy's coffin has been seen by crew and there are rumours of a Mummy on board. It also seems that there are a number of people saying that the whole ship is cursed and this is adding to their concern. Now, this last part is a worry."

"What?" asked Mallory.

"It seems that below decks is buzzing regarding the fact that some of the coal supply is on fire and has been since Titanic left Belfast."

139

"That sounds serious," said Mallory.

"Depends on how bad the fire is and if they are able to get it under control. She says that she will keep us informed," said the Professor as he put the note away. "Mallory, the fact that Jazmine is on board, and as a stewardess, giving her freedom to roam and hear things we cannot, puts us at a distinct advantage over the Von Brauns"

Without thinking, Mallory, who was looking after the scarab, reached into his pocket and pulled it out to take a look at it.

"No, quick Mallory," said the Professor seeing the scarab, "put it away you idiot! I don't want anyone to see it!"

"What?" said Mallory doing as he was bid, but it was too late.

"Blast it Mallory!" said the Professor. "Look over there, that man in the dark suit. I recognise him. This could mean trouble."

"Who is he?" asked Mallory looking round at a man with dark hair and a neatly trimmed beard sitting at another table who was now staring over at them intently.

"Edmund Kane, he is a dealer in antiquities, as crooked as they come. He deals in stolen goods, and thinks nothing of commissioning forgeries, good quality forgeries at that, then selling them off as the real thing. The problem is that somehow he has the reputation as one of the most honest dealers in London. Damn it he's coming over." He gave Mallory a furious look to underline the fact that it was his fault.

Kane walked up to the table. "Good morning Sirs, may I introduce myself? I am Edmund Kane."

"Pleased to meet you," said the Professor, almost through gritted teeth.

Kane quickly sat down at the empty seat next to Mallory.

"Forgive me for being so bold, but I saw you had an interesting necklace. Now, I am a dealer in rare and specialised items, and I was wondering if it was possible for me to take a closer look at it?"

"Um, oh it's nothing," said Mallory quickly. "Just a trinket that I picked up in Covent Garden, a present for my girlfriend, bought it for a song."

"Then I may have some good news for you," said Kane as though he were addressing an old friend. "I actually think that it could be of some value, possibly even a rare Egyptian artefact. Could I take a closer look for a moment?"

The Professor glared at Mallory for his incompetence.

"Oh, there is really no need," said Mallory, "but thank you for your kind offer."

Kane looked at the two and realised that he was not going to get what he wanted. "Gentlemen, I will bid you a very good day, if you change your mind feel free to contact me." From his waistcoat he produced his card and leaning over, placed it on the table between Mallory and the Professor, taking a pen he wrote something on the back. "There, my cabin number, just in case you change your mind." He then turned and headed towards the door of the dining saloon, not even bothering to finish his breakfast.

"Well done Mallory," growled the Professor.

"That was not my fault. How was I to know?"

"You were not, and that is the point. It's a valuable item so you need to be discreet. It's bad enough the Von Brauns know we have it without advertising the fact to everyone else on the ship, now give it here."

"What?"

"I said give it here so I can look after it. I can't have you flashing it about whenever the whim takes you." The Professor held out his hand.

141

Mallory was about to argue, but decided against it, instead he reached into his pocket for the scarab.

"What's wrong?" asked the Professor seeing the look of horror on his companions face.

"The scarab, it's gone."

"What do you mean gone?" said the Professor. "This is no time for jokes Mr Mallory."

"I'm not joking," replied Mallory as he made a frantic search of the rest of his pockets, but it was not there. "No, it's not there, it's gone!"

The Professor and Mallory looked at each other and then their eyes were instinctively drawn to Kane's card which still lay on the table.

"He must have picked my pocket when he leant over to place the card down."

"Well, your pockets don't seem to be a very safe place for things do they?" replied the Professor, the anger in his voice growing.

"They would be if people were to keep their sticky fingers out of them," said Mallory, his mind flitting back to when Jazmine had taken his ticket from him on the boat train. "Look, he gave us his details, we can track him down."

"Don't be a fool man!" grunted the Professor. "He gave us false details. That scarab is worth a fortune, and he knows it! I wouldn't be surprised if........." he stopped mid sentence.

"Wouldn't be surprised if what?"

"We are stopping in Ireland in a few hours time."

"Yes?" said Mallory. The Titanic was due to make a short stop in Queenstown, Ireland.

The Professor paused. "He's going to jump ship! That's what I would do if I were in his boots!"

"But he might be booked for New York," pointed out Mallory.

"Maybe so, but bearing in mind how valuable the scarab is he's not going to hang around. No, you mark my words, he's going to leave when the ship docks and make off."

"Oh my goodness!" said Mallory. "If he goes, we have got nothing to defeat the Mummy with!"

"Well come on man," said the Professor rising from the table, "there is no time to be sitting here like a stuffed kipper, we need to get after him!"

CHAPTER 25

The Professor and Mallory burst through the saloon door and out into the first reception room and looked around for their quarry.

"Which way did he go?" asked Mallory.

"I have no idea," replied the Professor. "We are going to have to split up. We have got to get that scarab back. Do whatever it takes." The Professor quickly looked at his pocket watch. "Right, meet me back at the room in an hour. If we have not got it back by then, we will have to work out another strategy."

With that the Professor bounded off heading towards the main staircase. Mallory decided upon a different tack and decided to approach a well dressed man in the reception, who confirmed that Kane had passed him and had headed up the staircase. Mallory headed upwards, only stopping to ask other passengers as he went which way his quarry had gone. Then before long, found himself in the stairwell of Deck A. He was about to continue upwards when from the right he heard the door leading directly onto the promenade deck slam shut. Instinctively he changed direction and headed outwards onto the deck. Looking to the bow he saw the figure of Kane, now running away.

"Come back!" yelled Mallory, but Kane ignored him and continued to sprint away, with Mallory in pursuit. The chase took him round the front of the promenade deck then back round towards the stern on the port side.

"Sorry, sorry," Mallory called as he dodged around a number of passengers startled by the chase that they suddenly found themselves part of. Kane pushed past an elderly gentleman and back inside the ship to the first class entrance where he ran up the stairs heading for the boat deck. The elderly gentleman, holding his walking stick up, temporarily stopped Mallory, giving him a piece of his mind, while Mallory apologised before continuing past. On finding himself at the first class entrance he saw the figure of Kane disappearing out of the door on the starboard side. He followed and back on deck looked from left to right trying to see where Kane had gone, but he was nowhere in sight. Then to his right he noticed that the door leading to the Titanic's gymnasium was open, swinging freely. Mallory realised that this was the only place that Kane could have gone. Quickly, he ran inside, stopped, and then looked around. There was no one there. No fellow passengers taking exercise, no staff in attendance but most important of all, no Edmund Kane. Mallory quickly tried the other door to his immediate right which would lead back into the first class entrance but that was locked too. Looking round again Mallory could see no other exit or entry point other than the one he himself had just used.

"I know you are in here!" he called out loud. "Show yourself!"

There was no reply.

Mallory moved further into the gym, scanning his surroundings. There were a variety of machines and equipment, exclusively for the use of the first class passengers; a rowing machine, wall bars, stationary cycles, vaulting horses, and a large piece of electrical powered equipment that resembled a camel, but no visible sign of Kane which meant that he could only be hiding in one possible place.

Mallory moved over to the large wooden cupboard which presumably held more exercise equipment and reached out, took hold of the handle and tried to open it.

The door rattled but would not open.

Mallory tried harder, but it was clear that the door was locked. Satisfied, he took a step back, and then looked around the gymnasium again. This time his eyes fell upon the wooden vaulting horse.

Mallory realised that it was the only other conceivable place that a man could hide. Kane must have hidden himself in the hollow wooden structure. Quickly he moved over it going to the far end, then grabbed hold of the soft padding on top of the horse and lifted up the very top of the structure so he could stare down inside.

Again nothing – it was empty.

Dropping the top of the horse back into place Mallory concluded that Kane must have just thrown the door open as he went past, hoping that Mallory would do what he had done, think he had gone inside and go and investigate. Kane would now be long gone, the scarab with him.

Annoyed with himself he turned his attention to the large camel like piece of equipment which had caught his attention before. It was like no piece of fitness apparatus that he had ever encountered. It was much like the electrical powered 'horse' that people could sit upon and 'ride' according to the settings. However, it was much larger and the high saddle over the arched back gave it the camel like appearance.

Then, from behind, there was a noise. Mallory spun round to see Kane emerging from the cupboard that he had tried a few moments ago. He had been in there all along, no doubt holding the door from the inside making Mallory think that it was in fact locked.

Mallory started to move forward, but in a flash Kane produced a small gun from his pocket and aimed it at him.

"Stop! Keep your distance."

Mallory, unarmed, obeyed. He considered trying to rush Kane, but he knew that he would not be able to cover the distance in time before Kane discharged the weapon and at this close range, even with the small gun Kane held, the wound could be serious, if not fatal.

"Give me the scarab!"

"Brave words considering that I am the one holding the weapon," said Kane as he started to edge around the gymnasium.

Mallory decided upon a different tack. "Fair enough. Keep the scarab, it's already stolen and on a number of lists. It will be easy enough to trace."

"Then it's just as well that I have a number of contacts who will happily buy it for their 'private' collections."

Mallory understood what this meant. Some items would be bought then displayed in secret by the buyer, with the intention of never being shown to anyone else. This applied particularly to stolen items as, of course, they did not want others to know they had it in their possession. In this case the scarab would appear to have disappeared off the face of the earth never to be seen again.

"Now the question is," said Kane, "what do I do with you? How about I kill you here and now and then hide your body in the wooden horse? That would get you out of my hair."

"You are forgetting my friend the Professor," said Mallory. "If anything happens to me he'll know where to come looking." He paused, holding Kane's gaze, cursing himself for his passive argument, which basically involved action after his demise.

146

"I would not worry yourself about that matter if I were you," said Kane. "I'm an expert at ensuring my tracks are covered. I will be able to deal with him. The only real concern I have at the present is what I am going to do with you."

Kane did not see the attack coming.

While they had been talking Mallory had slowly and carefully been slipping his foot loose from his right shoe. Then with pin point precision accuracy he kicked it off at Kane while at the same time diving to the right. The flying shoe hit the gun, knocking it out of Kane's hand and in the surprise, Kane's fingers brushed against the trigger setting it off. The bullet flew through the air past Mallory and slammed into the large wooden frame which housed an illuminated deck plan of the Titanic.

Mallory rolled to one side and onto his feet in a crouching position. Kane meanwhile scanned the floor for the dropped gun but Mallory saw it first and in one fluid movement took off his remaining shoe and hurled it at the weapon. The brown shoe hit it, sending it skidding across the floor, moments before Kane was about to grab it. Seeing his enemy was off guard, Mallory ran forward yelling. Kane jumped to his feet and darted to the wooden horse which he used as a barrier to separate him from Mallory.

"I will not surrender the scarab!"

"You are not going to have much of a choice in the matter," growled Mallory.

"Let's strike a deal! I sell the scarab and we go halves on the profit! We won't have to tell your friend!"

"Give me the scarab," repeated Mallory.

Kane shook his head. "You are going to have to take it from me!"

"So be it!" cried Mallory as he then ran forward and vaulted over the horse directly at Kane, who jumped back.

147

Mallory landed on the floor the other side of the horse and with the momentum gained, threw himself forward at Kane, yelling as he did so. But the acrobatic move cost him seconds, and allowed Kane the opportunity to brace himself. So when Mallory reached him he was able to grab him by the jacket and turn him around. Mallory in turn took hold of Kane in a similar manner and the two men, fuelled by Mallory's momentum travelled across the gym before crashing into the wall between the high arched windows that looked out onto the boat deck. Mallory took the brunt of the impact allowing Kane to take the advantage and propelled both of them back into the gym, over to the electronic camel. Mallory yelled out in pain as his back hit the machine.

"Bad luck," said Kane as he raised his clenched fist in the air ready to strike. "The scarab is mine and is staying that way!"

The next thing that Mallory remembered was being shaken gently on the shoulder.

"Are you alright?"

"Um, who are you?" asked Mallory as he slowly came to his senses and looked up at this spry little man.

"I'm Mr McCawley, one of the gymnasium stewards. What happened? You should not have been in here without one of us here to show you what to do!"

"Um, sorry," replied Mallory. He realised that there was no point in trying to tell the truth. "I was passing, the door was open so I thought I would come in and see what was what." He glanced up at the mechanical camel beside him. "I tried to have a go on that thing and fell off. I must have hit my head."

"Well you were lucky that you did not break your neck," replied McCawley. "To use this equipment you need proper instruction and supervision."

"Um, yes I'm sorry," said Mallory as he stood up and looked around. Kane was of course gone, and Mallory consoled himself with the fact that he had not decided to shoot him while he was unconscious.

"I think we need to get you along to see the Surgeon, Dr O'Loughlin," said McCawley, "and get you checked over."

But Mallory shook his head, he wanted to at least try and make one last effort to catch up with Kane before meeting up with the Professor. "No, no that won't be necessary. Um, I don't suppose you can help me find my shoes?"

CHAPTER 26

Otto Von Braun stood transfixed looking at the tall glass fronted bookcase that was in the first class lounge. The object of his focus was a small empty vase placed upon the top plinth. "It is almost beyond belief isn't it? A sacred canopic jar, used to hold the remains of an ancient Egyptian, from the small size I would say an infant if not a baby, can end up here as a mere decoration. Not that anyone will take notice of it up there, except the cleaning staff, who will think it 'just a pretty little vase, something else to dust'. It often amazes me how lost artefacts can end up in the strangest of circumstances, sometimes being used for the most mundane of purposes. I once heard that a priceless Samurai sword, lost for generations was found being used as a prop in a London theatre."

"You know, that's true," said Professor Charles Montacute, who had silently walked up to Von Braun while he stared at the jar, "as I was the one who found it and returned it to the Japanese authorities."

"A noble gesture. I, however, would have sold the sword to the highest bidder."

"Well that's the difference between us isn't it?"

"You need not try and take the moral high ground here Charles, I know full well what I am, I do not pretend otherwise." He paused. "Elisabeth told me you have the black scarab."

The Professor winced inwardly and hoped that Mallory had caught up with Kane. "That's right and we will use it to stop your Mummy."

"Oh, I doubt that very much. Still I hope that it brings you more good fortune than its previous owner."

"I will stop you," said the Professor, "you realise that, don't you? I will destroy the Mummy; don't think hiding him will stop me."

"Ah!" said Otto, almost excitedly. "You have already tried another attempt on the sarcophagus! How did it go? Not well I presume, looking by the state of you."

"Things went a lot better when I found the recall button for the locusts, especially for my colleague."

"Yes, your new friend. Elisabeth told me all about him. Is it true that you chose him to come with you over Jazmine? I wager she will not forgive you on that little matter. Such a wild young creature; back home in Vienna I had a horse like that, fierce, untamed, spirited. Of course it had to be broken, only I broke it a little too well and I ended up putting it out of its misery with a bullet. I would like to say it did not suffer much, but why lie? "

The Professor chose to ignore the remark, instead taking comfort in the fact that they did not know that Jazmine was onboard, a fact that they could turn to their advantage at a later opportunity. He looked up at the jar. "So, what are your plans for the canopic, Otto?"

"My masters have decided that is has to be destroyed. The three others have been sought out and obliterated from the face of the earth; the last one must join them."

150

"If your 'masters' asked you to jump through a flaming hoop would you do it?"

Otto smiled. "I love that witty British humour. Make no mistake my dear Charles, if there were not so many people around I would strike you for that comment." The last part of the sentence was spat out with venom.

"No, you would *try* and strike me, there is a difference."

"Have a care old man; you are an inconvenience that can be rubbed out at will."

"By sending your bandaged friend after me? Would you? It's going to save me the trouble of tracking him down and destroying him myself."

Otto chose not to reply to the comment, sending the Mummy directly after the Professor while he was in the possession of the black scarab was the last thing they were going to do. Even without the scarab, that action would only be considered as a total last resort. The Professor had proven in the past he was more than capable of taking on the Mummy and surviving, indeed he actually stood a chance of beating it totally.

"Of course," said the Professor filling the silence, "I'm not going to stand by here and let the canopic be destroyed. It is a valuable item that should be in a museum."

"But it's too late," replied Otto, still transfixed. "It is as good as gone, look!"

The Professor looked up again at the bookcase, the canopic was still there, intact, but then he saw it. A large five fingered spider moving down the panelling of the wall just above the bookcase. It was the detached hand of the Mummy moving freely by itself.

"What on earth!"

Otto smiled. "I wager you had no idea that the Mummy could do that did you?"

The Mummy's hand then jumped to the top of the bookcase behind the canopic. Then the jar began to move and judder towards the edge of the bookcase, being pushed forward by the mummified hand.

Anticipating what was about to happen, the Professor started to move forward, aiming to catch the ancient jar as it fell, but Otto was quicker and stuck his foot out causing the Professor to fall to the floor.

The canopic jar hit the ground a few moments later and predictably smashed into pieces. The sacred jar used to hold the kidneys of the newborn daughter of the High Priestess Altru was now destroyed forever.

"Let me help you up, Sir," said Otto in a loud, helpful tone as he bent down, mindful that some of the other passengers were starting to come over to see what had happened. Before the Professor could react he found himself being hauled to his feet, then in his arm he felt a sharp jab, which made him yell out in pain.

"What the....?"

The Count smiled. "I told you that I did not need the Mummy. That was Hydrathioderd, I don't have to tell you that the poison was a favourite with assassins in the Eighteenth Dynasty and I'm sure that you already are aware of what is to come?"

"You son of a........."

"It's alright!" said Otto in a loud voice, as a steward appeared by his side. "I think that he just missed his footing a bit as the ship moved."

"Are you alright?" asked the steward.

"Yes, never better," lied the Professor glaring over at Otto who was hiding a small container with a spike in the top, the method of delivering the poison, back in his pocket.

152

"Oh and I'm afraid that something broke, it fell off the bookcase, can you make sure that it is cleaned up?" said Otto innocently.

"Yes of course, Sir," replied the steward, looking round at the smashed blue jar now on the floor.

The Professor looked up at the top of the bookcase. The hand of the Mummy was nowhere to be seen; then out of the corner of his eye he saw it, the spider like creature moving away unseen across the ornate panelling of the ceiling.

"Here," said Otto guiding the Professor away from the now disbanding group, "have a sit down, the excitement looks as though it is getting to you."

Suddenly, feeling faint, the Professor found himself being propelled, then deposited down, into one of the saloon's tub chairs. Otto hovered over him like a bird of prey ready for the kill. "I'm sure that you are familiar with Hydrathioderd, by now it will have entered your blood stream and will be flowing through your veins; death usually occurs in twelve hours. A poison usually given in the late evening to the victim would have the appearance of falling ill just after they settled down for the night."

"The antidote?" gasped the Professor. "Assassins always carry a small vial of the antidote in case something goes wrong."

Otto ignored him. "At first you will just feel ill, a rise in temperature and general giddiness with the occasional vomiting fit. But don't be fooled into thinking that it will pass, for in about six hours your vital organs will be affected beyond repair and you will slip into a coma and then into the great beyond."

"The antidote you Bas…."

"Now, now, Professor; no need to resort to that kind of behaviour, especially as this situation can be sorted out so easily."

153

"How?"

"You have something that I want, while I have something that you very much want. What could be more apt in this situation but a simple exchange?"

The Professor stared at the Count. "The black scarab for the antidote?"

"The penny has at last dropped."

"Go to hell."

"Yes, most likely, but without the antidote you will be there much sooner than I."

The Professor took a deep breath, this was a very bad situation, for not only was he being forced to hand over something that, at present he did not have; but also the black scarab was the only thing he knew could stop the Mummy and without it, the Von Brauns would be almost unstoppable.

"Well, what do you say?" asked Otto, enjoying every second of having the upper hand.

"I say that you want me to sacrifice my Queen to save a pawn."

"Yes, yes!" replied Otto jumping upon the chess analogy. "I bet you are travelling with your set aren't you? Should you survive I would very much like to play you again, do you think that will be possible?"

"I think that is unlikely," replied the Professor thinking of his impending demise.

Otto nodded. "Well, do not rule it out totally. I am sure that you will come round to my way of seeing things." He paused. "Now if you would be kind enough to excuse me I must be getting along. I am booked in for a session of the Turkish Baths at one o'clock, deck F. Meet me there, a ticket of entry will be waiting for you. Bring the black scarab and I will bring your antidote." With that the Count stood up straight, nodded his head at the Professor quickly, at the same time

154

clicking his heels together before turning and abruptly walking off.

CHAPTER 27

The stop in Queenstown, Ireland proved a mixed blessing for those in the boiler rooms. Normally a stop of this kind allowed all the stokers and trimmers, of whom the latter were responsible for the management and distribution of the coal, a valuable respite as minimum activity was required due to the ships temporary inactivity. Today was different; today, a number of men who would normally use the time to chat or rest were instantly reassigned to coal bunker number six. Their task was to continue to try and get the bunker fire under control.

Leading Fireman James 'Jas' Keegan watched the activity with a keen eye, peering up through the large access hole which allowed some of the coal to spill out onto the floor of the boiler room before it was scooped up, then distributed into the furnaces. Three trimmers had been sent scrambling up the still massive pile of coal to ensure that the hoses being used to dampen the top of the coal were distributing water evenly and to try to detect any 'hot spots' or other changes that had taken place in the coal mass. At the access hole additional stokers, firemen and more trimmers were trying to move out as much coal as possible in the short time before having to return to their original stations. The coal, once loaded onto wheelbarrows, was being distributed into the furnaces around the engine room in order to maintain the overall pressure, which would soon be called upon once the ship was ready to leave Ireland. Once they had taken on passengers and mail, and allowing those passengers booked to Queenstown to depart.

Keegan stepped out of the way of a stoker moving past loaded down with coal, before looking back up the pile and calling to one of the trimmers scrambling over the coal. "Jack Dawson, you be careful up there!"

"Alright Sir, But it's Joseph, Sir! Joseph Dawson!" came the reply.

Keegan cursed himself for the error, Joseph Dawson was not normally on his section and so he did not know him that well. "Well, whatever your name is, watch yourself. It's dangerous work you're up to!"

"Will do, Sir!"

Keegan moved back and then took a look at his watch, noting the time. He anticipated that he would have another half an hour, maybe forty minutes until he would receive the order that they were ready to leave. Putting the timepiece away he again looked up at the coal stack. He was not sure how much the efforts that were being made would help overall, but it was something at least. He had heard a rumour that the order was to be given that Titanic would stop here overnight, allowing a concerted effort to deal with the fire properly. Fire boats would be called, along with an influx of men from Queenstown to dig out the coal to reach the internal blaze, but it did not materialise. Instead he had been told that it would just be a normal stop, and that he should use the time wisely to do as much as he could to fight the fire.

"Slide! Slide!" a call came out from within the bunker, accompanied by the sudden shifting sounds of coal. Everyone jumped back and a plume of coal dust billowed out of the hatch, followed a moment later by the blackened forms of two men half tumbling, half scrambling out to freedom. Keegan, with the others not far behind, rushed forward to help them.

"It just went!" coughed one of the men as he was pulled free. "Dawson's still up there!"

"Quick," called Keegan, "get these two clear and checked over." He then rushed back to the coal bunker hatch, waving his hand against the coal cloud to clear it, before ducking under the hatch door into the coal store itself.

"Dawson! Dawson! Where are you?" he called into the blackness. The sudden movement of coal in the bunkers was always a risk; one which increased as the pile was depleted allowing more scope for movement, a factor considerably increased with the movement of the ship, especially in turbulent weather. Normally because of this it would be forbidden for anyone to venture inside the coal bunkers; however the circumstances of the fire had changed that rule.

"Dawson! Dawson!" Keegan called again as he started to move up into the coal bunker.

"Take this!" called a voice from somewhere behind him. He looked back to see the shine of a safety lamp, which was being held out for him. He reached down and grabbed it, held it up to try and see if he could find the unfortunate trimmer.

"Dawson! Dawson!" he called again as he moved up the pile. As he moved higher up the coal pile he felt a thin stream of water hit him on the face. In order to help with the dampening of the coal an enterprising fireman had taken a hose and attached it to the roof of the bunker by a series of makeshift brackets, with the rest of the hose running over the steam pipe and back out into the main boiler room and down to the floor where it trailed to the supply of cold water. The system worked well, allowing a wide spray over the top of the coal, rather than concentrate the water in one place. It also had the added bonus of freeing up a man who could help empty out the bunker.

From somewhere nearby Keegan thought he heard a muffled cry. He moved towards it, moving the lamp around in the hope of seeing some sign of the missing trimmer.

Then he saw it.

To his left there was a section of the coal that seemed to be moving as though something or someone was buried underneath trying to get out.

"I'm coming lad! Take shallow breaths if you can!"

As Keegan moved over to the spot, the coal parted slightly and out emerged three blackened groping fingers. At the same time there was the unmistakable sound of a few pieces of coal trickling down the mound. Keegan looked up just in time to see a large section of the coalface start to shift and start to slide down towards him and the already buried Dawson.

Without thinking, Keegan dived forward to where Dawson's hand had emerged, landing on all fours. He briefly looked up at the coal that was fast approaching. Closing his eyes, he tucked his head down and braced himself for the impact that was to come.

A wave of black swept over him, but as far as he could make out it did not actually dislodge him from his chosen position, thanks entirely to his chosen stance that acted with the coal rather than against it. Then after a few moments the coal seemed to stop. It was a small slide not a large one and from the weight of coal on his back Keegan realised that he had not been buried deep. From somewhere nearby he thought that he heard a yell, probably from one of his men witnessing the incident. He ignored the temptation to cry out in response. Instead, slowly, he pushed down against the coal below him and tried to rise up. The weight of the coal on him subsided as it shifted and slid off his body, and with little effort he was free. Instinctively he tried to wipe the coal dust out of his eyes but only succeeded in putting more coal dust into them impeding his vision further. Keegan blinked a few times and shook his head.

"Keegan!" a voice called again.

"I'm all right!" he yelled back. Then looking down he saw the still moving fingers of Dawson. He started to claw and scrape at the buried hand. "I need some help here! Quick."

Two men entered the bunker and made their way over to Keegan who was now frantically digging at the spot where Dawson was. Soon the young man's arm was free, and digging on further they managed to expose his shoulder and then his head. Keegan put his ear to the boy's mouth. "He's barely breathing!" he yelled. "Quick, hurry lads."

The two men increased their frantic efforts until together they were able to grab at him and pull the rest of his body out of the coal. Once free he was dragged down the coal face and out of the wide bunker opening where he was laid out flat on the floor. Keegan again put his ear to the young man's mouth; around him an anxious group had gathered, to watch the proceedings.

"He's not breathing!" announced Keegan desperately. "Quick help me turn him on his side!"

Two men from the crowd came forward and helped turn Dawson over as Keegan had asked. Keegan then leant over and opened Dawson's mouth, sweeping his fingers inside. Out came some coal that the poor lad had ingested. Keegan then turned his attention to Dawson's back which he started to rub hard, intermittingly hitting him between the shoulder blades.

"Come on lad! Fight it! You are not ready to die yet!"

The men watched on with bated breath. Dawson's body remained still and lifeless.

"Come on!" cried Keegan. "You listen to me lad you're not going to die, you're going to live!"

Then, as if in reply, Dawson spluttered, coughed and was sick, spewing up a horrible black gunge before taking a deep gasping breath.

159

A cheer went up from the men and Keegan lifted Dawson into a sitting position. "How are you feeling lad? You alright?"

Dawson nodded and croaked a husky, "yes".

"Right," ordered Keegan, "get him off to the hospital and let the Doctor know what just happened."

The two men who helped with the resuscitation took hold of Dawson and lifted him to his feet. Keegan was able to stand unaided only to be greeted by one of the firemen who had just appeared onto the scene. "Sorry Sir, but we have just had the order from the bridge sir. We are leaving Ireland now; slow ahead."

Keegan nodded and inwardly cursed. The stop had done little to put the fire out and had only managed to put a man in the hospital. "Alright," he said out loud, "back to your positions men. And can someone please get me a mug of water?"

CHAPTER 28

A very bruised and fed up Mallory arrived back at his cabin well over the agreed time. As if things were not bad enough already, he knew that he was now going to have to face a fuming Professor.

"Mallory? Is that you?" called a voice from inside, as the cabin door opened.

"My goodness what happened?" called Mallory as he ran over to the Professor who he found slumped in the leather chair. "Are you suffering from sea-sickness?"

"I caught up with Otto Von Braun. Let's just say things could have gone a lot better."

Mallory stared at the Professor who had turned pale.

"He injected me with poison."

"We need to get you to the ship's Doctor."

The Professor spluttered, turned to the side and spluttered again before turning back to Mallory, shaking his head. "He won't be able to help me. It's a slow working poison. I'll be alright for the moment. Tell me that you have the scarab."

Mallory shook his head. "Sorry, I caught up with Kane in the gymnasium, we fought but he got away!"

"Blast it," said the Professor as he struggled to his feet. "Von Braun has offered an exchange, the scarab for the antidote. He wants me to meet him in the Turkish baths."

"But we don't have the scarab!" said Mallory.

"Which is why we have to get it back, and fast," said the Professor who had reached for his handkerchief to wipe his brow.

"But what if Kane has jumped ship at Ireland?" said Mallory, well aware that Titanic had already left the port.

"For my sake we must pray that he hasn't! We've got to assume that he is still on the ship and act accordingly."

Mallory smiled. "If Von Braun has the antidote, why not just take it from him?"

The Professor shook his head. "No, he's far too clever for that; the antidote will no doubt be well beyond our reach."

"But how do you know Von Braun will honour his end of the bargain? He could use it as a chance to get the scarab then refuse to give you the antidote."

"That thought had crossed my mind," said the Professor as he struggled to his feet, "but at present it is my only chance. Come on let's get going."

In about half an hour, after a brief stop at the Purser's office on deck C where they managed, via one of the Professor's convincing tales, to find out where Kane's cabin was, Mallory and the Professor found themselves standing outside the door.

"So how do we play this one?" asked Mallory.

The Professor shrugged. "No idea. Kane may not even be here." He then knocked on the door and waited.

No reply.

The Professor signalled to Mallory who called out, "Mr Kane? Are you in there?"

Still no reply.

Mallory then took hold of the handle and slowly turned it – the door was unlocked!

Quickly, before any other passengers or crew could spot and challenge them, Mallory and the Professor went inside closing the door behind them.

The sight that greeted them was like something from a Gothic horror novel. Kane was lying on the floor gasping for breath. His chest was covered in blood coming from what looked like a gaping wound. From the overturned furniture in the room it was clear that a struggle had taken place.

"Help me!" gasped Kane as he became aware of the newcomers in the room.

"Oh my......" said Mallory. He had seen the horrors of death before, in his army career, but seeing it here in such a strange setting seemed even more unnerving. Then from the wound, there seemed to be an unnatural movement; appearing out of it came what looked like a large five fingered spider.

"The Mummy's hand," cried the Professor. In one movement he pulled out the sword blade from his walking cane and lunged forward trying to skewer it, but the hand was too quick, scuttling away. Mallory rushed over to Kane as he lay on the floor, but it was clear that the man had but a few short minutes to live.

"Did you see that thing?" gasped Kane.

Mallory nodded. "Yes, I saw it."

"It was a hand, a hand of a Mummy!" wheezed Kane.

All Mallory could do was nod.

"This is my punishment. I have done many bad things. I'm sorry for what I did to you in the Gymnasium."

"That's alright," replied Mallory, the fight and anger he had felt towards the man seemed so unimportant now.

"I have wronged so many people," continued Kane, "all to line my pocket and for my own glory, and what has it gotten me in the end?"

"Well let me give you the chance to put some of that right," said Mallory, seizing the opportunity. "The black scarab that you took from me. Where is it? That alone can stop the creature that did this to you."

"Lost!" Then Kane moaned and closed his eyes, but Mallory shook him. "Kane! Kane! Come on, don't you dare! Kane! Kane!"

Edmund Kane's eyes suddenly snapped open. He looked straight up at Mallory.

"The black scarab," said Mallory realising that there was not much time before Kane died. "What do you mean 'lost'?"

"Lost," repeated Kane, "after we fought I realised that it was gone." He took another breath. "I even went back to the gymnasium after you had left to look for it, but it was not there!"

Mallory's heart sank. "Have you any idea where it could be? It's important, the Professor's life is at stake!"

Kane tried to speak, but all he could manage was a hoarse rasp, so instead he shook his head.

Meanwhile the Professor was having his own problems. The Mummy's hand, which despite its venture into Kane's body was strangely free from all traces of blood and gore, seemed to be taunting the old scholar. It scurried across the ceiling then down the walls, not really trying to escape. Seeing an opportunity, the Professor lunged forward at it, but the hand flew past him through the air. It landed on the floor then scurried on its fingers across the carpeted floor and

163

under the single bed where the Professor followed, dropping to his knees making another stab at the hand. He missed and somehow realising that he was off guard, the hand turned lunging towards him. Its fingers clawing into the old man's throat causing him to fall backwards. Dropping his swordstick he grabbed at the ancient hand and managed to dislodge it before flinging it away. Picking up the swordstick he again launched his attack, sweeping the blade wildly at the limb which again climbed up the wall and onto the ceiling.

Placing Kane gently on the floor Mallory went to the side of the Professor. "Oh my goodness!" was all he could say looking at the bandaged hand which seemed to be waving its two fingers at them in an insulting gesture.

The Professor snorted. "You wait till you meet the Mummy proper!"

A shiver went down Mallory's spine, realising that very soon he would end up meeting the rest of the creature, which would have to be defeated. "If the hand is here, how close by is the rest of the Mummy?"

"No idea," replied the Professor keeping a careful eye on the hand as it moved back and forth across the ceiling and then down the wall, "I have never come across this kind of thing before."

"I've got an idea," said Mallory quickly. He moved over to the table at the side of the room and picked up the lamp, wrenching it free from its electrical cord. "Get ready to lunge to the left." With that Mallory threw the lamp at the wall to the right of the hand, which instinctively moved the other way. Forewarned, the Professor was able to thrust forward and the blade found its target pinning it to the wooden panelling of the cabin. At the same time, from somewhere nearby, there was a strange screaming sound. The Professor drew back, letting go of the swordstick which was firmly stuck in the wooden panelling, the twitching hand on the end.

164

"That scream," said Mallory.

"I heard it," replied the Professor. "The hand must still be connected, if that is the right word, to the Mummy itself."

"But it came from close by," replied Mallory.

"I know," said the Professor looking at his colleague.

"Do you think that 'it' will come to reclaim the hand?"

"I'm not sure," said the Professor with honesty, "but I would advise to be ready."

"Kane's dead," said Mallory, "he claimed that he did not have the black scarab, he said that it went missing."

"We need to do a search, just to be on the safe side."

Mallory nodded. He believed what Kane had said but they had to be sure. Mallory made a search of the body itself while the Professor looked through the rest of the cabin, including Kane's travelling bag. There was no sign of the black scarab. All the while they kept a nervous eye out, half expecting the Mummy to burst in to reclaim its limb.

"No it's not here," said the Professor slightly exasperated. "He was telling the truth."

Just then there was a clattering sound which made the two spin round. The Professor's swordstick was now on the floor and the Mummy's hand was nowhere to be seen.

"Blast it!" cried the old man. "It managed to get free." He turned to Mallory. "Come on, we'd better get out of here."

"What about…?" Mallory nodded over to the lifeless body of Kane. "We should tell someone."

The Professor shook his head. "Sorry, if we do we will then have to answer a lot of very awkward questions. No, we need to slip away and hope that we are not seen."

"The body will be discovered at some point though," said Mallory.

The Professor moved over to the desk and picked up the 'Do Not Disturb' sign. "We'll put this on the door as we

165

leave. Hopefully that will dissuade any visitors and cleaning staff, for a while anyway."

"Poor Kane," said Mallory taking another look at the body, "he was terrified. He said that he had done some terrible things in his life."

"He had," replied the Professor, "but even he did not deserve to die like that. Come on Mr Mallory. We need to get out of here."

CHAPTER 29

Without warning there was a fierce knocking on the Professor's cabin door. Mallory, who was seated at the desk, stood up and moved over to answer it. The call was not unexpected as they had ordered some tea to be brought to the room, but as he moved closer, the rapping became increasingly more and more impatient. "Alright, I'm coming," he called as he opened the door. However, to Mallory's surprise it was not one of the stewards.

The woman standing outside was in her forties, wearing a long expensive dress and an oversized hat with feathers sticking out of it at all angles. She had a look on her face which indicated that she was not the type of lady to be trifled with. "Well I can see that you are not Professor Charles Montacute," said the woman as she abruptly pushed her way past into the room. To Mallory's surprise, behind her was Jazmine Montacute.

"You cannot barge your way in like this," said Mallory, as he closed the door.

"I certainly can if my life is potentially in danger," replied the woman, looking at Jazmine.

"Before you say anything," said Jazmine, "it was unavoidable."

"What was?" said the Professor as he appeared.

"Father! What's happened? You look terrible."

"We need to get you to a doctor," said the other woman. Moving over to the Professor, she went to try and touch his forehead to gauge his temperature, but he pulled away,

"And who might you be madam?" growled the Professor looking her up and down.

"My name is Margaret Brown, Maggie to my friends," she said as she returned the appraising look.

"Well Ms Brown," replied the Professor with curt politeness, "why, precisely, have you forced your way into my cabin?"

Maggie pointed over to Jazmine. "Your daughter says that my life could be in danger and you can help me."

"It was not my fault, before you say anything Father," put in Jazmine quickly.

"So why exactly would your life be in danger?" asked the Professor, although he could think of a few reasons.

"Because of this." From inside her large handbag she pulled out a small item wrapped in yellowing cloth and handed it to him. The Professor unwrapped the item, his eyes widening as he realised what it was. The figure was around eight inches in height and depicted a small mummy, although the features were well worn and there was damage to the turquoise glaze in several places.

"That's ugly," said Mallory, looking at the statue.

"Yes, very," replied the Professor, "but worth a fortune. Even in this state I can think of three museums who would like to get their hands on it. It's also extremely old, I would say 700 BCE."

"What's BCE?" asked Mallory.

"It stands for Before Common Era," explained Jazmine. "It's a term used for dating in historical circles."

The Professor turned his attention back to Maggie. "Where did you get this?"

167

"I picked it up from a dealer when I was holidaying in Egypt a couple of years ago. I carry it around as a lucky charm. Is it true what this girl tells me that there is an Austro-Hungarian Count and some kind of freakish monster on board who would possibly kill me for it?"

The Professor looked over at Jazmine, clearly annoyed.

"I'm sorry Father. I was taking some tea to Maggie's cabin when I saw the statue and realised what it was. I knew that by having it she might attract the attention of the Von Brauns so I tried to take it."

"But I caught her," said Maggie proudly. "I was going to hand her over as a thief, but she told me all about what was going on."

"And you believed her?" asked Mallory in surprise.

Maggie shook her head. "Not until she started speaking Latin to me, and telling me the detailed history of Egypt. No mere stewardess would be educated to that level."

"But you told her about the, um, monster?" pressed the Professor.

"I didn't really have much of a choice," replied Jazmine sheepishly. "Maggie is very persuasive and I had to ensure that I was not taken for a thief."

"These Brauns sound dangerous," said Maggie.

"Yes, very," said the Professor. "I have had the odd tangle with them before and they must be stopped."

"I think that we should call the ship authorities," said Maggie. "They will know what to do."

"No, they would never believe us," replied the Professor still looking over the statue. "Not many people are as accepting as you have been." He took a deep breath as the effects of the poison continued. He moved to the nearby armchair and sat down. The others followed.

"I think we need to get you some medical attention," said Maggie.

"They won't be able to help I'm afraid," replied the Professor. "Von Braun poisoned me."

Maggie looked shocked. "What!"

"He injected me with an ancient poison."

"Von Braun will have the antidote," replied Jazmine instantly.

"Yes, but I'm afraid that that is where things get a trifle complicated," said the Professor. "Von Braun wants to exchange the antidote for the black scarab."

"But is that the only thing that can stop the Von Brauns creature?" asked Maggie, based on what she had been told.

"Yes," replied Mallory, "but there is a problem, a crooked antiquities dealer is on board. He managed to steal the black scarab from me. We mounted a raid on his cabin, but he's dead. The Mummy got to him. The scarab was not there. Fortunately from his last words, it seems that the Von Brauns don't have it either."

"That's because I have it," said Jazmine, as from inside her pocket she produced a long gold chain, on the end of it was the missing black scarab.

"The scarab!" cried the Professor gleefully. "But how?"

Jazmine shook her head. "You men cannot be trusted for a second. I saw Kane pick Mallory's pocket at breakfast this morning. Before he left the Dining Saloon, I was able to go over and pick his pocket in return."

"But why didn't you let us know?" asked the Professor.

"Because by the time I had got it back off him you two were gone."

"But you could have come after us," said Mallory.

Jazmine looked slightly embarrassed. "Well, normally I would have."

"Jazmine?" asked her Father.

"I could not leave the Dining Saloon in the middle of my shift. I already have a verbal warning and did not want to make things worse."

"Verbal warning?" asked Mallory raising an eyebrow.

Jazmine tried to look innocent. "Apparently 'rude' to a passenger, but he was a self-opinionated idiot. Anyway, the point is I was tied up and could not get away. I could not even get a message to you."

"Oh that does not matter now," said the Professor visibly relieved. "We can keep the scarab, and I still have something to bargain with to get the antidote."

"My statue?" replied Maggie, clearly unhappy at what was being plotted.

The Professor nodded. "Or I could just let you keep it until the Mummy comes calling."

Maggie glared at him.

"Oh don't worry," said the Professor, "I can make sure that you are reimbursed."

"Well that was not really the issue," said Maggie. "I was more worried about your 'minor' flawed plan. You want to barter with a madman in charge of a monster, using a valuable statue to get an antidote back that he probably does not want to give you in the first place!"

"It is not the best of situations I grant you," replied the Professor, "but up until a few minutes ago things were a lot worse."

"Wait a second," said Maggie, suddenly looking at the scarab Jasmine held, "I've just remembered something. I've seen a scarab like that somewhere before on the ship."

"No you could not have," replied the Professor. "There are only three in existence. I'm guessing that somehow you saw that one."

"No," replied Maggie as she did her best to remember. "For one thing the scarab that I saw was a brilliant red."

170

The Professor stood up; could this be the fabled red scarab? "Think carefully, are you sure?"

"Yes," replied Maggie, "it was identical to that in every way apart from the colour. Now where did I see it?"

"Maggie, this is really important," said Jazmine. "The person who owns it could be in great danger, far worse than you were."

"I've got it!" cried Maggie. "It was a young pregnant woman. Astor! That was it. I saw them when I boarded at Cherbourg. She and her husband were talking to this tall well built European man. I was not all that close, so I couldn't hear what was being said, but I remember thinking that he was European."

"Can you describe this man?" asked the Professor.

Maggie nodded, and gave them a description. When she finished there was a muted silence.

"That sounds like Otto," said Jazmine.

The Professor nodded. "That means that they are aware of the red scarab and the Astors will no doubt be targets."

"Then the Astors will be in danger," said Maggie aghast. "My goodness, but the young thing is pregnant!"

"Let me assure you madam," said the Professor, "we will do everything we can to protect her."

"I can do my best to keep an eye on them Father," said Jazmine.

"Good," he replied thinking out loud. "Jazmine I want you to keep the scarab for the time being. That way if there is a problem you can use it against the Mummy."

"I don't think that she will be able to take on the creature," said Mallory with some concern.

"I was thinking more of her using it as bait to lure the creature away," said the Professor. "If Jazmine appears with the black scarab, the creature will register her as a threat and leave the Astors alone. Are you alright with that Jazmine?"

171

She nodded.

"Good, now the immediate concern is to get the antidote. I'm not going to be able to do anything dead. Then we can work out a realistic plan to protect the Astors and get their scarab, with it we can destroy that Mummy for good."

"I want to help too," said Maggie.

"Um, you can help by keeping a general eye out for the Mummy, and warning Jazmine if you see anything," said the Professor, determined not to have this strong minded woman interfering.

Maggie nodded.

The Professor took a deep breath. "Now if you will excuse me ladies, I need to rest in preparation for my meeting with Otto."

"Yes," said Jazmine putting the black scarab back in her pocket. "I have to be going too; I want to try and swap my afternoon duties." She glared quickly at her father. "So I can be nearer to the Astors."

As Maggie followed Jazmine to the door she turned to look at the Professor. "This creature," she said, "it can be stopped can't it?"

The Professor nodded silently, although secretly he knew that if his meeting in the Turkish baths was not successful it was unlikely that Jazmine and his new friend Mallory would be able to do it without him, and the Mummy would be free to cause boundless havoc and mayhem.

CHAPTER 30

Having arrived at the Turkish Baths on Deck F, Professor Montacute found that, as promised, an entry ticket was waiting for him leaving Richard Mallory to pay the four Shilling charge himself.

The baths actually consisted of five individual rooms, each with a different function of the bathing process, positioned opposite the Titanic's swimming pool, which was used to complete the bath before finally drying off. Having donned a towel which acted like a kilt, and then checking their clothes in with the attendant, Mallory and the Professor made their way into the main section of the baths. Being already forewarned that Otto Von Braun had decided to start his bath earlier than planned, the two passed through straight into the cooling room where their enemy was waiting.

"Ah, Charles, over here," called Otto who was reclining on a couch. "So glad that you could make it and it seems that you have brought your new 'pet' with you as well."

He looked up at Mallory who just stared at him silently.

"Well," continued Von Braun, "it seems that we have the room to ourselves and what a room it is! I wager that it matches any bath you will find in the East."

Mallory and the Professor paused slightly to look at their surroundings. The room had five couches in total as well as a weighing machine and a drinking fountain. The walls were lined with oversized tiles of green and blue. Everything had been done to give the impression that the passenger was in a real Turkish bath, from the Egyptian curtains right down to the original Arabian style lamps.

"Yes, very impressive," said the Professor as he sat down on the couch next to the reclining Otto. He was far more concerned about the matter in hand, as well as fighting the increasing effects of the poison.

"You don't look well at all," said the Count with a look of smugness on his face. "Now my dear Charles, where were we? Ah yes, I have your antidote and you have the black scarab. I would advise that you hurry up though, I would hate to say how long you have left!"

"The antidote," said the Professor. "Show me the antidote."

Von Braun reached down by the side of the couch and produced a small glass vial containing a clear liquid and held it up for all to see. "Here it is, now my scarab if you please."

"Not so fast," said the Professor. "How do I know that it is the antidote and not another dose of the poison or something else equally as fatal?"

"Charles Chester Montacute I am insulted and, if honest, a little hurt at your attitude," said Von Braun in a surprised voice.

"I don't trust you Von Braun," said the Professor.

Otto nodded. "I don't blame you, I certainly would not in your position, so let me put your mind at rest." With that he removed the stopper of the vial and took a small sip. "There! It tastes wonderful! Now hand over the scarab."

"Five minutes," said Mallory. "We want to see that you don't start to fall ill or keel over."

"As you wish," replied Otto almost bored." So, what are we to do to fill the time? Perhaps you will tell me how you intend to stop my Mummy. You must have a plan by now."

"Find him, insert the scarab, and throw him over the side of the ship," said the Professor simply.

Otto clapped his hands together. "Wonderful! You have no idea where he has been moved to! This puts you at a disadvantage."

"For the moment, yes," conceded the Professor, "but he is a conspicuous fellow and should not be too difficult to track down."

"But far more difficult to stop, even if you do have the scarab, but of course you won't for much longer will you?"

"We'll see," said the Professor, feeling more and more uncomfortable.

"Yes, we will," replied Otto as he paused to look around. "Look, my dear Charles, we have business to conclude. As you can see I am still in perfect heath which proves that the

174

contents of the vial are not poison as you suspected. It is time to conclude our business – the scarab if you please."

"The deal's changed," said the Professor defiantly.

"Changed? Very brave words considering that I hold your very life in my hands, all I have to do is smash the vial and you are finished! Alright then, my dear Charles I'll play along with your little game. So why has our agreement changed?"

The Professor brought out the small bundle that he had concealed in the folds of his towel and slowly un-wrapped it from the faded cloth and held up Maggie Brown's statue. Von Braun's eyes widened. It was the statue that he had been sent to recover and return to his agent.

"I will swap you this for the antidote."

Otto Von Braun remained silent as he considered his options. "Well, well. It now seems that you now have *two* things in your possession that I want. The deal has indeed changed; the scarab *and* the statue for the antidote!"

A look of horror spread over the Professor's face. He had not expected this.

"The scarab *and* the statue for the antidote!" repeated Von Braun, although this time he made it sound much more like a threat.

"That's not fair," said the Professor, wiping sweat from his brow. Even though this was a cooling room the effects of the poison were causing his temperature to soar.

The Count merely smiled.

"It seems the presence of the statue seems to be clouding the deal, it must be taken out of the equation," noted the Professor thoughtfully. "Mr Mallory, Please go and fetch the scarab and while you are about it, smash the statue to pieces." He handed Mallory the figure, as a look of uncertainty flickered across Von Braun's face.

"And, please bring back the fragments so my friend here can see that it is destroyed."

Von Braun shook his head. "You are bluffing Charles."

"No Otto, I'm really not." He nodded to Mallory who started to move off.

"Wait!" called Otto not wanting to risk the statue. "Alright, have it your way, the statue in exchange for the antidote."

"I would prefer it if you gave me the antidote first."

"The statue, or the deal is off and I smash the vial. Come, I have already indulged you so far; the statue."

The Professor nodded and after wrapping it back up, passed Maggie Brown's statue over to Otto, who smiled then in a loud voice called, "Come!"

Mallory and the Professor looked at each other, unsure what to expect. Then the door to the cooling room opened and in walked a large man wearing a long coat with a hat pulled down over his face.

"The Mummy!" cried Mallory. As if understanding, the creature turned, raised his head and seemed to stare at him with its glowing red eyes and gave a low pained grunt.

"Of course," said Otto, almost proudly, "you have not yet met my monster formally have you Mallory?"

All Richard Mallory could do was to shake his head, as he was lost for words.

"Well, Mr Mallory, this is my Mummy, a creature used for revenge on those who have violated my heritage."

"You were born in Vienna," said the Professor abruptly.

"A mere detail," said Otto, waving his hand dismissively. "It is a cause that is dear to my beloved Elisabeth and one which is more than profitable."

"You're sounding hen pecked."

"And how is *your* dear wife Charles?" replied Otto with a sneer.

A look of anger passed over the Professor and he tried to stand, but the effects of the poison caused him to sit back down again. Otto turned and gave the Mummy the statue.

"Go, take this and put it somewhere safe". The creature, in response, turned and moved out of the cooling room.

"You are fortunate that I value the statue so highly. I had considered using him to attack you straight away, still another time."

"The antidote," pressed the Professor.

"Yes, well, about that. I have decided not to give it to you. It seems that your instincts not to trust me were actually correct. You see….."

Before Otto could continue, the Professor lunged out his hand and grabbed at the bottle, ripping it from Otto's grasp.

He then pulled out the cork and drank down the contents in one go before Otto had the chance to react.

A look of panic crossed the old man's face as he took the bottle away from his lips. "It's water! You double crossed me!"

Mallory moved in as though he was about to attack, but Von Braun held up his hands almost as though he was surrendering. "No, please wait! Before you do anything rash, let me explain. This is not what you think, Charles you are not in any danger."

Mallory stopped. "What?"

Von Braun sat up a little straighter. "Charles, my dear old friend. As you are no doubt aware Hydrathioderd is a particularly difficult poison to create, even more so when the main ingredient, the Tanner leaf, is not in season, so I was forced to compromise. Sadly what I gave to you was a weakened and inferior form of the poison which is non- fatal, but good enough for my purpose, which was to make you think that your life was in danger!"

The Professor paused. The Tanner leaf was indeed out of season.

"How do I know that you are telling the truth?" said Mallory.

"One of the effects of the poison is vomiting," said Otto. "Now I wager, although feeling terrible, you have not actually been sick."

The Professor nodded, he had not.

"The extent of the poison is what you are feeling now, and have been feeling since I administered the dose; dizziness, high temperature, feeling sick and being generally unwell. After a good night's sleep the effects will pass, and sadly for me, you will be right as rain and no doubt trying to cause me more trouble."

"Professor?"

"Yes," replied Montacute nodding, "he's telling the truth."

The door to the cooling room then swung open and in came three men, all draped in towels.

Seeing the newcomers, Otto stood. "Well, I think that is about all don't you? I had better be going. Thank you of course for the statue that you have so kindly donated to my cause. That will save the Mummy a trip out tonight and will have no doubt saved the life of the previous owner." With that he turned and started to head towards the door. Mallory started to follow but the Professor grabbed him by the arm. "No, let him go."

"But...."

"Another time. This afternoon has been a success, of sorts, let's just settle for that. We still have the black scarab, have seemingly saved Maggie's life and I know that I'm going to make a recovery!"

Mallory sat himself down on the couch, seemingly lost in thought.

"Let me guess," anticipated the Professor, "you're thinking about The Mummy, eh? Well, impressive as he is, he will be stopped!"

Mallory nodded silently.

"Come on Mr Mallory. I need to get back to the room! I for one, need to rest."

CHAPTER 31

Mallory returned to the cabin to find the Professor sitting in the chair, engrossed in a yellow hardback book, with a trolley containing the remains of a cooked breakfast beside him. "You are looking much better," commented Mallory.

The Professor nodded. "I feel it thanks. A good night's sleep and the poison wearing off naturally, just as Otto promised."

"I did think that he might be lying you know."

"Yes, that had crossed my mind too," replied the old man reflectively, "but there was no other choice but to trust him, and well, as you can see I am alright now, if still fuming with my Austro-Hungarian friend!"

"What are you reading?" asked Mallory looking at the book.

The Professor smiled. "An old novel Jazmine found for me for a joke when she realised that we would be making the trip. It's called 'Futility' by Morgan Robertson. It's about a ship called TITAN which sinks on its maiden voyage across the Atlantic after hitting an ice shelf."

"That girl has a warped sense of humour," said Mallory, "if not actually ironic."

"How so?"

"There is a writer on board, Stead or something like that. He had a book published with a similar story. I ended up sitting with him last night as he was telling anyone who would listen about his work."

"Well I would not get too worried," said the Professor, putting down the novel, "I can't see that ever actually

179

happening. Anyway, how did you get on with the rest of your evening?"

Mallory shrugged. "Nothing really to tell. All was quiet. I caught up with the Von Brauns. They were having dinner with the Astors. I did not approach, just watched from a distance."

"Any sign of the red scarab?"

Mallory nodded. "Lady Astor was wearing it. From what I saw it was exactly the same as ours."

"Well I would not get too excited on that score if I were you," said the Professor. "It may be a fake or the spell that should have been cast over it may not have been prepared correctly which means that it won't do its job." He put the book down. "Have you seen Jazmine at all this morning?"

Mallory tried to hide a smile. "She has seemingly donned the disguise of a lady and has been following the young Mrs Astor at a distance."

"Good! She is going to be a valuable asset to us in this venture, make no mistake!"

"Not if she gets into trouble she won't. The dress she wore was 'borrowed'."

"Needs must Mr Mallory! Needs must! Our venture is of vital importance, lives are at stake, even possibly ours, so a slight bending of the rules, in my book, is justified."

"From what I see of your methods so far you don't just bend the rules you rip them up and substitute them with your own!"

The Professor could not help but smile. Mallory's description was pretty much what he usually did.

"Anyway," continued Mallory, "you did not mention the ship's library to me. That is bound to be of interest to the Von Brauns."

"Really?"

"You don't know?" said Mallory somewhat surprised. "I took a stroll there last night. It's Egyptian themed."

The Professor let out a low whistle.

"There are papyruses, statues, even an ornate sarcophagus lid attached to one wall."

"Are the items genuine?"

"I asked the library steward, and he seemed to think that they were. No expense spared for this ship it seems."

"I had no idea," said the Professor, taking in the revelation.

"It seems the idea was that there will be a different theme to the library every year or so," continued Mallory. "Apparently next year they are going with the whole nautical theme, even now there are people trying to get hold of authentic bits of old sunken tall ships and the like."

"That might be worth seeing," said the Professor.

"So what are you planning for the day? I'm presuming that you are not going to stay here with your feet up reading."

"Certainly not!" replied the Professor. "I think that today I will direct my attentions to trying to find out where exactly the Von Brauns have hidden the Mummy."

"Are you thinking of another midnight raid?"

The Professor shook his head. "No, a daylight one. I've been thinking about this all wrong. The creature needs to be kept out of sight as much as possible. A walking Mummy would attract all kinds of attention, so it is safe to reason that it is hidden during the day, and brought forth at night. If I can locate where it is, a day time strike will be required!"

"Why not approach the Von Brauns directly? They might slip up and give us some kind of clue; the location, who or what their next target is."

"Possible, but they are going to be on their guard."

"How about we try a raid on their cabin? There is bound to be some clue there. Perhaps Jazmine could use her lower deck connections?"

The Professor shook his head. "No, too risky! Knowing that we are on board, the Von Brauns would have done everything possible to protect themselves from one of my 'visits' "

"You think that they would have placed booby traps?"

"No, more subtle than that, I'm sure that they would have left a number of 'clues' that would lead us off in the wrong direction, if not directly into danger."

Knock! Knock!

Mallory looked over at the Professor before moving over to the cabin door and opening it slightly to see who was there. The figure on the other side was dressed in dark blue trousers and collarless shirt. On his head he wore a flat cap with a small black peak.

"Um, is this the cabin of Charles Montacute, the Professor?" said the man in an American accent.

"Who wants to know?" asked Mallory warily.

The man removed his cap. "My name is March, John Starr March. I work in the postal room. We have a problem and I was advised that Professor Montacute may be able to assist us."

"In what way?" The Professor, hearing the conversation, had left his chair and appeared by the door.

"Um, it's all a bit odd really," said March. "I went to one of the Officers for help and he remembered that there was a Professor on board and advised me to seek you out."

"You had better come in then."

March was admitted to the room; he quickly looked around. From the look on his face it was clear to both Mallory and the Professor that his quarters were nowhere near as opulent as this.

"I think that you had better start at the beginning," said the Professor as he sat back down in his chair.

"Well Sir," said March, a little nervous, "as I said, I work here in the post room. Sorting post, ensuring that it is ready for when we get to New York and the like. Well, in among one of the bags we started to hear strange noises. Moaning and scratching. We thought that it was a mouse or rat that had gotten into the post room, but on investigation we found that it was coming from inside a parcel itself."

"Someone trying to smuggle an animal?" suggested Mallory.

March shrugged. "Possibly, we're not sure. The noises don't sound like any animal that I have ever heard. Well anyway, because there was an obvious breach in rules about sending livestock, we, under the postal regulations, are allowed to investigate the package further; so we opened it."

"What did you find?" asked the Professor.

"A wooden box," replied Starr, "locked of course, although we could not actually find the lock mechanism that releases it. But the thing about it, and why I was advised to come to you, is that the thing was covered with Egyptian hieroglyphics."

There was a short silence as the Professor, his interest sparked by the story, pondered what he had just been told. Finally he asked, "Where is this box now?"

"It's still down in the mail room. Do you think that you can help? It's making us all really nervous."

"That depends on what's actually inside the package," replied the Professor with a smile. "Has anyone else been approached about it?"

The man shook his head. "No, apart from the fourth Officer, we went to him for advice and it was he who directed us to you."

"Good," replied the Professor, fearing that the Von Brauns or even Edmund Kane might have been sought out to help. "I shall come at once." He turned to Mallory. "Of course you had other plans for the rest of the morning didn't you?"

Mallory nodded, slightly annoyed as this sounded incredibly interesting, although the task that he was assigned with did have the potential for some excitement.

"Then, Mr Mallory, we shall meet later." With that he turned to March. "Alright, I think that you had better show me the way."

CHAPTER 32

"The one thing that I am really scared about," confided Madeleine Astor, leaning a little closer to Elisabeth Von Braun, "is actually giving birth."

Elisabeth smiled. "Women have been giving birth for thousands of years, and with the medical advances it is ever safer!"

"But that's easy for you to say," replied Madeleine, placing her hand on the swell of her stomach, "you are not going to have to go through it in a few months time."

Elisabeth smiled politely, then looked back into the dancing flames of the fire, in front of which they had positioned themselves, before making a visual sweep of the reading and writing room where they had decided to spend the morning until lunch. There was only one other person in this oversized room, a woman in purple by the big bay window, immersed in a book who had been there since they had arrived. Fortunately, owing to the sign which she had cunningly placed on the door, Elisabeth knew that there was no danger of them being disturbed, or more people coming in.

"Do you think that you will ever have children?" said Madeleine suddenly.

"No," mused Elisabeth, "for one thing I am getting too old and, well, it would not fit in with our lifestyle."

"But does your Otto mind not having an heir?"

"No," replied Elisabeth with a laugh. "We are more than happy as we are. If truth be told, a baby would just get in the way. I know we could get a governess to do all the work but....."

Her voice trailed off, Madeleine had taken it as a sign of secret regret, but Elisabeth's attention had again been caught by the woman by the window. Familiar eyes peeped out at her over the top of the pages.

"I must say, your life does sound fun," said Madeleine, unaware of her new friend's distraction. "I hope that after my baby is born I shall be able to travel more; there is so much of the world that I still want to see."

"I'm sure you will," said Elisabeth, her eyes now fixed on the woman at the window. The reading woman looked up yet again, then seeing Elisabeth stare, quickly averted her eyes back downwards. Elisabeth was now sure beyond any doubt as to whom this woman was – Jazmine Montacute. Somehow at Southampton the Professor's daughter had made it onto the ship and had been there all this time. Elisabeth's eyes looked over at Madeleine and then down to the red scarab necklace around her neck and realised that the Montacutes must be aware of its existence. It had to be the reason that Jazmine was here in the reading room.

"Are you alright?" asked Madeleine with concern. "You look a bit white. I'm sorry, was it the talk of babies?"

"No, no I'm fine," said Elisabeth quickly.

Seeing her friend was fine Madeleine leaned closer. "You will never believe this, but I've been approached by a reporter! On the birth of our baby they want John and I to tell them our story so they can publish it exclusively in exchange for a large sum of money! They even want to take photos of us all! Have you ever heard such a thing?"

"No," replied Elisabeth, preoccupied and realising the time to act was upon her. "Madeleine, would you like to see something very interesting?"

"Why yes, what is it?"

"Something that I picked up on my travels," replied Elisabeth as she reached into her bag plucking out a small stone palm sized tablet which she gave to Madeleine. Out of the corner of her eye she saw Jazmine rise and start to move over to them.

"Ah! That is amaz…….." Madeleine stopped in mid word, her gaze fixed upon the tablet as the spell took effect. Quickly Elisabeth reached forward, grabbed at the red scarab necklace and tore it from the girl's neck. She stood and held the necklace up high in the air showing off her prize. "You are too late Jazmine! The scarab is ours!"

Jazmine, now only a few feet away stopped in mid stride. "What have you done to her?"

Elisabeth looked down towards Madeleine. "She is not harmed. The spell on the tablet has merely frozen her in time. She will be fine when I choose to release her."

"Very clever," said Jazmine. "Suspend her in time, take the necklace, then let her go. As far as she is concerned nothing untoward has ever happened and when she realises her scarab is gone all she remembers is a delightful time in the reading room then assumes that the chain somehow broke and it fell off."

"Which I of course will reaffirm, when she asks," added Elisabeth smiling.

"But you are overlooking one minor detail. Your plan has gone awry."

"Because of you my dear? No, I do not think so. The scarab is now mine." She looked over at her prize, then back to Jazmine. "And I have the perfect opportunity to get rid of you for good."

"And how are you going to do that?" said Jazmine. She knew that she could take on the Countess and win, and was more than happy to do so.

The handle of the door to the reading and writing room slowly began to turn, and the door opened. In walked the Mummy in its disguise of the long brown coat and wide brimmed hat. The creature walked into the room and stood silently facing Jazmine.

"You are taking a great risk having him out like this," said Jazmine as she looked round the room, trying to work out her next move. "What happens if he is seen? Why not just conceal the scarab on your person?"

"Because if things had gone wrong he would have been needed to kill, then dispose of her."

Jazmine looked over at the frozen Madeleine as a chill ran down her spine.

"Of course, now he will be required to deal with you!"

Jazmine looked over at the Mummy. There was no way that she could match him physically. She was going to have to use her brains to get out of this one. Slowly she started to back up. With a nod from Elisabeth, the creature started to move after her, but not fast enough. Jazmine was over at the large bay window where she was sitting a little earlier. She grabbed the bottom latch and opened it, but the second one, much higher up, was still fastened. So, hampered by her long dress, she started to climb up onto the chair to reach it.

Suddenly around her throat she felt something wrap itself, and tighten. She turned round on the chair to see the Mummy standing around fifteen feet away from her, its left arm was reaching out, and from it a long strand of the bandage which it had cast out to her like a long yellow fishing line.

"Surprised?" called out Elisabeth. "You would be amazed at what he can do! Gone are the days of the ancient dead just stumbling along to get their prey!"

187

Jazmine grabbed at the twine, and tried to release herself but she could not. In fact the grip around her throat seemed to be getting tighter. Then without warning the Mummy yanked the bandage forward causing Jazmine to overbalance and fall to the floor. Quickly, and unhurt, she struggled to her feet, the Mummy allowing her to do so without trying to pull her towards him. All the time Jazmine struggled to free herself with no success. Then, letting out what sounded like a deep laugh, The Mummy yanked the bandage to the right and Jazmine found herself being pulled across the room, only stopping when she crashed hard into a set of table and chairs. Laughing, the Mummy then pulled hard on the bandage, and started to reel in the struggling Jazmine like a fish. A few moments later she found herself face to face with the creature, staring deep into its red glowing eyes.

"Enough of this," said Elisabeth. "Kill her, kill her now!"

The Mummy let out a groan and then took hold of Jazmine's throat with his bandaged hands and started to press down hard. However, Jazmine Montacute was not going to let herself succumb so easily. Reaching up to her own neck she managed to grab the one thing that could save her. The gold chain on which was the black scarab.

Tearing it from her neck she placed the sacred item directly onto the Mummy, and started to push it under the bandages.

Instantly the creature went limp and started to fall away. Jazmine jumped back, taking the scarab with her. Without the scarab's power the Mummy then came back to life, and was for a few moments dazed from its inactivity. Realising that she needed to deal with the tether, she turned and ran, then dived to the nearest writing table. Her fingers coiled themselves round a letter opener, which was on the table in a compartment containing an inkwell and writing paper, just then the Mummy started to pull her back.

This time however, things went very differently.

Still gasping for breath Jazmine severed the bandage holding her, with the letter opener, and held up the black scarab for the Mummy to see as a warning.

It worked, as the creature remembering what happened before held back.

"You are never going to get out of here alive you know," taunted Elisabeth.

"Oh I will," retorted Jazmine confidently, although she was aware that she had to do far more than that. She picked her moment and took aim directly at the Mummy, drew her arm back ready to throw the letter opener, but at the last possible second veered her aim off to the right.

The letter opener flew through the air, directly towards Elisabeth, who, fooled by the feint, was unable to move in time. It hit her in the arm causing her to yell out.

It was at this point that Jazmine struck.

Quickly, before either the Mummy or Elisabeth could react, decisively she ran over to the fireplace and pushed the Countess to the floor. She then turned and made a successful grab for the red scarab, before turning and continuing on towards the main door, opening it and disappearing out.

"Kill her! Kill her!" screamed Elisabeth in anger as she got up pulling the letter opener from her arm and throwing it aside. "Find that little witch, get the red scarab back, then kill her. Then afterwards return straight to your crate!" The Mummy turned and headed towards the opened door that Jazmine had just escaped through, watched by the Countess. She then turned her attention to her arm. The blade had just grazed her skin, but had ruined the sleeve of her dress, which would need to be mended. The Countess paused for a moment, wondering if she had done the right thing sending the Mummy after Jazmine. But it was now too late, the decision had been made and she would just have to hope that the creature's core orders that were programmed into him, to

189

avoid being seen and captured at all costs would be enough to safeguard him.

Taking a few deep breaths to compose herself, Elisabeth Von Braun sat back down in her seat and looked at the figure of Madeleine in front of her, still perfectly frozen, unaware of the battle that had taken place around her. When she felt suitably settled, Elisabeth lent forward, took the small stone tablet still being held by Madeleine, turning it over and quickly sat back.

"......zing," continued Madeleine in mid word, although of course she had no idea of the time that had passed.

"Yes," said Elisabeth continuing the pretence. "Each figure represents a word. Let me translate it for you............."

CHAPTER 33

It did not take Professor Montacute long before he and John March found themselves standing in the mail room of the Titanic, located at the bottom of the ship on the orlop deck.

The mail room was like any other, only it happened to be located on a ship, and it was the reason that Titanic was allowed to use the RMS (Royal Mail Ship) prefix. Professor Montacute looked round at the room with general interest. Along one wall there were numerous pigeon holes where mail was being sorted into, as well as large racks in the middle of the room containing various open sacks of mail which were being readied for their eventual arrival in New York. Three other men were also in the room, hard at work, sorting and checking the mail.

"Not a bad little set up eh?" said March almost proudly, as he too looked around.

"Very impressive," said the Professor nodding in agreement. "Now, where is the mysterious box?"

"Over there," said March pointing to a big sorting table.

The box was very much as described: a large box made out of a light coloured wood with no visible lock and covered with Egyptian looking Hieroglyphs. Its dimensions the Professor gauged by eye were around twenty inches by ten inches with it standing around eight inches high. Carefully he lifted the box slightly off of the table. It was not overly heavy, but from within he detected a sudden shift of weight as though something had moved position. Also there came a strange noise which caused him to drop the box back down on the table.

"See what I mean?" said March.

The Professor nodded.

"Here, this may be of some help," said March as he handed over a large sheet of crumpled brown paper. "This was what it was wrapped up in."

The Professor looked at the discarded paper. On the front there were a number of postmarks. The item had originally been sent from Egypt and had travelled via London. The final destination was a post office in central New York, the sender most likely opting to collect in person. Although no doubt that person would be hired specifically for the task, and paid handsomely for it too, for if the authorities got wind of the parcel, they would be taken in for questioning, not that they would be able to provide much information. Whoever had arranged this had taken great pains to stay anonymous.

"What does the writing, um, pictures say? Are you able to read them?" ventured March.

The Professor smiled. "Reading Egyptian Hieroglyphs is not like reading normal text. A symbol can have a number of different meanings depending on its position, and even what is written next to it. Given the right books, and time, I probably could translate most of it, but sadly, at the moment it's beyond me."

"Can you make out anything?"

191

"No," lied the Professor looking back at the box. Despite what he had said there were a couple of symbols that he was able to translate on the spot and they did not bode well.

Then, from the box came a noise, a scraping as though something was trying to claw its way out. By now the other mail room workers had moved over to the table, interested as to what was happening.

"I think that we need to open the box," said the Professor.

"Are you sure?" asked March.

"Yes."

"But how?" asked one of the postal workers. "There does not seem to be any way into it."

The Professor leaned forward and placed his hands on the box. "The box is a puzzle. An item of value would be put inside and the box sealed. Only the person who owned the box would know exactly how to open it."

"We could put an axe to it," said March.

"Do you have one?"

He nodded, and then disappeared, only to return a short while later with a large axe.

"Good," said the Professor, seeing the weapon. "I want to try and open the box without breaking it if possible, but keep it to hand."

March nodded, resting the axe on his shoulder.

The Professor laid his hands on the box, he was certain that he would be able to solve the puzzle box, in fact he had come across one similar a couple of years ago. In reality, the axe was more of a precaution for what lay inside. He ran his fingers across the hieroglyphs, every so often pausing, until eventually pulling his hands back totally. Some of the images were raised, very slightly. If he were to press down on them in the correct order the box would open.

"Well?" asked one of the mail room workers eager to find out if the box could be opened.

The Professor took a deep breath, before again placing his hands on the box. "Get ready gentlemen." As if in response there was an eager scratching from within. He pressed down on one of the images and there was a feint clicking noise.

"What was that?" someone asked.

"It's alright," answered the Professor, "there are a series of internal locks within. That was one of them dropping into place." He moved his hand to the side of the box and pressed another image. Again there was a click, but one in a different tone. The Professor suddenly had a feeling of dread sweep over him as though something was wrong. "Everybody back!" he yelled as he himself jumped away, as from three sets of holes, hidden from the naked eye, came three thin jets of a wispy green powder.

"Cover your mouths!" cried the Professor as he turned away.

The green mist hovered in the air in the area immediately around the box before dissipating totally.

"What was that?" asked March.

"A trap! Oh, don't worry," he added seeing the worried look on March's and the other mens faces, "we are quite safe now. It is designed to affect anyone who is in direct contact with the box, the person trying to break into it actually!"

"What would happen to the person who breathed it in?" asked March.

"They would die," he replied simply. Although he kept the fact that the death would be in agonising pain over several hours as the victim's inside was literally eaten away by bacteria in the green haze, to himself.

After waiting a few more moments to be sure that the mist had subsided, the Professor returned to the box for another attempt. Again, ignoring the movement from within, he placed his hands on the box and searched for the hidden buttons that would release the lid. Some minutes passed before he looked up from his task. "I think I've got it. Ready yourselves Gentlemen." Then from the box there came in succession four loud clicks as he pressed down in certain areas and the internal locks were released. The fourth lock had barely been released when a screaming sound erupted from the box and the lid flew open to reveal the singular occupant, who stood up on all four legs, hissed and looked around with its eyeless sockets.

"Dear God protect us," came the cry from one of the men as they stared at the thing in front of them. "What is that thing?"

"It's a cat," called out the Professor, "or more to the point, what is left of one after it has been mummified."

The creature seemingly looked around again hissing. Although identified as a feline because of the shape of the skull it was barely recognisable as such, the ears, like the eyes were gone. It was practically bald, exposing skin that was wrinkly and discoloured. The fur that was left hung in small matted clumps. There was also an unholy smell coming from the creature which was now growling ever louder.

"The axe!" cried the Professor. "Use the axe! Kill the beast!"

As if understanding the situation, the cat suddenly leapt from the table just as the blade came crashing down where the abomination had been a few moments before. One of the postal workers went after the creature managing to seize it by the tail, but the cat turned on him scratching him viciously causing him to cry out. The creature then ran behind a number of boxes which had been piled up to one side of the room.

"Don't let it escape!" cried the Professor as he moved to the parcels. Another of the men was by his side to help sort through the pile, while March positioned himself behind, the axe raised in readiness.

194

Suddenly they were distracted from behind. The door to the postal room flew open and in burst an excited looking man dressed in a mailroom uniform holding up a bit of paper. "Look what I've got!" he called. "There is an actress on board! She signed this for me."

The cat somehow sensed that this was going to be its chance for freedom. Quickly, while everyone was momentarily distracted, it burst from its hiding place, sped across the floor, and through the legs of the autograph hunter and away.

"After it!" called March.

But by the time that they reached the door and looked out down the passageway the mummified cat was nowhere to be seen.

"Well done Williamson!" snapped March. "You let the cat out!"

"That was a cat?" replied the unfortunate man, confused as to what he had stumbled into.

March grabbed the postcard, looked at it before thrusting it back into his colleagues hand shaking his head. "Dorothy Gibson – never heard of her! Hardly a Florence la Badie is she?" He turned to the Professor. "So what now? We cannot have that thing running loose."

The Professor nodded. "I think that we are going to have to report this and enlist help."

CHAPTER 34

Richard Mallory, in no uncertain terms, had been told by Jazmine Montacute not to interfere in her observation of Madeleine Astor and Elisabeth Von Braun.

"I am perfectly capable to keep watch on them without being seen, and intervene if required."

"But what if you need help?"

"Unlikely," had been the response, in a tone that echoed her Father's, "but on the off chance that I do need a message sent to my Father or the like you can remain nearby."

"I would like to remind you I was an Officer in his Majesty's Army, not a mere errand boy."

She smiled in a way that was almost flirty and completely dismissive. So, deciding not to press the issue further, Richard Mallory positioned himself on the promenade deck outside the reading and writing room, where he was able to observe both Jazmine and Elisabeth unseen through the large bay window.

Not wanting to be seen himself, he kept his observation to a minimum, opting to sit on the seat nearby and read, occasionally returning to the window to check that all was well. It was on one such check that he saw things had taken a dramatic turn for the worse with the Mummy in the room advancing upon Jazmine, who had some kind of cord round her neck. Instantly he sprang into action, running the short distance to the first class entrance, past the grand staircase and down the long corridor that would lead to the reading and writing room. He was barely halfway down the passage when Jazmine appeared, running towards him, the Mummy not far behind her.

"I've got the red scarab!" she called and threw it to him.

He caught it and momentarily looked at the little red object. "Quick, we need to get outside," called Jazmine as she caught up to him. "If we use the red scarab to destroy the Mummy in a confined space it will cause untold damage."

So with that Jazmine and Mallory, with the Mummy following them, made their way back down the corridor, then out onto the Starboard Promenade deck via the first class entrance where they headed towards the stern of the ship.

"C'mon!" cried Mallory as they reached the electric crane at the end of the deck, "up to the boat deck."

Jazmine nodded and followed, only turning to see the Mummy, now even closer. Mallory quickly ran to the ladder which would lead up to the boat deck and scaled it quickly. As he helped Jazmine up, he looked down to see the Mummy at the bottom of the ladder, and beyond the creature, on the poop deck, a number of third class passengers. He hoped that none would look up and see them. As the creature neared the top of the ladder Mallory punched down at him hard. He hit the Mummy square on the chin, resulting in the creature falling to the deck below, landing in a heap.

"C'mon Jazmine, run," called Mallory as he grabbed her hand and started to head towards the Bow, "I've got an idea!"

"What is it?" she replied, not happy about him taking the lead.

"You'll see," he said, as he guided her up a small ladder which led them to a raised section of the second class promenade deck, directly by the Titanic's dummy funnel.

He suddenly stopped and seemingly happy with the position turned to Jazmine. "Quick, down on the deck and play dead."

Jazmine glared at him and placed her hands on her hips. "You are joking!"

"No, now get down! With the Mummy's reduced mental capacity he is bound to fall for this old trick."

Jazmine shook her head. "If you think that I......Aaaah!" Her words were cut short as Mallory decided to 'help her'. Grabbing her by the shoulders he then hooked her ankles with his foot, and guided her to the floor as gently as he could, apologising as he did so. With moments to spare, before the Mummy appeared, he had pulled himself up onto the large raised square base on which the dummy funnel stood and moved out of sight using the curve of the funnel itself to hide behind. After a few moments he dared to look round and checked on Jazmine, who was still lying on the floor staring

197

back at him mouthing obscenities, furious about her current situation and her role as bait. Mallory quickly reverted his attention to what he thought would be the less dangerous Mummy.

The creature was now on the raised deck, and was moving ever closer to Jazmine before it suddenly stopped. It reached down to its left thigh then seemed to actually reach inside the bandages for something. Mallory stared in morbid fascination as the creature produced from its leg what looked to be a short sword.

The Mummy advanced towards Jazmine, the weapon raised in the air. "Kiiilllll."

Mallory gasped in horror. With no other option he threw himself from the raised section landing on the Mummy.

The creature dropped the weapon and fell away, landing against the guard rail, while Mallory landed heavily on the deck.

"This is our chance!" called Jazmine as she jumped to her feet, only stopping to pick up the Mummy's fallen weapon. "The scarab! Get ready to insert the scarab!"

"Where?" asked Mallory, climbing to his feet.

"Here!" cried Jazmine as she ran forward. The Mummy, sensing the attack, swung his arm out, but the girl was quicker and avoided the blow, then lunged forward as a fencer would. The blade hit home, just below where the sternum was and penetrated the creature's body. It let out a strange cry, one that was made worse when Jazmine quickly twisted the blade to the right to make the entry hole bigger before jumping back.

Seeing his chance Mallory advanced, the scarab in hand. The Mummy raised its right arm at him and the hand detached itself flying towards Mallory's throat, but he managed to sweep away the flying limb and was able to continue his attack. Again the creature tried to lash out, this time punching out with its right fist but as before, the attack was futile with Mallory dodging the blow, making it through to his desired target. In one movement of his fingers, the red scarab went into the hole that Jazmine had just created. Quickly he withdrew his hand leaving the scarab in the cavity.

"Get back!" cried Jazmine as she scrambled away. "If the legends are correct he is going to become a fireball!"

Mallory did as he was bid, his eyes focused firmly on the creature, who realising that something was seriously wrong started to claw at the hole in a vain attempt to remove the scarab before it caused his demise, but the bandaged fingers were too cumbersome and could not manage to reach inside the small hole.

"Jazmine?" asked Mallory with some curiosity.

She angrily shook her head. "It's not working! The scarab must be a fake."

"So what now?"

"We go to plan B."

Jazmine threw the sword to Mallory before reaching to her neck, producing the black scarab which they knew would immobilise the creature and ran forward to him. The creature, having learnt its lesson from its previous failed attacks, ran to meet her and before she could evade him he swept his arms around, picking her up in a bear hug and started to crush. With her arms pinned to the sides of her body there was nothing Jazmine could do except try and push against the vice like grip. Mallory tried to stab the creature with the sword, but the creature turned itself using Jazmine as a barrier, forcing Mallory to retreat. Again he advanced and again the creature turned using the human shield to protect itself. Then letting out a low roar he let the grip on the now semi conscious Jazmine slip, allowing him to pick her up in his arms. Before Mallory could react he turned to starboard to

199

face the sea and in one huge effort threw Jazmine as far as he could.

"Jazmine!" screamed Mallory as he watched her flight. She flew like a rag doll through the air, over the rail of the raised platform that they were on, over the small span of deck before landing on top of the covered material of lifeboat number 13 before bouncing once. She came to rest at the outermost edge of the craft, below her a drop of sixty feet into the freezing Atlantic waters. Seeing the new danger that Jazmine was in, Mallory ignored the Mummy, opting to run past it and using the rail as a launch pad, jumping towards the lifeboat. As he was airborne he saw to his horror Jazmine tip off the side of the lifeboat, but somehow she managed to reach out and grab the side to stop herself falling completely. Mallory landed on the lifeboat cover and quickly made his way over to her, his fingers wrapping around her arm just as her grip was about to fail.

"Help me!" cried Jazmine, stealing a look downwards at the sea below her dangling feet.

Using all his strength, Mallory pulled as hard as he was able, and slowly Jazmine was lifted up. As she did so she managed to grip onto the side of the lifeboat, before she was eventually pulled back onto the safety of the cover.

Panting, Mallory looked round back at the raised section of deck, but the Mummy had gone. "Are you alright?" he enquired, turning back to Jazmine who was staring at him.

"You saved my life!"

Mallory felt suddenly embarrassed. Before he could say any more, Jazmine leant forward to kiss him, but then suddenly without warning she tore herself away and pointed. "Look, over there!"

Mallory turned to where Jazmine was pointing.

Over at the dummy funnel, wedged in tight between the huge yellow cylinder and a pipe which ran down it, twitching slightly trying to get free, was The Mummy's detached hand.

CHAPTER 35

There was an uneasy atmosphere amongst the men in the boiler rooms, especially those concentrated at the bow. News of the fire in the coal bunker had spread among the men and the latest word was that it was far from being extinguished but was getting worse. The constant rotation of men had been doing as Joseph Bell had ordered, dampening down the fire with hoses at the top of the fire while at the same time emptying out the coal store with shovels directly into the furnaces, but it did not seem to be working.

Bell stood to the side of the bunker as he watched the firemen and trimmers hard at work scooping out coal from the bunker via the large access portal.

Leading Fireman Thomas Davies moved over to join him. "This is hell's work, and no mistake! Care to pick up a shovel and pitch in for a bit?"

Bell smiled. "I think that you have things under control here."

"I would not say that," commented Davies. "I've never known a fire this difficult to get under control, it does not add up."

"Yes, well you are right on that score," confided Bell. "Something is not right on this and no mistake and I don't like it one bit!"

"Have you noticed that the ship is listing very slightly too? A couple of people have mentioned it."

Bell nodded. In normal circumstances, the bunkers would be emptied out at a steady rate all at once. However the focus upon the number six bunker had lead to 'uneven emptying' which had caused the ship to list to starboard due to the weight of the remaining coal. "The Captain mentioned it too when I was updating him earlier."

"What did he say?" asked Davies.

"He did not seem overly worried, just so long as it did not get too noticeable for the passengers. You know how they tend to complain if their wine ends up tilting in the glass!"

"Ahh, I wondered why there was more activity around bunkers three and four. It's an attempt to address the balance isn't it?"

Bell nodded. Extra men had been relocated to those areas in the hope that their efforts would naturally counteract the rapid loss of weight from the tons of coals being moved from bunker number six. "Although it's also having a serious effect on our speed, because of the extra activity we have been averaging twenty knots so far."

Then from within the bunker there came a strange rumbling, the firemen nearby heard it too and look around unsure as to what was happening.

"Take cover!" yelled someone as they jumped away. "Fire spurt!"

Bell and Davies threw themselves to one side, away from the bunker opening and the other men tried to run for cover too. The rumble got louder, then from the bunker a pile of glowing red coals exploded out into the boiler room. One unlucky fireman who had not moved fast enough was caught by the burning rocks, and his arm was instantly set alight, his friend nearby turned and ran back to help him.

"No, get back!" another voice yelled, but it was too late, for the first spurt was just a forerunner, like a small earth tremor before the main quake. Again there was a rumble, followed by what sounded like a crash of thunder, then the main fire spurt erupted. A mass of fiery coal was blasted into the main boiler room at speed. The man with his arm already

202

alight and his friend were caught directly in its path. They ran screaming from the scene before they were both tackled by their friends and colleagues who managed to knock them to the floor and beat the flames out. Three other men had been caught too and were shedding their burning outer garments where they stood, as the floor in the immediate area was covered with burning coals and embers, meaning they were unable to roll to put out the flames. One of their colleagues appeared, seemingly from nowhere, with a hose and doused them with water. The bunker then made one final groaning noise and sent forth one weak trickle of coals, indicating that, at the moment at least, it had finished.

"Get that fire out!" yelled Bell as he stood up and pointed to the floor, but men not directly involved were already on the scene, ready to help. The two metal wheelbarrows that were being used to transport the coal from bunker no. six to other furnaces were instantly put to use with the burning coals scooped up and dumped in them while other men appeared with buckets of water and more hoses. The injured men were quickly removed to a safer area where they could be attended to, before no doubt being taken off to the ship's hospital.

Bell looked over at Davies, his face etched with horror at the scene from hell that he was now part of. "My god, I thought the whole thing was going to go up then!"

"It still might," replied Davies, seriously worried about the flammable coal dust that filled the air. If ignited it could cause an explosion which could literally rip the whole ship apart.

"Hoses!" yelled Bell urgently. "More hoses. I want this whole area saturated in water and I want it done two minutes ago!"

By now firemen and trimmers from bunkers five and four had arrived to help and were lending a hand wherever they were able to.

"Listen!" called out Davies. "Everybody quiet!"

Everyone stopped and strained to hear. There were more strange sounds coming from within the coal bunker.

"Second wave!" yelled Bell. "Second wave! Everyone down, down, down!"

Then just as he had finished speaking a burst of bright yellow flame shot out from the centre of the bunker into the boiler room. One trimmer at the edge of the flame briefly found himself engulfed, before the fire instantly retracted back into the coal pile. He stood there for a moment, astonished that only his face and hands had been burnt superficially, before collapsing to the floor in shock.

"The barrow," called out Davies. "Get a hose on it, there's a man under there!" He indicated to one of the metal wheelbarrows now upturned and covered with fire. The man concerned had turned the barrow over, hiding underneath to protect himself from the flames, an action which undoubtedly saved his life. Instantly men were upon it and the fire extinguished, the man underneath emerged shaken, but miraculously unscathed, and was quickly escorted out of the way.

"Keep going men," called Bell. "Get these coals cleared, get a hose on that patch there!" He pointed to a small pile of coal that was flaring up. One man with a hose moved in towards it and just as he did so the water jet from the hose seemed to dry up. Other men bearing hoses had the same problem with their jet of water becoming no more than a trickle.

"The water's gone!" a cry went up.

Bell looked over at Davies. "This goes from bad to worse!"

"There is no way on this earth that the tank should be empty already," replied Davies. He then turned to the stunned looking men. "Don't just stand there! Get shovelling, beat the flames out! Pull 'em out and pee on the ruddy thing if you have to! You men with the hoses stand clear!"

Immediately, the men resumed the task of fighting the fire, and those bearing hoses stood to one side giving their colleagues room to work.

Davies turned back to Bell. "What do you make of it? I'm beginning to think that this damn ship is cursed!"

Suddenly from nowhere a young man appeared.

"Ah! Mr Rouse," said Davies. "I trust you have an explanation for us as to the sudden loss of water?"

"The pump broke," replied the ship's plumber wiping his hands on a rag. "It just stopped, I've no idea why, a blockage maybe."

"That's not going to help us now though is it?" replied Bell looking round at the firemen and trimmers working to clear the flaming coals. "Anyway shouldn't you be doing something to fix it?"

"Give it a few more moments sir," said Rouse confidently. Then with a spurting sound the dormant hoses sprang back into life and the hose bearers ran back to the fires turning the water on the dancing flames.

"Well done Rouse!" said Davies to the grinning plumber. "What did you do?"

The Plumber suddenly looked nervous. "A few things that you will not find in any manual, Sir. I'm afraid that it is only a temporary fix. I'm going to have a hard time putting things right again."

"Understood," said Bell nodding. He was just relieved that they had water back and was certainly not going to give Rouse a hard time over what he had done. Rouse was a more than capable man and would no doubt be able to put right any damage he had been forced to make.

The bunker suddenly groaned yet again making the men brace themselves for the inevitable, but this time there was

205

just the sound of a low rumble and a jet of steam seeped out from the pile, followed by a splutter and a small section of the coal shifted.

"That's it!" called out Bell to reassure everyone. "It's over."

"Blast it all!" said Davies. "I've never known anything like it. What are your thoughts?"

But all Bell could do was shake his head. He too had never seen anything like that in all his years as an Engineer. All his experience told him that a fire should not behave in that way.

"Right," called out the Chief Engineer. "Enough is enough! I want that bunker emptied out in double quick time! Increase the hoses and double, no triple, the men on it at once."

"But that could lead to a further list to the starboard," pointed out Davies.

"After what's just happened that is the least of my concerns," said Bell. "We need that fire out as soon as possible. Ensure that it's done at once. I'm going topside to inform the Captain."

CHAPTER 36

The events in the mailroom had duly been reported to a rather stunned First Officer William Murdoch. As the Professor and March finished their joint report, a call came through from the engine room that a strange creature had been sighted roaming around, and had attacked one of the stokers, biting him badly on the arm.

Murdoch acted quickly and summoned five members of the Guarantee Group; Ennis Watson, Frank Parkes, Robert Knight, Alfred Cunningham and Henry Parr, arranging to meet them in boiler room number one near where the creature had been seen.

"Sorry we are late gentlemen," said Murdoch as he arrived, the Professor and March behind. "We had to find Mr King before making a stop at the Master-at-arms room."

"The Master-at-arms? We are being given guns?" asked Parr.

"No," replied Murdoch seeing the surprised faces, "I'll be armed of course, and so too will Professor Montacute here, and Mr March as they both have firearms experience."

"Ruddy hell, Mr Murdoch," said Knight. "What are you sending us into?"

"Gentlemen," said Murdoch in a clear loud voice, "there is an immediate problem which I need you to turn your attention to. There is an 'animal' for want of a better word loose on the ship and you must find it and capture it by any means.

"Well, that explains the blankets," commented Parr, looking at the pile of blankets which had been provided for them.

"Sir, what kind of animal are we talking about here?" asked Cunningham with concern in his voice.

"Um, well this is the thing," stumbled Murdoch. "It is er, um."

Seeing the First Officer's hesitance about a situation out of the realms of his understanding, the Professor stepped forward. "The creature we are hunting is a cat." He paused as he let the men react with some surprise. "But don't be fooled gentlemen. This is a dangerous animal that has already sent one man to the hospital. The creature was being transported illegally through the postal service. Moreover, it is unlike any cat you would have ever encountered before."

"That's true enough," said March, "I've seen it with my own eyes. It's not so much of a cat more a small monster, one that is not of God's making."

"Are you serious?" asked Parkes.

207

"Very much so," said Murdoch. "This man is Professor Charles Montacute, an expert in this kind of thing. He will be handling this operation."

"So how did it end up down here?" asked Parkes.

"We are presuming that it got into the vents," said the Professor.

"Which is why you have been summoned," said Murdoch. "We are going to split up and find this creature. It must be caught."

"Ideally alive," interjected the Professor wanting the opportunity to study it then pass it on to a colleague at the Natural History Museum in London. "Use the blanket provided as a net and try to gather the creature up."

"But dead if you have to," added Murdoch quickly, as one by one the men reached for a blanket.

"Now, Mr March, Professor, the guns," said Murdoch turning to address them directly. "You have a full chamber of six bullets, but only use them at close range to the creature, and only if absolutely necessary. A stray bullet down here could cause all kinds of trouble."

They nodded in reply.

"Ah Mr Dyer," said Murdoch, as a man approached from the stern.

Henry Dyer, Senior Assistant 4th Engineer was holding his arm which was bleeding. "What the hell is that thing?" he shouted above the noise of the engine. "It just jumped out and attacked me!"

"We are not totally sure," replied the Professor unwilling to get drawn into having to give a long explanation. "Where is it?"

Dyer pointed towards the section of the ship which housed the ships engines. "Back down there."

"Can you give me a quick idea of what's back in that direction?" asked March, wanting to get bearings on the ship.

Dyer did as requested and gave a brief overview of the layout, explaining that the next section of the ship was dominated by the two main engines, and beyond that was a smaller engine room housing the smaller engine turbines.

"Mmmm," said the Professor as he stroked his beard thoughtfully. "This is not going to be easy, there are plenty of places a creature of that size could hide."

"Alright, we'll take it from here; Mr Dyer make sure that you get that looked at."

Dyer nodded to Murdoch before heading off past them towards the bow and to seek medical treatment.

"Right then gentlemen are you ready?" asked Murdoch.

The men indicated they were.

"Good," said the Professor taking charge. "I'll take Watson and go portside. John as you too are armed you take Parkes and Knight and go starboard." He turned to address Cunningham and Parr. "Now, as for the rest of you, I want you to head down the middle of the engines with Mr Murdoch. If you see the creature, try to use the blankets as a net to catch it."

With that the three groups of men, those armed in the lead, headed off in their ordered positions.

"Professor Montacute?"

"Yes Watson," he replied, over the engine noise, as he carefully moved down the ship and looked back at the youth.

"Is it really as dangerous as you are saying? I mean it can't be that bad? It's only a cat!"

The Professor smiled. "I can assure you that…"

His words were suddenly cut off by a scream and the sound of a gun firing, followed a few moments later by the impact of a bullet hitting metal, and the screech of something that sounded like an animal. Then from between the workings of the engine itself came the mummified animal landing a few feet in front of them. The hairless creature, barely

209

recognisable as a cat, turned to face them and growled. The Professor was about to shoot when Watson ran forward and dived at the creature, trying to catch it in the blanket, but the cat was too fast, and in an impossible move jumped in the air, turned and ran towards the stern. Not to be defeated that easily Watson rose slightly, picking up the blanket and propelled himself forward again. This time, he was successful. The creature was caught under the material.

"Well done lad!" cried the Professor as he moved forward to help. Quickly he took hold of the barrel of his own gun so he could hit the creature with the butt of the weapon to render it harmless. However, as he came in closer to land the blow, the creature let out a growl and then suddenly appeared through the blanket, tearing a hole in the material with its teeth and claws. Watson reached out for the creature, and for his efforts received a cut on his arm where the cat scratched him as it bounded away. The Professor raised his gun to fire, but again had his aim spoilt, as ahead, Murdoch and Parr appeared directly in front of him having been drawn round the engine by the commotion. The cat cried out and continued towards the stern with both Murdoch and the Professor unable to fire through fear of hitting each other rather than the animal. Sensing that he, for the moment at least, had the advantage, the cat launched itself forward into the air directly at Murdoch and Parr who instinctively parted allowing the creature to pass between them.   Cunningham, who was just behind Murdoch, threw the blanket like a net hoping to entrap the creature, but it managed to evade it and continued on its way.

"Come on!" cried the Professor as he ran forward. Murdoch and the others followed, past the huge turbine engine and onwards towards the smaller turbine engine room where they were met by March, Parkes and Knight who were waiting for them.

"Where is it?" cried the Professor.

March shrugged. "Dunno, we saw it and fired and it ran off towards you."

"We know," replied the Professor. "Watson here almost got it didn't you lad?" Watson, still clutching his wounded arm, nodded.

"Did you see it coming this way?" asked Murdoch. "It double backed."

"No," replied March, "no sign of it."

"Look there it is," cried Parr pointing. The creature had somehow managed to hide from the search party momentarily before heading back towards the bow, in-between the two huge reciprocating engines.

Immediately the Professor with Murdoch, March and the rest, started to follow. This time, with no-one in front to spoil his target the elderly scholar was able to fire off a couple of rounds, but the creature managed to dodge them. At the end of the engines, the creature burst into number one boiler room and took a sharp right and headed portside.

"Get it! Don't let that thing escape!" called the Professor to a bemused stoker who found this strange creature running towards him.

The cat, seeing that its path was blocked, gave out a hiss and leapt up at the man, who in response swung the shovel to defend himself.

The cat hit the flat metal, and the stoker swept the shovel to the side, whereupon, more by good luck than any judgement, the creature was directed straight into the open mouth of one of the inactive furnaces, which the man was tending to.

The Professor jumped forward and grabbed the protective door, slamming it shut on the creature inside. Almost at once there was a clunking sound as the creature crashed against the inside of the door as it tried to escape.

"Well done!" cried March in congratulation as he and the others gathered round the closed furnace. From within there came a low crying sound.

"What the hell was that thing?" asked the stoker.

Murdoch smiled. "You would not believe me if I told you. I'm going to have a word with the Captain. That furnace is to remain locked and untouched."

"Good," said the Professor, "because I think that this is the safest place for our mummified moggy. I advise that it is kept in here until we reach New York. Then it can be placed in a suitably strong container and be dealt with appropriately."

"Yes," agreed Murdoch thinking of what he had just witnessed. "A very strong container indeed!" He turned to the men. "Well done lads! Very well done! I think that I owe you a drink!"

CHAPTER 37

It was some hours later when the Professor eventually made it back to his cabin to find Mallory and Jazmine waiting for him. He had been requested to make a formal report into the incident in the postal room, after which, as thanks, he was given a tour of the ship, and a complementary meal in the à la carte restaurant.

The Professor was astounded when he heard the events which had transpired regarding the fake red scarab and the battle on the boat deck. But his main curiosity was taken with the Mummy's detached hand which now stood on the table, housed in a large glass pickling jar which had been provided by Jazmine after a visit to the Titanic's stores.

The hand itself was frantically moving around inside as though it was trying to find a way out of its prison.

"Totally fascinating," said the Professor, who had crouched down to take a better look at the trapped hand. "It seems as

212

though it is almost in some form of distress at the separation from its main body!" He then slowly started to unscrew the lid of the jar. Immediately the hand tried to scramble up the side to freedom, but he slammed the lid down again hard, catching the fingers between the lid and the glass rim. He then started to prod and poke the protruding digits. The fingers almost seemed to fight back as they moved and extended before quickly withdrawing back into the jar completely.

"Amazing," said the Professor as he screwed down the lid tightly before standing up again. "I wonder if the other hand can detach itself too or is it just limited to this one? We've only ever seen the left one so far."

"Never mind that," said Mallory. "What are we going to do with it? We can't just keep it here as a souvenir."

"It would certainly make a good subject for a university lecture, Father," pointed out Jazmine with a wicked smile.

"True enough," mused the Professor, "but I have a far better idea"

"What have you in mind?" asked Mallory.

"A trap," replied the Professor simply. "The creature is going to want the limb back and we know from experience that any pain we inflict on the hand will be felt by the creature directly. That puts us at a distinct advantage."

Mallory nodded, remembering the yell when the Professor pinned the hand to the wall of Kane's cabin with his swordstick.

The Professor disappeared into his bedroom, only to re-emerge a few moments later with a large coil of thin rope. He then moved over to the table and swept up the jar. "Come along then, no time like the present."

"For you maybe," said Jazmine as she removed the black scarab from her neck and passed it to Mallory, "but thanks to you two I've got a long evening shift ahead of me."

213

"You are never going to let that rest are you?"

"No, Father, I'm not," she replied icily.

"Well we can discuss that later; come on Mr Mallory, I want to get moving. There is no telling if our ancient friend is already on the trail of his missing hand."

With that he moved out of the cabin door not bothering to see if Mallory was behind him.

"How on earth did I get myself into this?" muttered Mallory.

"Sheer good luck!" replied Jazmine with a wicked grin.

"This is good luck?"

"Compared to the alternative, yes, remember you could have been back in Southampton!" she replied. "Anyway my father does not normally let people just tag along with our investigations."

Mallory stared at her slightly shocked.

"There are a number of students who would give their right arm to be where you are now," she said leaning towards him.

"Well, this mission does have certain advantages," he said trying to keep a straight face.

"Oh, and what are they?" she replied.

"Well for a start….."

"Mr Mallory!" called the familiar voice of the Professor who had appeared back at the doorway. "Come on! We do not have a great deal of time!"

Mallory looked over at Jazmine, smiled, then went over to the door where the Professor was waiting impatiently for him.

"Right," said the old scholar as he set a terrifyingly fast pace down the corridor. "We need to find a place where we can lure our ancient friend, then deal with him without being disturbed."

"Professor!" called a familiar voice behind them. "Professor Montacute!"

Mallory and the Professor turned to see Maggie Brown running towards them.

"Oh dear!" muttered the Professor. "It's that infernal Brown woman!"

"Professor Montacute! I'm so glad that I have found you!" she called out as she caught up to them. "I've been looking for you all over the place. I was so glad to hear from Jazmine that you were alright and recovered from the poison."

"Yes, well, thank you, but I am afraid that I am in a bit of a hurry at the moment. If it's about your statue I can assure you I will take all the necessary steps to get it returned to you as soon as we are able."

"No, it's not about that, although I would like it back." She stopped, noticing the covered object that he was carrying. "What's that?"

Checking that no one was around and thinking it would be a good chance to get away, he lifted the cloth. "We managed to capture the Mummy's hand." Maggie stared at the bandaged limb jumping around in the jar like a giant spider. "The creature will no doubt be keen to retrieve it, so we are going to set a trap for it. So I'm afraid that we cannot stop. He might already be on our trail." The Professor dropped the cloth back over the jar to hide it.

"Um alright," said Maggie, slightly taken aback at the sight, "but this could be very important to you."

"Alright, but make it quick."

She nodded. "Well, after you told me your story I became fascinated by the whole concept of what was going on, so I decided to go to the library. Did you know that it was Egyptian themed?"

"Yes I had been told," said the Professor looking over at Mallory, "but as yet I have not had a chance to investigate myself."

"Well anyway," continued Maggie, "the library is mainly made up of fiction, but there was a set of Encyclopaedia Britannica, some world history books and a small selection of books on Egypt due to the theme of the room itself. So I started to look up various things. Mummies, Pharaohs, and the like, then after a while the library steward asks me why I am so interested in that particular subject."

"You did not tell him about the Mummy or the Von Brauns?" asked the Professor.

Maggie gave him a stern look. "Of course I did not! Credit me with some sense! No, I told him that there was a friend of mine on board who was a Professor in history and an Egyptian expert."

"So you and the Professor are friends?" quickly put in Mallory much to the Professor's embarrassment.

Maggie ignored the remark. "Well, the steward asked who it was so I gave him your name. Then his whole attitude changed. He went pale as a ghost, became very evasive towards me, then suddenly became busy with other passengers, and was no longer able to attend to me."

"Interesting," said the Professor thoughtfully. "I don't suppose that you know the name of this man?"

Maggie nodded. "After his behaviour I made a couple of enquiries. His name is Harold, Harold Turley."

"Turley!" gasped the Professor. "That little snake in the grass, he's onboard Titanic?"

"You know him?" asked Mallory.

"Of sorts, yes. He was an Archivist with the British Museum up until last October. He took off, taking with him a number of books and other artefacts. It caused quite a scandal in academic circles."

"Did he take any Egyptian items?" asked Mallory.

"Quite possibly, but the list of what was taken was hushed up."

216

"A library steward sounds like the perfect job for an archivist on the run," said Mallory.

"Yes," said the Professor, "and a ship's library the perfect place to hide his booty."

"We need to take a closer look at that library," said Mallory.

"Agreed," said the Professor, "but at the moment our main priority is the Mummy's hand. I doubt he will be up to much mischief without it, and this is our best chance so far to really get at him." He turned back to Maggie. "Maggie, thank you, you have been a great help, but I need to impose on you one more time."

"Certainly, do you want me to make some more enquires about this Turley or to keep an eye on these Von Brauns?"

"Neither," said the Professor looking at the large feathered hat upon her head, a sudden thought coming to him. "I need to borrow a hat pin."

CHAPTER 38

The Professor and Richard Mallory were attracting attention. The Poop Deck was used for third class passengers and it was clear from the way that they were dressed and their demeanour that they were not. Positioning themselves on one of the seats at the stern, the rest of the passengers would occasionally look over but give the two a wide berth.

"How long are we going to have to wait here?" asked Mallory, glancing down at the cloth covered bundle between them which was the jar containing the Mummy's hand. "We've been here hours and I'm getting hungry."

"As long as it takes I'm afraid," replied the Professor, his own belly growling. "We need to wait until this section of deck is clear before we can act."

217

"But what if the Mummy decides that he cannot wait that long?" replied Mallory.

"Oh, I really don't think that he will chance anything with so many people about. No, we have to wait."

"Well in that case can I go off and get some food while you stay here?"

The Professor paused and, deciding that there would be no harm in the idea, agreed. So Mallory passed the Professor the scarab, and went for some food. He returned just under an hour later and with the deck still busy it was decided for the Professor to do the same. So the scarab and jar was given over to Mallory allowing the Professor to leave.

"Good to see you," said Mallory with a smile as he saw the Professor return a little later. "The deck suddenly started to clear. I thought that I would have to face our friend on my own."

"Sorry," replied the Professor looking round at the nearly deserted Poop Deck. "I got waylaid. I'm presuming that it is the third class dinner sitting in progress."

Mallory nodded as the last of those on the deck passed them, heading away. As soon as they had left, the Professor reached into his coat and produced two signs on chains, the signs read 'CLOSED'. "Here," he said, passing them to Mallory, "the reason why I was waylaid. Put these over the two entrance ladders to this section and it will ensure we are not disturbed until the Mummy shows up."

"Where did you get them from?" asked Mallory. "Um, on second thoughts I'd probably be better off not knowing!"

Quickly, before anyone else had time to approach the raised deck, Mallory placed the signs over the stairways, before then joining the Professor, who had positioned himself with the now uncovered jar on the raised docking bridge used by crew to get a better view of the stern when the ship was being brought into dock.

"Good work, Mr Mallory," said the Professor. "Now I have tied one end of the rope to the rail. While I was off acquiring the signs I was also able to acquire a bottle of brandy which I poured over the rope so it is quite flammable. As you can see the other end of the rope is firmly tied to the jar."

"What have you got in mind?" asked Mallory warily as he passed the scarab back to the Professor who quickly put it in his pocket.

"When the Mummy comes, I set the rope alight then throw the jar over the rail; that will give him a dilemma."

"Lose his hand or be turned into a fireball?"

"Yes, but it will also allow us time to rush him, insert the scarab then tip him over the side."

"But what if our ancient friend decides not to come?"

"Oh, he will!" said the Professor with an evil grin. From his jacket he produced the hat pin given to him by Maggie Brown. Then carefully he unscrewed the jar lid. The Mummy's hand jumped and tried to get to freedom, but the Professor was quicker and he plunged the pin into the hand as hard as he could before replacing the lid. Inside the jar, the hand twitched and convulsed, then from somewhere nearby there came a corresponding wail.

"The Mummy!" cried Mallory. "He must have been nearby all the time!"

"Look there he is!" pointed the Professor as the figure of the creature dressed in his normal long coat and wide brimmed hat came stumbling into view from the sunken aft deck.

"Haaaand!" wailed the creature as it moved forward, climbing up the short ladder, bypassing the 'CLOSED' sign, and stepping onto the Poop deck.

The Professor held the jar high in the air for the creature to see, then with his other hand he lit a concealed match, and set the rope alight. "I've estimated that you have about a minute before the rope burns through totally," called out the old man before turning and throwing the jar towards the stern of the ship.

The Mummy screamed out in terror as he watched the jar, and his hand within, sail over the Titanic's rail.

"Get ready, Mr Mallory! We are about to solve our Mummy problem once and for all!"

But the creature clearly had other ideas. Reaching out his arm he launched a section of bandage which sped across to the figures on the bridge. The target was Mallory, and the Mummy hit the mark with frightening effect. The impact hit Mallory with such force that he was knocked back and over the side of the Docking Bridge. One end of the bandage somehow wrapped itself around his neck as he fell, while the other end attached itself to the rail, and Mallory found himself suspended in the air, being hung by the neck like a condemned man on the gallows. The Professor instantly produced his pocket knife from his waistcoat and tried to cut through the bandage, but the blade was dull. The material would not break. Meanwhile Mallory was somehow able to reach up with one hand and grab hold of the rail, alleviating the weight from his neck, but still leaving him dangling in mid air.

While they were distracted the Mummy, seeing his chance, ran forward and, unchallenged, made his way over to the stern rail where he looked over to where his trapped hand in the jar was hanging.

"No you don't!" called out the Professor who had now jumped to the deck and headed over to the Mummy, his swordstick drawn. He thrust the blade into the creature's back. In response, the Mummy swung round, his clenched fist catching the old man and knocking him to the floor. The creature then pulled out the sword and raised the blade, meaning to use it to finish off the Professor once and for all.

But the old man was faster, managing to roll out of the way as the blade came crashing down into the wooden deck. Seeing his chance, the Professor scrambled to his feet pulling out the black scarab from his pocket. He squared up to the Mummy, who, seeming to realise that if he did not act soon his hand would be lost forever, turned his attention back to the rail.

The creature leant over the rail outstretching his arm and sending out a strand of bandage down the back of the ship. The cloth hit and attached itself to the jar, just as the rope burnt through. At the same time the Professor reached the ancient creature and put one arm round its neck pulling it backwards while with the other he reached round trying to place the scarab into the creature's chest to immobilise it forever.

"I'm going to send you back to hell where you belong!" cried the Professor as he grappled with the creature who, without warning, lifted both feet into the air, placed them onto the rail and with all his strength pushed hard sending both himself and the Professor sprawling back onto the deck floor. A few seconds later, the jar containing the Mummy's hand appeared over the rail and smashed onto the deck into pieces, freeing the hand. The Mummy let out a whine of triumph and the hand returned to the empty stump attaching itself. With its other hand the creature removed the hat pin that had caused him so much discomfort and threw it to the deck.

Meanwhile the Professor, still holding the scarab, had scrambled to his feet, but seeing the new situation that was suddenly developing moved back. The long strand of bandage that the Mummy had sent out to retrieve the jar was now on fire; most likely as it had made contact with the burning rope at some point. The strand of bandage was acting like a fuse and a trail of fire was heading up towards the Mummy.

"Fiiiire," yelled the creature in alarm as it suddenly became aware of the heat of the flames, but it was too late, for the creature's hand was alight and the flames started to move up its arm. The Mummy threw itself to the deck and started to roll. After a few moments the flames were extinguished. Seeing his chance the Professor ran forward, but the Mummy was on its feet and roared like a wild creature before lunging forward pushing his enemy back. Then the creature, not wanting to risk further confrontation, ran and in one leap jumped then scaled the Docking bridge, where it stood on the rail, momentarily looking across at Mallory, who had only just now finished freeing himself from the bandage that was threatening to strangle him, and was pulling himself up to safety.

The Mummy then raised his singed arm and shot out a long strand of yellow bandage which eventually attached itself high up the rear mast. Then with a giant leap the Mummy threw himself off the side of the raised bridge and swung in a wide arc over the edge of the ship, then back round until he landed back on Titanic in the sunken aft deck.

By now the Professor had made his way back up onto the docking platform and after checking Mallory was alright, looked to see the Mummy had disappeared from sight. "Blast it! I was so close to making him inactive! Another second and we would have had him!"

"So what next?" asked Mallory, rubbing his throat. "How about mounting a search for the Mummy?"

The Professor shook his head. "I'm sad to say that I don't think we are ever going to find its hiding place. The Von Brauns have it hidden too well. No Mr Mallory, I think that the plan for tonight should be rest and a game or two of chess while we try to work out our next move!"

CHAPTER 39

Thomas Andrews looked over at Joseph Bell with a look of grim concern on his face, a look that Bell was returning with equal seriousness.

It was now mid-morning on Saturday, and the fire which had started just before the sea trials, and had raged for so long was finally out, due to the combination of dampening and coal clearance. However, as the two men inspected the bunker there were concerns that there was still great danger ahead of them.

"I don't like the look of it at all," said Bell holding up his lamp to look at the damage left behind by the blaze.

Andrews nodded in agreement, his own lamp raised also.

A large section of the starboard hull was severely buckled out of shape as well as still glowing red hot.

"It would be interesting to see what damage the outer hull has if any," said Andrews with professional curiosity.

Bell nodded. "Well, that will have to wait 'til we get to New York. I'm more concerned about the damage here." He jabbed a finger at the section of warped metal.

"Do you think that there is a danger of structural failure?"

Bell moved closer to the bulkhead and cast his eye over the warped metal. "I think it will hold," he confirmed. "Of course, I will feel a lot happier once it has cooled down totally."

"We could put some hoses on it," suggested Andrews.

"No," said Bell, "I think that we should let it cool naturally. A rapid temperature drop could cause us even more problems later on."

Bell turned to look at the bunker wall which backed onto the coal storage of bunker number five. His attention was fixed on a large metal plate that had been hastily welded in place.

"Of course," he said, "that made the situation a whole lot worse."

Andrews nodded.

The large hole had created a link directly between the bunkers. As efforts were made to empty out number six, unbeknown to them, coal was slipping through from bunker number five.

Bell shook his head angrily. "I should have realised sooner! The level of number six was hardly moving. No wonder it took us so long to reach the fire."

"Don't be too hard on yourself!" said Andrews. "Even if you had have realised, there was nothing that could have been done until enough coal was cleared to get to the breach anyway!"

"Perhaps," answered Bell, although he was not convinced.

"What worries me is why that hole was there in the first place," continued Andrews. "As far as I knew all the bunkers had been checked and signed off as completed; a gaping hole certainly was not on my blueprint!"

This made Bell smile. "Well at least I am not the only one who has had problems."

"Problems that could have been worse," replied Andrews. "It was a miracle that the fire did not spread through into the other bunker; by rights it should have."

"Yes, that certainly would have…."

Bell's words were cut off dramatically by the sound of a tremendous thud coming from the cherry red bulkhead, which then echoed around the hollow bunker.

"What the hell was that?" said Andrews.

"I've no idea," replied Bell, his eyes fixed upon the glowing metal. "It sounded as though something hit us, probably a whale or something of that type." He turned to the bunker entrance hatch where a number of blackened faces, drawn by the crash, had gathered. "Someone call up to the Bridge. Find out if they know what just happened."

"Will do sir!" cried one of the men before dashing off.

"That was quite a knock we took," said Andrews, sounding slightly concerned.

"I know," replied Bell, "and it sounded as though it was right outside the damaged section of hull too. Why the hell did it have to be there?"

"The outer hull is an inch thick," pointed out Andrews, "I'm sure that it will hold."

"What if it's a gash though?" replied Bell. "What if the outer hull is breached or cut most of the way through?"

"It sounded more like a thud than a gash," pointed out Andrews. "But if there has been a breach we will soon know about it!"

"That's no comfort," replied Bell, his mind racing at the prospect.

"Look, you know the construction of this ship almost as well as I do," said Andrews. "If there is a breach we simply seal the affected bulkhead, engage the water pumps and carry on, monitoring the situation hourly."

"Sir," called a voice from the bunker door, "message from the bridge. Nothing abnormal to report, they did not even feel anything. "

"Well that's a good sign," said Bell.

Just as Andrews was about to reply, from somewhere nearby there came the sound of a groan of metal and an ominous creaking sound.

"That did not sound healthy," commented Bell, looking up.

Again there was another creak and groan from outside, then from the top of the bunker came a small hiss, then a thin train of steam started to appear and slowly move downwards.

"A breach?" said Bell, although from the sound of his voice it was clear that it was more of a question than an observation.

"I don't know," replied Andrews scanning the area. "I cannot see any obvious traces of water flowing. Can you?"

Bell shook his head. A leak, especially considering the pressures involved would soon be apparent. A small dribble of water would soon be replaced by a spurt and then gushing as the water exploited any weakness.

The trace of steam continued to travel down the metal at a steady rate. Andrews moved closer, lifting up his lamp to try to throw light on the problem. "This does not seem right."

"Careful!" warned Bell. "I don't like the look of it at all."

Then from above, out of the gloom something fell. It was a long hose with a large metal nozzle. The hose landed on Andrews, the metal end catching the side of his head. He dropped the lamp, and pitched forward. Bell jumped, grabbing Andrews by his jacket, pulling him back before he was able to burn himself against the glowing metal of the bulkhead.

"What happened? What hit me?"

"Just a hose," replied Bell sounding relieved. He picked it up from the floor. "I remember now, one of the lads said something about rigging it up over the bunker to make it easier to dampen the coal, but it must have gotten forgotten and left up there."

"Yes, well I'm not likely to forget it," replied Andrews rubbing the side of his head. "By the way, thank you." He motioned over to the glowing bunker wall. "That could have been very nasty."

Bell shrugged indicating that it was nothing. He looked down at the hose then back at the bunker where the steam had appeared. "No breach," he said relieved. "The remainder of the water in the hose must have leaked out onto the bunker."

"What caused the hose to fall?"

"I'm guessing that it was something as simple as the ties breaking," replied Bell throwing the hose to one side.

As soon as he finished speaking there came another groan and a creak from the bulkhead. Both men stopped and stared at it in anticipation, but nothing happened. There were no signs of any further buckling or traces of water. The two men stood in silence waiting and watching, but nothing more happened.

After some minutes Andrews spoke. "I think that if there was any danger, it's past now."

Bell nodded. "But I think we will still need to keep a close eye on it."

"Agreed," replied Andrews nodding.

"I'm going to detail a man to check on the bunker every fifteen minutes and notify me at once if there are any changes."

"I'm going back up top soon to report the current situation to the Captain, but if there are any changes I want to be notified at once."

"Of course," said Bell. "Come on let's get out of here." With that he and Andrews moved over to the bunker hatch where they ducked down and moved back out into the boiler room.

"Sirs, sorry to interrupt you."

Bell and Andrews turned to see a soot covered fireman, cap in hand in front of them, looking worried. "We've got a problem."

"Yes?" replied Bell expectantly.

"There seems to be uncommon heat patches in bunker no. five. We think that the fire has spread after all."

"Right then," replied Bell grimly. "The usual routine if you please. Clear out the coal as fast as you can into the furnaces and get hoses on the coal."

The fireman nodded and dashed off, to ensure that the orders would be carried out.

Bell turned back to Andrews shaking his head. "We need to get to New York as soon as possible. If there is another fire it could damage the bulkhead further."

"What about lighting the remaining furnaces?" suggested Andrews knowing that not all of the ships 159 furnaces were in use. "We could squeeze out another knot or two and I don't think the extra speed would adversely affect the weakened bulkhead."

Bell shook his head. "One we cannot use, and if we light the others it would affect the digging out of bunker five. My men are already tired out through the efforts in number six."

"Why is one furnace out of use?" asked Andrews.

Bell paused, the words 'well it is currently being used as a makeshift prison for a mummified cat' sprang to mind, but instead he opted for the more plausible, "There is a fault with the temperature gauge. I don't want to light the thing if I can't tell if it's going to overheat and potentially blow up."

Andrews nodded. "Right, I had better report this all to the Captain. I'm going to recommend that we make all possible haste to New York."

"Well," said Bell, "in the circumstances I think that it is the safest option."

CHAPTER 40

Harold Turley looked up with expectancy, and some resignation, as Richard Mallory and Professor Montacute entered the Titanic's library. The former British Museum Archivist rose from behind his desk to greet them. He was a small slight looking man, dressed in a dark three piece suit and looked nervous to the point of being scared. "Professor

Montacute. I've been expecting you. Please allow me to close the Library while we conduct our business."

The Professor nodded and pulled the swordstick slightly from its sheath. "Alright, but if you try to run….!" he said, but from the look of defeat on the man's face it was clear that the threat was unnecessary. As Turley moved to the door to close the room, watched keenly by Mallory, it gave the Professor a chance to look round at the Library.

It was indeed Egyptian themed as he had earlier been told, and was decorated with various artefacts to enhance the topic. The Professor was particularly impressed with the wooden sarcophagus attached to the wall, although he recognised instantly that it was a reproduction.

"As soon as I realised from that woman I spoke to that you were on board, I knew the game was up," said Turley returning to his desk. "You have a fierce reputation Professor Montacute. I know that it is no good me trying to make excuses or even trying to run, not that on this ship there are many places I could go."

The Professor nodded courteously to the complement, while Mallory tried not to laugh.

"Yes, I confess. I stole a number of items from my time at the British Museum. I had been doing it for over a year. You see, at first, I was being blackmailed." Turley paused, bracing himself for the inevitable question which would come next which was asked by Mallory. "Blackmailed over what?"

Turley looked to the floor, took a deep breath and spoke. "I'm homosexual."

The Professor and Mallory paused. Homosexuality was against the law, and could even result in a prison sentence.

"I stole to keep my Blackmailer quiet," said Turley.

"But you said 'at first'?" noted the Professor.

Turley nodded. "The man who was blackmailing me was doing the same to a number of others with my, um,

229

orientation. Anyway, it seems that one of us was not so nearly as obliging to just keep handing money over. Do you remember that story about the unidentified naked man who was found dead, tied to a tree, in Hyde Park last Summer?"

The Professor nodded, it had been all over the London papers.

"Well, that was my blackmailer. I can't begin to tell you how relieved I felt when I heard. But the problem was, having started stealing from the Museum I found that I could not stop myself! It was so easy; a coin here, a book there! Through my role as Archivist I could move freely among the back stores and catalogues, helping myself to whatever I pleased. It became an easy way to supplement my modest income."

"So what went wrong?" asked the Professor.

Turley smiled. "I simply got greedy. There was a jade stone which I came across. I just had to have it! I knew that, unlike the other items I took, there was a chance that it might be missed, but it was a chance I had to take so I took the gem!"

"And I presume that it was missed?"

Turley nodded. "But the irony of it all was that it was lost to me within an hour of me liberating it from the museum. There was a hole in my waistcoat pocket. I retraced my steps of course, but to no avail, it was lost!"

The Professor smiled, it was indeed sweet, natural justice.

"Anyway," continued Turley, "a few days went by and the jade was found to be missing. The police were called and questions started to be asked, and it was realised that other items had gone. I knew that it would not be long before the finger of suspicion would be pointing at me."

"So you decided to run?"

Turley nodded. "But not before I made one final visit to the stores of the British Museum. I grabbed as much as I was able, and then went into hiding. With the police looking for me I dared not try and risk selling any of my booty, so I decided that I would escape abroad where I would be beyond their reach, but I was critically short of actual funds so I decided I would have to work my passage."

"And you ended up here on Titanic as a library steward," said the Professor, mentally filling in the rest of the story.

Turley nodded. "Imagine how my heart leapt when I found the position was vacant! With my knowledge and expertise of the workings of a library I sailed through the interview with ease and was easily able to falsify a reference. The job was mine! I could hide here aboard the ship, doing a job that I loved, hidden, until we reached America where I could jump ship with my stolen booty and then disappear forever."

"A good plan," commented the Professor.

"Now tell me," said Turley. "How did you find me? What clue did I leave behind?"

The Professor smiled, not wanting to reveal that he had been found by chance. "Turley. Tell me about the items that you took."

"A mixture," he replied; "some books, jewels, and the like."

"Anything Egyptian?" pressed the Professor, keen to find out if Turley had inadvertently brought himself to the attention of the Von Brauns.

"Yes, a few bits, they are easy to sell abroad, especially in the United States."

The Professor nodded. "The items that you stole. Where are they now?"

Turley smiled and looked around. "Here, I hid them in the library. I wanted to keep them close by. As I knew that I would be spending most of my time here anyway, it seemed practical."

"Hiding them in plain sight," said the Professor, "very clever!"

Turley nodded and turned to a pile of books on his desk. He picked one up which had been marked 'reserved' and opened it. The inside had been hollowed out, and inside the well was a variety of Egyptian jewellery.

The Professor took the jewellery and started to sort through, then deciding that there was nothing of significance there, handed them back. "Is there anything else?"

"Yes." Nodded Turley as he moved to one of the bookcases. He reached up and brought down a statue that had been half hidden between the books, before returning to the desk. Professor Montacute's eyes widened in a mixture of excitement and terror, as he saw the object clearly for the first time. "My goodness Turley! Do you know what you have here?"

"I think that it is a statue of Osiris, Lord of the Dead. A funny looking chap isn't he?"

The Professor, still staring at the statue, nodded. The figure stood nine inches tall and was set upon a large wooden base. Dressed in a white robe the figure had its arms crossed and on one hand held a flail and in the other a small crook. On its head was an elongated crown with what looked like wings coming from it.

"Alright Professor," said Mallory. "You are going to have to help us out here. What's wrong?"

"In Egyptian mythology Osiris is the god of the afterlife. A righteous Pharaoh, he was murdered by his brother Seth, but was brought back to life by his son Horus and his consort Isis. Anyway, a movement grew over time to worship his brother Seth, the god of darkness and chaos. However, statues of Seth were banned; in fact it became illegal to worship him, so his followers went underground. Meeting in secret and hiding all traces of their true allegiance."

"So? What has this got to do with the statue?" asked Mallory.

"Everything, as I do not believe that this is a statue of Osiris in its truest form."

The Professor then started to run his fingers over the statue as though feeling for something. He spent a few moments checking the base before moving back to the main body itself. Then to both Mallory and Turley's surprise he gripped the two arms of the statue and pulled them free.

"What have you done!" cried Turley. "You've broken it!"

The Professor ignored him and, discarding the arms, gripped the head and pulled that off too. He then started to feel at the base pushing in hard at certain points until there was an audible click and from the base a hidden drawer shot out.

"What the....!" gasped Turley.

From the drawer the Professor pulled out a small head, which looked like that of an anteater and placed it on the statues neck. Back at the drawer he then pulled out two arms, one was holding a cross while the other was empty. Looking back in the drawer, the Professor pulled out three small rods which he put together to make a sceptre which he placed into the empty hand before taking both arms and placing them back on the figure and stood back. "That was not a statue of Osiris," announced the Professor, "it was a hidden statue of his brother Seth."

"Oh my goodness!" cried Turley in amazement.

"The Osiris version would be on display for all to see and then later, in secret, the limbs would be swapped round to show Seth. A cunning way of keeping the owners true beliefs hidden!" explained the Professor. "I'm presuming that you had no idea of the true nature of the item, Turley?"

"No I just liked the look of it and I thought that it ….." Turley's words were cut short. A silver blur flew past the

Professor and Mallory as a dagger flew through the air and embedded itself into Turley's shoulder. He fell backwards gasping then, again from behind, a long strand of yellow bandage shot out and wrapped itself round the statue of Seth before pulling it clean off the table and over to the door of the library where stood the Von Brauns' Mummy in its long coat and hat. "Kiiillll Turley! Get statue!" said the creature as it caught the statue and smoothly dropped it into his leather satchel.

From his coat the Professor pulled out his revolver and fired it at the Mummy. The bullet hit the creature knocking it off balance slightly, but it regained its footing. Again the Mummy unleashed a strand of bandage from his hand. This time his target was the section of bookcase behind the desk. The yellowing binding latched onto the top of the bookcase, and then in one movement the creature started to pull it forwards. There was a cracking sound as the screws that held the bookcase were pulled away from the wall and it started to pitch forward. At the same time the Professor pulled his swordstick free from its sheath, while Mallory dived forward onto the desk and picked up a pair of scissors. Each made a swipe at the bandage to cut it, but it was too late. The bookcase had tipped forward too far, and gravity had taken over and it started to fall freely towards them. The Mummy roared out in triumph and, as he turned to leave, the sound of the crashing bookcase filled the Library.

CHAPTER 41

Slowly Mallory pulled himself free from the mass of books and other items which had been on the shelves. The bookcase had partially landed on Turley's desk, which had acted as a barrier and had stopped them from being crushed completely. Then the Professor appeared from the debris, carefully dragging the unconscious Turley with him. "He was very lucky!" said the Professor examining the knife wound. "A little lower and it would have been a very different story!"

"I'm going to go after the Mummy," said Mallory.

"Alright," said the Professor handing him the black scarab. "Take this and be careful. I'll ensure that Turley is alright then I'll catch you up."

Mallory left the library and started to walk around the deck hoping to find the creature, which he did with little effort. In fact the creature almost seemed to be waiting for him down a long passageway. Mallory stopped wondering what action he should take next. The Mummy raised his right arm. Mallory watched it keenly, waiting for the hand to detach itself and than launch an attack, but it did not happen. Instead the Mummy just collapsed on the floor.

Slowly, Mallory edged his way forward, mindful the creature could easily be copying the ruse he had tried on it earlier. As he got closer the Mummy's hand started to twitch slightly, making Mallory almost turn and run, but the movement stopped and after a long pause Mallory continued.

Almost at the body, Mallory reached out his foot and tapped it to see if there were any signs of life.

The creature remained motionless.

Mallory kicked it again only this time harder.

Still nothing.

Keeping his eyes firmly on the Mummy, Mallory went for the black scarab in his pocket, aiming to deal with this creature once and for all. As he did so the door to his right flew open and two hands reached out, gripped him by the throat, before dragging him inside the cabin.

In the semi-darkness of the compartment Mallory punched out at his attacker, realising as he did so that he was no longer holding the black scarab. In retaliation his assailant returned the attack, a punch, hitting him hard in the stomach causing him to double over. From somewhere nearby he heard the door of the cabin being closed, then the electric lights were turned on and Mallory was pulled upright and for the first time able to see who had attacked him.

Mallory's eyes widened in total disbelief at what greeted him.

Standing before him, some six foot tall was the figure Seth, behind him, over by the closed door, was the Mummy.

"What the …………"

"I am Seth, or rather a living effigy of the god that I was made to resemble," the creature replied.

"No, that's impossible!" said Mallory trying to get his head around what he was seeing.

"Is not my bandaged friend here an impossibility?" said Seth in perfect English as he turned to point to the Mummy who grunted in acknowledgement.

"But you, you were just a wooden figure a few inches high, stuck on a shelf!"

"But now, as you can see, I stand here before you, alive of sorts. Free at last!"

"Free?" said Mallory, realising that this could be his chance. "I doubt that very much. I cannot see the Von Brauns releasing you back into the wild as it were. You will end up as their puppet just like the Mummy here."

Seth moved forward. "The plans for my future are of no consequence to you. But the question is what should I do with you?"

"Let me go with a stern warning?" quipped Mallory.

Seth sneered. "No, I think not. You are a danger which must be dealt with in as painful a way as possible!" He looked over behind Mallory's shoulder and nodded.

The Mummy responded by reaching out his arm, a strand of bandage flew out and wrapped itself around Mallory's chest, pinning his arms against his side. As Mallory struggled with his bonds the Mummy moved forward and seized him. Then with one hand it grabbed Mallory by the hair pulling his head backwards.

Seth moved forward holding up something long and thin in his hand that he had produced from somewhere on his person. "Do you know what this is?"

Mallory stared at the long thin piece of metal with a bend at the end into a hook. He had an uncomfortable feeling he knew exactly what it was and tried to struggle free, to no avail.

"It is called a 'brain hook,' " continued Seth. "It was an implement used in the process to create a Mummy. The hook would slowly and carefully be inserted up the nostril, ultimately pushed up into the skull, where the brain would be pulled down and out through the nasal passage."

Mallory stared at the hook, now being held a few inches in front of his face.

"It was a noted fact among embalmers that the best time for this procedure to take place was when the person, who would eventually become a Mummy, was still slightly alive. Of course, actual death usually occurred in the middle of the procedure. Did you know that it was also carried out in specially created rooms with extra thick walls that muffled the screams?"

Inspired by what he had just been told, Mallory took a deep breath, about to scream out, but Seth, anticipating the yell, hit him hard in the chest, causing Mallory's intended cry to turn into a choked splutter.

"Gag him," ordered Seth to the Mummy. "I don't want our work to be overheard." The Mummy responded by detaching a small section of his own bandage from his hand and stuffing it into Mallory's mouth, before renewing his vicelike grip.

Mallory struggled again but the Mummy pulled his head back even further.

Seth moved the implement and placed it just under Mallory's right nostril. "Embalmers were divided throughout our history as to which nostril to use as entry to the brain. Which should I start with?"

Mallory tried to turn away, but the grip of the Mummy was too strong.

"The left or the right?" said Seth as he slowly moved the hook from one nostril to another to prolong the mental agony. "Believe it or not the decision does make all the difference, of course I could just start with a simple castration? What do you think?"

Mallory suddenly pushed his weight back on the Mummy and tried to kick out at Seth, who jumped to the side before, in retaliation, plunging the brain hook deep into Mallory's leg, causing him to yell out loudly despite the gag.

Seth wrenched the instrument free then placed it in Mallory's left nostril. "Enough of this! It is time for you to die!" He then pushed the hook upwards into Mallory's nose until it came to a natural rest at the top of the nasal passage. A smile seemed to cross Seth's face as he readied himself to push the brain hook upwards.

The door to the cabin flew open, and the figure of Professor Montacute filled the doorframe. Seth paused for a moment, then was about to push the brain hook up as far as he could, but the Professor was quicker, bringing his gun up and firing at the creature. The bullet hit its target sending splinters of wood flying into the air, and causing Seth to stumble backwards. The Professor fired again, the second bullet flew into Seth and passed right through as he launched his counter attack by picking up his sceptre which had been resting against the wall and throwing it like a spear. It flew through the air grazing the Professor on the arm causing him to drop the gun. Rather than stoop down to retrieve it, the scholar opted to run forward at the life-size effigy.

Meanwhile the Mummy released his grip on Mallory and brought his arm up to try and snare the Professor by shooting out a strand of bandage. However, Mallory, now free, pushed himself back into the creature spoiling his aim. Then, despite his bonds, he managed to place a well aimed kick at the Mummy's knee which sent the ancient creature to the ground. He looked round to see the Professor, who was locked in battle with Seth, before turning back to continue his own battle with the Mummy. But in those brief few seconds the Mummy had scrambled to his feet and was heading out the cabin and was away. Mallory considered going after him, despite his bonds, but was then distracted by Seth who had raised both arms in the air in a dramatic fashion and lifted his head upwards as though calling out to the gods themselves.

"I am the effigy of Seth! I represent the god of storms, chaos and the desert itself. I invoke the powers of the ancient gods to destroy you!"

Grabbing the fallen sceptre, the Professor swung it round in an upwards direction at Seth. The tip of the rod caught Seth under the long snout which formed its nose. The effect was totally unexpected. The wooden head, which was in reality only placed upon the body, lifted off and fell to the floor. As it did so, it, along with the body, began to shrink back to its original size of just a few inches high.

The Professor ran forward and instinctively slammed his foot down on the wooden figure which smashed under his boot. He stamped down several more times to ensure that the stature was totally destroyed before turning to Mallory. "Are you alright?"

Mallory nodded and mumbled.

The Professor moved over to him pulling the bandage from his mouth, dropping it on the floor.

"Thank you!" said Mallory. "That was close! But how did you find me?

239

The Professor smiled, reached for his pocket knife and began to cut through Mallory's bonds.

"I heard a yell, well more of a muffled cry."

"That must have been when I was stabbed in the leg with the hook," reasoned Mallory, looking down at his bleeding thigh.

The Professor nodded. "That certainly helped, but it was really this which showed me where you were. It was on the floor outside the door." He held up the black scarab on its chain.

"Sorry, I dropped it when I was grabbed by Seth," said Mallory.

"Well in this case I would say that it was a very good job you did. Because if you had not, I would still be stalking the corridors looking for you, and when I did eventually find you, all that would have been left was a brainless corpse."

Mallory and the Professor moved over to the shattered pieces of the statue of Seth and stared at the wooden debris.

"Could that thing really have invoked the ancient powers of the Egyptian gods?" asked Mallory.

The Professor shrugged. "I'm not sure. He certainly thought that he could and I did not want to take the chance."

"And you just stopped him by knocking his head off!"

The Professor smiled. "That normally does work, even with enchanted creatures!"

Mallory smiled. "We'll have to bear that in mind with the Mummy! What are we going to do with the pieces?"

"Gather them up and toss them into the nearest fireplace. We also need to get you to hospital."

"Oh, I'll be alright," said Mallory, looking down at his leg wound.

"I'm afraid that I was not thinking of you," replied the Professor. "Turley is now in the hands of the Titanic's

240

medical staff and I have the feeling that our bandaged friend
may still want to finish him off!"

CHAPTER 42

Richard Mallory sat up in the bed and reached over for a glass
of water. As he did so he glanced over to a nervous looking
Harold Turley who was trying to concentrate on a magazine.
The door to their room opened and Turley nearly jumped out
of his skin.

"Are you alright Mr Turley?" asked the nurse.

"Um, yes, yes I'm fine," he said trying to calm himself.

The nurse moved over to the third bed in the small room
and checked on its occupant who was asleep, before smiling
and leaving.

"I don't know how much more of this I can take, my
nerves are in shreds!" said Turley. "Do you really think the
creature will come after me?"

Mallory nodded. "The Professor seemed quite clear on its
intentions Mr Turley. Recovering the statue of Seth was only
part of the mission."

"The other being to kill me!"

"Look, it won't come to that. Should he come for you we
are more than prepared to protect you."

From the third bed there came a cough and the occupant sat
up, having coughed himself awake, grabbed some tissues
from the cabinet beside him and held it up to his face. "I can
still feel the coal dust in my throat!" he spluttered.

"Hardly surprising," replied Mallory to Joseph Dawson,
"from what you said I feel that you had a lucky escape, but
one you will recover from."

"Yes, well I got off lightly!"

Mallory nodded, aware that most of the remaining beds in
the small hospital were filled with other victims of the coal

bunker fire, some of whom had extensive burns, and would need further medical attention. Because of the influx of patients, they had been placed in the part of the hospital normally reserved for infectious illnesses. The dividing wall which normally separated the two sections had been opened up to create one large space, the idea being that an extra bed could be squeezed in.

Just then the door to the room was opened and in came a nurse. Behind her were two orderlies, between them a heavily bandaged man. "Room for one more?" the nurse said cheerily.

Turley and even Mallory stared at the newcomer with some reservation. The man's arms, legs and head were covered in clean white bandages, sticking out of his pyjamas, giving him a Mummy like look.

"Oh, don't be alarmed at his appearance," said the nurse to the occupants of the room, seeing the reaction to the man. "It looks a lot worse than it is. He only suffered flash burns, covered his whole body they did, burnt his clothes right off! He was so lucky, they should heal totally in a few weeks. He wanted to be moved to a room with a window, so here he is."

In response the bandaged man tried to lift his hand in acknowledgement to everyone as the orderlies helped him over to the vacant bed just by the window.

"Now, Mr Smith here did sustain some damage to his vocal cords, so he won't be up for conversation," announced the nurse. "Now if you will excuse me I have other patients who need my attention." With that she and the orderlies left the room closing the door behind them.

Mallory was out of his bed in an instant, and had reached under his mattress for the concealed wooden stick that he had smuggled in, and quickly made his way over to the newcomer looking at his face before drawing back.

"It's alright," he confirmed. "It's not him. The eyes are the wrong colour, normal blue instead of glowing red."

Turley sank back in his bed. "For a moment I thought that it was, you know."

"Well, you were not the only one," commented Mallory, looking over at the bandaged Mr Smith as he hid the stick and returned into bed.

"Are you two sure about this?" asked Dawson. "It does seem a bit far fetched for my liking. A killer dressed up as an Egyptian Mummy going after people!"

"Oh, I'm afraid that you don't know the half of it!" said Mallory. Because of the possible attack on Turley and the close quarters of their accommodation, it had been decided by the Professor that Dawson should be told of the potential danger, although the version that they had told him had left out some of the more fantastic details.

"Why don't we just tell the Officers about this madman and let them deal with it?"

"No," said Turley quickly. The last thing that he wanted was officialdom involved, especially as the Professor had promised him freedom on the condition that he helped them and turn over all the stolen artefacts to him so they could be returned to the British Museum.

Again the door to the room opened and in walked the Professor.

"How did it go?" asked Mallory.

"Much better than I thought," came the reply. "I ended up dealing with the 2nd Officer, Lightoller, and Thomas Andrews the ship designer. I was able to convince them that the bookcase just came loose due to shoddy workmanship. The library is going to be closed while they make some temporary repairs." He then pointed to the bandaged Mr Smith. "Who on earth is that?"

"A Mr Smith," replied Mallory. "He's an injured fireman. Took a fire blast pretty bad by what we were told. I know what you are thinking, we did too, but he isn't."

"I'd rather be the judge of that if you don't mind," said the Professor as he went over to the injured man and looked at him closely.

"He won't be able to answer you if you talk to him," said Mallory and then went on to explain about the man's injured vocal cords. The Professor grunted, opting to lean in closer to the man's face.

"It is alright," reassured Mallory, "I checked his eyes. They were totally normal."

"And how do we know The Mummy has not got the ability to change his very eye colour too?" asked the Professor. "He does seem full of surprises!"

Mallory paused, and Turley suddenly looked scared – they had not considered that.

The Professor continued his visual examination of the man, before gently prodding at the body in certain areas, making Smith grunt and move in discomfort.

"Well?" asked Turley.

Smith made a groaning sound, unhappy at the examination.

"Same height, same build," said the Professor thoughtfully. "Let's try a different approach." He then went to his pocket and produced the black scarab and held it over Smith's face. Again Smith grunted.

"He's not liking that at all is he?" said the Professor.

"No, he's probably wondering what on earth you are doing," pointed out Mallory, still unconvinced. "Besides if it was the Mummy, surely he would have been up on his feet by now spoiling for a fight?"

"Mmmm, that is a good point Mr Mallory," the Professor conceded. "So I think that there is only one way to be certain." Before anyone could say anything the Professor returned the scarab to his pocket, then in one movement ripped open Smith's pyjamas to gain access to the bandages beneath. Smith protested, as did Mallory and Turley, but before anything could be done the Professor had parted the bandages on his chest to reveal tender red skin that had been burnt from the bunker fire.

The Professor paused, embarrassed at his actions. It was clear that this was not the Mummy but a brave man who had been burnt in a fire. He turned to a stunned Smith and apologised before carefully replacing the bandages.

"So, not the Mummy," said Mallory.

"No, it's not," replied the Professor solemnly, "but we must be on guard! I am certain that an attempt will be made on Turley's life and we must be ready for it!"

"I really cannot cope with any more of this!" cried Turley as he reached over to his side table where he poured himself a drink of water. "Are you sure that there is no other way to protect me?" He took a big swig from the glass. "Why, oh why, did I think that this was a good idea?" The Archivist suddenly convulsed, dropped his glass, and then clutched at his chest.

"Turley!" The Professor was over to him in an instant as was Mallory, while Dawson called out for a nurse.

"Cannot breathe…..chest hurting, tightening."

"I think he's having a heart attack," observed Mallory.

"He's a bit young for that," said the Professor with suspicion.

"Water…." gasped Turley.

Mallory picked up the fallen glass and then reached over to the jug to fill it, as he did so he suddenly stopped, noticing something at the bottom of the glass. "Professor, take a look at this."

The Professor took the glass and peered into it. Stuck to one side of the glass were the remains of a thin yellow powder. "Poison," he said simply. "A rare poison derived from certain dried out reeds only found growing along the lower parts of the river Nile. Ingested it has the effect of instantly clotting the blood, which when it tries to pass through the heart causes a cardiac failure."

Turley grabbed both hands against his chest and gave one final gasp before sinking back into his bed, dead.

"So how did it get in the glass?" asked Mallory. "They were all brought in at once and I saw him drink from that very same glass not an hour ago."

"It must have just happened," said the Professor looking around the small room.

Then he noticed it.

Up above Turley's bed there was a small grill covering an air vent. The bottom two screws were missing.

"The Mummy's hand!" he cried. "It's here somewhere!"

Then, on cue, the hand appeared, scampering straight up the wall to the vent. Before anything could be done, the hand had disappeared under the grill into the vent where it escaped, to return to the Mummy itself.

"Damn and blast it!" cried the Professor. "I was so convinced that Smith over there was the Mummy that I did not even notice the vent!"

Mallory silently moved forward and respectfully closed Turley's eyes and shook his head. The Mummy had managed to claim another victim.

CHAPTER 43

"No, blast it!" said Jack Phillips as he sat back at the small telegraph desk. "Nothing, totally dead!"

"So what do we do?"

Phillips looked over at his colleague, the fresh face of Harold Bride, and was about to make a rude comment when he was interrupted by a knock at the door. "Come."

The door to the Marconi wireless room opened, and in walked a grumpy looking Jazmine Montacute, carrying a tray on which were balanced two mugs of coffee and a plate of biscuits.

Bride smiled. "Cheer up, your face is interfering with the radio waves."

"I had just finished my evening duty shift, and was about to go to bed when I was told to go to the kitchen and fetch you this," she explained. Her anger at being turned into a stewardess was growing by the day and she was thinking of ever more cruel ways to make her father and Mallory pay for the indignity.

Phillips grunted at her, not really concerned at her problems when there were far bigger issues at stake. "Well, thanks anyway." He turned to Bride. "Look, there is nothing more that can be done here. You drink your drink then get to bed. I'm going to do the same, after I've had a word with the Bridge, fill them in."

"Anything wrong?" asked Jazmine, her curiosity roused at the snippet of conversation.

"The radio's broken," said Bride.

Phillips shot him a disapproving look before turning to Jazmine. "It's not strictly broken but we are having a few problems with it, and have had to make a few adjustments."

"Have you tried running it on just battery power?"

Phillips and Bride were taken aback at the unexpected question.

"Um, yes that's what we are doing at the moment," said Phillips.

"That's going to reduce the range severely to about fifty miles would you say?"

247

Phillips nodded. "How the hell would you know that?"

Jazmine smiled. In truth she loved all new technology, and did her best to find out as much about it as she could. Through her father she was able to get her hands on all the latest journals and periodicals, which kept her up to date with new developments, but of course she could not reveal that to the wireless operators. "My father likes to dabble in all things science," she replied simply.

"So what do you know about this then?" asked Phillips pointing at the wireless set, wanting to test her.

"I know that this is a Marconi wireless, rotary spark design powered by a 5 kW motor alternator, with a standard range of two hundred and fifty miles."

Phillips whistled, impressed by the reply. "Not bad, not bad at all!"

"Are you going to try and fix it?" asked Jazmine.

Phillips shook his head, taking her more seriously than a few moments ago. It was clear that she was more than just a stewardess. "No, we've just checked it, changed the battery, and completely shut down the system before then restarting it."

Jazmine nodded at the reply. "You would be amazed how many times that turning if off and then on again works."

"Well not in this case," said Bride.

Phillips took a look at the telegraph desk, and the mounting piles of telegraphs from important passengers waiting to be sent. "Which is a shame as the messages are piling up and the passengers are not going to be pleased about it. Captain Smith was extremely concerned about it not working. He wanted us to do as much as we could to get it going."

"Isn't there anything else that you can do?" asked Jazmine.

Phillips shook his head. "No, our instructions from Marconi, who employ us, are clear in this type of situation. Do the basics, and if that still does not get things working, leave well alone until we get to port then an actual Marconi engineer will fix the problem."

Jazmine gave a coy smile. "And do you always do what you are told?"

Phillips and Bride looked at each other.

"Look," continued Jazmine, "despite what you think, it's probably something really simple that has gone wrong, something that will take just a few seconds to fix. Why not at least investigate a bit more, get an idea of what the problem is?"

Bride looked almost hopeful, but Phillips was not so sure. "I don't know."

"We could poke around a bit more," suggested Bride.

Phillips gave him a disapproving look. "This is sophisticated equipment lad, you don't just 'poke about' in it." He paused and scratched his head. "Although it could be possible to open her up and make more of a proper visual inspection. Get a real idea of what's happened."

"But think if we can get it fixed," said Bride, "we can get all those messages out, and also you never know who might be trying to reach us. For all we know there could be an emergency that we need to help with!"

The thought of the ice warnings passed through Phillips mind. If another ship was in trouble, Titanic could be their only hope. He looked over at Jazmine. "You seem to know a bit about these things. Are you prepared to act as another pair of hands?"

Jazmine nodded eagerly. "Of course."

"Right then let's get started!" said Phillips, moving over to the main wall panel and switching off the power to the wireless system. "Let's get the floor hatches up and take a look at the heart of the beast!"

Bride responded by kneeling down and carefully lifting the wooden hatches in the floor to gain access to the actual workings of the radio, which sat in specially constructed wells in the floor, with Jazmine and Phillips gathering round.

First they made the visual check, only to find that some of the connections had somehow managed to work their way loose. It was an easy fix, and one that took no more than a matter of minutes. With these fixed firmly back in place they tried the radio again but it remained dead. Jazmine pressed Phillips and Bride to go further, and enthused by the fact that they had successfully solved one possible problem they agreed. Using what tools they had, they explored the complex workings further, going so far as actually taking sections of the radio out of the floor section completely for examination.

Eventually they found the root cause of the problem. One of the secondary coils had burnt out, which had shut down the entire machine. The coil would have to be replaced totally; certainly a job for the Marconi engineers in New York who would have the know-how and more importantly a fresh coil itself. Phillips and Bride thought that they had gone as far as they could, and were ready to call it a night, but Jazmine, using her knowledge of technology, felt sure that she could instruct them on how to disconnect the broken coil and bypass the safety override so it could function on the remaining ones.

Phillips and Bride agreed and after an hour's work, which took them into the early hours of Sunday morning, Bride restored the power to the wireless for a test.

"Right," said Phillips as he took his seat at the desk, "let's see if it worked. Harold, boost the signal." Bride responded by moving to the electrical control panel where he turned the lever which boosted electrical output of the radio, and Phillips started to try to transmit. After a few moments a smile crossed Phillip's face. "Got something!" But the joy was soon short lived as he soon deduced that the range of the signal had been severely reduced. "Seventy miles!" he exclaimed tossing the headset onto the desk, "seventy ruddy miles! My grandmother can shout that far!"

"I think that we are lucky to get anything at all," said Bride. "I mean without that second coil, we cannot expect too much." Phillips looked at him with some annoyance, but realised that he was right. He was about to agree and suggest that they call it a night when he caught a wicked glint in Jazmine's eye. She smiled. "The power for the transmitter is powered just through the ship's lighting circuit."

"Yes, that's right," confirmed Phillips.

"Well, why not rig just one coil up to that lighting circuit and hook up another coil to another electrical system? That should boost the signal."

Phillips nodded. "Possible, but then you run the real risk of blowing each coil which will put us in a worse situation than we are already."

"Not if we use the broken coil as a dampening filter to modulate the currents," said Bride.

Jazmine smiled, that was the idea that she was about to suggest.

Phillips looked over at his young colleague and nodded in approval. "I see that I'm going to have to watch you! Yes, that would work."

"But it would take a lot of work," said Bride, "and I don't think that we have all the parts that are needed."

"Oh, I think that we can manage with the parts we have," said Phillips. He then looked up at the wall clock to see that it was twenty past one in the morning. "As for time, well that's up to you two. I'm certainly up for it, we've come this far. But if you want to call it a night I'm sure that we could resume early in the morning."

Jazmine shook her head. "I'm on breakfast duty. I've got to be in the kitchens at six this morning."

"We could ask for her to be released from her normal duties to help us do it later," remarked Bride. But Phillips was not happy for this. Despite Jazmine's obvious talent and ability, at the end of the day it would still be viewed that they had to call upon an humble stewardess to mend the equipment, which would ultimately reflect badly on them, aside from the fact that they should not even be attempting to modify the equipment in the manner on which they were planning.

"No," said Phillips. "If we do this it has to be done now."

He looked at Jazmine who, excited by the challenge, nodded.

It was nearly five in the morning when they were finally happy with the modifications and Phillips again took his seat at the desk to send a test transmission.

Eagerly Jazmine and Bride looked on as a message was received. They could tell from the look on Phillip's face that their work had paid off.

"Well done people," he announced, placing the headset down on the desk. "It is not only fixed but better than before! We now have an operating range of four hundred miles!"

"But remember that you are going to have to keep a close eye on that bypass coil," said Jazmine. "If that goes there is no reprieve!"

Phillips nodded, then started to laugh. He pointed to the thing that was causing him such mirth. The two cups of coffee that Jazmine had been asked to bring them the night before were still sitting on the tray, totally untouched and now stone cold.

CHAPTER 44

Otto Von Braun moved quickly across the Titanic's thawing room to the long crate which had been carefully placed at the far end. The chilled room, which was used to store fresh meat, before being taken to the kitchens, was now also the temporary home of the Mummy. At the crate, Otto knelt down and removed the sacking which had been placed over it, before taking the crowbar he had brought with him to slowly lever up the wooden lid to reveal the inactive Mummy lying within. From his pocket he took out the telegram and read it again. It had arrived Saturday afternoon; a communication from their superiors, saying that they had found out that a golden Egyptian ceremonial axe was being smuggled to America aboard the Titanic. The location of the item had been identified as under the seat in a car that was being transported in the cargo hold. It was to be acquired as soon as possible, and confirmation sent via telegram when it was secured.

Even though the location of the Mummy and the hiding place of the axe were at the opposite ends of the ship it was decided by Otto that the new task could be carried out straight away without using night as a cover. He was confident that using the ship's passageways and corridors he could get from one end of the ship to the other without being seen.

Otto leant down over the creature and, where its ear was, whispered the chant which would awaken the Mummy. The creature's eyelids flickered open to reveal its glowing red eyes beneath. It then sat up in the crate, before rising to its feet.

"Maaaster!"

A slight chill went down Otto's spine. More and more the creature seemed to be exhibiting human characteristics. The attempts to speak had only occurred in the last few months. He had mastered no more than a few simple words, but it was a sign that the creature was gaining some form of self awareness, and was no longer the mindless automaton that they had been given by their Egyptian contact some two years ago.

"Don your coat and hat, and replace the lid; we have work to be done," said Otto. The creature nodded and then did as he was told.

Carefully Otto led the Mummy, unseen, through Deck G to the bow whereupon they were able to gain direct access to the car storage section via hatch number two.

Only two cars were in the hold: a new red Renault and a dark green 1910 Austin. Both vehicles, which were on a small wooden plinth, were tied down by a number of ropes attached to metal rings set into the deck floor.

"Search the red car first," ordered Otto. The car containing the axe had not been identified to him in the correspondence, so both would have to be looked at. "Check under the seats."

The Mummy nodded before moving forward to the car where he climbed into the open front seat of the Renault, and started to look for the weapon.

It was not there.

Climbing out, the Mummy then opened the door to the passenger compartment and climbed inside, closing the door behind it. Otto waited and looked on.

"Oi!" called out a voice. "You should not be down here!"

Otto turned to see a man dressed in a White Star Uniform, no doubt checking that all was well with the cargo. The Count discreetly turned back to look at the Mummy who, alerted by the man's voice, was now peering back at him through the car's window. Otto motioned his head to the crewman then drew his finger across his throat indicating that the man was to be killed. For a moment it seemed to Otto that the Mummy's red eyes seemed to twinkle at the prospect, another sign that the creature was becoming more than just a mere animated tool.

"Oi!" repeated the crewman moving closer. "I said that you should not be down here. This is strictly off limits. Staff only."

The door to the Renault opened and the Mummy stepped out.

"What the….?" said the crewman looking the creature over, slightly baffled at the sight which greeted him. "What are you doing in that get up?"

"Kiilll," said the Mummy and reached out his right hand. From it a stream of bandage flew out, aimed directly at the crewman who somehow managed to dodge out of the way before turning on his heels and running. The Mummy instinctively retracted the bandage which flew back through the air and wrapped itself back round its wrist and arm, before aiming and again firing another bandage bolt outwards. This time the bandage found its mark and caught the unfortunate crewman round the neck where it wrapped itself tightly. The Mummy then yanked hard on the bandage and the crewman was jerked into the air backwards with the sound of his neck cracking, before landing on the floor in a heap. The Mummy then withdrew the bandage back to its arm before looking back at its master.

Otto went over to the crewman and checked that he was dead, before making a quick search of the body where he recovered a watch, some coins, but most importantly of all a set of keys. He did not know what they were keys to, but were certainly keys that related to locks on the Titanic somewhere, which may be of use to him later. "Did you find anything in the Renault?" asked Otto to the Mummy.

The creature shook his head.

"The other car," instructed Otto pointing. The Mummy nodded and then went to the green Austin where it started to make a search. As before there was nothing in the open front seats so the Mummy went to the rear of the vehicle to search the back. While the Mummy was occupied, Otto dealt with the body of the crewman, opting to stuff it in the boot of the Renault. It would of course be discovered but hopefully not until the ship's arrival in New York when the car was eventually unloaded. Finishing his macabre task Otto turned back to the Austin, just in time to see a strange golden glow filling the inside of the car. The door opened and the Mummy stepped out, bathed in a pulsing light that was radiating from the axe he was holding. The axe itself was the size of a normal short handled axe. It was, however, the blade that set this implement apart. The blade was made from solid gold and sections of it had been deliberately carved out, leaving the shape of what looked like two men locked in battle.

Otto looked at the Mummy, unsure what was happening. "Give me the axe."

The Mummy ignored him, too enveloped in the power of the glowing weapon.

"Give me the axe now," repeated Otto but this time as a firm order.

The Mummy let out a roar, throwing its arms out, its head back and started to shake. The halo of light around it started to change colour from gold, into green, to blue, violet and then a dark grey. The Mummy cried out and then the aura seemed to be sucked up, going directly into the Mummy's mouth itself before it was gone completely.

Otto stared for a few moments, unsure what had happened. His eyes were drawn down to the axe. The blade was no longer gold, but black. The Mummy's hands slipped from the handle and it fell towards the deck. As it hit the solid floor the weapon simply shattered and dissolved into a pile of black ash. Otto looked back to the Mummy who was now looking at him, its eyes still glowing red. "We had better get you back to your packing case," he said uneasily.

"No," the Mummy replied.

The clear response took Otto aback. "Come, we must get you back to your packing case before you are seen."

"No. Dark in there, do not want to go back. Want my freedom."

A shiver ran down the Count's spine. The Mummy has spoken a coherent sentence, and worse still had expressed a clear opinion on something. "No, you must return to your packing case." Otto felt that his voice was shaking, and realised that he was actually scared.

"Not return. I want to be free."

"Well you can't," said Otto. Understanding that the creature must be stopped, he recited the chant that was used to send the creature back into its dormant state.

Nothing happened.

The Mummy just stood there.

Otto repeated the chant again, just in case he had said it incorrectly, but instead of the Mummy falling to the floor, forced slumber induced, it just stood there.

"Enchantment no longer works. I want freedom."

"That's impossible!"

"I am impossible! Should not live but I do! I want to be free!" The creature then reached out with both hands and grabbed Otto by the throat, then slammed him into the side of the Austin. "Freedom, no matter who tries to stop me!"

Otto started to pull at the Mummy's arms, but the creature was too strong. Three thoughts suddenly crashed into his mind, the irony of his impending death, killed by his own creature; a sudden empathy with those who he had seen die in this way before and to him the most disturbing of all, that he would be separated from his beloved Elisabeth.

Otto's attention was suddenly brought back to his present situation by the sound of something whizzing nearby and the yell of the Mummy as it abruptly flew to the side. Otto turned to see who his saviour was. A large bearded crewman stood a few metres away; his arm outstretched holding a smoking revolver. Before Otto could react, the Mummy rushed past him to attack the newcomer. The bearded man stood firm and fired again. Each of the bullets passed directly through the Mummy as he continued, this time ready for the onslaught. For the last few feet the Mummy launched himself into the air and hit the newcomer, both falling to the floor. The bearded man tried to slam the gun into the side of the Mummy's head, but the Mummy took the blow before opening his mouth and with a low roar breathed down on his foe. From the Mummy's mouth a haze of black wispy smoke was breathed into the crewman's face, the Mummy then stood up to watch his handiwork unfold.

The smoke enveloped the bearded man's face. He tried to yell but only succeeded in drawing the mist down into his lungs.

Using the distraction, Otto was able to run round the Austin and start to make his way over to the open door of the cargo hold. Looking back, he could see the shape of the crewman slowly dissolve into nothing, and the Mummy look up at him, his red eyes almost shining with delight.

CHAPTER 45

The Professor and Mallory were taking tea in the Palm Court Café situated on the Port side. The café itself, attached to the first class smoking room, was actually two separate rooms, either side of a staircase and lift.

The Professor looked round quizzically at the decorated surroundings. "I don't like this," he announced. "We are on a ship in the middle of the Atlantic, not in some Mediterranean square." He shifted in his seat. "And these wicker chairs are not the most comfortable or practical. White! Who thought of that? It won't be long before they fade to a yellow or are stained with someone spilling tea over them!"

"I'm sure that the White Star won't let the place end up looking tatty," replied Mallory, trying not to laugh at the Professor's grumpiness.

Suddenly two figures appeared through the large revolving door looking around frantically.

"Charles!" called Otto as he, Elisabeth a few paces behind, ran over to their table and seated themselves down as though they had just come upon old friends.

"Make yourselves at home," said the Professor curtly, "and what do we owe this unexpected honour?"

"Charles, there is no time for animosity. We have a problem and desperately need your help."

"Well, sadly for you we have to be going." With that the Professor started to rise, Mallory following his lead.

"No, please," said Elisabeth, clearly concerned. "This is very serious. At least hear us out."

The Professor paused then sat back down.

A look of relief passed over Otto's face. "Thank you Charles. It is the Mummy; it is loose, and out of our control! We need your help to stop it."

The Professor shook his head. "You're lying. This has to be some kind of ploy, one which I'm not going to fall for."

"No it is true!" cried Elisabeth. "We are serious, we need you to help us, let me show you that we are genuine." She reached inside the bag that was on her lap and produced a bundle of cloth and placed it on the wicker table in front of them. "There, it's yours; take it as a gesture of our goodwill, a peace offering if you will."

Mallory reached forward, picked up the cloth bundle, opened it, gasped in surprise then passed the contents to the Professor for closer examination.

It was the small statue that belonged to Maggie Brown.

259

"It is yours now," said Otto. "I'm returning it to you."

The Professor looked over the small statue. It was indeed the one that Otto had taken in exchange for the fake antidote. Silently he wrapped up the statue and put it in his pocket. "Tell me, Otto, were you responsible for the death of Lord Rainsbury?"

The Count was taken aback by the question, but realised that answering it could secure the required help. "No, that was our contact at the Embassy, Ahmed."

Mallory and the Professor exchanged a look.

"What about all the other similar robberies that have taken place?" asked Mallory thinking of the client list at his insurers Oldfield & Harper. "The ones where other such artefacts were taken?"

"Again all down to Ahmed," said Otto, before pausing and shrugging. "Well, we might have been involved in a few of them."

The Professor paused. "Alright, you have my full attention."

Otto breathed a visible sigh of relief.

"So what happened?"

Between them the Von Brauns recounted the story of the telegram, and the hunt that followed to find the ceremonial golden axe. When they came to the end of the tale, Professor Montacute said nothing, just reached for his cup, took a sip and then placed it down again.

"Well?" asked Otto.

"Well, you are a fool, that much is certain," replied the Professor. "An item like that usually comes with some kind of enchantment attached to it. Why did you not take appropriate precautions?"

"All we were doing was going by the orders from our superiors," protested Elisabeth. "Besides, the creature has a natural protection from curses and the like."

"But not from the black scarab I take it," said the Professor. "It's not just our knowledge and experience with the Mummy that you want is it? It's use of the scarab."

Otto nodded. "Yes, that is correct. I fear that the power of the scarab is the only thing which will be able to stop it."

The Professor paused. "Say I agree to help and we stop the creature, what then?"

"I think in the current circumstances it is safe to say that your mission has now become our mission," replied Otto. "You did not see the creature the way I did. It is now fully self aware, and has this new, new ability, this… this, 'breath of death' which it was not afraid to use. I fear that all on this ship are in danger."

The Professor nodded. "Alright, but this is done my way not yours. We find the Mummy, overpower it, insert the scarab to deactivate it, then weigh it down and throw it over the side."

"But can we not try and remove the enchantment?"

"And have the creature still on the loose for you to use for your own ends?" pointed out the Professor. "No, the creature is to be destroyed. If you want my help, this point is non-negotiable."

The Von Brauns paused before nodding in agreement.

"Agreed," said Otto nodding. "We will go along with what you say."

The Professor smiled, settling back. "Now, we have to work out exactly where he will be. I know that his main sarcophagus was placed at the bow, but the Mummy itself was hidden elsewhere. where?"

Otto hesitated.

"Come Otto," said the Professor sternly.

"Alright! It was hidden on Deck G, in a crate in the thawing room."

"You think that it may return there?" asked Elisabeth.

261

"A possibility," replied the Professor. "Either there or to the original sarcophagus are my first thoughts. It would want somewhere where it could stay hidden and even familiar. There is of course one other option open to it."

"What?" asked Otto eagerly.

"It might decide that it would continue with the tasks that it was being given and continue to carry them out."

Otto paused. "We only gave the Mummy the 'tasks' one at a time. He would not know what was coming until he was awakened then told."

"No, wait Otto!" interrupted Elisabeth. "Don't you remember when he was raised, when you took him to the Turkish Baths on Thursday, we mentioned the possibility of taking him straight to deal with Simon Munro afterwards, so he would know about him."

"Who is Simon Munro?" asked Mallory.

"A photographer," replied Otto. "He took a number of pictures of the Sphinx at Giza then manipulated them; adding the missing beard and nose, he even made the image in colour! His efforts were not welcomed, and we were instructed to pay him a visit with the Mummy and scare him; so far though we have not been able to find him."

"Right, well in that case," said the Professor, "I think that we need to enlist the help of Jazmine too. She can keep an eye on this chap while we monitor the storage areas. That's where I think he will be heading, if he is not there already."

"A logical plan," complimented Otto. "Elisabeth and I will take the stern. Can we have the scarab?" He held his hand out hopefully.

The Professor stared at him. "I take it you are joking?"

Otto withdrew his hand and smiled sheepishly. "I can understand why you do not trust me!"

"Now, Elisabeth, those small enchanted stone tablets that you use. Do you have any that can repel the Mummy?"

"No, but I have some blank ones. I can 'make up' a couple which could have an effect on it."

"Good," said the Professor. "There is no guarantee that they will work now, but it might be useful to have some on hand. Now, I propose that we will split ourselves up," announced the Professor. "It will give us the opportunity to cover more ground that way."

"Agreed," said Otto. "Now I think that …………"

"Otto!" interrupted Elisabeth pointing to the wall behind the Professor and Mallory. "Look up there in the vines! It's the Mummy's hand!"

Everyone turned round to see a small section of the vine move, then, a few moments later, everyone was on their feet.

"Be careful everyone!" called out the Professor as he withdrew his swordstick from its sheath and then threw the wooden sheath itself to Mallory who caught it to use as a club. "Mr Mallory, if you would be so kind as to act as a beater for us!"

Mallory nodded, moving forward to the wall where he warily poked at the vine where the hand had been.

"Careful" called out Elisabeth.

"It's alright," replied Mallory, "just as long as I can keep……" the stick then prodded the hand, which instantly started to move across the vines.

"Blast it!" said Mallory "Where did it go?"

"There," cried Otto pointing.

All eyes turned to the spot where he had indicated and at that exact moment the hand flew out from its hiding place, in the direction of Otto.

Mallory was too far away, but the Professor acted instantly, slashing at the flying bandaged limb, missing it by a matter of inches. The hand landed momentarily onto Otto's shoulder before the hand, using the shoulder as a launch pad, propelled itself onwards to the right where they found their intended target.

Elisabeth Von Braun.

The bandaged hand wrapped itself around her delicate throat, and started to crush it causing the Countess to fall to the ground. Otto, the closest, was the first to be there and managed to pull the thumb away from Elisabeth's windpipe, but the rest of the digits dug in hard.

"Elisabeth!" called out Otto in despair.

By now the Professor and Mallory were by his side. Mallory reached over and tried to place the discarded sword sheath under the slightly raised hand to pry it off, while the Professor managed to pull up the little finger and attempt to break it. Then without any warning the hand released itself, and was flung into the air where it landed on one of the tables before flying towards one of the big arched windows. It smashed its way through one of the small upper panes and out onto Deck A.

"Elisabeth, Elisabeth my dear are you alright?" asked the visibly upset Otto as he cradled her in his arms.

"Yes, yes I will be alright," she replied as she rubbed her throat. "Can I have some water please?"

Mallory went to fetch some, returning a few moments later.

"Well, then, what did you make of that?" asked the Professor.

"What do you mean?" asked Mallory.

"The behaviour of the hand. It singled out the Countess deliberately did it not? It even opted to leave Otto totally unharmed in order to go for her."

"By goodness you are right," said Otto, "but why?"

The Professor paused. "I think I know. I think that it was because Elisabeth is the only one who can create the spell tablets. I think the Mummy, through the hand, somehow understood my request to her, and seeing her as a real threat tried to kill her!"

"In that case," said Elisabeth, her voice wavering slightly, "I suggest that we go to my cabin with haste so I can make the required tablets before The Mummy's hand tries anything else!"

CHAPTER 46

The Von Brauns took Mallory and the Professor straight to their first class cabin. Once there, Elisabeth set about the task of inscribing two plain tablets with an ancient enchantment that she said should incapacitate the Mummy. Elisabeth explained that the creature need only have the briefest contact with the tablet for it to work and would result in the Mummy becoming slow and disorientated, if not totally immobilised. Although Elisabeth was careful not to make any firm promises as to how long the effects of the tablets would last for.

It was decided that they would split up into two groups. Because of the Mummy's interest in Elisabeth it was agreed that she would stay with the Professor who, armed with the black scarab, would investigate the bow where the main sarcophagus was stored. While Mallory and Otto, with the newly created enchanted tablets, would examine the crate that had been stored in the stern. If the Mummy was there they would use the tablet, then seek out the Professor and Elisabeth before jointly attacking the Mummy with the scarab.

It did not take Elisabeth and the Professor long to reach the sarcophagus, stopping only to drop a note off to Jazmine regarding the current situation, and to request that she try and catch up with the photographer Simon Munro. Then to the

Professors cabin, where he secured Maggie Brown's statue, before eventually arriving down at the orlop deck.

"Well, everything seems to be exactly the same from the last time I was here," said the Professor looking round the cargo bay. He moved over to the large crate, and carefully prised off the lid to reveal the sarcophagus that lay within.

He then looked over at Elisabeth. "The booby trap."

"Yes," smiled Elisabeth, "you must have had a terrible time with the locusts!"

The Professor grunted, not wanting to be reminded of the close escape that he and Mallory had had. "Yes, thank you, we did. Anyway, can you disarm that trap, and any others that may be waiting for me when I open the lid to check if our friend is inside?"

Elisabeth nodded. "There were actually three other traps held within the case. I'm surprised that you did not spring them before though." She moved forward to the stone coffin and ran her hand over the lid, then pressed down hard on one of the figures that decorated it. From inside there was a click and she stood back. "There, all done! All the traps are deactivated. It's safe now."

"Safe? Well I think that depends on what we find inside," said the Professor as he braced himself against the lid. "Can you give me a hand? This thing is heavy!"

"I certainly will not," cried Elisabeth in surprise. "I am a Countess and a Lady! I certainly do not do manual work in any form!"

The Professor was about to reply with a cutting comment when she leant forward pressing another figure on the coffin, and the lid, by itself, moved, creating an opening. "There you are Charles! The ancients thought of everything!"

The Professor grunted, opting to ignore her, instead looking inside the coffin. "Damn and blast," he cried. "Empty, he's not here!"

266

"Are there any signs that he has been here at all?" asked Elisabeth. "Is his disguise or bag there? He might have gone off somewhere without them."

"No," replied the Professor. "Wait a moment though, there is something, it's not totally empty." He leant into the stone box and reached down, appearing a few moments later with a pair of broken spectacles. "Interesting," he mused, holding them out towards Elisabeth. "Do you recognise them?"

The Countess shook her head. "No. So what do we do now?"

"The only thing that we can do in the circumstances," replied the Professor dropping the glasses back into the sarcophagus. "We wait, and see if he comes back, and while we do, I want to try and put the odds a bit in our favour."

With that he moved over to a pile of nearby wooden barrels, and using his pocket knife proceeded to cut the ropes which held them, before re-arranging them in a tall stack near the sarcophagus. Finally he tied a section rope around the bottom barrel and trailed out the remaining length across the floor. One hard tug and the barrels would tumble down.

"I'm not sure that will stop him," said the Countess, looking at the Professor's handiwork.

"Oh, I don't believe for one second that it will. However, it is better than nothing and it is bound to cause him some injury if he is hit."

"I think that 'if' is the key word there," replied the Countess smiling.

The Professor shrugged. "If he wants to get back into his sarcophagus, he will have to pass the trap, that's when we strike! Now, we'd better conceal ourselves."

With that the two retired a safe distance, opting to hide behind a large wooden crate to wait.

"Did you hear that?" said Elisabeth after about ten minutes. The Professor, gripping tightly the end of the rope, turned to hear. "I think so, footsteps?" Elisabeth nodded and pointed in the direction of the door which led to the other section of the cargo hold. The movement became louder and louder until the familiar sight of the Mummy, bound head to toe in bandages, staggered into view. The creature stopped and turned as though by some mysterious power he realised that something was amiss.

"Do you think he realises that we are here?" asked Elisabeth.

"He might do," whispered the Professor. "There is no telling what the power of the axe has done to him."

"Look," whispered Elisabeth. "He's heading towards the sarcophagus." Sure enough, the Mummy staggered towards the crate before suddenly stopping, just in front of the impromptu booby trap.

"This is no good," said the Professor gripping the end of the rope in his hand, "he is not close enough to the barrels."

"Never mind, just do it!" urged Elisabeth. "Do it, before he moves away."

"No," replied the Professor. "They will barely touch him, he needs to be closer."

"Look he's turning! He's moving away from them altogether, it's now or never!"

"Blast it! Alright here goes!" said the Professor as he started to pull hard on the rope. Over the other side of the cargo hold, the barrels that it was attached to suddenly started to move from their position and overbalance. The Mummy turned just in time to see the barrels start to fall towards him. He tried to move out of the way but he was too late, ending up on the floor among the fallen casks.

"Quickly," cried the Countess producing a hidden knife. "Use this on him, cut him open and insert the scarab!"

"No there is already a hole in his chest from an earlier encounter," replied the Professor, thinking of the event

Mallory had told him which had taken place by the dummy funnel.

Elisabeth shook her head. "No, he has the power to heal himself, you must use this."

So taking hold of the knife the Professor sprang up from behind the barrels running to the Mummy who was now rising to his feet. He dived towards the creature landing on top of it, stabbing down hard in the chest.

Almost instantly, he realised something was not right. The Mummy convulsed as though in agony, then slumped back down. Where he had stabbed turned crimson with fresh blood. The Professor froze in horror. "This, this is not right!" he gasped. "There should be no blood." He then looked to the Mummy's eyes and noted that they were not glowing red, but pale green. Carefully using the knife, he started to cut down the bandages around the Mummy's face, then very slowly he put his fingers in the slit and pulled the cloth apart to see what was underneath.

The Professor gasped in dismay as he was confronted, not with the mummified face of the ancient dead, but that of a clean shaven middle aged man. "That's not the Mummy!" cried the Professor turning to Elisabeth, who stood calmly and gave a satisfied smile.

"No my dear Professor, it's not."

"Then who is he?"

"Simon Munro, the photographer that we told you about. It looks like our Mummy caught up with him after all."

"You knew didn't you?" hissed the Professor.

"Yes," confessed the Countess, "I recognised the spectacles as belonging to Mr Munro. Then when 'The Mummy' appeared, I knew instantly it was not ours."

"But you still let me kill him didn't you? You even encouraged it!"

269

"Yes," replied Elisabeth calmly. "He still had to pay for his crimes."

The Professor looked down at the body. "This needs to be reported."

"Oh, you know that that cannot happen," said Elisabeth sternly. "For one thing you would be tried and no doubt hung for murder, assuming that you were not thrown into an institution for the rest of your life, if you tried to tell the truth."

"You've turned me into a murderer!"

"Oh come on Professor!" replied the Countess almost dismissively. "You've killed before! I've read about your antics!"

"Yes, but only ever in self-defence, when there was no other alternative, this is totally different!"

"Well it's done now." She looked down at the body. "Now we need to get rid of him, come on, hurry up, the noise that was made with those barrels might have attracted someone. Put him into the sarcophagus."

Reluctantly the Professor grabbed hold of the body of Munro, lifted him up then dropped him in the sarcophagus, dropping the knife in after him on the Countess's instructions. Then with the lid closed Elisabeth pressed a symbol on the side and from within immediately came the sound of hundreds of tiny feet. "There, I have just activated the locusts. In a few minutes there will be nothing left. No trace of Mr Munro at all!"

"The perfect crime, eh?"

Elisabeth shook her head. "As far as I am concerned no crime has been committed, only the carrying out of a sentence that was already passed." She paused. "Well, I think that there is no more that we can do here, apart from a quick tidy up," said Elisabeth looking around at the spilled cargo before

270

allowing her eyes to settle back onto the Professor. "I wonder how the others are getting on?"

The Professor Just stared at her.

"You know Charles," she continued quite casually, "Otto and I have an invitation to the Captain's table tonight. If he and that Mallory fellow have not found, and killed the Mummy, it might be an idea for me to use my charm so you can dine with us; safety in numbers until we can work out our next move."

Professor Montacute nodded. He did not want to let this evil scheming woman out of his sight for one moment.

CHAPTER 47

It took no effort at all for Mallory and Otto to gain access to the stores area. In the time that they had been aboard the ship Otto had perfected a route which ensured that he would not be seen by Titanic staff when he needed to rouse and then return the Mummy from its missions.

"It's colder than I expected!" said Mallory as he rubbed his hands together as they walked through the stores passageway.

"Yes," replied Otto. "Much of what is down here is kept in refrigerated units until they are required by the cook. Ah, here we are." He stopped outside a door which was marked 'Thawing Room'. "My dear Elisabeth managed to arrange for him to be relocated here when she realised you and the Professor were in pursuit."

"Yes, very insightful," replied Mallory.

Otto reached up to the door frame and produced a hidden key which he used to open the door. The sudden chill hit Mallory making him shiver.

"A bit chilly I'm afraid," said Otto almost apologetically, "but it did its job and the Mummy did not seem to mind!"

271

"I would not worry about that," replied Mallory. "If he's here we will kill him and then get rid of him once and for all."

The room was larger than Mallory expected. Down one side was a row of carcasses hanging on hooks being thawed ready for use, while opposite was a large chopping table with a variety of cleavers and other large knives hanging above on a rail.

"Oyster?" said Otto, holding out one of the shelled creatures that he had plucked from a tank just behind the door.

"Maybe at dinner," replied Mallory dismissively. "Now, where is the Mummy?"

Otto dropped the Oyster back into the tank then motioned to the other end of the room to a large coffin like crate covered over with sacking. "In there, assuming that he came back."

"Well there is only one way to find out," replied Mallory. "Have you got the stone tablets?"

Otto reached inside his pocket and produced one of the small stones that Elisabeth had hurriedly created and held it up.

Mallory, followed by Otto, moved over to the crate, pulled off the sacking and then lifted the lid.

Inside was the Mummy lying with its arms folded across its chest.

Mallory and Otto looked at each other and smiled.

"He's reverted to his sleeping state," said Otto.

"How long will he stay like that for?"

Otto shrugged. "Normally until he was woken, but due to the power of the golden axe I would not like to wager how long he will stay that way."

"Well no matter," said Mallory, "we have him where we want him. The tablet if you will." He motioned to the sleeping Mummy.

Otto moved forward and placed the tablet on the Mummy's chest. Instantly the creature's eyes flicked open, looked around, making Mallory and Otto step back. The Mummy tried to rise, but slumped back down as though the weight of the tablet prevented him from doing so, then the red eyes seemed to fade and the creature remained still – the tablet had worked!

Mallory looked down at the sleeping creature. "Right, now we need to get the Professor. We know that the scarab will stop it for certain and it looks as though we have the time to get it."

"But we don't know for sure how long the tablet's power will last for," pointed out Otto.

"Alright, one of us stays here with the second tablet while the other goes and fetches the Professor."

Otto shook his head. "I say we act now!"

"What?"

"We deal with the creature ourselves," replied Otto indicating over to the knives and cleavers on the wall.

Mallory shook his head. "We need to use the black scarab, the Professor said….."

"Oh, the Professor said!" replied Otto imitating the voice of a young child. "Let's try this my way. The Mummy will be dealt with immediately and we will not end up losing such an important piece of jewellery!"

Mallory paused, his mind swaying, after all, his original mission that had led him to this was to recover the black scarab and with this course of action he could do just that.

"Come on! A few cuts and that will be that and we can all get on with enjoying the voyage!" encouraged Otto.

273

Before Mallory could respond there was a moan, the Mummy's eyes had flicked open again and it tried to move but could only manage a shuffle, then in frustration let out a cry of anguish, then shuffled again, this time moving up further than before.

"I think the effects are wearing off," said Mallory. "Quick, the other tablet!"

Otto responded by producing the second tablet and dropping it on the Mummy's chest. Instantly the creature stopped moving, but this time its eyes stayed bright and clear.

"It's working," observed Mallory, "but I don't think as well as the last one."

"The creature must somehow be building up an immunity to the enchantment," said Otto. "We don't have much time, we must act now!" With that he then turned and ran to the chopping board, returning with two large knives, one of which he handed to Mallory.

"Alright," said Mallory wanting to seize the moment, "let's do it."

Otto took the blade and placed it over where the heart of the creature would be. "I am sorry old friend, but this has to be done!"

The Mummy tried to move realising what was to come but it was too late. Otto plunged the knife into the creature up to the handle and then wiggled the blade around before withdrawing it out. The whole time the Mummy moaned and tried to struggle but to no avail.

"It's still alive!" cried Otto.

"You've been reading too much Bram Stoker! It's not a vampire it's a *Mummy*," replied Mallory. "We need to cut its head off!" He grabbed the knife from Otto, ready to make the cut, but then pulled back as the eyes of the creature started to glow even brighter.

"What's happening?" asked Otto.

274

"I have no idea," replied Mallory. "Oh no, Otto, look at the tablet!"

The second stone tablet that had been placed on the Mummy's chest had started to crack and break, within a few moments it was no more than dust. Free from the enchantment, the Mummy sat up in his crate. Mallory swung forward with his knife but the Mummy brought up his arm and stopped it, before pushing him away. Otto moved in but the Mummy snapped its head round and let out a piercing yell making the Count retreat allowing the Mummy to stand up.

"You tried to kill me!" the creature yelled. "You must both pay, pay with your lives!"

Mallory, now recovered, threw his knife as hard as he could. It landed with a thud into the Mummy who simply grabbed the handle, removed it from its body before throwing it back. Mallory dodged out of the way, the blade missing him by inches.

"We've got to get out of here!" cried Otto as he turned and started to make for the door, but the Mummy had other ideas. Holding out his left hand he shot out a stream of bandage which wrapped itself around Otto's ankles. The Count was brought to the floor and the Mummy started to reel in its catch as Otto desperately tried to claw at the floor to stop himself. "Help me Mallory! Please help me!"

Mallory responded by running to the chopping table, picking up a super sharp cleaver and in one move swung down at the bandage, freeing Otto, who instantly got up and moved to one side then onto his feet, kicking the bandage remnants away from his ankles. "What do we do now?" cried the Count, staring at the Mummy who was looking between the two men, trying to work out which one to make his move on.

"Only one option," cried Mallory rushing forward. "We get him!"

Mallory grabbed The Mummy from the left while Otto did the same from the right and together they managed to lift the Mummy off the floor.

"The meat hook!" cried Mallory, as he started to propel the creature towards the row of hanging carcasses, aiming specifically for an empty one. Otto followed Mallory's lead, and together they heaved the creature higher into the air towards the hook. The Mummy screamed with pain as the metal point plunged into the back of its neck while Mallory and Otto just stood back. For a moment the Mummy just hung there suspended on the hook before there was a ripping sound and the creature's own weight pulled it free. It landed on the floor before standing upright straight away, but it was clear to see that the damage was done. The head of the Mummy lolled unnaturally to one side, a big gash exposed.

"Finish it off," cried Otto, "quick, before it can regain its wits."

Mallory moved forward, but the Mummy, although injured, was able to let out a roar, block the blow and lift Mallory, throwing him across the room.

Otto ran over to Mallory to see if he was injured, and the Mummy seeing its chance lurched over to its packing crate, stooped down and retrieved its coat and hat before heading unchallenged to the door of the thawing room where it escaped into the corridor.

By the time Mallory had recovered his wits and made it over to the door, the creature had disappeared, and was nowhere to be seen.

"Why didn't you go after him while you had the chance?"

"I went to check that you were alright," replied Otto, who in truth only did so as he did not want to tackle the creature on his own.

"You let him get away!"

"Oh, is that all the thanks I get?"

Mallory stared at the Count, his rage rising.

"Look," said Otto quickly. "You saw his head, it is almost off!"

"But not actually off!" replied Mallory, "he's still active."

"True, but he is not going to last long in that state is he?"

Mallory paused, realising that was probably true.

"Come on," said Otto, "let's get out of here; we need to tell Charles what happened."

CHAPTER 48

"Are you alright Professor?" asked Captain Smith, turning directly to his right. "You have hardly touched your soup and you do look a bit off colour."

"I'm fine thank you," replied Professor Montacute throwing a quick look over at Elisabeth, and then to Mallory, who was seated next to her. The events that had just taken place in that cargo hold had made him lose his appetite altogether. Elisabeth smiled back to him and raised her glass and took a small sip. "I'm not sure the Professor here has gained his sea legs yet!"

This raised a small round of polite laughter from around the table. Elisabeth placed her glass down. "But Captain, I must thank you again for extending your invitation to my friends Professor Montacute and Captain Mallory here." She glanced over the table at Otto, who was the other side of the Professor and nodded, for it was really he who had managed to arrange it.

"Not at all, it's my pleasure," replied Smith, although the first that he knew about it was when the guest list and background information regarding his dinner companions had been given to him a few minutes before the meal had begun. Although a list of dinner guests was not the only thing that he had been given. At the same time he had been passed another message stating that the build-up of ice in the area was increasing; a telegram which he noted and duly passed on, although he was not overly concerned.

Smith turned to the Professor. "So, your trip, is it business or pleasure?"

The Professor looked across the table at Elisabeth. "Business I'm afraid. There is an ongoing matter that I really need to sort out, and it is causing me real problems."

"Oh I am sorry to hear that, and you have joined up with the Von Brauns as they can help you?" said Smith trying to make the connection between the two.

"Yes, something along those lines," replied Mallory, as he leaned back slightly to allow Jazmine, who had been assigned to the Captain's table that evening, to remove his empty plate.

"Tell me Captain," said Elisabeth quickly before they could elaborate any further, "how is our journey progressing? Otto and I have done our fair share of trips and we seem to be going very fast."

"Yes Captain," said a deep voice from further down the table, "the rumours are that we are going for the Blue Riband."

"A prize, Colonel Weir that if we do get will not be a deliberate one!" replied Smith in truthfulness.

"Well it was a happy accident that brought me to Titanic in the first place," replied the Colonel, thinking of how he had been transferred to Titanic because of the coal strike in Southampton, "so I'm sure that I can cope with another intervention of fate putting me on a record breaking ship!"

"Yes, well, we will have to see," replied Smith evasively, he turned to the Von Brauns wanting to quickly change the subject. "So how are you enjoying the trip so far?"

"Oh it's wonderful," replied Elisabeth. "The ship is amazing!"

"Thank you, a lot of people have spent a lot of time trying to make it that way."

"Well they have done a wonderful job," replied Elisabeth, "and the crew members are so professional." She threw a glance at Jazmine who quickly looked away. "When I came aboard and had to have my request to have a certain piece of luggage moved into a different section they were most helpful."

The Professor looked up realising that she was talking about the Mummy. Smith nodded in reply to the Countess understanding too what she meant. As Captain he had to be informed fully of any special requests of dangerous or unusual cargos, signing the final paperwork himself. "Anything to accommodate, but I have to admit in all my years I have never had to transport something so old or as unusual. Tell me, what are your plans for The Mummy when you reach New York?"

"It will go on display at a number of locations including the New York State Museum, before going to the main university where it will be studied for a few weeks," lied Otto.

"Aren't Egyptian Mummies normally cursed?" asked Colonel Weir. "You know, 'don't disturb my tomb or death will follow' and all that?"

"No, not at all," said Elisabeth trying not to giggle.

"I did hear about a dig a few years ago," continued Weir, "where a Mummy was removed from a tomb and everyone who handled it died."

"It was my understanding that a poisonous fungus was later found on that particular Mummy which caused the deaths," explained Elisabeth, "only it seems that the media neglected to report that detail, only focusing upon the initial deaths, and a possible curse. They decided that would sell more newspapers."

Smith smiled. "I don't think I've ever seen a real Egyptian Mummy before, and it is certainly creating interest among the other senior staff. Would it be possible to arrange a private viewing?"

"Yes," said the Professor with a wicked smile, staring directly at Otto. "That sounds like a good idea! Is it possible to see this ancient creature, in the flesh as it were?"

Otto glared back. "Um, I'm afraid that will not be possible."

"Oh, why is that?" replied the Professor, trying to sound innocent.

"It's to do with the wrappings," replied Otto in a pre-planned response that he had used over the years to put people off seeing the Mummy. "It is coated with a special liquid to prevent the bandages drying out. To expose it for viewing now would mean we have to treat the whole of the creature again and that would cause us a number of problems."

"Oh that is a shame," replied Smith who had been quite looking forward to the prospect. "I suppose then I will have to make do with the planned dog show tomorrow!"

This raised a polite laugh from those at the table. The show had been hurriedly devised for entertainment as there was a number of quality breeds on board brought on by the first class passengers.

"I think that is something that I will miss," said Elisabeth leaning back as Jazmine placed a plate of roast duckling in front of her. "I've always been a cat person myself. Oh, Stewardess!"

"Yes Miss?" replied Jazmine returning to the table.

"I think that there has been a mistake," said Elisabeth holding the plate up to her. "I ordered the lamb shank with rice and boiled potatoes."

"So sorry," said Jazmine taking the plate, but throwing the Countess a snide look. "I'll see to it straight away." With that she hurried off. Elisabeth looked over at Otto and gave a wink.

"So Captain," said Colonel Weir trying to restart the conversation, "I overheard that there was some trouble with the ship, a fire or something."

This made The Professor and Mallory look up. Jazmine had kept them up to date with the situation and knew that it was out, but were never the less interested in what the Captain would say about the subject.

Smith quickly shook his head. "I fear that just like the story about the Mummy, things have been somewhat distorted!"

"So no fire?" asked Otto.

"Well, only a tiny one," said Smith, trying to play things down, "but it was soon under control. People don't realise it, but fires are quite a common occurrence, but they are quickly dealt with, and are just a minor inconvenience."

"Excuse me for interrupting Captain, might I have a word?"

The Captain looked up. It was the Fifth Officer Harold Lowe.

"Of course," Smith replied, grateful for the intrusion as it would put off any further questions. "Ladies, gentlemen if you will excuse me, I will be back shortly." With that the Captain stood, nodded to his guests and left the table.

"Alright what's going on?" said the Professor to Otto as quietly as he could so he was not overheard. "I saw that wink you gave to Elisabeth. You two are up to something."

"Oh Charles! What a suspicious mind you have!" Otto replied.

"I know what you two are like. What's going on here?"

"I have found a temporary solution to our Mummy problem!" said Elisabeth smiling sweetly.

"Which is?" asked Mallory, having a feeling that the reply was not going to be good.

Elisabeth leaned forward and whispered to ensure that she was not overheard. "While I was getting ready for dinner I had just enough time to create a very special tablet, one which I have just been able to plant on Jazmine."

"What!" cried the Professor. "What does the tablet do?"

Elisabeth grinned wickedly. "The Mummy is now under the impression that Jazmine is in fact the living reincarnation of his lost bride and that she is in danger."

A look of sheer horror spread across the Professor's and Mallory's faces.

"Now the creature's sole intention will be to catch up with her, and spirit her away somewhere and keep her safe."

Mallory and the Professor were on their feet and frantically looking around the first class dining room to try and find where Jazmine was, so they could warn her but she was nowhere in sight.

"Look over there!" said Mallory pointing to a nearby table. He ran over to her, the Professor following and reached out and grabbed her by the arm. "Jazmine!"

"No," came the reply in a soft Irish accent, as the woman turned round. "I'm Violet."

"I'm sorry!" replied Mallory, quickly seeing his mistake. "I was looking for Jazmine, Jazmine Montacute."

"She's over there," said Violet pointing.

Mallory turned to see the familiar figure of Jazmine disappearing through two double doors which led into the service section of Titanic's Galley.

CHAPTER 49

Jazmine Montacute moved past the big wooden table and over to the dresser to retrieve a number of new cotton napkins. Around her was a hive of activity, as from the kitchen, plates of desserts were being brought out and placed on the long serving tables, ready to be picked up by stewards who would then take them out to the diners.

"Jazmine! Jazmine!"

She turned around, surprised to see her father and Mallory standing there. "What are you doing here? This is off limits to passengers."

"Never mind that; we, or rather you, have been set up by the Von Brauns."

"What?" she said, looking around uneasily at the kitchen staff, who were now staring at them, wondering what was happening.

"Elisabeth has set an enchantment on you," said Mallory, unaware of the attention that they were drawing. "The Mummy thinks that you are his lost bride and is going to come after you."

"She told us that she slipped one of those stone tablets in your apron," continued the Professor.

Jazmine reached into her pocket and produced it. Just before it disintegrated into dust she was able to see the markings which were the curse which now marked her out.

"We've got to get you to safety........."

"I'm sorry, but is there a problem?" said a loud gruff voice belonging to the Chef who had appeared from his small office.

"No, no, um we had to speak with this stewardess."

"I was not actually talking to you," said the large man and turned to Jazmine to address her directly. "Are these two men troubling you?"

283

"Um, er no Chef."

The man nodded and turned to Mallory and the Professor, who were slightly taken aback. "Now listen here you two, first class passengers are not allowed, this is *my* domain, and you do not burst in here and start harassing my staff! I want you to get out now!"

"I'm sorry, but we needed to ………."

"Well *I* need you to leave my kitchen immediately! And if I find you have been anywhere near her, or any other member of my staff again, I will report you straight to the Captain."

Mallory was about to respond, but the Professor grabbed him by the arm, apologised and dragged him off, the Chef's eyes following them out the door, before turning back to the slightly flushed Jazmine. "What was going on?"

"Um, it's complicated."

"Yes it would be, anyway you can give me the full story after the last dinner sitting has finished, in my office. Until then I'm taking you off of front line service." He turned and grabbed a tray of food from a passing stewardess and passed it to Jazmine. "Do you know where the first class Barber shop is?"

"Deck C towards the stern, by the staircase."

"Good, then take this tray of food there. Arthur is working late, then report back to me directly."

"Um actually Chef, I'm not feeling overly well," said Jazmine quickly. "Is it possible for me to be excused the rest of service?"

The Chef looked at her sternly. "I and I alone will tell you when you are ill! Now, get that tray taken to the Barber Shop, quick smart!"

She nodded, resisting hard the urge to answer back. "Yes Chef!"

A short while later Jazmine arrived at the Barber shop on C deck. Balancing the tray on one hand she knocked at the door. "Mr White, I've been sent from the kitchen."

There was no response.

"Mr White, are you there?"

A sudden chill ran down her spine. Could the Mummy be inside waiting for her?

"Mr White?"

Still no answer came. Jazmine wondered if the creature had somehow overheard the conversation in the kitchen and managed to get here ahead of her. If this was the case Mr White could be seriously injured or more likely dead.

Carefully Jazmine placed the tray on the floor, then took hold of the handle and opened the door peering into the darkened room. Her eyes were automatically drawn to the number of dolls, souvenirs to be sold to passengers that were suspended from the ceiling; but to her looked more like shrunken bodies like the kind that she had seen on a trip with her father to Borneo three years before. Then her attention was caught by the outline of a figure sitting in one of the barber chairs, slightly reclined with its head back and covered totally by a shaving towel.

"Mr White?" Slowly she moved deeper into the room, ready to turn and run at the first sign of trouble. "Mr White?"

The figure jerked and one hand ripped the towel from its face, while the chair itself spun around.

"Oh great! You must be the girl with my supper! I'm sorry miss, are you alright?"

Jazmine, who's heart was pounding as she thought she was about to have a direct encounter with the Mummy, slowly nodded as she caught her breath. "Yes, I'm fine, it's just that you startled me."

"Sorry about that," said Mr White, "I was just having a snooze. I had orders from one of the Officers that the shop

285

here had to be cleaned from floor to ceiling as one of the passengers claimed that it was not up to standard! I've been at it for ages. Um, did you have any food for me?"

"Oh yes, sorry. It's just outside…."

The door to the Barber shop burst open without warning, and before either Jazmine or Mr White could react, the Mummy had come inside and had slammed the door shut behind him.

Mr White took one look at the creature with its partially severed head from which were two glowing red eyes, and promptly fainted, hitting the side of the chair on the way down.

"Jazmine!"

"Get away from me!" she replied backing away.

"I have come for you! I will look after you – my bride!"

Now pressed against the far wall of the Barber shop she waited for the creature to get slightly nearer before making her move. Quickly she darted to the right past the Mummy and ran to the door. She opened it, but something flew past her head, hitting the door and slamming it shut again. Looking up she could see the bandaged hand of the Mummy, its fingers spread and somehow managing to keep the door shut. Responding instantly Jazmine removed a hairpin from her hair and stabbed it hard into the hand. From the other side of the Barber shop the Mummy screamed, and Jazmine again pulled at the door, but this time it opened. She tried to move through but suddenly felt herself being pulled backwards, as a long strand of bandage wrapped itself around her waist. The hand, now recovered, pushed hard on the door again, slamming it shut, then flew back down where it hovered in the air for a few moments in front of Jazmine's face before striking her hard on each cheek.

"Bride! Do not do that! Must submit to me, your husband and master!"

The hand then grabbed her by the throat and she found herself being turned around, and being slammed back against the door slowly. While the hand's grip tightened she gasped for breath, but very quickly things started to go dark and she blacked out completely.

Jazmine awoke to find herself being carefully lowered to the floor, being placed on a number of empty White Star mail bags that had been deliberately placed in the arrangement of a bed. Looking around she saw that she was in some kind of large alcove. To one side stacked to the ceiling was a huge pile of crates. Beyond the creature that stood over her was a number of expensive looking trunks and matching luggage cases all piled up and held in place by netting. She quickly realised that they must belong to first class passengers, which must mean that she was being held in the baggage compartment of Deck G. The Mummy stepped back and nodded to her. "You will be safe here my Bride, until we can formally be joined together forever."

"Forever?"

"Yes," replied the creature, sounding happy. "Forever."

Jazmine looked the creature up and down shaking her head. "No, I'm sorry. There has been a mistake."

The Mummy's head moved as though it was trying to nod. "Yes, bride…..I did not see it before…….but you are the incarnation of my dearest beloved."

"No, I'm really not," replied Jazmine getting to her feet. "Please, you must let me go."

"No!" said the Mummy, the suggestion of the stone tablet taking hold of his thoughts. "There is danger……Must keep you safe…….You will be safe here…….No one ever comes down here."

"Danger? What danger?"

The Mummy paused, he did not know. Elisabeth's tablet did not have exact details, it just gave him an overwhelming feeling that his love was in danger.

"Danger," repeated the Mummy. "Must keep you safe…"

"Mr White, what did you do to him?"

The Mummy paused looking unsure.

"The man in the barber shop, did you kill him?"

The Mummy shook his head. "Tried to, but he had already passed to afterlife."

She winced realising that the poor man must have died of fright.

"I put him in his chair…..He will duly be judged!"

Realising that time was running out, Jazmine tried to run past the Mummy but he caught her and pushed her, causing her to fall and land on the sacks.

"Must stay here." He then grabbed at the crates, which were piled up to the very top of the store ceiling, and started to pull them over the opening. Jazmine ran to them and tried to push against them, but it was no use and within seconds she found herself sealed inside.

"Let me out of here!"

"In time," replied the Mummy.

She pushed at the crates which were acting as a door to her prison, but they did not budge, being too heavy for her. They were jammed in tightly.

"Let me out of here! I'll scream!"

"Go ahead!" came the reply. "No one comes down here now!"

Jazmine cursed to herself, she knew that that was true.

"But chef will realise that I am missing, and they will make a search."

"They will not find my bride!"

"But I'll starve down here," she said desperately.

"No, catered for, look."

288

Jazmine looked round her small makeshift cell and saw for the first time that in one corner was the tray that she had been instructed to take to Mr White. The Mummy, in a loving gesture, had brought it down for her so that she would have something to eat and drink.

CHAPTER 50

"Ice?"

"Sorry?" said Captain Smith lost in thought.

"Ice," repeated Bruce Ismay as he held up his glass. "Do we have any more ice?"

"Sorry, no," replied Smith, "I think Thomas here had the last of it."

Ismay looked over at Andrews who shrugged apologetically. Smith had invited Andrews and Ismay to his private sitting room for a nightcap, but was now wondering how long the two were going to stay. Ismay had settled himself down and looked as though he was planning to be here for a while.

"Oh well, never mind," said Ismay taking a sip of his whisky, "I'm sure that I can survive without it. So Captain, what do you make of our present situation?"

Smith moved away from the bookcase and sat himself down in the leather tub chair, placed his mug of tea on the table and looked directly at Ismay. "Well I cannot pretend to be happy or comfortable about it."

"But if the fires are out in the bunkers as you have said," replied Ismay, "surely any potential danger is past?"

"One fire," corrected Andrews. "It turned out the other bunker was not on fire after all. It was just a mixture of paranoia from the crew and false heat readings."

"Well one fire then," said Ismay, "but it amounts to the same thing, as I said, the issue is that the main danger has passed."

Andrews shook his head. "We don't know the full effect that the fire has caused on the ship itself. There is visible interior damage to the hull, but until we get her to New York and divers go down and check her, we will not know how much, or what other problems there could be."

"Which is why I am trying to get her to New York as quickly as possible," said Smith.

"Well," said Ismay with a slight smile, "I'm certainly not going to be complaining about the speed of the ship. How are we doing anyway? Are we on course for the Blue Riband, could it be possible?"

Smith paused. "I am not concerned with the Riband, my concern is with the ship and those aboard her."

"But we are on course for breaking the Olympic's maiden voyage time aren't we?" said Ismay with a hungry look in his eyes.

Smith slowly nodded his head, in working out the calculations for their overall arrival it had been realised that Titanic could beat its sister ship's time. "Yes we are, but I must make it totally clear to you that that, for you, just happens to be a fortunate side effect of our present situation!"

"And what a side effect that is!" said Ismay with a broad grin. "This is going to be a feather in your cap Smith!"

"I'm not interested in feathers."

"Well maybe so," said Ismay, "but it looks like a distinct possibility! Anyway, that aside, the issue that I am concerned with now is the return journey. We have a full list of passengers booked from New York back to England next week. I don't want Titanic stuck in New York."

"The passengers can easily be transferred to the Olympic if required," pointed out Smith.

"But surely it would be far better for us to return Titanic to Southampton," said Ismay. "At least get the return journey over with. Then if there is any real cause for concern, which I seriously doubt, it will be easier to get her back to Belfast where any repairs can be made at Harland and Wolff."

"I really think that we need to make a full assessment of the ship in New York before we attempt to sail her back to Britain again," pressed Andrews. "The fire damage, added to the mysterious impact that we encountered when Bell and I were inspecting the bunker, could have caused damage and weaknesses to the ship that we are not immediately aware of."

"But I doubt there is any real cause for concern," said Ismay.

"Is that your expert opinion?" replied Andrews, trying to be as polite and as sarcastic as he was able in the same breath.

Ismay grunted, taking the jibe. "But look how well she's running, twenty to twenty three knots for most of the journey so far. Surely that is an indication that everything is sound?"

"I think you misunderstand the situation," said Smith. "There has been a certain haste to get to New York. Initially, as we could not get the fire under control and it seemed to be spreading, and now, as a precaution, to ensure that if any problems do develop we are not in the middle of the Atlantic."

"I think that you are being over cautious," said Ismay.

"And I am happy to be that way," replied Smith. "I know you are concerned with headlines, well consider what would happen if something were to go wrong. I would also like to remind you that should a situation arise where an evacuation was to be required, that not everyone would be able to leave!"

Ismay paused. "This is harping back to the lifeboat thing isn't it?"

291

The Captain paused and Andrews took a strategic sip of his drink to avoid saying anything. He had stated all along that Titanic should have more lifeboats but had been overruled.

"We have been over this a number of times before," pressed Ismay. "I grant you that there are not enough lifeboats for everyone on the ship, but I would also like to point out that the Titanic *exceeds* the amount of lifeboats required by law."

"Maybe so," replied Smith, "but you cannot argue with the simple maths. There is only capacity for one thousand one hundred and seventy eight souls and we have over two thousand people on board!"

Ismay shook his head. "I am not going through this again! We are not going to need to use them. You have been quoted yourself saying how safe the ship is!"

"In our present situation I am not so sure!" said Smith, trying to stay calm.

"In addition," said Ismay, "you have to remember that it is not as though Titanic is the only ship in the Atlantic! The place is teaming with them! If, in the unlikely event we did need to evacuate, a radio message could be sent and help from a nearby ship could be called upon.

"But what would happen in a situation if radio contact were to be broken?" asked Smith. "I would like to point out to you that the Marconi wireless did break last night, and for many hours we were unable to call or receive. What would have happened if an incident were to have occurred then?"

"There are other methods of signalling other ships," said Ismay, "but all this is a moot point anyway is it not? Nothing is going to happen? Let's just get Titanic to New York and then bring her home again!"

"Look," said Smith, "I feel that there is some middle ground that can be reached." He paused, knowing the wording would have to be crucial to persuade Ismay. In the end he was the owner of the ship and if he insisted upon it, Titanic would not stop in New York as he and Andrews wanted. "If we break the Olympic's record, it means that we are going to be ahead of our intended schedule when we arrive in New York anyway am I right?"

Ismay nodded. "Yes, but not by a great deal."

Smith nodded. "Well why not use that extra time for a more comprehensive inspection of the damage? That way a decision can be made on whether to continue back or not. If we do have to postpone we can say that the damage was caused by breaking the Olympic's record. There will be no shame in that, especially as it will lead people to think that we are in reach of the Riband."

Ismay paused, considering the notion. "Alright, but we will have to break the Olympic's record! Can you guarantee it?"

Smith nodded. "I think so. We have had to make a slight southward course change already which has added a bit of time and another deviation may be on the cards."

"Why is that?" asked Ismay.

"We've been receiving a number of warnings regarding ice from other ships," explained Smith.

"Not totally uncommon at this time of year or bearing in mind our position," said Ismay casually.

"No, that is true," replied Smith, "but the ice seems to be drifting further south than normal. We are keeping a watch on the situation. So far there is no cause for concern or even any sightings. The course change ordered was only slight to give us a bit more leeway, and if I had to admit it, not as severe as I would normally have made."

"More worried about phantom fire damage than icebergs, eh?" replied Ismay.

"If you want to put it in those blunt terms then yes, I am," replied Smith, almost through gritted teeth. He then reached for his pocket watch. "Gentlemen please, it is getting late. I think that it's time I turned in."

"Nine twenty?" said Ismay looking over Smith's shoulder to the clock on the mantle.

"Late for me!" replied Smith. "It has been a very long day and I want to be up early tomorrow."

Ismay and Andrews quickly downed their drinks and said their goodnights before leaving Smith alone in his sitting room. Smith moved over to the fireplace and looked momentarily at the flames that were dancing in the hearth. He had won a reasonable victory with Ismay in getting him to agree to have Titanic examined in New York, but that all hinged on the fact that they beat the Olympic. He stabbed at the flames with the poker, and a sudden thought crossed his mind. What would happen if another ship encountered problems with the ice flow? If close by they would have to respond, and that would cost them valuable time on the record which could also allow any unseen dangers with Titanic to develop further. Smith shook his head trying to put the thought out of his mind and with that went to retrieve his mug from the table before then heading to the door which led directly to his bedroom.

CHAPTER 51

After their ejection from the kitchens the Professor and Mallory returned to the Captain's table to find that the Von Brauns had made their excuses and had left. Hoping that Jazmine would return to the table they stayed for a while, but after fifteen minutes there was no sign of her, so Mallory hit upon the idea of writing a message and asking the other stewardess Violet to pass it on to her. However, the Irish girl seemed reluctant to take the note, so skipping the remainder of the meal, Mallory and the Professor tried to find another way of making contact with Jazmine, but realised they could not. There was no way back into the kitchens and no staff member was willing to assist them.

"This is very annoying!" grunted the Professor as he stormed down the corridor heading back towards his cabin.

"Well, we have got to do something!" replied Mallory.

"Don't you think I know that," barked the Professor.

"Professor Montacute!" called out a familiar voice.

"Oh no!" said the Professor dejectedly, looking down the passageway, "it's that Maggie Brown woman, and she's got company with her."

"You know Professor, I think she likes you!"

"Oh shut up Mallory, we don't have time for this!"

"Um, perhaps she has seen Jazmine or the Von Brauns?" added Mallory, quickly trying to change the subject.

"Mmmm, possibly, but don't tell her about what has just happened... Ah Maggie, how delightful to see you!" He quickly looked over at the nervous looking man who was with her.

"Yes, yes," she said. "Look I need to speak with you both."

The Professor nodded and ushered them into his cabin. "Right, first things first," said the Professor moving over to the small safe which he opened and brought out a small package which he passed to Maggie.

"My statue!" she cried in delight. "You managed to get it back for me, but how?"

"A long story," said the Professor. "Out of interest have you seen Jazmine or the Von Brauns at all?"

Maggie shook her head. "Why, is something wrong?"

"No nothing," he replied. "So who's your new friend?"

"This is Mr Terence Corman," announced Maggie. "I started chatting to him, and he told me something very interesting that I thought you should know about." She turned to the nervous looking man who cleared his throat. "Go on, you tell the Professor."

The man stepped forward. "I own and run a bookshop in Salisbury. We specialise in rare books and manuscripts. Anyway a few weeks ago we purchased some copies of Egyptian Hieroglyphs. It was a job lot, including books and maps. Anyway, one of the hieroglyphs particularly caught our attention. It seemed to be….." He stopped, looking nervous as though he was about to make a fool of himself.

"Yes?" said the Professor, urging him on.

"Well it looked like a large light bulb." He winced, as though waiting for a rebuff and to be told that it was impossible and not to be so stupid, but none came.

Instead the Professor looked thoughtful.

"Tell them about the robbery," urged Maggie.

"What? Oh yes. Well a few days after we acquired the hieroglyphs there was a break in at the shop."

"The picture of the light bulb was taken?" said Mallory.

"Yes," replied Corman, "among other things, but that was what was odd about the robbery. There was no attempt to force the till or gain access to the safe and the secure area where the valuable books were left untouched, the things that were taken were of no real value at all."

"Seems the robber got what he wanted, then took a few other things to hide his true purpose," suggested Mallory.

The Professor nodded. "Were there any suspects?"

"There was a strange man seen in the area that the police did want to trace, but he seemed to disappear and there was not a clear description of him."

"Apart from being big built and wearing a long coat and hat?" put forward the Professor.

Corman nodded in surprise.

"Tell them about the door!" said Maggie.

"That was another thing," said Corman, slightly more confident as he realised that he was being taken seriously. "The robber gained entry to the shop by literally ripping the front door off its hinges!"

"That does sound like our 'friend'," said Mallory cautiously.

"Yes, it does," said the Professor stroking his beard. "Mr Corman, can you remember the details of this 'light bulb' you saw on the hieroglyph?"

"Yes I think so."

"Good." He then crossed the cabin to the writing table and fetched a pencil and some paper and gave it to Corman. "Here, make a sketch of it, as accurate as you can, try to leave nothing out."

Corman made the sketch and passed it back to the Professor. "There, I've tried to make the two figures that were carrying the 'bulb' as accurate as possible, as well as some of the background detail."

The Professor looked over the sketch carefully before passing it to Mallory who shook his head. "Well I know that you are the expert, but it looks to me just like a flower blowing a bubble with a snake inside."

The Professor nodded. "Maybe so, but it seems that someone went to a lot of trouble to get the sketch if that was all it was."

"Look Professor, since I have hooked up with you I have seen a lot of strange and disturbing things, but do you really expect me to believe that the Egyptians created a gigantic light bulb thousands of years ago?"

"At this point I'm not sure what to believe," said the Professor taking another look at the picture. "Is this totally accurate?"

Corman nodded. "Yes, as far as I can remember."

"Mallory, take a look at that square on the wall," said the Professor pointing to a particular spot.

Mallory took another look and gasped. "My goodness, it looks like, like some kind of switch!"

"Yes, that's what I thought, a light switch," echoed the Professor.

"Have you come across anything like this before?" asked Mallory.

"Well there have been theories put forward, mainly from the lunatic fringe, that the Egyptians were visited by people from other worlds who gave them information and knowledge beyond their time. This is how it is explained that they were so advanced for their age, and were able to build the pyramids."

"But a light bulb?" ventured Maggie sounding doubtful.

"Mr Corman, who did you actually buy the original hieroglyphs from?"

"They were bought from an auction house. I think that it was part of a house clearance. I'm not sure of whom they originally belonged to though."

"Right," said the Professor. "Well I think that this is going to have to be investigated further. I will need the name of the auction house, and any other information that you can give us."

"But there is something else," Corman said nervously. "I've had a strange feeling that over the past few days that I have been, well, been watched, and I did hear that some people were asking after me."

"The Von Brauns?" suggested Mallory.

The Professor nodded then looked down at the sketch. "Mr Corman, let me be honest with you. I think that you have stumbled upon something quite unique and important that certain elements do not want others to see."

"Could he be in danger?" asked Maggie worriedly.

"Possibly," replied the Professor, "although if the danger was real I don't think that you would be standing here talking to us."

Corman's eyes widened in fear at the implication.

"Right, there is only one course of action to take," said the Professor. "Mr Corman, I am going to keep this sketch. I also want you to start spreading the word that you have found a strange Egyptian drawing which resembles a modern piece of technology."

"People will think that I am mad."

"Well, that is a risk that you must take. But also tell people that you have passed the details on to academics that have taken the matter seriously, and are investigating the matter further."

"Let the proverbial cat out of the bag?" said Mallory smiling.

"Precisely!" said the Professor excitedly. "No point in coming after Mr Corman to keep him quiet if the secret is already out, eh? Now I want you to start doing this straight away, go to the smoking room, the receptions, make a point of telling anyone who will listen, and don't be afraid to draw more sketches either!"

Corman nodded, seeing the sense of what was proposed. "My travelling companion will have to be warned too."

"Good," said Mallory. "Get him to do the same."

"Oh it's actually a 'her'. I'm hoping that one day she will become my wife."

The Professor smiled. "That is very nice, but get to her, let her know what's happening, like yourself she should not be in any danger, but it will be best to act as fast as you can."

"I will, at the moment she's….um …don't worry, I'll tell her."

"At the moment she's what?" asked the Professor, sensing that there was something more.

"Um, well nothing!"

"Mr Corman! I advise you to tell me what's going on!"

The man paused but from the look he was being given he realised that he had to say what was going on. "Well my intended has an item of jewellery, Egyptian in origin, and we have found a buyer for it. The deal is being made now, even as we speak, on this ship in secret."

"Secret? Why?" asked the Professor.

Corman looked even more uneasy "Um, well it seems that the item, a bracelet, may have been smuggled out of Egypt without the authorities knowing. We did not know that until afterwards and it seems that the Egyptians are within their rights to demand it back from the owner without any form of monetary compensation. Anyway, to cut a long story short we found a buyer who was happy to make the transaction knowing this."

"Did you ever keep the bracelet at your shop?" asked Mallory.

Corman nodded. "Why yes, in a hidden safe."

The same thought entered Mallory and the Professor's mind almost at once – The Mummy most likely had been sent to the shop to retrieve both items but had only found one.

"Who's buying the bracelet? – Oh don't bother answering that, I've an idea who," said the Professor.

"Where is the deal taking place?" asked Mallory quickly.

"The First Class Lounge."

With that the Professor and Mallory headed towards the door leaving a stunned Mr Corman and Maggie Brown.

CHAPTER 52

Mallory and the Professor burst through the doors of the First Class Lounge. The Von Brauns were there, standing by the fireplace with a rather startled looking young woman.

300

"Otto, you have gone way too far this time!" cried the Professor as he marched up to them.

The young woman looked nervous as though she was about to go, but Otto held up his hand to indicate calm.

"Professor, if you will just let me conclude my business here."

"In front of someone?" the young woman sounded surprised.

Otto smiled. "My friends here are of no consequence." To emphasise the point Elisabeth held up a large roll of banknotes.

The woman, seemingly assured, nodded, then from her bag produced a large thick bracelet. She paused, then held it out to the Countess who grabbed it, while allowing the woman to take the roll of notes.

"That will be all," said Otto sternly.

"I do have other items of jewellery," the woman said eagerly.

"I said that will be all," repeated Otto, this time in a stern dismissive manner. The woman taking the hint turned, then headed towards the door of the lounge as fast as she could. Elisabeth instinctively placed the jewellery on her wrist snapping it shut.

"Now," said Otto, "I am presuming that you are not here for a late night drink, so what can I do for you?"

The Professor drew his swordstick and held it up menacingly. "First things first – let's talk two thousand year old light bulbs and smuggled bracelets."

A look of surprise crossed Otto's face. "So I take it you have met that girl's beloved, Mr Corman? And it is a *three* thousand year old light bulb."

"Well, whatever the dynasty, I have put wheels in motion to protect him and his intended, so you can just leave the both of them alone!"

301

Otto, clearly annoyed, nodded. "So be it, is there anything else?"

"Yes," snarled the Professor. "Thanks to you, your creature has kidnapped my daughter. You must have some idea where it could have taken her and I want answers!"

"Oh put that thing away!" said Elisabeth sounding particularly unimpressed. "First sign of trouble and you are always bringing your sword out! It is getting tiresome."

"As well as so outdated!" replied Otto, who was now pointing a small pistol at the Professor. "Thank you my darling!"

Elisabeth smiled, her outburst had allowed her husband to reach for his gun.

"Now Professor," continued Otto, "let me put your mind at rest. The enchantment Elisabeth placed on Jazmine was to make the Mummy think that she was his intended bride and she was to be protected. All he has done is track her down, and taken her off to what he believes is a safe location, probably an unoccupied cabin or small storage area somewhere that no one goes to. He will keep her there and no doubt watch over her, and of course while he is doing that he will be keeping out of sight and not causing any trouble anywhere else."

"Not good enough," said the Professor, "and what happens when we get to New York? He can't stay on the ship forever."

Otto and Elisabeth shrugged. In truth they had not thought that far ahead, they just wanted to ensure the Mummy was occupied for the rest of the journey.

"Look, just tell us where she could be and we will take it from here," ordered the Professor.

"But I don't want to," said Elisabeth, almost in the tone of a spoilt child. "Seeing you like this is far more fun!"

"We can't leave Jazmine at the hands of this creature. Anything might happen!" said Mallory.

"Oh such concern!" said Elisabeth "But I'm sure that she will be alright."

"He thinks that she is his lost bride!"

"Are you worried about her safety or her honour?" replied Elisabeth, making Mallory quickly look to the floor in embarrassment. "Well," continued Elisabeth, "I can assure you that it is far too late to save the latter. That went a while ago, the shameless hussy!"

Mallory looked shocked, while the Professor fought the rage that was rising within him.

"As for the Mummy," continued Otto, "well, he is in no position to act in that manner. It seems the puritan Victorians got hold of him at some point and a certain appendage was removed."

"I'll explain later," said the Professor seeing the confusion on Mallory's face. He turned to Otto. "Look, all we are interested in is Jazmine's safety. You must have some idea where it could have taken her."

"The spell I cast on the tablet was vague and deliberately non specific," replied Elisabeth. "I'm afraid that he could be anywhere."

"Just give us an idea," pressed Mallory.

Elisabeth shrugged. "Well there are a couple of possible places that are likely." She then laughed out loud, "but I am certainly not going to tell you!"

"Why you……!"

Mallory's exclamation was interrupted. From somewhere there was a scream followed by the door of the lounge flying open and the Mummy, wearing its long coat and hat, staggered in carrying the unconscious form of the young woman who had just sold the bracelet. The Mummy unceremoniously placed her down on a tub chair before stumbling over to the fireplace, its half severed head flopping around. "Golden bracelet!" it moaned. "Want the golden bracelet! A present for my Jazmine!"

"She is not your Jazmine," said Mallory defensively.

The Mummy turned its body to face him. "My Jazmine! Not yours! My lost bride!"

"Whatever," cried the Professor grabbing Mallory and hauling him to one side. "Anyway, you want the bracelet, take it!" and pointed at Elisabeth, who realised that the object of the creatures desire was now around her wrist.

The Mummy started to advance and the Countess tried to remove the bracelet but was unable to. "The clasp! It's stuck," she cried, as she wrestled with it. Otto moved in to help.

"Otto!" cried Elisabeth desperately.

"I'm doing the best I can," he replied, looking up to see the Mummy moving ever closer. "Professor, help! Use the scarab. That will stop him."

"I'm sorry old boy, but I can't do that. You won't tell me where Jazmine might be so things are going to have to happen the hard way. I am going to have to let the creature get the bracelet, then follow him, presumably he will lead us straight back to Jazmine."

Otto then turned, aiming his gun at the Mummy, firing wildly. The bullets hit the creature, causing it to jerk and stagger, but it regained its footing, then continued to advance.

"Come on Otto," cried the Professor who was now holding up the black scarab as a taunt. "Where is Jazmine? Give me a likely location."

"He's got her stashed in a lifeboat! I'm not sure which one."

"That's a lie," replied the Professor instantly, "that's far too impractical! Now where is she?"

304

"Beyond your reach for sure now!" cried Elisabeth triumphantly, holding up the bracelet which she had finally removed from her wrist. Then before anyone could react she turned and threw the bracelet into the blazing fireplace. The Mummy reacted by trying to fire out a thread of its bandage, but it missed and the golden bangle landed in the hearth. The Mummy ran over to the fireplace and tried to reach into the fire to get it, but soon pulled his bandaged hand back through fear of setting himself alight.

"You are a fool Countess," said the Professor. "The gold will melt and the bracelet will be destroyed."

"Oh I think not," replied Otto. "That was not all it seemed to be. It was actually an experimental type of metal made by the ancients, then plated with gold. The gold will melt off yes, but it's that alloy itself which holds the real value and that will be safe, all we have to do is fish it out from the fire."

The Mummy gave out a roar seeing that it had been outwitted, and turned. "Taken away! My Jazmine's gift taken away! You must pay!" The creature lifted its arm and before anyone could react, the Mummy's hand flew across the room and landed around Elisabeth's throat and started to choke her. Otto responded instantly by going to help and somehow managed to start prising back the creature's fingers. Meanwhile the unconscious girl who the Mummy had brought in with her had recovered her wits, and seeing the situation had decided to flee.

"Come on Mallory," said the Professor moving forward to help. "I was hoping the Mummy would scare them into telling us were Jazmine was, this was not my intention."

The Professor was by Otto's side in moments and the two of them managed to pull the hand away from Elisabeth's throat.

Otto threw the Mummy's hand far across the vast space of the Lounge. However, as it flew through the air, it seemed to

305

take on a life of its own, moving in a wide controlled arc back to the Mummy's waiting outstretched arm where it reattached itself.

"Must pay!" cried the Mummy slowly, moving towards them. "You all must die!" He then started to inhale ready to expel the black breath which he had used before to kill.

Then without any kind of warning the whole ship seemed to judder and shake, everyone stopped, unsure as to what had happened, even the Mummy itself seemed to pause, momentarily caught off guard by the events.

"My God!" cried Elisabeth pointing to the windows. "Look at that."

Everyone turned just in time to see what appeared to be a large tower of white ice pass by.

"What in the world…?" asked Otto. "That looked like an Iceberg."

"I think you could be right," replied the Professor, "it is possible….."

He was interrupted by Elisabeth letting out a scream and pointing to the Mummy who had resumed his attack. The creature, using the confusion, had come even nearer, leaning forward and breathing out a wispy wave of smoke.

"Cover your faces, look away!" cried Otto.

But it was too late, for the smoke drifted straight over to them and despite their best efforts, they were unable not to breathe in the poisoned air. Otto and Elisabeth fell to the floor almost instantly, while the Professor fell moments later. Mallory tried to cover his face with his sleeve, but was aware that he had already taken in a lung full of the Mummy's poisonous smoke. With his last seconds of consciousness and all his remaining strength he lunged out grabbing the Mummy by his arm and pulled the creature towards him. As Mallory hit the floor he looked up to see the Mummy waving its arms in the air trying to beat the wispy smoke that surrounded him but it was too late. As darkness took over, the last thing Mallory was aware of was the Mummy, too, falling to the floor, and the pleasant thought of how the creature had been caught in its own trap.

CHAPTER 53

Captain Smith practically burst into the wheelhouse. The scene that greeted him was one of panic.

"Captain on the Bridge," a voice said automatically.

"Report," he ordered, ignoring the formality.

"An Iceberg Sir!" came the reply. "It scraped the starboard side."

"I know," replied Smith. "I saw it from my quarters through the porthole. Report Mr Murdoch."

Murdoch, who was clearly shaken by what had happened took a step forward. "The lookout spotted an iceberg Sir, dead ahead, and rang down. I ordered a hard to starboard and then full reverse." He paused. "But it was too late, it was too close, we hit along the starboard side before we could turn clear."

"How close were we when it was spotted?"

Murdoch paused. "Less than a mile, I think, Sir."

"Speed?"

"Twenty two knots."

Captain Smith paused. All his years of experience told him that the wrong decision had been made. If a turn of this type were to be attempted it needed to be made with full forward power which aided the angle of the manoeuvre, not while the engines were in reverse which slowed the speed. However, in a situation as the one described, it would have been far safer to aim towards the iceberg to collide with it straight on while at the same time ordering a full stop. Trying to steer around such an obstacle and failing to do so exposed the broadside for an impact and even if the ship did appear to have missed,

307

there was the danger that they could be hit below the waterline by sections of unseen protruding ice. But then another thought entered his mind. How many ice warnings had been received during the previous day? His mind briefly drifted back to a conversation with Ismay and Andrews less than three hours ago in his sitting room. Danger to the Titanic had been perceived, but it was in the form of damage caused by the bunker fire, danger from ice had been considered, but had been the lesser, more unlikely evil, one that could be dealt with using tried and tested methods.

"Thank you Mr Murdoch," said Smith finally, although he wanted to say a lot more, regarding Murdoch's decision making process, but he decided against it. It did not do well for Bridge crew to see their Captain openly berate the First Officer. Smith would deal with Murdoch at a later date. No doubt there would be an enquiry into what had happened where he could vent his full dismay at the situation. "I want this all accurately entered in the ship's log."

"Already done Sir," replied Murdoch.

Smith nodded in approval. "Close all the bulkhead doors."

"I gave the order as soon as we hit," replied Murdoch.

"Good," replied Smith, as he looked up at the display board, lit up to show that all the bulkhead doors were closed. "Full stop!"

The order was repeated and carried out.

Smith then moved out of the starboard door of the wheelhouse onto the boat deck and over to the small gap between the first lifeboat and the small viewing compartment where he looked down. Far below all he could see was the blackness of the sea and the white spray of the water that was being thrown up. Any damage, he concluded, was below the waterline. He tried to look back, past the lifeboats, and in the distance half hidden he thought that he could make out the outline of the Iceberg that they had hit. Quickly he moved away from the rail past the wheelhouse to the navigation bridge. Below him in the forward well deck a number of passengers had already gathered, trying to see what had happened. Some were picking up and examining the various chunks of ice that now littered that part of the deck. A shiver ran down Smith's spine. All of the people were smiling, talking, even joking, united in the shared experience of a seemingly unexpected event.

Quickly he returned to the wheelhouse.

"Message from below Sir," said Murdoch as he moved away from the internal telephone panel. "There is severe damage. Big gashes along the starboard side below the waterline, the forward compartments are flooding."

Smith nodded, he had expected as much, everything now depended on how bad the damage was.

"Mr Boxhall."

"Yes Sir," said the Fourth Officer suddenly appearing by the Captain's side.

"I want you to make a visual inspection of the damage and report back immediately."

"Aye Sir," he replied before turning and disappearing.

"Is there anything else that we can do sir?" asked Murdoch.

Smith looked out of the main wheelhouse window, and noticed that the bow of the ship was no longer level. "No," he replied finally, "at the moment all we can do is wait until a full assessment has been made."

They waited for nearly twenty minutes in silence, watching the bow of the ship slowly start to dip before, through the wheelhouse door, Boxhall appeared, with a shocked looking Thomas Andrews, clutching rolls of paper with him, presumably plans of the ship. The third man with them was Bruce Ismay who had spotted the two men while heading to the Bridge.

Smith nodded and headed towards the chart room, followed by Andrews, Ismay and Murdoch, where they could talk without being overheard by the rest of the bridge crew. Inside with the door shut Andrews placed a large plan of Titanic on the main chart table and quickly unrolled it. "I'm not going to beat about the bush. The inspection I made was limited but only one possible conclusion can be drawn. Titanic is going to flounder completely and in not very much time."

There was a moment of shocked silence.

"No, that is impossible!" said Ismay in disbelief.

Ignoring him Smith moved forward and looked down at the plan. "Explain."

Andrews indicated on the plan. "We hit the iceberg along the starboard side there, below the water line, the damage is around 300 foot long, possibly in a series of long rips, it's impossible to say for certain."

"The ice has gashed us open?" asked Ismay.

"No," replied Andrews carefully, "I don't think it has. What I think has happened is that the smashing into the ice has caused the steel plates of the hull to bend and buckle out of shape, putting unreasonable stresses on the rivets, causing them to burst, causing the rips. Anyway, the first five compartments are flooding. Titanic can stay afloat with damage to four compartments, but not five, and it's going to get worse."

"But how?" asked Ismay. "What about the bulkheads, surely they should stop it."

Andrews shook his head. "The bulkheads only go up to Deck E. As the ship is pulled down the water goes over the top and into the next compartment. This is then repeated and so on and so on down the length of the ship." To indicate this he tapped each section on the plan.

"What about the pumps?" asked Smith, hoping for some kind of reprieve.

Andrews shook his head. "They cannot cope with that amount of water. All they will do is buy the ship a matter of minutes. Titanic is sinking and cannot be saved."

"How long do we have?" asked Smith his mind racing.

Andrews looked down at the plans. "At best an hour and a half, maybe two if we are lucky."

Smith pointed at the plan, specifically to bunker number 6, a thought suddenly entering his mind. "Your theory about the buckling, there was already possible damage to that section of the hull where the bunker fire was. What effect could that have had, if any?"

Andrews took a deep breath. "Impossible to say, it depends on how bad that damage was in the first place, which of course we don't know. I have a feeling that we will never know for sure how much it contributed. All I can say is that, by rights, the bunker should have been about half full, but was totally empty because of the fire. The weight and mass of the coal might have helped ease the impact, in much the same why it is harder to crush a full metal can rather than an empty one; but again that's just speculation."

"This is a cruel irony gentlemen," whispered Smith. "Our present course and speed was all initiated to get the ship to the perceived safety of New York, but instead all we have seemed to do is put the ship into direct peril!"

"Captain," said Murdoch after a pause, "the lifeboats."

"Yes," replied Smith, nodding, "of course, we must launch the lifeboats at once!"

Andrews nodded, stealing a look at Ismay. "Good, but referring to what we were talking about earlier. There are not enough places in the lifeboats for everyone on board."

Smith nodded. "Then we must pray that Ismay's assertion, that there are bound to be other ships in the vicinity to help, is true."

Ismay looked as though he was about to say something in his defence, but then thought better of it, opting to nod silently.

After a short stop in the Marconi room, where he told Phillips and Bride the situation, he asked them to send out a distress call and got them to report what ships were in the vicinity. Smith, followed by Andrews and Ismay, re-entered the wheelhouse, where all eyes turned to them, hoping for good news.

"Gentlemen," said Smith trying to keep his voice steady, "it is my sad duty to inform you that Titanic is sinking and will be lost in a little over an hour's time. A call for help has been issued although it does seem that the nearest ship will not reach us until after Titanic has sunk."

He paused, registering the looks of surprise and terror on the crews faces.

"Mr Murdoch, send the order for all crew to report to their emergency stations and for the lifeboats to be lowered, women and children first; we are abandoning ship."

CHAPTER 54

"Help me!" screamed Jazmine as she pounded against the boxes and crates which served as her small prison.

The seawater was already up to her ankles and was rising fast. The crates wedged in the alcove entrance, floor to ceiling, by the Mummy, was acting as a makeshift barrier, keeping out the majority of water that was rapidly filling the cargo hold. But it was by no means completely watertight and some of the freezing water was finding its way in. Jazmine estimated that she had less than ten minutes before the water was over her head and five minutes after that, unless she could escape, she would drown.

"Help me! Father! Richard! I'm down here! Help me!" She wiped a tear away from her eye.

From the other side of the boxes there came a noise.

"Help me! I'm in here!" She cried again with new vigour.

Suddenly a gap appeared in the wall of crates above her head and the body of a man, followed by a tide of rushing water swept in. The man bobbed to the surface and gasped for breath. "Quick, take a deep breath, the biggest you have ever taken, because you are in real trouble, then follow me!"

Jazmine did as she was told, just as the freezing cold water filled the small area where she had been hidden. The mysterious man disappeared through the hole that he had come through. Jazmine, fighting the cold and the fear that was rising inside her did the same, keeping as close to her saviour as she possibly could. The man swam through the now flooded cargo hold, towards a section of what looked like solid wall and then appeared to disappear inside. As Jazmine got closer she saw that there was in fact an opening leading to a shaft. Quickly she moved inside and looking up saw the feet of the man kicking frantically away from her. Pulling at the water above her head and kicking her feet she began to rise upwards moving faster and faster until eventually, after what seemed like an age, she broke to the surface and gasped for air.

"Over here Miss!"

She turned to see a hatchway with the legs of the man who had saved her disappearing through, then two faces filling the rest of the opening with an outstretched hand reaching for her.

"Come on Miss, this way!"

Still gulping for air she nodded and moved towards the hatch where she reached up and was grabbed by two strong

313

hands which pulled her through, finding herself on the floor gasping for breath, surrounded by mailbags with two surprised looking men staring down at her. By their dark trousers and collarless shirts she immediately took them to be the Titanic mailroom clerks. The man who had saved her sat up and addressed his colleagues, shaking his head. "It's no good! I could not find either of them."

There was a silence from the two men as they realised that their fellow co workers, William Gwynn and John Smith were lost.

"Damn it!" cried one in an American accent. "I told them not to go back! It was just too dangerous and by now anything would be damaged due to flooding!"

He nodded over to Jazmine.

"Where did you find her?"

"First class baggage Deck G behind a load of crates. They sort of acted like a dam," replied the man trying to shake the excess water from his clothes.

"Well good work Williamson," said the American, "but I don't want you going down there again!"

"No way! Not on your life!" He then looked down at Jazmine, who had now caught her breath and was rising to her feet. "Are you alright? What were you doing down there in the first place?

"You would never believe me if I told you," she replied. "Thank you, you saved me!"

Williamson looked down slightly embarrassed.

"Could someone please tell me what's going on and where I am?"

"Deck E and as for what's going on, well, we hit an iceberg and if you had not already worked it out the ship is sinking," said the third man. "By the way I'm Oscar Woody, the chap who saved you is James Williamson and our American friend here is Mr John March."

Jazmine nodded at the men individually.

"You had better get yourself out of here," said March sternly to her. He pointed to the nearby staircase. "Get to the lifeboats as quickly as you can."

"But what about you three?" asked Jazmine.

March looked down at the mail bags and the piles of parcels which had already been saved, and littered the floor around them. "We are going to try to get these up top and then hope we can find room for them in a lifeboat."

"Look John, I'm sorry, but I don't think I've got the energy left to manually haul this lot up," said Woody who was visibly tired from his exertions. "Is there any other way?"

March pointed back to the shaft. "If the hatch cover up on deck was open we could use the small winch by it to tie the bags together and haul them up that way, but it's locked firm."

"How do you mean locked?" asked Jazmine.

"Well, what I said - locked. There is a padlock on the outside. I went up and checked."

"Does the hatch cover lift up at all?"

"Well yes a bit," replied March.

Jazmine smiled and then produced a small hair pin. "I've got an idea!"

"Pick the padlock of the hatch?" asked Willliamson.

"No," she replied. "I've got a better idea." She motioned over to an unmarked heavy looking brown door. "I'm going to pick the locks of *that* room, or try at least."

"Why?" asked Oscar.

Jazmine smiled. "Because it's the Master-at-arms-room."

"A pistol," cried March, "if we had a pistol we could just shoot the hatch lock off!"

"Exactly!" cried Jazmine as she ran to the door to examine it.

"Well," asked March, "can you do it?"

"I'm not sure," replied Jazmine. "It's a reinforced lock for obvious reasons, but I can give it a go." Kneeling by the door she placed the hairpin in the keyhole and started to probe inside, trying to move the unseen lock mechanism. After a few moments there was a ping and Jazmine cried out in dismay, "My hairpin's snapped!"

"Do you have another one?"

"No," replied Jazmine looking annoyed.

"Move aside Miss," said March. "This requires some good old fashioned direct action!"

Jazmine did as she was asked. March eyed up the door, and taking a deep breath lifted his leg and kicked it as hard as he could. "Dear Lord!" he cried as his foot practically bounced off. "What the hell kind of wood is that door made from?"

He kicked at it again and again but nothing.

"It must be re-enforced somehow," replied Jazmine. "After all, the last thing that is wanted is for someone to get hold of guns and ammunition."

"Come on Woody," said March, "we'll try together."

Oscar took his place and after the count of three, the two of them kicked at the door with no effect.

"We'll try once more," said March.

"Oh no you won't!" called a voice, "get away from that door at once."

They turned to see four men walking towards them, all dressed in senior officer uniforms.

"What's going on here?"

March stood almost to attention. "Sorry Mr Murdoch, we needed a firearm. We are trying to get the mail out through the bunker hatch, but the cover is locked. We figured that if we could get a firearm we could shoot the lock off."

"Sorry that's not possible, move back." Murdoch moved to the door, produced a key and opened it. The three men disappeared inside only to reappear a few moments later all carrying pistols.

"One of you could quickly come with us up the shaft," said March hopefully.

"I'm sorry," replied Third Officer Pitman, locking the door behind him. "We've got to get back on deck. Best you use the stairs and get as much as you can up that way."

With that he and the four men headed away.

"Damn it!" cried March. "Now what?"

Jazmine looked down at the broken hairpin. "It might be enough to release the padlock on the hatch. I'm going to need some help though; can one of you come with me to hold up the hatch as far as possible so I can reach the lock?"

March stepped forward. "It will be a pleasure Miss."

So Jazmine and March moved back to the open hatch and climbed into the shaft.

"The water's still rising," commented Jazmine as she took firm hold of the ladder which ran up the side of the duct, and started to ascend.

"I don't think that there is going to be a great deal of time before the ship is totally lost," commented the American following Jazmine step for step.

"Then we better hope that this works!"

At the top of the ladder Jazmine moved over to one side as far as she was able, allowing March to move up beside her and brace himself against the top of the hatch. On the count of three he pushed upwards allowing Jazmine to slide her hand outside and try to reach round for the lock. "This is going to be difficult," she observed.

"But can you do it?"

"I think so," she replied, "but it's going to take time."

Jazmine struggled with the padlock, usually a lock of this type would not be a problem, but the angle she was attempting it from added to the fact that the hairpin was broken was making it almost impossible.

"I cannot hold the hatch for much longer!" cried March.

"I think I'm nearly there………..No!"

"What's wrong?"

"I've dropped the hairpin!" said Jazmine as she pulled her hands back inside.

"Oh blast it!" cried March as he let the hatch down.

"I'm sorry," said Jazmine. "This is my fault, if I hadn't suggested trying to break into the Master-at-arms room and had gone straight for the padlock…."

"Don't worry Miss you did your best…."

Then, just overhead there was the sound of a gun being fired and the sound of a bullet bouncing off of metal, causing them both to duck and almost fall from the ladder. Then the hatch above them lifted up and was opened to reveal two familiar faces. One was Officer Murdoch and the other was Pitman, who helped the two onto the tilting deck.

"Thank you," said March to the senior officers.

Murdoch nodded. "That's alright. But I warn you there is not a lot of time. Are you going to be able to work the winches?"

March nodded, and with that Murdoch and Pitman turned and headed off.

"You better go too Miss," said March. "Get yourself to a lifeboat and off this ship as quickly as you can and thank you for your help."

Jazmine smiled at March and as she did so a shiver ran down her spine. She had a terrible feeling that he and what remained of the Titanic's postal team were not going to make it off of the ship alive.

CHAPTER 55

"My man, you there, Steward!" called Maggie Brown as she moved past the other passengers.

"Yes madam?" replied the steward turning to face her.

"Surely what we've been told is not right, we cannot be sinking, this ship is like a floating city, it is just not possible!"

The steward, not really understanding the situation himself declined to answer, instead just handing Maggie a lifejacket. "Please, just put this on and report to the boat deck and board the first available lifeboat."

"But my things!"

The steward shrugged, this was the reaction he was repeatedly getting from passengers. "Please, it's Captain Smith's orders, put the lifejacket on and report to the boat deck."

Maggie, slightly annoyed, took the lifejacket. "Buddy, if you think that I am just going out like this you have another think coming!"

She then turned and, grumbling all the way, moved through the ship back towards her cabin, but then stopped, suddenly she had a feeling that something was wrong; then she realised what it was. The floor was tilting; in fact the whole corridor as she looked down it seemed to be at a slant. She looked round, other people had not seemed to have noticed it, but she had. Then it hit her – the ship really was sinking!

With that realisation she quickly hurried the remaining distance to her cabin.

The orders that she had originally been given by the steward who had knocked on her door some fifteen minutes earlier, before she decided to go off and find out what was going on herself, had been clear. 'Don't attempt to pack a bag or bring personal possessions.' However, as she had to get some more suitable clothing she certainly was going to take advantage of the situation. After she changed into some warm clothes, putting the lifejacket on over them, she quickly gathered up the small silver framed picture of her husband, and her jewellery. She then moved over to the chest of drawers where she had her green glazed Egyptian statue hidden among her clean undergarments. On opening the drawer she immediately realised that something was not right. From underneath the material was a strange glow. Carefully Maggie moved the clothing to expose her statue, which was no longer green but light orange.

Cautiously, with some trepidation she touched it to find that it was no longer cold to the touch but slightly warm. Then, feeling brave, she picked it up, and it seemed to glow stronger in her hands. She stared at the statue for a few moments before a strange feeling seemed to come over her; a feeling that she was in danger and must leave as soon as possible. Instinctively, she put the statue in her pocket and straight away abandoned an attempt to gather any more of her belongings, instead moving straight out of her cabin and, almost driven, headed as fast as she could towards the boat deck and the waiting lifeboats on the port side of the ship.

Out on the deck she moved down through the gathering people, being careful not to lose her footing on the sloping deck, the warm feeling of the statue with her all the time. She made her way to the first set of lifeboats opting for the one at the end, almost level with the second funnel. As per orders, women and children only were permitted to board. The crewman in charge pointed at her and ushered her to board. Maggie moved forward in response, and was helped in, opting to sit right at the back of the small craft which was suspended in mid air over the sea, held in place between ropes connected to arc-like metal arms called davits. As she watched other passengers boarding, she suddenly felt the statue in her pocket had become much warmer, almost hot. Taking the ancient artefact out to examine it she was horrified to see the statue had changed in colour again, no longer orange, but glowing red. A feeling of panic and trepidation suddenly swept over her. Something was wrong, very wrong. "I've got to get out of this boat!" she said, suddenly standing up, much to the surprise of those within and the members of the Titanic's crew who had been placed in charge. Ignoring the calls for her to keep in her seat she moved across the lifeboat, passing a woman in a dark red coat who, seeing the chance, took Maggie's vacant place, while Maggie herself was helped back aboard the sinking ship by stunned crew.

"Right," called out the Titanic's crewman almost straight away, "that's enough, lower away!"

"But the boat's half empty!" protested Maggie.

"What do you care?" someone beside her responded. "You did not even want to go in it!"

Maggie chose to remain silent, after all the observation was correct, so instead, she looked back at the boat as it was slowly lowered down the side of Titanic. Again Maggie checked the statue, this time it was much cooler, back to warm and had returned to a light orange colouring. Had she imagined it? Was the danger of the night affecting her mind? Then from the left hand side davit, there came a snapping sound with the remains of a rope flying through the air, and from the lifeboat itself came a chorus of panicked screams. Instantly crewmen rushed forward to secure the secondary rope, but it was too late. Looking over the side Maggie could see that the stern end of the lifeboat had tipped and lurched downwards, sending passengers crashing into each other and, even over the side of the boat. Maggie's eyes were drawn to the woman in the red coat who had eagerly taken her seat. She was now hanging over the edge of the boat crying for

321

help, then her grip failed and she was gone, to the further gasps and cries of horror of those around her.

Looking again at the statue, Maggie realised what had happened. It had warned her of the danger. It had changed to orange because of the danger the ship was in and then to red to indicate the danger of the lifeboat. This was no mere ornament, it was a warning device that could detect danger for the owner, and it had saved her life.

Quickly she moved up the boat to another lifeboat, from which a number of people, having just seen one such craft tip, had decided that it would be far safer on the sinking ship and were climbing out.

"No, please get back into the boat!" cried one of the crewmen, as yet another person pushed past. "It is perfectly safe, what just happened was a glitch!"

Stopping, an idea hit Maggie and she quickly went to the lifeboat, boarding it, but not taking a seat. She quickly looked at the statue, which was a very light orange with flecks of green in it, with almost all of the heat now gone.

A smile crossed her face. The colour change in the statue must mean that this lifeboat was not going to come to any harm, and she would be safe, and by extension, any one else in it.

"Madam, please," called a crewman to her. "Please take a seat, if no one else gets in we are going to launch!"

"Oh no you are not!" cried Maggie, and before anyone could stop her, the statue was thrust back in her pocket and she had again jumped back into the ship. "Hey you, over here!"

A rather startled woman in a white dress pointed at herself, unsure if she was being addressed.

"Yep that's right honey, it's you I'm talking to, come with me, this lifeboat is your ticket outta here and you are going to take it."

"Oh no, I'm not sure!" she replied, but it was too late. The formidable Maggie had grabbed the woman and was gently propelling her to the lifeboat where she was met by the crewman who helped her aboard.

"Come on sister," cried Maggie grabbing a woman with a small child. "You two next, they can't wait all day!" Maggie then spied two women standing and looking at each other unsure. "Come on you two!"

One of the women shrugged. "Um, I think that there were other people here before us."

"Oh no you don't," said Maggie holding her finger up at them. "I'm not having any of that British politeness here! Manners to one side tonight, the both of you are getting in that boat." In response the women nodded and stepped towards the waiting lifeboat.

Seeing Maggie's activities, some people who had been hanging back slowly began to move forward, encouraged by this brash American woman's sheer will of character.

"Come on people," she called out loud. "There is plenty more room here! Hey where do you think you are going?"

"Um back to my cabin to fetch my stole," the woman replied in a European accent.

"Oh no you're not!" replied Maggie sternly, "into the boat now!"

Then without warning Maggie, who had started to move away down the deck to find more people, suddenly found two arms being wrapped around her from behind and her feet left the deck. "What on earth? Put me down! You can't do this."

"Oh, I can and I am," came the reply from the large crewman, who had decided to take matters into his own hands literally. "You're going in that lifeboat too!"

"I shall report you to the Captain, this is assault!"

"Oh shut up woman," he replied as he moved towards the edge of Titanic where the lifeboat had just started to be lowered. "I'm trying to save you!"

"I don't need saving, put me down you oaf! I've got to find my friends, ahhhhhhh!"

Her cry stopped as she landed in the lifeboat practically on top of two other women. Recovering herself she looked up to see the crewman who had thrown her off peering down with a satisfied look on his face before disappearing.

"Right you!" came a cry.

Maggie looked round to see a Titanic crewman looking straight at her.

"Sit down and shut up!"

Maggie's eyes narrowed, her anger rising, then in a quiet voice she said, "Right it's time for me to finish my glass of champagne and to start to cause some trouble."

"But you don't have a glass of champagne," pointed out the woman next to her.

"I know," she replied, looking firmly over at the crewman. "Sister, I think that you had better brace yourself, I'm going to make sure that you are in for a hell of a ride! - Hey you boy!"

"My name is Hitchens and I'm not a boy!"

"Well Hitchens, are you planning to row us to safety all by yourself?"

He looked round, and realised that he was the only man in the boat.

"I think you better stop this boat and get some more men in here quick smart!" continued Maggie.

Under his breath, Hitchens cursed, he had the feeling this woman was going to cause him a lot of trouble.

CHAPTER 56

"This is hopeless!" said Jazmine to herself as she made her way back onto the starboard side of the boat deck via the door from the first class entrance. "Richard! Richard Mallory! Charles Montacute!" she called at the top of her voice in desperation before pausing to look around, hoping that they would hear her cries and show themselves, but of course they did not. Jazmine had gone straight to their cabin but they were not there. She had tried to ask a few people who were around, but none had seen them. Could it be possible that they had left the ship? Had they come off worse with a direct encounter with the Mummy? Could they be trapped or injured somewhere?

"Jazmine? Is that you?" called out a voice with a slight French accent. "You look like a drowned rat, what happened?"

Jazmine turned, smiled, then moved down to the band that had gathered on deck just outside the gymnasium and had just finished playing. "I took a dip down in the cargo hold," she replied to the man who had spoken and whom she recognised as Cellist, Roger Bricoux. "It was very bracing if a tad too cold."

A look of horror crossed his and the rest of the band's faces.

"How bad is it down there?" asked Bricoux. "We are hearing all sorts."

Jazmine paused. "Bad, very very bad. You better think about getting yourselves to a lifeboat."

"Can't do that I'm afraid," said Wallace Hartley, the band's leader, with a smile. "We've been given strict orders, make ourselves visible and play cheerful tunes to calm the passengers." At that point a man rushed past shouting to a woman not far behind him, trying her best to keep up, but hampered by a small boy almost tripping over the adult size lifejacket which swamped him.

"I'm not sure that music is going to work," commented Jazmine shivering.

"Look, you are going to catch your death," said Roger putting his cello to one side then standing up and taking off his coat. "Here, take this, you need it more than me."

Jazmine took the coat and pulled it round herself gratefully. "Thank you."

"So any requests?" asked Hartley as he put his violin under his chin.

Jazmine paused. "If you want cheerful, how about some Ragtime? 'Frog legs rag', that's one of my favourites."

"Oh, good choice," he replied approvingly. "Gentlemen, on my mark!" and with a nod of his head the band started to play. Over the music Jazmine smiled, wished them well and headed off towards the stern, keeping an eye out for Mallory or her father.

The scene which Jazmine walked through along the starboard side was one of polite chaos. People were now gathering on the ever sloping deck, trying to find out information as to where they should go, and what they should do. Around her she noticed some familiar faces, passengers which she had served in her role as stewardess as well as fellow staff. A small smile crossed her lips as she thought of Jack Phillips and Harold Bride who were no doubt in the wireless room sending out distress signals. Thank goodness they had gotten the radio working the day before, and not just working, but working at a greater range than it had been. No doubt help would soon be coming from other ships in the area. Her thought also momentarily turned to her friend Violet, with whom, among others, she shared a room.

Jazmine remembered Violet's account of the Olympic crash that had taken place last year and which ultimately caused her to end up on Titanic. This Irish girl was turning into something of a Jonah and Jazmine could not help but remember the joke one of the other stewardesses had made. 'Well now Violet I hope that you are not going to cause this ship to crash too!'

By now Jazmine was almost halfway along the ship's deck. Looking ahead she could see a large gathering at the lifeboats, the nearest of which was already being launched.

"Richard Mallory! Professor Montacute! Where are you?" she called out again in desperation. Then over in the distance, through the crowd, next to one of the lifeboats she noticed with relief the figure of her father, although Mallory was nowhere to be seen. She also noted with some irony that it was lifeboat No. 13, the one that she had ended up clinging to earlier when the Mummy had tried to throw her over the side. Breathing a sigh of relief, but also annoyed that her father had chosen to leave without finding her, she made her way through the crowd and to the very edge of the ship.

"Father, Father it's me Jazmine." She reached out and grabbed the man by his arm, making him turn around.

"Oh I'm so sorry," she said as she gazed upon the stranger's face. I thought that you were my father."

The man shook his head and Jazmine turned to move away trying to push her way back through the crowd when she felt her arm being suddenly gripped. "What you doing Miss? You are going the wrong way." She turned back to see a crewman in a long overcoat. "Get in that boat while you have the chance." She tried to pull away, but the crewman gripped harder onto her sleeve and yanked her back. "Don't be a fool Miss." The man leaned closer to her and almost in a whisper said, "Come on, you're White Star, you know the score! As soon as the order is given to abandon ship, all Staff are instantly dismissed. Also there are not enough lifeboats for everyone."

What the man had said about staff being dismissed was true, it was company policy, but as she was not really staff she did not care. As for the issue of the lifeboats, well that made her more determined to find Mallory and her father to ensure that they were safe.

Breaking free from the man she again turned and tried to push her way through the increasing crowd around the lifeboat, but a large man blocked her way. "Outta my way," he said as he shoved past her, intent on getting into the small boat and to safety. Another man pushed his way forward and Jazmine found herself being carried backwards, and in doing so accidentally placed her foot half over the edge of the ship. She yelled out in pain as her ankle rolled over, causing her to fall off the ship and into the lifeboat where she was caught in the arms of a well dressed man.

"My ankle!" she cried as she automatically reached down to hold it.

"Here, let me take a look at that Miss," said a man with dark hair. "It's alright I'm a Doctor." The man moved forward and made a quick examination of Jazmine's ankle, which already had started to swell and bruise.

"Well, good news Miss, it's not broken, just badly twisted, and you will probably need to rest up for a few days but you should be fine."

"I've got to get off," said Jazmine. "My father and my, my friend, are still onboard."

"Not a chance Miss," said the Doctor keeping a firm hold of her shoulder. "You are staying put!"

"But…." She tried to move again, but at the same time the lifeboat jolted as it started on the sixty foot journey to the sea below. She fell back onto one of the seats and looking up she

328

could see the edge of the deck moving further and further away.

As the lifeboat came level with the opening of the first class promenade deck she saw her chance and tried to stand up, with the intention of launching herself over the side and back on to Titanic, but as soon as she put weight on her injured foot, pain shot through it, sending her back to her seat. Tears filled her eyes as she realised that she was in no position to do anything with her injury, apart from just sit and allow events to unfold around her.

Slowly the lifeboat continued downwards until it eventually hit the water hard jolting those inside. The crewmen immediately started to wrestle with the ropes that were attached to the lifeboat but could not seem to free them. As they struggled, the small craft slowly began to drift towards the stern and right into the path of lifeboat number 15 which was being lowered in a jerky motion. The passengers in number 13 soon became aware of the danger and started to scream out loud as did the crewmen, but for some reason those in number 15 did not respond and the craft continued downwards directly on top of them. Abandoning the idea of untying the ropes, pocket knives were produced by crew and some passengers alike, and frantic attempts to cut the ropes started. While some of the male passengers picked up the oars, pushing against the lowering lifeboat and Titanic itself. All the time the passengers called out to make their plight realised. Lifeboat number 15 was barely six feet away, and number 13 was still directly underneath when it suddenly stopped, and then seemed to jolt downwards another two feet to the screams of those below, who ducked down as they thought that the craft that was intended to save lives would drop on them and kill them by crushing them totally. Then with a triumphant yell the ropes connected to lifeboat 13 were finally severed, and the boat started to drift away. It had barely moved clear, when lifeboat number 15 dropped the final few feet and hit the water, sending freezing water into the air and drenching some of the terrified passengers in number 13.

Taking up the oars, lifeboat number 13, with 15 just beside it, started to move away from Titanic. Jazmine looked up at the giant ship wondering if her beloved father and Mallory were still on board, safe or even dead. Bending down to pretend to examine her ankle so no one could see her, she started to weep.

CHAPTER 57

Bruce Ismay stood on the port side promenade deck breathing heavily, his heart pounding against his chest with his mind trying to take in, and make sense of, the events which were going on about him.

The ship, his ship, the Titanic, first conceived back in the summer of 1907, launched in 1911, now on its maiden voyage, the pinnacle of human endeavour and engineering, the new standard of luxury and opulence for sea travel, was soon to be lost, destined for a watery grave and due to the lack of lifeboats hundreds upon hundreds of souls would be taken along with it. There would no doubt be an enquiry, an investigation, questions would be asked, hard questions. The name of White Star would be dragged through the mud. Then there would be the law suits, in abundance. Any hint of blame, and the claims would come rolling in and there would be no shortage of law firms, on both sides of the Atlantic, happy to sue, everything from loss of life, to people stubbing their toe when they got into the lifeboats. This could even result in the eventual demise of the business totally.

Ismay momentarily thought back to the interview he had given to the press just before they had set sail and his bravado and pride, his dropping hints that the Blue Riband was in his grasp. Then the words of the woman arguing with her husband entered his mind, the one who at the last minute decided that she did not want to travel. *'This is an unlucky ship, and I want us to get off as soon as possible!'*

Had she somehow seen what was to come? If so why didn't she warn him?

"Mr Ismay!"

The voice brought him back to the present.

"Mr Ismay!"

"Mr Astor," said Ismay looking at Mr John Jacob J Astor, with his young scared looking bride Madeleine, slightly behind him.

"This is a bad business Ismay. I really don't understand how this can be happening."

"Nor me," said Ismay in all truthfulness.

"But abandoning ship? Is that really the only option we have?"

"I'm afraid that it is." He paused. "Mr Astor, there are limited lifeboats, I would advise that you hasten."

John stared at Ismay for a moment and then nodded, understanding the implication that with the order for women and children first, he was not likely to make it off of the ship.

"You there," called out Ismay to a steward who straightaway responded. "Now I want you to take Mr and Mrs Astor here to a lifeboat. Ensure that Mrs Astor is boarded and is comfortable."

The man nodded and proceeded to lead them away.

Ismay looked around, unsure what he should do next. He had been trying to rally round and help people. He had even tried to help in organising the boarding and lowering of one of the lifeboats, but despite his position, had been told firmly where to go by a crewman. His thoughts suddenly turned to his wife Julia, and his children, and he realised that he was not going to see them ever again, he would not even get to say goodbye. Then an idea struck him. He could send them a note. He would go to his stateroom and write a note to his wife. There were still lifeboats to be lowered, and after the note was complete he could give it to one of the crewmen with strict instructions it was to be passed on to her – he would be able to say goodbye after all!

Then from nowhere a man appeared, running and screaming, he ran straight into the White Star Owner. "Hey steady there!" said Ismay, gripping the man by the arms, mainly to prevent himself from being knocked over onto the deck.

"I saw him! I looked into his eyes!"

"What? Who's eyes?" said Ismay confused.

"The Mummy, I saw him!"

"The Mummy?"

"The Egyptian Mummy."

"What? There's no Mummy!" cried Ismay, thinking that the present situation of the sinking of the ship had unhinged the man's fragile mind.

"He's in the Lounge - covered from head to toe in bandages!"

"No, no!" replied Ismay, realising what had happened. "It's not a Mummy it's a man! There are some injured people in the hospital. I expect they were brought up to the Lounge. I heard someone say something along those lines was being planned. What you saw was an injured man, burnt from one of the furnaces."

The man grabbed Ismay and pulled himself closer so they were just inches apart. "Beware the curse of the Mummy, Ismay! It has doomed the ship and damned us all to hell! The wrath of the ancient gods is upon us!" With that the man broke free, ran straight to the side of the ship where he threw himself over the rail to his doom.

For a moment Ismay just stared at the empty spot where the man had thrown himself, then, despite the danger of the current situation he found himself turning and walking down the slope of the ship towards the First Class Lounge.

Inside there were still a number of people milling around, all first class passengers. Some were just sitting, waiting, while others were standing and talking about the night's events.

Then to one side he noticed on the floor, covered by a number of coats the outline of a figure, with some people standing over it.

"Move aside, let me have a look," said Ismay as he pushed his way through the crowd and knelt down. The figure had not been covered totally and Ismay could clearly see bandaged parts of the body protruding out; bandages which looked decades old. This was certainly not a fire victim from the hospital. Ismay took hold of the coat which was covering the upper body of the prostrated figure and pulled it back.

"What, in the name of all that is holy, is it?" he said, staring at the sight of the Mummy that was before him.

"No idea Sir," said one of the crewmen who had been assigned to the lounge and had come over. "Never seen anything like it before in my life."

"Who found it?"

"One of the stewards, when he was letting people into the lounge under orders; there are other people over there all unconscious." The crewman pointed over to the fireplace, but Ismay ignored him, his attention captured by the bandaged man in front of him. "My goodness! The head is almost severed."

"I know," said the crewman, "but there is no blood and it's still alive, look how the chest is moving."

Ismay looked down to see the gentle rise and fall of the chest before moving his hand and placed it on the creatures forehead, pausing, before then placing his thumb through a gap in the bandage on the right eye, his intention to lift the eye lid and look at the man directly.

"Oh Sir I would not do that!" said the crewman quickly.

"Why?"

"Someone just did it, and well, they went a bit funny."

Ismay remembered the ranting man who threw himself from the ship. "No, I must look!" And with that Ismay lifted the eyelid and looked into the Mummy's red eyes.

Instantly, he was gripped by a sudden fear, and a feeling that he was looking upon something ancient and even wrong. Suddenly images started to fill his mind.

The image of a stone Sarcophagus - a man in a fez talking – a man that (he?) appeared to be strangling – a bandaged hand running freely around a wooden floor – a view of the pyramids of Egypt - staring down at a man clinging to the rail of a balcony before falling to his death – someone firing a gun repeatedly at him(?) with no effect – a library filled with books – standing in a road with a car swerving to avoid him – a tall man with an Austro-Hungarian accent and a stunning English woman with long flowing hair – an old man with a swordstick – the man with the fez giving orders.

"Mr Ismay Sir!"

Ismay suddenly found himself being grabbed by the shoulders and pulled back, breaking the gaze from the Mummy.

"Mr Ismay, are you alright? Quick, get that thing covered over."

Straight away someone replaced the coat over the Mummy, hiding the creature's face.

"Mr Ismay are you alright?"

"I, I don't know," he replied. His heart was pounding and the images that he saw seemed to be burned on his mind as

334

well as fragments of others which randomly started to appear. "I need to get some air."

Ismay stood up and left the lounge, without a word. Out on the boat deck, almost overwhelmed by what he had seen, he slowly sat down on the sloping deck floor. He was confused, almost dazed. The images he had seen were through someone else's eyes, but at the same time seemed to be his own.

"Ahmed Hawass," said Ismay out loud. That was the man in the Fez he had seen in the visions. He had never met him, but at the same time had a feeling that he knew him. Then another name came to him, Otto Von Braun and another, Charles Montacute, again they were strange and yet familiar.

In the near distance Ismay's eyes seemed to settle on a single lifeboat. People were getting into it. Slowly he got to his feet and moved over to it. He looked around, there was no-one nearby.

Then calmly, with more images coming into his mind he moved towards the edge of the ship and stepped into the lifeboat where he took a seat without anyone raising an objection. A few moments later the order was given and the boat started to descend, although to Ismay the descent barely registered. He was trying to cope with the new images and memories that had invaded his head, as well as the fact that his ship, along with hundreds of people, were about to be lost.

CHAPTER 58

Slowly, very slowly, the Mummy became aware of voices coming from somewhere nearby.

"What is it?"

"I tell you it is a chap in costume!"

"You mean fancy dress?"

"Must be!"

"But I did not hear that there was a costume event!"

"Well I didn't hear that there was going to be an iceberg either!"

"Oh Gerald do be quiet!"

"Sorry dear!"

"Bet it's one of the crew dressed up for a jape!"

"That must be why it's wearing a coat and that natty hat!"

"Yes, but look at the head, it's hanging off"

"All part of the costume, easy enough to do. I bet it's a small chap. The head part must be a fake!"

"So why is it asleep?"

"Bet he's drunk, like those other people over by the fireplace!"

"Oh, put the coat back over its face! I don't want to look at it any more!"

"Gerald, look, its eyes, they are moving."

"By George, so they are!"

The Mummy opened its eyes and slowly rolled over to see a number of people standing over him peering down.

"Um, are you alright down there?"

Holding his head, which although still almost severed, was starting to heal and reattach itself, the Mummy sat himself up and then rose to his feet, the coats that had been used to cover him falling off. The small party that had gathered around him stood back unsure what to do.

"I say old chap, what's going on? Why are you in costume?"

The Mummy ignored him, surveying the scene around him. There were a number of people milling around wearing big padded jackets that the creature somehow registered were lifejackets. He also realised that the ship was now sloping downwards.

"Um, would you like me to get you a lifejacket?"

The Mummy turned to stare at the man who spoke.

"Um, it's just a precaution, we have been told to gather here, some sort of bother."

The Mummy looked round to see the slumped figures of the Von Brauns and the old man with the beard and the younger man who was always with him. Around them were other people trying to wake them. Then beyond them the dancing flames of the fire caught his eyes and he remembered the bracelet that was now in the hearth protected by the flames, the bracelet that he had tried to get for Jazmine.

Jazmine!

The Mummy reached out and grabbed the man who had spoken by the throat and lifted him, to the protests of the other people who were standing around.

"Jazmine! Jazmine! Where is she?"

"Never heard of her," said the man gasping for breath.

A White Star Crewman, seeing the incident, came running over. "Hey, what are you up to Sir?" But he was silenced as the Mummy punched out with his other hand, knocking him to the floor.

"Jazmine!" repeated the Mummy.

"I've never heard of her," choked the man, desperately grabbing at the Mummy's arm. "But the ship is in trouble, perhaps she has gone to a lifeboat?"

The Mummy let out a roar and swung the man around before hurling him to the floor. He then ran over to the fireplace, looking down into the dancing flames; realising that the bracelet was beyond him, he turned to leave. But then he noticed on one of the tables a large vase of flowers. He shot out a thread of bandage to the vase, and in a few moments the blue and white urn was in his hands. He tipped the contents into the fire before dropping the vase to the floor. There was a hiss as the flames were extinguished and he reached down and grabbed at the remains of the bracelet. Putting it into his jacket pocket he stormed towards the port side, and using a

337

tub chair as a makeshift launch pad, jumped through the window, landing on the deck to the surprise of the passengers who were milling about the ever increasingly sloping deck. The Mummy casually lifted its lolling head in place, back on his shoulders and pulled down the wide brim of his hat to try to hide his face, before turning and running towards the bow of the ship.

Pushing past the people who were now at the lifeboats he tried to make his way onto the navigation deck, aiming to climb down to the forward well deck when a large man wearing an officers jacket blocked his way. "I'm sorry Sir, but you cannot go down there!"

The Mummy grabbed the man by the jacket and lifted him into the air. "Must save Jazmine!"

The Officer looked down into the Mummy's glowing red eyes and suddenly realised that this was no mere passenger. Stunned by what he was seeing he simply asked where she was.

"Safe down in the cargo hold!" replied the Mummy.

The Officer shook his head and gulped. "It's all under water, has been for a while!"

"What!"

"I'm sorry!" said the Officer trying to gain composure. "It's all flooded; anyone down there will be dead by now!"

A feeling of despair and grief washed over the ancient creature; he had 'found' his lost bride after all this time only to have her cruelly taken away. With a wail of despair he dropped the man to the floor and turned towards the lifeboats. He knew instantly that he would not be able to board with the rest of the passengers, he needed another method to get off the ship, and then it came to him. His coffin like crate in the thawing room, made from solid wood, it would float and act as his own private skiff. Almost smiling at his own cleverness he turned and ran towards the stern of the ship.

About halfway up the ship, almost level with the third funnel the Mummy was greeted by a group of dogs on leads, practically pulling along a man behind them, who realising the ship's fate had decided to release them to give them a fighting chance. On seeing the sight of the Mummy in front, the man tried to stop, but the hounds pulled free and, barking and growling, headed straight towards the ancient creature, almost sensing evil which had to be stopped, while the man himself, unsure of the sight before him, decided to head in the opposite direction.

The Mummy looked upon the lead hound, a large grey brute, and for some reason, the words 'Irish Wolfhound' entered his head, although he had no idea where from as he had never seen such a creature before. The Mummy reached out with his left arm, and the hand detached and flew towards the throat of the wolfhound. But the dog, used to playing with flying objects merely jumped into the air, turned and sank his teeth into the flying limb, biting down hard, growling and snarling as he did so. The pain was excruciating, bringing the Mummy to its knees, allowing the rest of the pack to jump up at him and start their attack. Frantically, the Mummy tried to get them off by hitting and pulling at them, but the dogs just seemed to grip on tighter. One small dog tore at his pocket which ripped open, and then grabbing at the strange bit of metal that fell out, turned and ran.

The bracelet was gone!

The other dogs continued to grab at him. He looked down at the nearest dog, a small Jack Russell and breathed the wispy black breath onto it which would either kill it or render it unconscious. The effects were immediate and the little dog let go and fell to the deck. The other dogs sensing a new danger seemed to back off just enough for the Mummy to get to his feet. Even the Irish wolfhound seemed to hesitate in its attack, allowing the Mummy to recall his now mauled hand back to his wrist. One of the dogs, a terrier, seeing a chance, tried to lunge forward and made it to the Mummy's ankle where it grabbed hold with its teeth. Caught by surprise the Mummy took his eyes off the rest of the pack, turning his attention to dislodging this one dog, allowing the others to surge forward. With one sharp shake, the brave little terrier was dislodged, but realising he was about to be set on again the Mummy turned and ran up the nearby flight of steps which led to the square base, where a funnel was mounted. The dogs continued their pursuit, the wolfhound taking the lead.

With no other option open to him, the Mummy headed straight to the ladder which ran up the side of the yellow funnel. He started to climb as fast he was able, only stopping briefly to look down to see the large wolfhound, its two front paws on the base of the ladder as though he was going to attempt to climb, with the other dogs milling around him waiting. The Mummy continued to climb, only stopping when the ladder eventually finished. He looked down again, the dogs were still there but it did not matter, as he had a plan to escape them.

Lifting his left foot and hand off the ladder he turned outwards to face the second funnel now directly in front of him. Holding his left arm straight out he shot out a strand of bandage in order for it to attach itself, and use that as a means of escape. He would tie the bandage off and climb hand over hand across to the second funnel where he would descend and then double back past the dogs to the thawing room where his crate-boat awaited him. The strand of bandage flew across the gap, but fell slightly short. Instantly the Mummy recalled the material back to his arm ready to try again. With the wolfhound's barks getting louder he leant out even further to try again, but the second shot also fell short, and again he recalled the bandage. He pulled himself back in towards the ladder, ready to prepare himself for a third attempt. Then disaster struck, for his bandaged foot slipped off the rung of the ladder and his bitten and mauled right hand was unable to keep its grip. He slipped from the ladder and started to fall downwards, his body turning outward towards the second funnel as he descended. The Mummy screamed, fearing that he would be delivered straight into the jaws of the waiting dogs below, but his journey was short lived as the belt of his coat suddenly became snagged on something which brought him to a sudden stop, making his already damaged head jerk wildly, and almost caused it to sever completely. The Mummy, his back now against the ladder, tried first to struggle free, but was unable, so he tried to untie the belt, but his own body weight pulled it even tighter, making it impossible.

The Mummy looked down and let out a grim yell, realising that he was trapped and that there was not going to be anyone to help him.

CHAPTER 59

"Come on, wake up!"

Mallory's eyes flicked open and he slowly sat up. The Professor was standing over him shaking him awake.

"What happened?"

"We have serious problems!" said the Professor.

"Oh good," said Mallory trying to gather his senses. "Situation normal then."

"Oh no it's not!" replied the Professor. "Things are very un-normal and are about to get a lot worse."

"Why, what's going on?" said Mallory, suddenly realising that the previously deserted lounge was now full of people milling around, many of them wearing lifejackets.

341

"The ship is sinking. They have already started launching the lifeboats with women and children."

"But that's impossible," said Mallory getting up. "Are you sure?"

"Yes," replied the Professor. "From what I've gathered, that Iceberg we hit has gashed the hull open and we are going down."

"The Mummy," said Mallory suddenly. "I managed to grab it and pull it into its own trap. Where is it?"

"Gone," confirmed the Professor. "Seems that it woke up just before we did and escaped. Caused quite a stir, it was seen by a number of people, as they were put in here by the crew. They had no idea what to make of it. Anyway the creature woke and made off, but not before causing trouble." The Professor nodded over to a crewman who was nursing a broken arm. He then moved over to Otto who was doing his best to rouse a still unconscious Elisabeth.

"She's not waking!" he said urgently. "Help her!"

The Professor moved in closer to the sleeping Countess.

"So what happened?" asked Mallory. "I mean with the Mummy? I thought that we were goners."

"My best assessment is that with its head half severed the 'Breath of Death' lost its potency, so rather than being killed we were only knocked out, then while we were unconscious he used the opportunity to escape."

"The alloy!" said Mallory, as he quickly moved over to examine the fireplace.

"Oh you won't find it," called the Professor, as he gently patted the Countesses face. "I woke first, and checked; it's gone. See that discarded vase of flowers? The Mummy used it to dampen the flames and allowed him to get it."

Mallory cursed, and returned back to the Professor.

At this point Elisabeth started to wake up. "Otto, what's happening?"

342

The Count grabbed her and held her in his arms. "It's alright my dear, we survived. The ship is sinking and we need to get to a lifeboat." With that he helped the still dazed Elisabeth to her feet and started to move off.

"But wait," called Mallory, "what about Jazmine and the Mummy?"

"What about them?" replied Otto coldly. "The Mummy is doomed; he can hardly take a place in a lifeboat can he? As for Jazmine, well I am sorry but that is of no concern of ours. That is your problem. The ship is going down and it is every one for themselves!"

"Now you look here," said the Professor, "if it was not for your enchantment on my daughter, she could potentially be safe now! As for the Mummy, it is technically immortal. If it was to jump into the sea it would eventually wash up somewhere, alive and still capable of causing trouble!"

"Then I wish him all the luck in the world! As for Jazmine." He shrugged. "I'm sure that many people will end up dying this night. If you want my advice, get to a lifeboat and ensure that you are not one of them."

"Why you….," said Mallory, as he started forward towards Otto, his fist clenched, but the Professor held him back.

"That's enough Mr Mallory!"

Without warning, a steward appeared clutching a number of lifejackets in his arms. "Lifejackets! Could you put these on please?" He tried to sound calm, but there was a trace of fear in his voice. Otto grabbed one of the lifejackets and handed it to Elisabeth who immediately put it on, Otto followed her example. The steward turned to Mallory and the Professor.

"Perhaps later," growled the Professor, his eyes firmly fixed upon Otto who was struggling with the straps. The steward, seeing the look in the old man's face then decided to

343

beat a retreat, and started to head over to a small group of other passengers nearby.

"Alright," said Mallory, "we cannot appeal to your sense of dignity so how about your sense of greed?" He held up the black scarab.

"Mallory!" cried the Professor realising what was about to happen.

"The black scarab in exchange for Jazmine's location!"

Otto's eyes widened in delight at the sight of the scarab, realising that it could be his.

"Don't be a fool man," said the Professor. "That's our only chance to destroy the Mummy for certain, and there is no guarantee that they will give the correct location!"

"Sorry, but at this point we are running out of time and I'm happy to take the chance." He turned to the Von Brauns. "Come on Otto, where is Jazmine? This is going to be your last opportunity to get the scarab ever."

"Throw the scarab to me! I'll only tell you once it's in the air!"

The Professor made a reach to Mallory to stop him, but it was too late, the black scarab was airborne. Otto reached out and caught the scarab, pocketing his prize.

"Come on Otto," called Mallory, "where is she?"

But instead of revealing the location of Jazmine, he remained silent.

"Why you double crossing....!" cried Mallory, lunging forward grabbing the Count by his jacket.

"Well what did you expect?" replied Otto, repelling the attack with a violent shove, pushing Mallory back.

"You idiot," growled the Professor to Mallory. "I knew that he would not keep his part of the bargain!"

"However, fortunately for you I will!"

Everyone, including Otto, looked at Elisabeth in surprise. "Look Otto, it does make sense. The last thing we need is

344

those two buffoons trying to stop us escaping. I have a feeling it's going to be difficult enough as it is getting off the ship without any added difficulties." She turned to the Professor to direct him. "There is a cabin in C deck, that's where he will most likely hide her."

"The number?"

"C100," replied Elisabeth.

"Why?" asked the Professor suspiciously. "He could take her anywhere, why there?"

"Because when Otto was out and about with the Mummy on the first night, he was nearly spotted and had to use that cabin to hide in. The creature knows it's empty and a place where he is unlikely to be disturbed."

"It does make some kind of sense," said Mallory.

The Professor nodded in agreement. "Right, you can come with us, prove what you say is true."

"Oh no we won't," replied Otto firmly, "from now on you are on your own!"

"Oh I think that you will!" replied Mallory.

Elisabeth suddenly reached out to a passing crewman. "Oh please help!"

"What's wrong?"

"It's these two men, they are troubling us!"

The crewman looked at the Professor and Mallory with an air of suspicion.

"No, no!" said Mallory quickly, "It was our mistake. We thought that they were someone else. I'm sorry!"

The crewman looked back at the Von Brauns who smiled indicating that things were after all alright. Happy, he left them.

Elisabeth smiled. "There, I think that we have that sorted out don't we? All I have to do is grab a crewman, spin them a story and you two are in trouble!"

With that the Count looked over to Mallory and then to the Professor, bowed his head, and clicked his heels together. "Goodnight gentlemen, although I am sure with your resourcefulness and luck you will both survive, but should you perish, I would like you to know that it has been an absolute displeasure, and should you have a final resting place, I will seek it out, only so I can spit on it."

He and the Countess then turned and pushed their way through some of the other passengers milling about, and disappeared from sight.

The Professor turned to Mallory and pushed him hard in the chest in sheer frustration. "You damn fool of an idiot! Now we will never be able to destroy the Mummy. I could ring your ruddy…." The Professor stopped in mid threat as Mallory held up a small black scarab and gold chain which he had hidden in his hand.

"The scarab!" cried the Professor in surprise and relief.

Mallory nodded. "Having had my pocket picked so many times I thought I would put the experience to good use! I got it back when I attacked him."

"But giving away the scarab in the first place was a dangerous gamble, Mr Mallory!" said the Professor seriously. "It was only by the Countess's intervention we got the information, and you may not have been able to have gotten the scarab back from Otto so easily."

Mallory shrugged. "Sorry, but there was no other choice. The scarab was all we had to bargain with. What about the cabin where they said Jazmine might be being held?"

The Professor shrugged. "An empty cabin does sound plausible. I can't see the Mummy wanting to stash his new bride in a crate down in the cargo hold."

Mallory winced at the idea. "I'm sure that Jazmine would not put up with that!"

"Sadly," replied the Professor, "with the Mummy's strength and deranged mind, I don't think that the poor girl, with all her feistiness and strong will, would have any kind of a choice in the matter."

"Then we had better get to her as quickly as we can," replied Mallory with grim determination.

CHAPTER 60

Captain Smith returned to the bridge, after making a short patrol of the boat deck, ensuring the launching of the lifeboats was going smoothly. Standing alone, having ordered the remaining bridge crew to emergency stations, he was still trying to take in what was happening.

His ship, the mighty Titanic, was sinking!

"Edward, Edward!"

Smith turned round to see that Thomas Andrews had entered the wheelhouse via the back entrance.

"Come on, we need to get out of here," said Andrews with a sense of urgency in his voice.

Smith shook his head. "You of all people should know that it is traditional for the Captain to go down with the ship."

"Don't you think that there is going to be enough loss of life this night without deliberately adding to it?" asked Andrews.

"Oh, I'm all too aware of that," replied Smith, "which is why I am staying here. I'm not going to take up room in a lifeboat at the expense of someone else!"

Andrews paused. "Captain, you are still in charge and responsible for the safety of those on board. Your guidance and leadership is still needed! Soon there are going to be a number of lifeboats adrift in the Atlantic and you should be there to command."

"It is my so called leadership that has gotten us into this mess in the first place!" said Smith bluntly.

"On what grounds?" said Andrews. "You thought that the ship was in danger through the effects of the fire and were pushing hard to get to a safe port."

"And by doing so put us in the path of an Iceberg, through not taking full notice of the evidence in front of my eyes. There were enough warnings of ice."

"Warnings which were heeded and addressed with a course change."

Smith paused and shook his head. "Thomas, my mind is made up. I stay here, now please go, there is still time for you to go and save yourself, please do so."

"But Edward, people will need to know what happened!"

"Which is why you must survive! You know this ship better than anyone and you are fully aware of what has happened on this journey. You will be the best witness to stand at the enquiries that will follow, now go!" said Smith sternly.

Suddenly the door that Andrews had entered through again burst open, this time the figure was that of Sixth Officer James Moody, who paused for a moment realising that he had interrupted something, before quickly saluting. "Sorry to disturb you, sir, but there is a problem, and I have been sent for help and I cannot find anyone."

Smith smiled at the young officer. "This certainly is the night for problems, what is it?"

"It's the electrical elevator sir. It has become stuck between floors and people are trapped inside!"

"What!" cried Andrews in dismay. "People were actually using it, in our present circumstances?"

Moody shrugged. "Some of the first class passengers were going back to their rooms and did not want to walk."

"Where is it stuck?" asked Smith.

"Between decks C and D, Sir, but there was something else."

"Isn't there always?" said Andrews.

"There was a snapping and jolting sound from the shaft, we think that one of the cables has snapped."

"Go on Andrews," said Smith. "Go, you have no time to lose."

Realising that it was pointless to try and continue to try and persuade Smith to leave, Andrews nodded and left.

It did not take Andrews and Moody long at all to reach the scene that had been described by Moody on Deck C. First Officer Murdoch was already there, his coat and hat piled to one side and his shirtsleeves rolled up, trying to open the concertina gating door with the scared looking occupants peering up at him from the stuck lift.

"No luck at all with the door then Murdoch?" asked Andrews.

Murdoch shook his head. "No, it's that ruddy safety feature that was built in, it's impossible to open the doors when it's between floors."

"I wonder if we would be better moving down a floor?" asked Moody, thinking it would be easier to tackle the problem from below.

"It's exactly half way, I'm not sure if it would make any difference at all," replied Andrews.

Suddenly there was a cracking and straining sound and the lift jolted slightly.

"We need to act fast," said Andrews.

"Agreed. Someone fetch me an axe," ordered Murdoch, looking at the lift door.

"There is an emergency manual crank and winch at the top of the shaft," said Andrews. "I can use it to secure the cabin and move the lift upwards."

"Good," replied Murdoch. "See to it at once, but be careful; it is a dangerous thing that you are going to attempt."

Andrews nodded then headed off. Just after he disappeared Moody came up with an idea. "Mr Murdoch Sir, why not shoot the lock?"

Murdoch paused, not keen on the suggestion. "Dangerous, the ricocheting bullet could end up anywhere!"

Then from the shaft there came a strange noise and those trapped inside started to scream and panic. Realising that he would have to do something quickly Murdoch decided he would have to take the chance. Calling for calm, he went to his folded up coat and produced his revolver. Shouting to everyone to stand back, he raised the gun, then fired once into the lock which seemed to disintegrate as the bullet hit.

Murdoch moved forwards and tried to pull open the concertina door. It opened about nine inches before getting caught up for an unforeseen reason.

"Help me!" called Murdoch as he quickly discarded the gun, dropping it on his coat, before grabbing hold of the door and trying to pull it open. Moody and a sinister looking crewman appeared by his side and grabbed hold of the metal grating door. They started to pull, but with no luck. Try as they might they could not get the door open any wider.

"My ten year old son!" called a woman inside the trapped lift, "he's small. He could fit through."

"No madam I think that…."

But it was too late, seeing that at least one of them could escape, the boy was picked up by two men in the lift and raised up to the gap, where he started to try to squeeze through.

"Alright," said Murdoch seeing that it was too late to stop them. "Try to open the door a little more." Immediately Moody and the other crewman grabbed at the concertina door again and started to pull at it, trying to make the gap as wide

350

as possible to let the boy through. Despite the tightness of the opening, the combined efforts seemed to be working, as the boy's right arm, head and shoulders were through.

"Keep going," called Murdoch, taking hold of the boy he pulled as hard as he could. The effort was rewarded, as the young lad came free from the gap and landed in a heap on the deck floor. Seeing the success of the venture there was a jostling from those left inside the lift as a young woman was lifted up and propelled towards the gap in the door, hoping that she too could benefit from a similar rescue.

"Please ladies and gentlemen," called Murdoch. "You cannot all be rescued like that. Please move back from the door and remain calm! We are working on having the lift moved up as we speak, just wait a little longer."

But it was no good, one man, panicking, pulled the girl back inside the lift and practically jumped at the gap and got his arm and shoulder through before being dramatically pulled back by another passenger who tried to take his place.

"Move back and remain calm," called Moody in a loud firm voice. "Your movement is causing the lift to move!"

He was right, the jostling was causing extra strain in the remaining cables, then from above there was a creaking sound and the sudden pinging as strands of the lift cable started to peel off. This however caused the trapped occupants of the lift to panic even more and make further attempts to get out via the gap.

"We've got to get that door open, and open now," said Murdoch to Moody, who responded by grabbing hold of the door and pulling frantically at it with the other crewman.

Murdoch tried to look up the shaft to see if there was any sign of Thomas Andrews and the winch. "Mr Andrews are you alright up there?" He waited but there was no response. He was about to call again when the lift door suddenly moved open before again becoming stuck. The gap was now just

351

over a foot wide, just wide enough for a person to squeeze through. At the same time more strands of cable broke and the lift jolted downwards.

"Right!" yelled Murdoch quickly, before panic could take over. "You first!" He leant down and grabbed a young woman who he dragged up and out of the lift. Trying a different tack, Murdoch moved back to the door and leant into the gap, placed his hands on the frame while placing his shoulder on the edge of the door.

He pushed back with all his strength trying to free the door further, as below him, the passengers were pulled one by one to freedom through the now slightly larger opening.

"Come on quick!" called Murdoch; he looked back, four more to go. Then without warning Murdoch's efforts finally paid off and the doors sprang open totally, causing him to almost fall forward into the shaft, but he managed to regain his balance. He was about to shout the order for those inside to get out as quickly as possible when the remainder of the cables snapped and the lift started to plummet down the shaft to the screams of those inside. Still in the jaws of the lift door Murdoch was about to yell out in despair at what he had just seen, when something caught him across the face, it was the snaking train of one of the lift cables. The force of the impact caused the First Officer to tumble forward into the shaft, Moody tried to reach for him, but failed.

First Officer Murdoch was lost.

There was a moment of silence before somewhere above, in the shaft, a horrifying yell could be heard and seconds later the figure of a man fell past the open door, following the lift on its last journey.

"My God! That was Andrews," said Moody in stunned surprise, turning to look at the sinister looking crewman who had appeared to help. "Mr Murdoch and Mr Andrews are gone!"

The crewman stared at Moody for a moment before suddenly stooping down and picking up Murdoch's cap, coat and firearm before running down the corridor.

"Hey come back! What are you doing?" yelled Moody.

"Getting off the ship!" the man replied, putting Murdoch's coat on as he ran. "I'm not stupid. Officers always make it off okay and I intend to be one of them!"

Moody cursed the man, knowing in harsh reality this was not the case. Putting this fake 'Murdoch' out of his mind, he then turned his attention to those passengers from the lift, wondering if he had really just delayed their death rather than actually saving them.

CHAPTER 61

Otto ran hand in hand with Elisabeth along the sloping corridor which led to the main staircase, then downwards to B deck, where their cabin was located.

"What do we take?" said Elisabeth looking round the room.

"The essentials," replied Otto, as he moved over to the small safe, which after a few turns of the dial opened. "Whatever danger the ship is in we have to remember that we are servants of a greater good." He turned to Elisabeth and passed her a number of jewellery boxes containing the Countess's prized gems. "Get rid of the boxes. I'll deal with the documents."

Elisabeth did as she was told and placed the jewellery in her handbag while Otto sorted through papers that they had been provided with by Ahmed back in London regarding their missions. Happy he had them all, he moved to the metal waste bin and dropped them in, followed by a lighted match. The papers took instantly and blazed away. "There! All traces of our association with our masters gone!"

353

"We could have taken them with us and hidden them," pointed out Elisabeth.

"No, too risky," replied Otto shaking his head. "We cannot chance them falling into the wrong hands, it is best this way!"

"It's a shame that we are going to leave empty handed as it were," said Elisabeth referring to the outstanding items they had been requested to recover as well as the items they had already been thwarted in trying to recover.

"Yes, but at least some of what we intended has been achieved," replied Otto referring to the murders that the Mummy had carried out. "That will certainly go in our favour when we report back!"

"Otto, do you really think that the Mummy is doomed as you said? What if it does somehow manage to survive in its present state?"

"Do you really want to spend time trying to hunt it down now?"

"Of course not!"

"Then we have to go! Let the Professor and Mallory worry about that."

"And speaking of which, I wonder if they will pay our cabin a visit?"

"You mean in their search for the Mummy?"

Elisabeth nodded and at the same time reached for her small gun hidden in her purse, holding it up. "Just in case they do, I would like to leave them a little parting gift!"

Within minutes of setting the trap, Elisabeth and Otto appeared on the boat deck to a scene of chaos. There were people struggling with lifejackets, trying to get information from crewmen as to what was happening, as well as people wandering around trying to find loved ones from whom they had been separated.

"Otto, look at the angle of the ship!" said Elisabeth, in partial disbelief. The entire ship was dipping downwards so far, that people actually had to lean against the tilt to balance themselves.

"Come on we have no time to delay," said the Count as he quickly pulled Elisabeth over to the nearest lifeboat. Once there he managed to push her through the crowd to the edge of the ship while following behind. Amazingly the people around did not seem to object, some even stood to one side to let them pass.

"Women and children only," called out a crewman as he helped a young woman with long dark hair dressed in a long black velvet dress over the small gap between the ship and the lifeboat. Making sure she was alright and seated he then turned and held out his hand towards Elisabeth. "Come along Miss you're next."

Elisabeth paused. "Actually, it's Mrs." She looked over at Otto. "My husband?"

The crewman shook his head. "I'm sorry, we have got strict instructions. At the moment it's only the women and the children." He moved his hand to the woman standing next to Elisabeth and quickly helped her aboard before again holding his hand out to Elisabeth. "Come on, we are getting full here."

"Yes, go on Elisabeth," said Otto, "I need to make sure you're safe!"

"Quick, hurry," called out the woman in the velvet dress. "She moved over and tapped the seat to indicate there was room. Don't be scared."

"I'm not scared," replied Elisabeth, "I just don't want to leave without my husband!" With that she stood back and a small child was handed to the crewman, who realising that this woman was not going to be persuaded, called to someone else.

"You should have gone," said Otto almost angrily, but Elisabeth responded with a quick kiss.

"Not without you!"

Otto smiled, touched by the display of love and loyalty. He grabbed her hand and started to pull her back through the crowd. "Come on, I think that I have an idea."

Otto ran across the deck to the gymnasium, opened the door and went inside, with Elisabeth following. Surprisingly there were still a number of people inside being given demonstrations of the equipment. Ignoring them Otto ran over to the set of cupboards that were against the wall and opened them. One of the instructors saw what he was doing and immediately came over to challenge him "Um, excuse me Sir, what are you doing?"

Otto ignored him moving to the next cupboard, Elisabeth watched on in curiosity.

"Look Sir, I really must protest!"

"Got it!" replied the Count as he pulled out what he was searching for, a large white dust sheet which was sometimes used to cover the equipment.

"You can't take that!" protested the instructor.

Otto responded to the man with a look of stern fury which made him take a step back. "Alright, calm down. There is no need for that." There were more important things to be concerned about at the moment than a mad passenger wanting to have a dust cover. "If it you makes you happy just take it and go." He then turned and headed back to the other passengers.

Keeping tight hold of the white cover, Otto grabbed Elisabeth by the hand and led her out of the gymnasium into the first class entrance where he moved over to a corner away from prying eyes. Then from his waistcoat he took out his pocket knife, knelt down and set to work. In a few moments he had cut a large square from the dust cloth, then proceeded to fashion it into a sling. Quickly he took off his lifejacket, dropping it to the floor, before putting the sling over his

356

shoulder inserting his left arm. To increase the effect Otto lowered his left shoulder giving himself a crooked appearance.

"Oh, Otto darling," said Elisabeth with a twinkle in her eye. "You are deliciously wicked! You look terrible!" She moved forward and kissed him firmly on the lips before drawing back. "But let me make one thing totally clear. We leave this ship together or not at all. If this fails we find another way, but we leave together."

"Agreed," replied Otto. "Although I seriously doubt with the act that I am about to put on that any crewman would dare to turn me away!"

"So, which lifeboat?" asked Elisabeth. "We cannot go back to the one we just tried."

"Agreed," replied Otto, "we try the ones on the other side. Come on." So with that he started to move across the reception to the door on the opposite side.

Out on the port side there was a similar scene to that of the one they had left on the starboard side, with people milling about, trying to find loved ones while others were joining the increasing throng which were gathering around the remaining lifeboats.

"I don't fancy our chances here." Elisabeth looked at the crowd almost directly in front of them gathering at the lifeboats.

"Me neither," replied Otto. "Come on, we will have to try the stern."

So, fighting the tilt of the ship, Otto and Elisabeth, as fast as they were able, dodged around people heading to the stern and the four lifeboats that seemed to be their only chance off of the ship.

"Oh, my goodness!" cried Elisabeth, suddenly stopping and pointing. "Up there Otto, on the funnel!"

"Yes I see it!" he replied looking at their Mummy, still trapped and struggling to get free. "How on earth did he get himself stuck up there?"

"What shall we do?" asked Elisabeth wondering if they should try and somehow deal with the creature. But Otto shook his head and moved forward, Elisabeth following. Stopping to save the creature was the last thing that he intended to do. Although not as crowded as the lifeboats that they just left, there was still a large number of people gathering around them. Elisabeth slowly managed to weave her way towards the front of the crowd, Otto following as best he could, making a point of trying to mind his 'damaged' arm and even yelling out when someone accidentally stepped into him. People, realising that there was an injured man, actually started to step aside allowing him more room. Otto thanked them and prayed that the crewman allowing people into the lifeboats would be as sympathetic.

As a woman, clutching a baby no more than a few weeks old, was helped into the safety of the lifeboat, Elisabeth took her place at the front of the queue. From the boat a crewman reached out his hand to her and started to help her carefully into the lifeboat. Otto tried to follow but the crewman shook his head and held up his hand. "I'm sorry Sir, women and children only at the moment."

Otto tried to look shocked. "But damn it man look at me!" He motioned down to his arm resting in the sling. "I'm totally incapacitated, I can hardly lift my arm! My wife had to dress me for dinner this evening! I can't put a lifejacket on let alone swim if needs be!"

The crewman paused, unsure what to do and looked over at the White Star Officer, who was standing by keeping an eye on the growing throng. He returned an equally puzzled look, unsure if he should follow his orders to the letter.

358

"Please," pressed Elisabeth, sounding genuinely desperate, "he broke his shoulder some weeks ago, it's healing badly and he is in constant pain. We are going to America as there is a specialist in New York who says he may be able to help."

The crewman looked at Otto, then to Elisabeth's pleading eyes. "Alright," he said reaching out to help Otto. "Stand clear! We've got an injured man coming aboard."

Otto gave an inward sigh of relief, knowing full well that this was probably his only chance of getting off of the ship and reached out for the crewman with his 'good' arm and let himself be helped aboard, being careful to wince with pain as he moved his 'bad' arm too much. Safely in the boat Otto took his place next to Elisabeth, who, relieved that he was safe put her arms round him and held him.

Three more people were allowed into the craft before, much to the dismay of those still waiting, it was declared that no more people would be allowed in, even though there were a number of spaces left. Then the lifeboat slowly started to be lowered to the sea.

As the boat descended Elisabeth and Otto looked at each other and smiled, the ploy had worked, and they would both live.

CHAPTER 62

Despite the fact the watertight bulkhead doors had been activated as soon as the Titanic had hit the iceberg, dividing the lower part of the ship into sealed compartments, Chief Engineer Joseph Bell, via the escape ladders and hatches, was still able to move freely through the lower sections of the ship.

Many of the stokers and firemen, with permission, had already left their posts, to allow them to make it topside and hopefully find means of escape. Others had decided to ignore

359

this and had opted to stay, trying to help out where possible, in the vain hope that the ship could somehow be saved or at least somehow have its life extended.

Bell stood looking at the now silent reciprocating engines that powered the ship. The metal of the engine still looked bright and new, just as it had been when he had first seen them assembled in the Harland and Wolff workshop for testing, before being dismantled then rebuilt in the ship's skeleton.

With most of the furnaces that fuelled the boilers under water and, of course, extinguished, the massive engines had fallen into total silence. The remaining furnaces were unable to keep the engines even on standby power, not that it mattered mused Bell sadly, as the next trip the ship would be taking would be straight down. What did matter however was the fact that the smaller turbine engines were still functioning, thus still keeping the electrics aboard the ship working.

"Sir, Sir!"

Bell turned and recognised the man now beside him as the trimmer Joseph Dawson, who, recovered from the coal slide in Queenstown, had returned to duty.

"Dawson."

"I was sent to find you, you are needed."

"Where?"

"The electrical switchboard platform on the Orlop. There is a problem!"

"You're injured," said Bell as he noticed for the first time Dawson's arm, the clothing was torn and burnt with a big red patch on his skin. "What happened?"

"Some burning coals fell out of one of the furnaces. The furnace door was not closed properly. With the tipping of the ship a load fell out and started a fire."

"Anyone else hurt?"

Dawson nodded. "A few of us; Leading Fireman Keegan took the brunt of it, he rushed forward to close the door as the coals were spilling out – he's in a bad way, some of the lads have taken him up to the hospital."

Bell nodded, although he knew that in all likelihood there would be little that could be done. "Alright lad, you've done well. Better try and get topside and try to find yourself a lifeboat."

Dawson nodded and turned and headed off towards the bow and the escape ladder that would allow him access to the upper decks. Bell paused for a moment, trying to take in one last look of the mighty engines, when he was distracted by hideous screams. Quickly he made his way towards it, negotiating his way through the extended route via the bulkhead until he found himself in sealed compartment number ten which housed five furnaces.

Bell looked around, expecting to see a man or men in trouble, horrendously injured, but the area seemed clear. Then the lights flickered off and then on again. Remembering his presence was needed at the switchboard he started to leave, when the screams came again.

This time it registered with Bell straight away – it was the mummified cat which the old Professor and the Guarantee group had trapped.

The screams came again and Bell moved towards the redundant furnace staring at it for a moment. Screams? Bell thought that was impossible, there had only been one creature caught in there, or so he had been told. He moved the 'Out of use' sign off of the door, then paused. Should he open it? He recalled the account of what he had been told regarding its capture and the viciousness of the creature, but did it really deserve to be left here, trapped in the furnace until it filled up with water and it drowned?

Again a number of screams came from within.

Making a decision, Bell moved forward, took hold of the door handle and opened the door, stepping back quickly expecting the creature to jump out, but nothing happened. Instead a number of cries came from the furnace and Bell warily peered inside, gasping at what he saw.

On the furnace floor were three kittens: one tabby, one black and white and the other ginger. Beside them, the mother, the mummified cat lying motionless on its side, now truly dead, with a hole in its belly where its offspring had appeared from.

One by one Bell lifted the now purring kittens out of the furnace and placed them on the floor. Each instantly ran off, sensing that although free from being trapped, there was a far greater danger present.

Again the lights flickered, bringing Bell back to reality. So leaving the kittens to their fate he started to work his way towards the orlop deck and the Titanic's electrical switchboard.

The scene that greeted Bell as he finally moved into the narrow switchboard room was one of chaos. Two men whom Bell instantly recognised as Frost and Campbell of the Guarantee group were lying on the floor. Campbell was dead while Frost gasping, barely alive, was being made comfortable by young Parkes. Two other Guarantors, both electricians by trade, Watson and Parr were frantically working alongside one of the Titanic's regular electricians, Alfred Allsop, trying to keep the ship's failing electrics alive.

Bell moved to Parkes. "What happened?"

"When the ship hit, we, that is the Guarantee group, came down to see if we could help," he replied, visibly scared, but trying to keep his voice steady. "We ended up here, but there was some kind of surge and Frost and Campbell here got hit. Mr Chisholm has gone for help."

"Never mind that!" called Allsop. "It's help I need here and fast!"

"Coming," said Bell as he stood and went over to Allsop.

In front of him was a large wall covered with electrical switches and gauges. This was the main switchboard from which all the electrics aboard the Titanic could be controlled. Bell marvelled at the fact that it was still functioning, and looking at the gauges they still seemed to be operating, most of which within acceptable parameters.

"I'm trying to shut down non essential circuits to stop the power from surging," said Allsop, "but I'm getting feedback! She was not designed to work under these circumstances!"

"Quite," agreed Bell.

"It's a losing battle!" responded Allsop. "I don't think that I can keep her going for much longer! But if we can cut some of the main electrical flow and pass it through the auxiliary, it should keep stable, under its own power for another twenty, to twenty five minutes. After that there is no more that we can do, but get the hell out of here!"

"What do you want me to do?" asked Bell.

"I'm going to turn off some more of the power switches, mirror what I do on the opposite panel there, but watch out she has a kick to her does this one!" He paused, looking back briefly at Parkes before returning to the matter in hand. "Right, Mr Watson, how is it going?"

Watson looked up. He had a section of panel open and was working with the wires. "Alright Sir, nearly finished!"

"Good. Now then everyone, this could be very dangerous! If anything goes wrong, and you will know if that happens, that big red switch will change whatever power is left to the auxiliary, if anyone is left alive, it must be thrown! Right, let's go!"

Allsop then proceeded to move around the switchboard, throwing various switches. Bell watching him keenly, copied, turning off the corresponding ones on the panel he had been asked to man. Every so often, one of the switches would throw out a small spark, making them jump back momentarily before continuing.

"Nearly ready!" cried Allsop, getting excited. "This is gonna work!" Then just as he was about to warn the others to stand back, disaster struck. From the far left section there was a loud bang and a small fire seemed to erupt from the panel.

"I've got it!" cried the young Parkes, jumping up from his injured colleague, grabbing his discarded coat.

"No lad, don't do it!" cried Allsop, but it was too late.

Parkes had reached up with the coat to try and smother the fire, but as soon as he touched the flames he was consumed by an electrical surge, dead before his body hit the floor.

"Look!" cried Allsop, "it's sparking!"

"Shut it down!" cried Bell, looking at the panels, all of which now discharged tiny forks of electrical power. "Shut it down! Cut the power."

"No!" cried Allsop. "The auxiliary, the auxiliary" He moved to the switch, but as he did so the panel seemed to explode, sending out massive electrical bolts into the small room.

Screams filled the air, which were suddenly cut short.

Allsop died instantly, as did Watson and Parr. Bell fell to the floor, a bolt had passed right by him and had hit the already injured Frost. However, despite not having direct contact with the electrical charge, the damage was done. Lying on the floor Bell tried to move, but could not, he felt strange, totally drained and giddy; his entire body seemed to tingle with the electrical charge. He tried to call out, but his words came out slurred and barely more than a whisper.

His eyes looked up at the switchboard, focusing on the auxiliary switch that Allsop had pointed out earlier. It was upright, in the 'OFF' position.

Bell tried to move again, feeling was coming back into his limbs, but it was limited. Then he noticed that the needles on the dials were rapidly moving upwards into the red 'DANGER' sections. If he did not pull the switch soon the electrics would fail totally and Titanic would be plunged into darkness, causing chaos and hampering those trying to escape.

With a superhuman effort he managed to roll onto his side. Slowly he started to somehow pull himself across the short distance to the auxiliary switch which mercifully was not too high up the switchboard. Straining every muscle in his body he pulled himself up onto his knees and started to reach his hand upwards, ignoring the still sparking panel. His fingers touched the lever and with a renewed strength he grabbed it firmly and pulled it down, Bell collapsing to the floor as he did so.

Instantly the sparking stopped, and there was a steady humming noise as the backup power took hold. The last thing that Joseph Bell, the Chief Engineer of Titanic, saw as he slumped back to the floor was the many needles on the gauges and dials returning to normal.

CHAPTER 63

Richard Mallory stood silent, as Professor Charles Montacute finished his rant. As an Ex-Captain of the British army, Mallory was used to hearing explosive, expletive outbursts, but the scholar seemed to elevate it to a whole new level. "Oh that blasted Otto and his evil witch of a wife!" finished the Professor looking round the empty cabin which the Von Brauns had said that Jazmine was being held captive in.

"Look Professor, we took a gamble and it did not pay off. What we need to do now is find where Jazmine is and stop the Mummy."

"Wrong order, Mr Mallory," said the Professor turning and moving past, back into the corridor.

"I'm sorry?" replied Mallory slightly confused.

"We have been going about this all wrong. We have been focusing on finding Jazmine first, through the von Brauns. Well the reality is there is only one person on board this ship who knows where she is."

"The Mummy!"

"Exactly Mr Mallory, the Mummy. We find him. That is our direct route to finding her."

"Blast it! Why on earth didn't we think of that before?"

"Because, Mr Mallory, we are both complete idiots, that's why!"

Mallory chose to ignore the remark. "So where do we find the Mummy, back to the cargo holds?"

The Professor paused, "No, we go to the Von Brauns' cabin."

"You think that the Mummy could have gone there?"

"Possible," replied the Professor, "but I think that it's much more likely that we will find ourselves a decent clue as to where the creature actually is."

It did not take long for them to reach the Von Brauns' cabin. "Right then Mr Mallory, we have got to be quick, the rate the ship is tilting I really think that we do not have much time!" With that he grabbed and turned the cabin's door handle, pushing it open – and in the process sprung the Von Brauns' booby trap.

A shot rang out and the Professor screamed as he fell forward into the room, Mallory following.

"Professor! Professor!" cried Mallory and he went to the floor to see if the old man was alright. The first thing that he saw was blood.

"Damn it! It was a trap!" growled the Professor through gritted teeth as he rolled over clutching his right arm above the elbow.

"How bad is it?"

The Professor took a look at the wound. "Well, being shot is never good! As far as this one goes I think I got off lightly! Quick, help me into the chair, and dismantle that ruddy trap."

Mallory carefully helped the Professor to his feet, then into a wicker tub chair before quickly dismantling the crude trap which consisted of thread tied between the door and the carefully positioned gun. Once this was done he moved back over to the Professor. "Well?" he asked looking at the wound.

"The bullet grazed my arm. Hurts like hell but I should be alright, no real damage done. Thank god it was only that pea shooter of a pistol. I'm going to have to bind it up though. Can you find me something? Also check in the bathroom, I'm hoping that there are some pain killers."

Mallory did as he was told. As the Professor hoped, there were pain killers left behind and as for something to bind the wound, the most suitable thing available was one of Elisabeth's cotton petticoats which Mallory tore into strips and passed to the Professor who insisted on tending to the wound himself. "Right Mr Mallory. While I am doing this, you take a look around to try and see if there any clues as to where the Mummy has been stashed."

"So what am I looking for exactly?"

"No idea!" said the Professor as he started to wrap the wound.

Mallory shook his head. He doubted he would find anything, especially after noticing the burnt papers in the waste bin. He was afraid that this was a fool's errand that would just waste time that he did not have. As if to emphasise this, items on the table and mantle shelf started to slide as the ship's tilt got steeper. Despite this he made the search, not worrying about being too tidy in the process. "How are you getting along, Professor?" he called as he rifled through the papers on the desk.

"Almost done, I just need to tie the end off and I'll be with you. Oh, be sure to check the underside of the drawers, I've known the Von Brauns to hide things there before."

Mallory moved back to a chest of drawers and pulled one out, totally turning it over.

"Stand where you are!" shouted a voice.

Mallory and the Professor turned round to see a White Star Officer standing in the doorway, a pistol in hand pointing into the room. "What are you doing?"

"This is not what you think," said Mallory quickly realising that with the state of the room and the frantic search the Officer probably thought that they were looters, breaking into cabins, taking whatever they could before trying to make their escape.

"Oh, don't you tell me what to think!" replied the Officer sternly. "I know exactly what I am seeing here!"

"Good!" replied the Professor quickly. "Don't let the blaggard get away with this!"

The Officer looked over at the wounded Professor sitting in the chair. "Is this your cabin Sir?"

"Of course it's my cabin! Mine and my wife's," he added, noting the Officer looking at the discarded dress which, of course, belonged to Elisabeth. "We were on deck waiting for a place in the lifeboats but I was getting cold so nipped back down to get a sweater when this fiend jumped me and shot me!"

The Officer looked over at Mallory. "Right that's it, hands in the air."

"But look, you don't understand!"

The Officer responded by pulling back the hammer on the pistol which clicked into place. "Hands on the back of your head, you are coming with me."

"Where?" replied Mallory, taking a look over to the Professor who was eyeing the Officer.

The Officer paused slightly, unsure himself as to what the best course of action should be. "Just keep your hands up." He moved into the room and quickly positioned himself behind Mallory, he looked over to the Professor. "Are you alright?"

"Oh yes fine," he replied. "What are you going to do with him?"

"Um," said the Officer, still undecided.

"I'm sure that there must be senior staff still on the bridge," said the Professor helpfully. "I'm sure that they will know what to do."

"Yes, yes of course," said the Officer, "well sir, you had better get yourself back to the lifeboats. I'm sure your wife must be getting worried."

"Oh, I'm coming with you," replied the Professor rising from his chair, "I want to see what happens to the cad and besides I may be needed to give a statement."

The Officer nodded. "Right, move slowly, keep your hands up and remember one false move and I shoot!"

So the three of them left the cabin and slowly started heading towards the bow of the ship, Mallory in front with the Officer directly behind and the Professor bringing up the rear.

"You are making a big mistake," said Mallory. "I was not looting."

"Don't listen to the fiend," said the Professor, drawing level with the Officer. "He is a cad and a bounder, with *unnatural tendencies*. After he shot me he insisted I tell him where my wife kept her *used* undergarments so he could take them for himself!"

The last statement made the Officer turn to look at the Professor in surprise. It was the reaction that the wily old man had wanted. He threw himself at the Officer knocking him into the wall. This was followed up by a punch to the jaw. "Run Mallory!"

Mallory needed no encouragement and he, followed by the Professor, ran as fast as they could down the corridor until they eventually found themselves in the first class entrance. Pausing near the main staircase they turned round to confirm that the Officer was not following them.

"Well thank you very much Professor," said Mallory angrily, "*'unnatural tendencies' 'used undergarments'* the man thinks I am some sort of deviant!"

"Oh Mr Mallory," said the Professor trying to keep a straight face. "I just said the first thing that came into my head to distract him, or would you rather be marched up to the bridge and branded a thief?"

"Out of the two, quite frankly, yes!"

The Professor's mantle slipped, and he broke out into a grin. "Oh cheer up Mallory! It's not the end of the world! That happens in 2012!"

"What?"

"2012. That's when the Mayan calendar ends and the world is supposed to finish along with it."

"Are you serious?" replied Mallory, forgetting the undergarment incident.

The Professor shrugged. "Who knows? But we have more pressing matters to worry about."

Suddenly from overhead there was a gun shot. The Professor and Mallory instinctively ducked before looking up expecting to see the Von Brauns or even the Mummy itself. Instead they saw a dark haired man in a dinner suit leaning over the banister rail, gun in hand. His targets were apparently a young woman with flame red hair in a low cut beige dress underneath a long dark green man's coat, hand in hand with a young man in a granddad shirt and brown trousers, who were running for cover. For a moment Mallory thought the running man had the remains of hand cuffs around his wrists.

"Come on Mallory," said the Professor as he placed his hand on Mallory's shoulder, "I'm afraid that there is not time to worry about what is going on there. We have a Mummy to find!"

"So what is the plan of action?"

"I'm presuming that you found nothing that could help in your search of the cabin?"

Mallory shook his head. "There may be something, but I doubt that we can go back to check."

"Agreed," replied the Professor, "and time is running out, I think that we need to get to the boat deck and make a visual sweep, and hope that we get lucky."

It did not take them long to make their way to the boat deck which was sloping heavily towards the bow.

"This is very strange," commented Mallory, looking upwards towards the elevated stern.

"I don't think the ship has got long at all Mr Mallory," said the Professor worriedly. "If we don't find the Mummy soon I think it's going to be too late."

But Mallory ignored him, staring towards the stern.

"Mr Mallory! Are you alright?"

"Yes, sorry what were you saying?"

"I said we need to find the Mummy soon."

371

"Um, he's over there," said Mallory calmly.

"What?"

Mallory pointed up towards the third funnel and there, hung up on the ladder was the struggling figure of the Mummy.

CHAPTER 64

"Oh bloody, bloody hell!" cried Jack Phillips.

"What is it?" asked Harold Bride as he tapped away, sending out the distress signal again.

"This," said Phillips as he held up a piece of paper from the pile that he had been looking through. "It was an incoming message, warning about ice. I don't think it went up to the Bridge!" He looked down at another message that he was holding, taken at the same time, but hurriedly written down on a plain sheet of writing paper. The message had been taken in this way as the Marconi telegram pad had just run out and the sheet of clean paper was closest to hand. It was for a Professor Charles Montacute, and like the ice warning, had never been passed on.

Bride paused before continuing to tap out the distress call. "I would not worry too much, other ice warnings were sent up to the Bridge, they did know about it!"

Phillips looked at the two messages, before screwing them up and throwing them aside, then placing the rest on the desk. "Yes, I guess that you are right. Here, let me take over."

The two men swapped positions and Phillips continued to send out the call for help while Bride stood on and watched eagerly.

"Mr Phillips, Mr Bride."

Both men turned to see Captain Smith standing in the doorway and instantly stood.

"How goes it men?"

Phillips shrugged. "The best we are looking at is help arriving in a couple of hours, everyone is too far away."

"Which ship?"

"Carpathia."

"What about the other ship, the California? You said that they were closer."

Phillips looked glum. "Sorry, no response. They must have their radio off or have forgotten to have charged it."

Smith nodded. "How is the new S.O.S. signal fairing?"

Phillips shrugged. "Difficult to say, I'm not totally sure if anyone receiving it are fully aware of what it is."

Smith paused, thinking. "Well gentlemen, I don't think that there is much more that can be done, you have exceeded what was expected of you. The ship will be lost shortly. Please, both consider yourselves relieved from duty with honour and my personal thanks."

"Let us stay a bit longer Sir," said Phillips. "At least let us send out one more message of our last known position."

"As you wish," said Smith nodding, "but then please go! Now if you will excuse me, I have to return to the Bridge." With that he turned and left them.

"He's going to go down with the ship," said Bride.

"Yes," said Phillips. "Come on, let's get this message out and then go, otherwise we will too! Wait! I think I'm losing the signal."

Bride moved to the electrical power switches and checked the gauges. "We're losing power, in fact, I think I can smell faint burning."

"It's a wonder that the electrics have lasted this long," commented Phillips frantically hitting away at the message key, "or that the signal mast has managed to stay up all this time; when that goes we've had it."

"I'm going to have to boost the power," commented Bride.

Phillips nodded. "Go ahead lad, we are on borrowed time anyway, might as well give it one last go."

Bride took hold of the power lever and turned it to full power, there was a sudden spark from the machine but it stayed on.

"Ah that's better," said Phillips, "go get the life jackets, I'll send out a couple more messages."

Bride did as he was asked, and by the time he returned to the Marconi room, Phillips was still at his post tapping away at the message key. "Nearly done," he said, looking up.

Bride placed one of the lifejackets down on the floor before taking the other and putting it over his head. As he did so, a man with a coal stained face and coal covered clothes came into the room. Seeing the lifejacket on the floor he moved forward towards it.

"Hey, what are you doing?" called Bride.

"Can't find a lifebelt, they are all gone," said the stoker scooping it up from the floor.

"Well you can't have that one," said Bride. "It's his." He pointed to Phillips who was watching while he continued to tap out the message.

"Sorry, it's mine now," said the stoker as he dropped it over his head and moved towards the door.

"Hey, you, give that back!" said Bride as he jumped in the man's way. The stoker paused for a moment before, without warning, unleashing a punch aimed at Bride's stomach. The wireless operator took the blow, and although automatically doubled over, the padding of the lifejacket cushioned most of the impact, stopping him from being winded. Bride responded by reaching out to push the man away but found his outstretched arm grabbed and was pushed down to the floor where the stoker kicked him hard. Again the lifejacket stopped the full force of the blow, but this time he found himself gasping for breath. The stoker then tried to step over

374

the body, heading towards the open door, but Bride had just enough left in him to grab onto the man's feet preventing him getting away.

"Oh no you don't!" cried the voice of Phillips, who had now abandoned the wireless set and joined the affray. Taking hold of the stoker he pulled him back into the room, turned him and threw him against the wall. The stoker came forward throwing a right hook, but Phillips was quicker, dodging the blow and planting his own fist firmly on the man's jaw, who then collapsed to the floor.

"Blimey!" said Bride coming over, "that was one heck of a punch!"

"Yeah, more to the fact that he had a glass jaw," replied Phillips as he bent down and took the lifejacket back.

"What are we going to do with him?" asked Bride, looking at the unconscious figure of the stoker.

"Not a lot we can do," said Phillips as he finished tying the life jacket's fastenings. "Come on, let's go!"

"But we can't just leave him there!" protested Bride.

Phillips looked at his friend sternly. "Do you want to pick him up and carry him?"

"No."

"Well come on then, there is not much time. We have to get going."

"He's going to die you know."

"So will we if we delay any longer!"

Bride paused for a moment, torn by the terrible decision that he was facing, before silently turning and moving towards the door, Phillips a few paces behind.

Outside on the port side boat deck Phillips and Bride got to see for the first time the full extent of the situation in which they found themselves. The bow of Titanic was totally submerged, with the water almost level with the top of the Bridge. Looking towards the stern they could see the back of the ship which was now raised into the air. About them there was frantic activity. On the roof of the Officer's quarters, directly by the first funnel, were a number of men struggling to free the small portside lifeboat. All around them there were people, most of them trying to work their way up towards the stern trying to escape the approaching water.

"Get me a bloody knife!" a gruff voice called out. It was a rough looking man standing by the small lifeboat, who was struggling with one of the thick ropes which held the craft in place.

"Come on, give me a leg up," said Phillips, looking towards the boat.

Realising what he meant, Bride moved to the side of the Officers' quarters and bending down slightly cupped his hands together and placed them outwards. Phillips used it as a step and quickly climbed onto the roof of the small structure and instantly leant back down to grab his friend and hauled him up beside him. Bride was about to thank his friend when from somewhere nearby a shot rang out and then another, followed by a scream and yet another shot.

Then from around the side of the funnel four men suddenly appeared, no doubt trying to escape what was going on from the other side of the ship.

"What's going on?" asked Bride to one of the men who was wearing a steward's uniform.

"Some Officer shot into the crowd before killing himself!"

"Who?" asked Phillips.

"By the coat I'd say Murdoch."

"Bloody hell!" exclaimed Bride.

"Oi, are you three up here to help or what?" called a broad Scottish voice.

"Yes," replied Phillips reaching into his pocket producing a large pocket knife, before opening it and moving towards the nearest guide rope which was holding the boat in place.

Bride and the steward produced their own knives before also moving in to help. Below them other men were trying to prop oars so the lifeboat could slide down onto the deck.

"Someone get the cover off!" cried a voice.

The young and athletic Bride responded by jumping directly onto the boat and proceeded to start to untie the holding ropes which held the protective covering in place. Another man jumped on to help him.

"Hurry up there!" shouted Phillips to Bride, "it's gonna go!"

Just as Bride and the other man finished removing the protective canvas, and had jumped clear back onto the roof, the boat started to move and tip over. From below there was a yell and the people on the deck scattered away as the lifeboat tipped, landing upside down with a crash on the deck. The craft had barely come to rest when the freezing sea water finally swept onto the deck, within moments the small boat was afloat and being moved towards the open sea, half guided by those around it and half pulled by a sudden wave.

From behind Phillips and Bride came an ominous creaking and straining sound, and threads attached to one of the lines attached to the first funnel started to fray and unravel. Then another line went altogether, causing the funnel to lurch forward.

"Come on!" called Phillips, "we've got to get off, and that lifeboat is our only chance!" With that he ran forward diving off of the roof, landing in the water where he started to swim among the other people towards the upturned boat, which by now had been pulled into the sea and was being swamped by people trying to grab hold of it and clamber aboard. With no other option Bride followed, launching himself into the air before landing in the freezing cold water. He started to swim straight for the lifeboat, not stopping until his hand was able to grab hold of the white wood.

377

CHAPTER 65

Mallory and the Professor raced along the ever rising deck until they were by the funnel. There, far above them, was the Mummy, struggling hard to get free but with no success. Below him was a group of dogs barking and growling up at the creature.

"Oh my goodness," said a voice from somewhere behind. "What, in the name of all that is holy, is that thing?"

"A resurrected Egyptian Mummy," replied Mallory, turning to see a startled White Star Crewman.

"A what?" replied the man, thinking that he had miss-heard.

"Hey, is that thing loaded?" asked Mallory looking at the object the crewman was holding.

The crewman lifted the flare slightly. "This? Yes, why?"

Mallory quickly reached for the gun and took it out of the man's hand. "I just need to borrow it for a moment."

"Hey, you can't!" protested the crewman, but it was too late, Mallory had adopted a shooting stance and was lining the Mummy up in his sights.

"Aim well," said the Professor realising what his friend had in mind.

"Don't worry, this is going to be an easy shot!" With that he gently squeezed the trigger, sending a flare streaking into the air towards the funnel, where it hit the Mummy who was instantly turned into a screaming ball of flame.

"Well done Mr Mallory," congratulated the Professor with a slap on the back. Mallory casually turned and passed the gun back to the startled crewman.

"Right then," said the Professor, his eyes fixed on the still blazing creature. "It's not going to be long before the flames burn through the coat and our ancient friend falls to the deck."

The old scholar drew his swordstick and discarded the sheath to one side, somehow knowing that it would never be needed again. "Come on!" he yelled, heading towards the funnel, "we need to be there ready for him."

Quickly he and Mallory moved onto the raised section of deck that the funnel stood on. As soon as they appeared, the waiting pack of dogs, sensing that their vigil was no longer required, dispersed. Mallory opted to stand to the left of the ladder while the Professor the right; the Mummy would fall straight down, so they would be able to make a joint attack from either side. Both found themselves leaning at an angle to compensate for the sloping deck.

"Get ready Mr Mallory," said the Professor calmly, his eyes fixed on the still burning and struggling Mummy above them. "Not long now."

Then as if in reply, the Mummy dropped slightly, the fabric holding him to the ladder almost totally burnt through.

"What's he up to?" asked Mallory noticing that the creature was suddenly behaving oddly.

"I'm not sure, it's almost as though he is trying to position himself to jump clear."

"Well he's not going to be able to do that," replied Mallory.

Then with a yell the Mummy, his body still ablaze, seemed to push himself clear of the ladder, to the starboard side of the ship, his arms outstretched and began to fall. It immediately became clear what the creature was intending. He was not trying to get clear, but rather use his body as a weapon, hoping to land on and crush one of his enemies below.

"Mallory!" yelled the Professor. But Mallory had already seen the falling danger, and without looking, dived, rolling forward to the right, straight into the Professor, knocking him over. Both slid down the sloping deck before coming to a halt.

The Mummy slammed into the floor with such force that it actually splintered, creating an indentation. Then, despite the fall, and the continuing flames, now fuelled by the creature's ancient flesh, he rose to his feet and headed to the starboard side of Titanic, jumping down from the raised section directly onto the boat deck.

"Get off me you blithering idiot!" yelled the Professor as he scrambled to his feet from under Mallory, and ran to the edge of the raised platform where in one leap he threw himself off, landing on top of the Mummy, causing it to fall.

By the time Mallory had gotten to his feet and had made his way down to the boat deck the Professor and the Mummy were squaring up to each other, both balancing to compensate for the ever tilting ship. The Professor, with his back towards the stern had the advantage, as he had still kept his sword, which he was now pointing to the flaming Mummy menacingly. The Mummy let out a hoarse roar and in response reached down to its thigh where it produced, hidden in its bandages, the short sword.

"Professor," cried Mallory from behind. "Look out, behind you!"

The Professor looked, just in time to see the figure of a man sliding down the deck towards them at speed. In one jump he leaped over the man and watched it continue on towards the Mummy, who at the last second was able to leap over the sliding body avoiding disaster. Landing back down onto the deck with a thud, the Mummy then lifted up his right hand which detached itself and flew out towards Mallory, but Mallory was faster and grabbed at the flying hand, catching it and then, keeping a firm hold, dropping to his knees and slamming it into the deck, over and over again. The Mummy itself screamed out in pain as its hand bore the brunt of Mallory's fury.

"The fingers!" cried the Professor, "break the fingers!"

Mallory responded to the instruction, ignoring the Mummy's cries and then suddenly the screaming stopped and the hand went limp. He looked round expecting to see the Mummy slumped on the deck, unconscious from the pain, but instead the Mummy just stood there.

"It's somehow managed to sever the link with the hand!" cried the Professor. "Blast, we have lost the advantage."

With that Mallory stood up and threw the lifeless hand over the side of the ship, where it was to be lost to the sea forever.

Meanwhile the Mummy had moved in for the attack, slashing with his short sword, while the Professor expertly parried blow after blow, trying to launch his own attack.

"The scarab!" yelled the Professor as he lunged at the Mummy pushing it back. "You must use the scarab! Get ready!"

Mallory watched the Mummy as it danced around the deck, the flames getting worse. He would have to act soon, otherwise the heat would make it impossible for him to get near. From his pocket he pulled out the scarab and waited for his chance.

With a yell the Professor lurched forward and plunged his sword. It went deep into the Mummy's flaming chest, before drawing the blade down slightly, then withdrawing it and jumping back. Mallory then dived forward, arm outstretched to the creature that had been the cause of so much trouble and death. Mallory winced with revulsion as his entire hand disappeared into the creature's chest, before withdrawing it without the scarab.

The power of the ancient artefact worked instantly, and as predicted. The Mummy stopped its frantic movement and first dropped the short sword, before the still burning body sank to the deck in an unconscious heap, defying the laws of gravity by staying put, rather than sliding down the deck.

381

"It worked!" cried Mallory in disbelief, as he was still checking his hand which remarkably had escaped from being burnt. "It actually worked!"

"Of course it worked, Mr Mallory," said the Professor coming to his side. "My research indicated that it was created by one of the most powerful priests of the time! Very well done, Mr Mallory, well done indeed." With that the Professor again slapped him on the back in congratulations, before looking back down at the blazing body. "Right, now we need to wait until the flames have died down so we can remove the scarab and wake him up again!"

"What?"

"Jazmine," replied the Professor.

Mallory cursed himself. In the excitement of the battle he had forgotten the primary reason for chasing the creature. It was not to destroy him, but to get him to reveal the location of Jazmine.

"Oh don't worry, Mr Mallory," said the Professor seeing the look on Mallory's face, "as soon as we have that information, back goes the scarab and we destroy this abomination for good!"

"It's not that, Professor, the ship, Jazmine, I think that it may already be too late."

"Don't you think I already know that!" hissed the Professor, his attitude changing in an instant, "but we have to at least try, there may still be hope!"

Then from nearby there came a flickering noise and a strange buzzing and all the electric lights along the ship suddenly blinked out.

"The electrics have failed," commented the Professor.

Mallory was about to reply, when from below there came a long ominous creaking. Looking down at the deck they could see small splits appearing in the wood, some of the boards around them started to slowly crack and spring up.

"Professor?"

"I think the ship's breaking," came the reply. "It cannot take the weight of the stern in the air and it's splitting apart. We need to get to the stern!"

"The Mummy?"

"Oh, he's coming with us, but you are going to have to be prepared to get yourself a bit singed." With that he moved to grab the Mummy's flaming arms. Mallory moved towards the creature's feet to do the same when there came another long whining sound and the area of the boat deck where they stood started to tear apart beneath them. Instinctively Mallory jumped back towards the elevated stern avoiding the hole which suddenly appeared, but for the Professor and the Mummy it was too late, both started to disappear into the growing rift. As he fell, the Professor somehow managed to reach up and grab a long deck board, still attached to the stern, which left him hanging in mid air over the void.

The break in the ship seemed momentarily to stop growing, allowing the Professor to look down to see the lifeless, still burning body of the Mummy, falling into the oblivion of the tangled mass of wood and metal far below.

He realised that the Titanic's Mummy was no more.

"Hold tight, I'm coming!" called Mallory, as seeing his chance, he started to move forward to try to save his friend, but the Professor turned and realising the futility of his position shouted to him to stop, causing Mallory to freeze in his tracks.

The Professor looked up at Mallory with a mixture of steely determination and anger at his own situation. "Run! Run you fool!" With that the deck board that he was holding broke, and Professor Charles Montacute, Historian, adventurer, traveller, swashbuckler, disappeared into the void after the Mummy which he had fought so hard to defeat.

383

Then there was a deep cracking sound and the ship and stern section suddenly seemed to accelerate on its journey backwards causing Mallory to dive to the side where he grabbed on to the twisted metal that was the lifeboat davit.

The stern of the Titanic smashed back into the water with a mighty crashing sound, causing Mallory to let go. With the remainder of the ship now horizontal, Mallory was on his feet and instinctively moved to what was now the very edge of Titanic.

CHAPTER 66

For a brief second Mallory stood transfixed, looking down at the mass of tangled metal that was below him. He could see that the ship had not totally broken in two, but the bow section was still attached. He was even able to make out some of the different floors of the ship, and more chillingly was able to see some people in the cross section, still alive and moving around. Then, the bow section slowly started to move away, sinking back into the Atlantic waters. The effect was instant, and Mallory felt the stern section slowly starting to tip upwards again, a direct result of the two broken sections still being joined. With no other option Mallory turned and started to run upwards, the angle increased quickly as he went; his goal, to reach the rail at the end of the upper boat deck and the relative, if only temporary, safety it would offer. A figure of a man tumbled towards him, and Mallory dodged around him straight into the path of another unfortunate passenger who had lost their grip and was sliding towards what was now the end of the ship. With no other option, Mallory jumped into the air and the man passed under him barely missing him. Mallory landed back down on the wooden deck continuing his battle upwards. Another two people fell past him, and as they did so his feet started to slip and he fell forward on the ever rising deck. His hands hit the now almost vertical deck, and rather than try to fight to stand up he pushed himself onwards in a frantic crawl. Looking upwards he realised that there was no hope of reaching the rail, as in a few moments the stern would be upright, impossible to climb, and he too would fall backwards. So, with no other option, he dived to the left, his arms wrapping themselves round one of the empty lifeboat davits. Using all his strength, he managed to pull himself up and stand up on the now horizontal davit.

For a few moments the stern of the Titanic hung totally upright in the air bobbing up and down. Mallory looked up to see people clinging onto the two electric cranes, the docking bridge, and beyond that the curved rail at the very end of the stern far above him. Then with an ominous creak, what remained of the stern started to fall back into the water, first slowly then gaining speed. Mallory looked down to see the sea rushing towards him and then back up to the top of the stern where people were clinging on in terror. Realising that there was nowhere to go he readied himself, then with only a few metres between him and the sea, took a deep breath and jumped as far as he could to try and put as much distance between himself and the sinking stern as possible.

Mallory hit the water, and his whole body convulsed with the sudden change of temperature, causing him to gasp, nearly taking in a mouthful of the freezing water. Fighting to keep afloat he suddenly became aware of bodies hitting the water, and the vast mass of the remainder of the stern thundering past him into the sea a few feet away. For a moment he feared that the force created by the sinking of the mass of metal would cause him to be sucked under, but his fears were unfounded, for a few moments later, the enormous stern disappeared from view, destined for the sea bed while he remained on the surface.

Then a strange eerie silence filled the air. Mallory looked around and a shiver went down his spine. Not through the freezing cold waters, but of the thought that the Titanic was gone, a ship that had been one of man's greatest achievements, which had promised so much, was no more. All that is left is a few lifeboats and numerous bits of shattered wreckage. All around him there were people floating in the water, bobbing up and down in lifejackets, some started to call for help. He knew that in these freezing waters they, and he, would not last long, and he must act soon if he was to survive.

Quickly Mallory started to swim over to a large piece of wood that was floating nearby, and fighting the numbness that was in his fingers, managed to climb on top of it. Looking around he saw that some other people had followed his example and had done the same with varying degrees of success. Reaching down he picked up a floating piece of debris that was drifting by, then looking around in the distance, no more than two hundred feet away, he could see the outline of one of the lifeboats. This was to be his salvation. Using the plank of wood as a makeshift oar, he started to paddle towards the nearest one. At first he made good progress, covering fifty feet without incident, but the people in the water on seeing the success of the makeshift raft started to paddle their way over to him and, very quickly, Mallory found himself surrounded.

"Help me!"

"Save me!"

"Let me climb aboard too!"

"There's no room!" called Mallory. The wreckage was barely supporting his weight let alone anyone else's. So, trying to shut out the cries for help he paddled on. Suddenly Mallory felt the oar being grabbed. He looked down into the face of a terrified young man. "For God's sake, let me on!"

Mallory tried to pull the oar free. "I can't, there is no room! There is still large amounts of wreckage about, you can still find some around."

But the man refused to release his grip, and Mallory was forced to violently pull the wood free before frantically trying to paddle away.

"My baby," cried a woman, desperately trying to hold a baby, no more than a few weeks old, up to him. Mallory nodded, realising that it would be possible to take it, and reached down for the infant. As he did so he felt the entire raft tip up, he looked round to see that a middle aged man had tried to use the opportunity to try and climb on from behind. Then before he could react, either by protesting or by getting a firm grip on the baby he felt himself being tipped off the wood, landing back in the icy water.

When he broke the surface he looked around, his first thought was for the baby and its mother, but neither was in sight. Then he became aware of a commotion nearby. The man who had tipped the raft was now clinging on to one side, while another two men in the water, who had grabbed his feet, were trying to pull him from the wreckage. Seeing possible salvation, other passengers were now trying to make their way over, but Mallory knew that this was futile, as ultimately no-one would be happy to let someone else take the raft and go to safety.

Mallory turned, realising that he would have to try and find some other way to freedom. Then in the distance he again spied the lifeboat he had been trying to make for. The oars were moving and he realised with horror that the craft was actually moving away; he guessed through fear of those in the water catching up with it and swamping them. Mallory cursed, he knew that he would not be able to catch them. Then looking around he spied the outline of another small craft, this one was upside down with people standing upon it. He realised that this would be his only hope of survival.

So, fighting the ever increasing cold, and trying to ignore the growing distance, he started to swim as hard as he could over to it.

His plan to travel in a straight line was soon thwarted, as wreckage and people, both those still clinging to life and the bodies of those who already had succumbed to the icy waters, drifted across his path. Carefully he picked his way through, trying to focus upon the upside down lifeboat, while trying to block out the cries for help of those around him. Then, dodging round the floating corpses of an elderly couple who were holding each other, disaster struck. In his lower left leg he felt a twinge of discomfort which then exploded into agony, as cramp took hold. He yelled out in pain, only managing to close his mouth in time as his head disappeared under the water. Kicking with his good leg and arms he fought his way to the surface, taking in a lung full of cold air before again disappearing below the waterline. He emerged from the salty water again, his leg still throbbing, made worse by his attempts to kick. Straight to his left was the floating corpse of a man in what looked like a bathrobe covered by a lifejacket. Reaching out for it Mallory managed to grab it and with no other option pulled the corpse closer until he was able to wrap both arms around it in a bear hug to stop himself from going under a third time. Mallory winced as he looked straight into the pale face of his saviour, the only consolation was that he did not recognise the poor man. The pain in his leg seemed to be subsiding, and was more bearable, but fearful it could return, Mallory kept trying to move and stretch it. "Come on Mallory," he said to rally himself, "you are doing fine." Then without any warning the eyes of the corpse sprang open and the man gasped in a long wheezy breath, "Help me!"

Mallory instantly let go and screamed out in shock, throwing himself backwards to escape the man. He flew backwards, his head hitting a large chunk of floating wreckage.

The last thing Richard Mallory saw before he blacked out and disappeared under the water, was the twisted face of the 'corpse' he had tried to use as a buoyancy aid. Its eyes wide open, almost smiling at him.

CHAPTER 67

The first thing that Richard Mallory became aware of was the feeling of his fingers trailing through icy cold water, followed by a view of the clear night sky littered with a mass of stars directly above. Then from somewhere a voice spoke, but he could not make out what was being said. He tried to reply, but could not, for under his chin was a hand.

Someone was saving him; and that someone had placed him on his back and was pulling him along by his chin. To aid the unknown rescuer he began to kick out with his legs to help propel them along.

The rescuer spoke, but as he did so the words were washed away, as the freezing water lapped over Mallory's ears. Mallory continued to kick and even tried to paddle as best he could with his arms. Again the voice spoke, but Mallory could not make out what was being said. In the background he became aware of more voices from somewhere nearby, then without warning the rescuer seemed to stop.

"Made it," said the voice. "We're at an upturned lifeboat. I'm going to let you go. Turn yourself around and grab hold of the side while I climb up. Then I'll help you aboard."

Mallory did as he was told, and a few moments later found himself holding onto a small overturned lifeboat, on top of which about fifteen souls had climbed. Others were either hanging onto the edge, or trying to pull themselves up. Then before he knew it, he found himself being lifted out of the water by the mysterious man who was now on top of the capsized craft.

"Glad you could make it Mr Mallory!" said the man, an almost cheerful voice. "I thought that you were a goner when I saw you go under, luckily I was able to get to you! Now don't try and stand, this thing is not stable!"

"Professor Montacute!" cried Mallory trying not to slip back into the water. "You're alive! When I saw you disappear I though that was it."

"You were not the only one!" replied the Professor solemnly.

"What happened?"

"I think I ended up in some air vent, and the pressure of the escaping air blasted me to the surface. Then I started to swim for the nearest lifeboat, even if it did happen to be upside down. That was when I saw you flapping about and came over. What happened to you?"

"Tried to climb up to the stern, but realised that there was nowhere to go so got off! Um, so what of our friend, um you know….?" He left the question hanging, not wanting to say the words because of those around him.

The Professor smiled realising that he was referring to The Mummy. "We have seen the last of him, of that I am certain. There is no way that he would be able to survive after the way he was dealt with!"

Mallory paused. "A shame about the scarab though."

The Professor nodded. "A shame indeed, but a necessary sacrifice."

"I wonder if…"

Mallory's words were disturbed by a commotion coming from the other side of the overturned lifeboat. Looking around Mallory could see men clinging to the side and trying

390

to board, causing the boat to dip in the water, while others on the boat were trying to push them away with oars.

"Go away!" cried one man with an oar, trying to dislodge the man who was frantically trying to gain purchase. "There is no room!"

"Let us on!" cried another man trying to climb up by grabbing onto the leg of one man on the boat, who kicked him away.

"No, there are too many of us here already."

"You'll sink us," said another man frantically. "Can't you see that? You'll kill us all!"

"Please! I'm light," called up one man in the water.

"No! Go away!" The man with the oar jabbed out hard, hitting one of the men on the side of the head, who disappeared under the water for a moment before bobbing back up.

"Come near again and I'll do it again, only harder," said the oar brandishing man. "Go and find your own piece of wreckage! Now bugger off!"

With that, the man and some others who were approaching, realising that they were not going to be helped, turned and started to swim away, swearing and cursing as they left, as they knew they had most likely been condemned to death.

"Was that really necessary?" asked the Professor, breaking the sudden silence. "I'm sure that some sort of compromise could have been reached."

"Yes," echoed Mallory, who was now standing up, "surely something could have been done"

"No, actually it could not," said a man in a White Star Officer's uniform sternly. "This boat is barely supporting our weight, any more and it would sink and we would all be doomed."

"And who are you to say that?" called out a man further down the boat, who was clearly disturbed by what he had just seen.

"Second Officer Charles Lightoller," was the reply.

"Second officer of what?" responded the man. "In case you had not noticed you don't have a ship any more!"

Lightoller's eyes narrowed. "Titanic may be gone, but as far as I know I am the most senior of the Bridge crew still alive, and therefore in charge!"

"Explain that to the men who you just killed!"

Lightoller was just about to reply when the lifeboat suddenly tipped downwards.

"It's sinking!" yelled someone.

"Spread out!" called Lightoller. "Quickly move round, and spread out."

Everyone did as they were instructed, and the upturned boat seemed to level out and although lower in the water than it had been seemed to remain stable, not sinking any further.

"Look!" came a sudden cry, "over there in the water! Is that Smith? It is! It's Captain Smith!"

People turned to look at where the man was pointing. In the distance was a man in his fifties with a neatly trimmed white beard, and seemingly wearing a black jacket. The man who had been coming towards them stopped, treading water on the spot before turning and swimming away.

"Captain Smith!" called Lightoller. "Captain." But the man was gone, disappearing into the waves.

"Was it him?"

"I don't know," replied Lightoller, "whoever it was they must have realised that we could not take them, and decided to swim away!"

"Sir!" called a voice, "another one dead."

"Alright Bride," said Lightoller to the young wireless operator, "push him off and move up. How are you doing Mr Phillips?"

Mr Phillips, the other wireless operator looked up and nodded, but it was clear that he was in a bad way.

"This is intolerable!" said the Professor, suddenly looking around at the bobbing shapes of the lifeboats around them. "The other boats can see us, why don't they come and help?"

"Some of the boats are half empty," said someone.

"I saw a boat being lowered with just a handful of people in it," said another.

"Well I saw a load of men climbing aboard another, so much for women and children first!"

"Mr Lightoller, Sir."

"Yes Bride."

"I think Mr Phillips has gone, Sir."

Lightoller turned to look at the figure of Mr Phillips, who had turned a deathly shade of white.

"Give him a shake lad."

Bride took hold of Phillips's arm and shook it. Phillips did not respond. Bride shook him again only harder, then harder still.

"I'm sorry lad," said Lightoller solemnly.

Bride nodded his head and quickly wiped a tear from his eye.

"Harold," said Lightoller softly, "I'm afraid that we need to let him go. The lighter we are the more chance we stand."

Bride nodded, and with the help of two others the body of Phillips was carefully and respectfully lowered into the water, where it was taken by the waves. Shortly afterwards two other men died, and again they too were placed into the sea, the loss of their weight actually seemed to make a considerable difference to the stability of the boat, and even allowed some of the men who were standing, room to sit

393

down. Mallory suggested that with the extra room a call was given in the hope that someone else could be pulled aboard, but looking around it was clear that there was no-one who would benefit from this. All those in the water that could be seen had already passed away and were just floating corpses at the mercy of the sea.

Exhausted and shocked by what they had gone through, silence took hold of those on the craft, the only thing that could be heard was the sea lapping against the boat as each tried to make sense of what had happened, with private thoughts turning to those who had been lost.

After what seemed an age and the realisation that they probably would not survive, someone suggested that they should pray. After a short discussion it was decided that they would say the Lord's pray. Lightoller stood, and trying to keep his voice from wavering led.

"......For thine is the kingdom, the power and the glory...."

"Look!" interrupted Bride, "over there, in the distance. It's coming this way!" Everyone turned, fearing that there was some new danger approaching, but instead, it was the shape of two of Titanic's lifeboats, drawing closer.

Slowly the two craft approached, coming nearer and nearer, eventually drawing alongside, so those atop the upturned boat could climb aboard to safety.

Mallory and the Professor were among the last to leave, helped aboard by a huge man in a White Star uniform who reached across and practically lifted them into his boat.

Now both safe, they took a seat, and dry coats were produced and given to them which they accepted gratefully, pulling them tight around themselves to try and keep warm. As they were doing this they both suddenly became aware of two sets of eyes staring at them intently.

On the seat, directly in front of them, were Otto and Elisabeth Von Braun.

CHAPTER 68

A strange morbid silence filled the air as the lifeboat bobbed up and down in the sea, only interrupted by the faint sound of sobbing.

Mallory looked around at the other lifeboats nearby. "How many do you think?" he asked.

"You mean saved?"

Mallory nodded.

The Professor shrugged. "I would not like to say, but judging by the boats I would say it will be a few hundred."

"My god," said the woman to Mallory's right, joining in the conversation, "but there were thousands of people on board!"

The Professor nodded, he did not know the exact figures and did not want to work them out either.

"There just were not enough lifeboats," said someone.

"And those that were launched didn't come back for those left in the water or clinging to wreckage," said a bitter voice. "Many more could have been saved!"

"We came back," pointed out a well dressed woman to the man.

He held her gaze before saying, "Eventually."

The woman looked away, aware that their return could have been earlier and many more could have been helped.

"You know Professor," said Mallory reading the old man's face, "I'm sure that Jazmine will be alright."

"Thank you," he replied.

"She managed to get on the ship against the odds, so I'm certain she would have ensured that she would have been able to get off too with the circumstances against her." Mallory continued trying to convince himself as much as his friend.

"Or she could be dead," taunted Otto, "her lifeless body floating in the sea, the fish starting to eat away at her!"

"Oh shut up you evil man," said a woman holding a small child close. "My husband is probably dead too! I don't want to think of him that way."

Otto looked around the boat and saw the angry faces looking at him, then, realising that he had gone too far, stopped. Carefully, he took his arm out of his sling and started to stretch it out to get the circulation going.

"I see your arm's looking much better," said the Professor. "What did you do to it?"

"Oh, just sprained my wrist," he replied without thinking.

"Hold on," said a voice accusingly, "I heard you say that your shoulder was broken! I was standing by you on deck when they tried to turn you away!"

Otto Von Braun turned to look at the woman. "I also sprained my wrist."

The woman stared at him. "You coward! You are not injured at all are you? You made it up to get on the lifeboat, while other good men stood by to let women and children go first."

"Madam, I can assure you that I am injured."

The woman leaned forward and grabbed him by the shoulder and shook it, caught off guard the Count failed to react.

"You monster!" she cried, "you evil monster!"

With the pretence exposed Otto just shrugged, and to the amazement of those around calmly took off the sling then started to fold it. "Well," he announced, "I am sure that I am not the only man to employ a little deviousness to survive, isn't that right?" The last remark was directed to a young man who started to look uncomfortable. "If I remember events correctly you jumped ship and climbed down the lowering cables."

"Damn it, the boat was half empty when it was launched!" he responded. "It didn't seem right." He looked down. "I was scared."

"And what about you eh *Miss*?" said Otto, turning round to single out one individual who quickly bowed their head to avoid the unwelcome attention. "You are one very ugly woman if I may be so bold, either that or a man in a dress!"

"Oh shut up you despicable man," said the woman getting angry. "I think what you did was far worse, making a scene, broadcasting the fact that you were injured to the whole world!"

"I don't see you complaining about those two," responded the count, pointing to Mallory and the Professor.

"We were pulled from an upturned lifeboat you son of a ...."

"Enough!" broke in one of the White Star crewmen pulling on the oar. "Things are bad enough without arguing like this! I don't care who got in the lifeboat, and what tricks they used to do so! There is still the small matter that we are adrift in the Atlantic, we are not out of trouble yet by any means!"

"But surely it's just a matter of waiting till we are picked up by a rescue boat?" asked someone.

For a moment the crewman looked uncomfortable, before reassuring the passengers that everything would be alright and that they would no doubt be rescued soon.

Picking up the man's uncertainty, Mallory looked over at the Professor, who looked glum, and leant over so no-one else could hear. "I am afraid that we are needles in the proverbial haystack. We have also no doubt moved from the position of where Titanic went down, which is where any rescue vessels will be making for. We are exposed in open sea at the mercy

397

of the currents, without food, and no means of communication. I'm afraid that it does not look good."

"No!" cried out Otto suddenly. Everyone looked at him as he hurriedly searched his pockets. He had decided to taunt the Professor and Mallory with the black scarab, but of course it was not there. "It's gone, it's gone and *you* must have taken it!" hissed the Count, his eyes finally settling on Richard Mallory.

"I'm surprised that you've only just found out," said the Professor, not even trying to hide the broad grin that was spreading across his face.

"I had other things on my mind at the time," said Otto through gritted teeth.

"Like scamming your way off the ship perchance?" added Mallory quickly.

"Alright, where is it?"

The Professor smiled. "The one place that we needed it to be!"

Elisabeth gasped, Otto's eyes narrowed, realising the implication; The Mummy had actually been defeated, placed into an eternal sleep, and was no doubt at the bottom of the sea. Despite the fact they already knew that their implement of death would be lost, at hearing the news, Otto could not help himself from lunging forward at Mallory, who seeing the attack rose up to meet it. The two men clashed and grappled, to the cries of alarm from those stunned passengers in the lifeboat, which started to rock with the sudden movement.

"Stop it you two!" yelled the White Star crewman. "Stop it!"

But still the two men continued to grapple with each other. Standing up, the crewman pulled the oar from the water, he knew there was only one way to separate the two men and the choice of target was not a difficult one.

The butt of the oar hit Otto firmly on the chin causing him to let go of Mallory with one hand, as he started to overbalance.

"Otto!" cried Elisabeth, but it was too late, for the Count, with no room in the small craft to move his feet to steady himself, fell over the side of the craft, still holding onto Mallory who was dragged after him.

As the boat started to tip, the occupants inside screamed out in terror, and instinctively lurched to the opposite side in an attempt to steady the small craft. As he fell, Otto somehow managed to throw out his arm and by sheer good fortune managed to grab onto the side of the craft. Mallory however, was not so lucky, finding himself plunged back into the icy Atlantic sea.

"Quick, do something!" cried the Professor leaning out to try and grab his friend.

"Get rid of that German," someone shouted.

"I'm Austro-Hungarian!" cried Otto as he clambered back into the boat, being helped solely by Elisabeth, while the other passengers deliberately held back.

"He's drifting away!" cried the Professor, trying to reach out to Mallory who was suddenly pulled back by a wave.

One of the men in the boat extended out an oar, but it was short, and then another wave took Mallory even further away.

"Swim for it man!" cried out the crewman, aware that they did not have the time to steer the boat around. "Swim for it, it's your only chance!"

Mallory started to swim, but only seemed to succeed in keeping himself from drifting away.

"Quick!" yelled the Professor. "I need all your belts and braces, now!"

The response from the men in the boat was quick, realising what the old man had in mind, the required items were produced. The Professor quickly tied them together using a variety of knots which were noticed by the seaman with professional admiration. Then he stood, and with one huge effort threw the line out towards Mallory.

"It's still short!" cried a woman seeing the line land into the water just out of Mallory's reach.

"I notice someone who didn't donate a belt!".

All eyes fell on Otto who, not wanting to aggravate anyone any further, silently removed his own leather belt which was then passed to the Professor, and added to the makeshift line before being cast out again.

The addition of Otto's belt made all the difference and Mallory was able to grab hold of the very end just as another wave threatened to drag him out even further beyond their reach.

With the help of some of the other men in the boat, Mallory was pulled back in and then hauled back onto the lifeboat like a stranded fish. Where upon he found himself wrapped up in coats donated by some of his fellow passengers.

Mallory fixed an angry gaze on Otto, and was about to say something when from the distance there was a yell.

Turning they could see a commotion in the furthest lifeboat. Some people in it were standing up, shouting and waving frantically. One of the crewmen had lifted an oar in the air and was moving it around as though there was a flag on the end.

"Look," said the Professor pointing into the far distance, "over there."

On the horizon was the unmistakable outline of a ship.

CHAPTER 69

With the large passenger liner in sight, the lifeboats started to head towards it, with the occupants inside realising that safety, and an end to their nightmare was at last in reach.

The ship, a Cunard passenger liner, on seeing the small flotilla, blasted its horn repeatedly to signal that they had been spotted, before slowly steering towards them. Although the lifeboats had done their best to stay together, they had inevitably drifted away from each other due to the waves and currents of the Atlantic, and it was to these outward fringes the Cunard headed first, picking up the survivors, then securing the empty lifeboats before making its way to the main group of boats which had managed to stay together.

"I once had to go there to do some research," said the Professor to Mallory pointing up to the name 'Carpathia' on the side of the ship that was now less than a few feet away.

"Ah yes," said Elisabeth, "I did hear about that. Tell me Professor, did you ever find Dracula?"

The old man's eyes narrowed and he was about to make a defensive remark about the adventure which had seen him nearly staked through the heart through suspicion of being a vampire, and Jazmine almost thrown off of the battlements of Bran Castle, when he was distracted by a familiar voice calling out to him.

"Father! Richard! Over here."

Both men turned around to see one of the nearby lifeboats that were slowly moving towards them and the ship, with a figure trying to stand up, waving, to attract their attention.

It was Jazmine Montacute.

Mallory and the Professor frantically waved back and shouted that they were alright, while Jazmine replied that she had nearly broken her ankle. However, realising that a continued conversation was not practical at this time, the

Professor pointed towards the Carpathia; indicating that they would meet up onboard.

"Thank God she's safe!" said the Professor sitting back down, a look of relief visible on his face.

"Yes, I'll echo that," added Mallory, who had secretly been convinced that she had been lost.

"Oh how sweet," goaded Otto, "the little whore survived!"

"I would shut up if I were you," said Mallory.

"Or what?" replied Otto, who was disappointed that Jazmine had not perished.

"*Oar* this!"

Suddenly the edge of an oar was placed firmly against the Count's throat, with a stern looking White Star man on the other end. "I've had just about enough of you. I'm going to make sure that everyone knows of the scam you pulled, and the way you attacked that man and pulled him over the side. That was nearly murder and you can swing for that!"

"But that's not how it happened," protested Otto. "I admit we were fighting, but you hit us with the oar!"

"Yeah and when you went over you made sure he went with you!" replied the crewman, "and there are witnesses! Now if another word passes your lips I'll smack you again."

Otto, fuming mad, but understanding that things could turn nasty, just nodded his head and remained silent. Elisabeth drew in close to her husband, and grabbed him protectively by the arm.

"Good," said the White Star man, "glad we understand each other." With that he returned the oar to the water.

One by one the group of lifeboats were slowly steered into position against the side of Carpathia, allowing the passengers to disembark, and to climb up the rope ladder that had been lowered down for them. The Von Brauns' lifeboat was the fifth from last to be guided into position, and one by one the still stunned and confused occupants climbed up the

402

ladder to the open doors in the side of the ship where the gangway was normally mounted. At the top they were helped aboard by the ship's crew and were immediately given a blanket and hot drinks by some of the ship's passengers who, hearing what was going on, had volunteered to help. Then the rescued people were separated out into three different groups, first and second class, third class and Titanic crew. The figure of a White Star crewman could be seen marshalling the crew members off to one side hurriedly.

The Von Brauns disappeared off as quickly as possible, hoping to be forgotten, while Mallory and the Professor opted to wait for Jazmine to board. She was in the next lifeboat which was being manoeuvred into position.

Jazmine, due to her damaged ankle was unable to climb the ladder, so, much to her annoyance, found herself being picked up and placed over the shoulder of a strapping Carpathia crewman, who ascended the ladder with little effort. Carefully she was deposited down and the crewman, with a polite nod and a wink, left her.

"Oh, thank goodness you are both alright!" she said throwing herself at Mallory, holding him tightly. She then moved to her father and held him fiercely, before moving back, slightly flushed, suddenly realising that she had instinctively gone to Mallory first. "Um, what about, you know, did it….?"

"Mummy's dead, gone for good! At the bottom of the sea by now, all things considered!" said the Professor with a smile.

"Oh, thank goodness for that!" she said smiling, before catching the gaze of a startled Carpathia passenger, who, overhearing the conversation, thought that her happiness was due to her actual Mother being lost in the disaster. The woman quickly turned away, focusing upon a little girl who was clutching three small kittens, one tabby, one black and white and the third ginger.

"Right then," said the Professor with fatherly concern, "we need to get that ankle attended to properly and catch up as to what happened."

The Professor turned round trying to work out where they should go when a crewman quickly approached them. "You there! Miss, over here! All White Star crew are to immediately muster over in the forecastle for a briefing."

"But she needs medical attention," protested Mallory.

"More to the point," said the Professor quickly, "she is not crew but my daughter."

"I hardly think that's possible," replied the man.

"She's crew, a stewardess."

"No I'm a passenger," lied Jazmine quickly, not wanting to be separated from Mallory or her father. "You must be mistaken."

"I recognise you as crew and you are wearing a jacket belonging to one of the band."

"One of them gave it to me to keep warm," said Jazmine truthfully.

"Look, you are crew, you have got to go over there." He pointed to the group of White Star staff, who had quickly been identified and moved away from the surviving passengers. The crewman was about to reach out and grab Jazmine by the arm. He was stopped by a cutting voice.

"What's going on here?"

Everyone turned to see the familiar face of Maggie Brown.

"Nothing," replied the crewman, "except a stewardess trying to pass herself off as first class."

"But she *is* first class," said Maggie without a second's hesitation.

"Not you as well?" said the man. "She is a stewardess. I've seen her dishing out breakfast, attending to passengers and the like!"

"Are you calling me a liar?" replied Maggie quickly, with a hint of anger in her tone.

"Well of course not," replied the crewman quickly, "it's just that you must be taking her for someone else."

"Oh I can assure you that I am rarely mistaken; this woman is no more crew than I am," said Maggie sternly. She then noticed a familiar figure that would be able to help her. "Bruce! Bruce! Mr Ismay!"

They all turned to see the hunched figure of Bruce Ismay, wrapped in a blanket and slowly being helped away by a man, who they presumed by the uniform and black bag he was carrying, was in fact the Carpathia's doctor. Ismay briefly looked round to see who had called, but it was clear that, at the moment at least, he was not going to be of any help. He was as white as a sheet and had a vacant far off look in his eyes. The doctor leant forward, spoke to him and then continued to help him away.

"Sorry, but I don't think he's going to help you," said the crewman, before turning back to Jazmine. He was about to speak again but Maggie reached forward and grabbing Jazmine by the hand, pulled her away. "I am not putting up with another word of this codswallop! Jazmine, you, your father and Mr Mallory are coming with me."

"Hey, you can't do that!"

"I can and I will!" growled Maggie, "unless of course you are going to try and stop me."

The crewman looked at Maggie and realising that he was not going to get anywhere with this overbearing woman, he waved them away. "Oh go on then, do what you like!"

"I usually do!" replied Maggie with a look of grim resolve on her face. "You there!" She signalled to a Cunard officer

405

who, holding the lead of a large Irish Wolfhound, had been keeping his eye on the events from afar, but had decided that it would be far wiser not to get directly involved, rather staying back at a safe distance. "I need your help. We need a cabin or cabins at once."

Not wanting to take on this woman, the man nodded, passed the dog to another member of crew and signalled them to follow him.

CHAPTER 70

Due to the fact that the Carpathia already had passengers aboard, and that they of course had not been expecting to become a rescue ship, spare cabins were not freely available. However, the Cunard Officer did manage to find two twin rooms next to each other with an interconnecting door between. So it was decided that Mallory and the Professor would have one, while Jazmine would share the other with Maggie. The Cunard officer left them, explaining that a meal would be provided and that some fresh clothes would be brought to them, but might take a while. With that, the man nodded and left them in one of the twin rooms.

Once alone they sat down in the room, which was noticeably Spartan compared to that of Titanic. The Professor, Mallory and Jazmine exchanged accounts of their individual stories which led them to escape from Titanic.

"So the creature, the Mummy, is it dead?" asked Maggie, scarcely believing the stories that she had been told.

"As good as," said the Professor. "The scarab has rendered it into a state of suspended animation, and after the ship broke up the way it did, I'm sure it's at the bottom of the sea by now."

"Well from what you said, that's where you should be too," said Maggie, "but you're here."

"'And the sea always gives up its dead,'" quoted Mallory. "That's what a friend of mine in the navy said. Is it possible that the Mummy could be washed up somewhere at some point?"

"Well, yes," conceded the Professor. "I'm sure that the sea will be throwing bodies from this for months to come, but I doubt our friend will be among them."

"Oh don't sound so glib Professor," scolded Maggie. "These are people we are talking about, and from what you were saying you were very nearly among them!"

"I'm sorry," he replied, almost sheepishly.

"But what happens if the Mummy does wash up somewhere?" pressed Mallory. "What do we do?"

The Professor shrugged. "I don't think that there is much that we can do. I doubt that we will even get to hear about it. At best they will just take one look at the body, and remember, there are no personal effects on it, and due to the damage there would be; the head almost severed, severely burnt and being in the water; well on seeing the state of it I'm sure they will just bury it without too much of an investigation."

"But what if this scarab somehow falls out?" asked Maggie. "Won't the, the thing come back to life?"

"Well, um yes, it would," confirmed the Professor, "but Mallory inserted it deep into the chest. I don't think that it will just work its way loose! As far as I am concerned the Mummy is gone. Well that one anyway. We have no idea how many others have been created all over the world and are wandering around causing chaos!"

"But what of the Von Brauns?" asked Jazmine. "The Titanic's Mummy may be gone, but they are certainly still around and are bound to be up to no good, even though they have been denied the creature."

"Very true," said the Professor. "I'm sure that they will make contact with their masters as soon as they can."

"The Carpathia's wireless," said Jazmine. "I could go and have a chat with Harold Bride, the Titanic's wireless operator. I'm sure I could persuade him to keep an eye out in the radio room and to ensure that any message by the Von Brauns is not sent."

"Well that is one option open to them," said the Professor.

"It's the only option!" said Maggie.

The Professor shrugged. "I'm not so sure. We have already seen Elisabeth use supernatural forces in the shape of those stone tablets. I think it is safe to assume that they will be able to make contact with their masters one way or another."

"So what is our next move?" asked Mallory.

"Well," said the Professor, "I'm afraid that so far we have nothing directly on the Von Brauns at all, but let us not forget that we do have their confession, the one made regarding the murder of Lord Rainsbury."

"Maybe so," said Mallory, "but the murderer is a 4000 year old Egyptian Mummy which is at the bottom of the sea. I hardly think that the police are going to be able to make an arrest, more likely we would end up locked in a padded cell for the accusation."

"Ah, but you forget," said the Professor. "The Mummy did not act alone! He was acting on the orders of that Ahmed chap, who Otto let slip was their London contact. If he is brought to justice it is very likely that he can be used to implicate the Von Brauns themselves.

"True," agreed Mallory.

"I think," continued the Professor, "that with a carefully worded telegram, things can be set in motion to bring some sort of justice."

"A good idea," said Mallory. "I really need to give some kind of report to Oldfield & Harper too."

The Professor nodded in agreement. "Now, when we do arrive in New York we still need to keep close to the Von Brauns. Even without the Mummy they may still be up to something and we have all experienced first hand that they are most dangerous."

Mallory and Jazmine nodded in agreement.

"My statue!" cried Maggie, suddenly producing the small green figure from her coat pocket. "I had forgotten all about it." She then explained how it had changed colour and had, in effect, led her to safety.

"I have heard stories of such statues," said the Professor thoughtfully. "Enchanted to keep the owner safe from harm. No wonder the Von Brauns were after it."

"Oh my goodness!" said Maggie. "What if they realise that I still have it and it's here on the ship? They might come after me and try and steal it!"

"We could use it as bait," said Jazmine suddenly, her eyes lighting up. "Set a trap and lure them into stealing it!"

But the Professor shook his head. "I'm not sure after what's happened that they would dare to attempt anything. Anyway I think that after everything we have been through, a few days quiet would do us all good."

Maggie looked down at the statue. "I'm not sure that I want it now, I think my interest in Egyptology is wavering."

Then there was a knock at the door, before it was thrown open, and in walked a tall serious looking man.

"And who do you think you are bursting into a ladies room like this?" asked Maggie.

"Captain Arthur Rostron," was the simple reply.

"Oh!" said Maggie, noticing the stripes on his uniform for the first time. "Well if this is about the girl, I can assure you…"

409

"No, it's not about the girl. It's about him," said Rostron, as he indicated over to Mallory.

"Me?" said Mallory in surprise.

The Captain nodded. "I have received a report that you shot a man with a flare gun on Titanic, and there was some trouble in the lifeboat. What's going on?"

"Let me handle this," said the Professor. "The man who he shot was actually an ancient Egyptian Mummy brought back to life, and used aboard Titanic by an unscrupulous couple called the Von Brauns. It was Otto Von Braun who Mr Mallory fought with in the lifeboat."

"And by the sounds of things nearly came off worse," said Rostron smiling slightly.

"Yes, but fortunately it was through the Professor's quick actions that saved me," said Mallory, who was taken aback by how much information the Professor had provided.

"Yes, well, old Charlie boy here has a habit of thinking on his feet like that."

The Professor winced. "I wish you wouldn't call me that Arthur, you know I can't stand it!"

"You two know each other?" said Maggie, also suddenly realising Rostron's lack of reaction on hearing such a fantastic story.

The Carpathia's captain nodded. "Yes, we are old friends, met back in '05, in the Russo-Japanese war when I was serving with the Naval Reserve. I ended up giving Charlie here a lift out of trouble, seems that some things never change, eh!"

"Yes, and as usual I am very grateful!"

"And by the sound of things, still up to your neck in trouble of one sort or another."

"More than you could ever know!"

"These Von Brauns," said Rostron. "Want me to do anything?"

410

"No, but thank you Arthur," said the Professor. "I think that we can handle things from here, although in truth there is not too much we can do at the moment."

"Very well then." He paused. "I'd better get going, as you can guess it's going to be a busy day for me! We are going to make one more sweep of the area to check that there is no-one left, and then head straight for New York. I trust you all will be able to meet me this evening for dinner?"

"We had nothing else planned!" said Maggie with a slight smile.

Captain Rostron nodded and then started to leave.

"But what about me?" asked Mallory.

Rostron paused and smiled. "You? Oh yes, well you are clearly not the man that I was looking for! See you all later!" and with that he left.

"That was fortunate!" said Mallory. "I thought for a moment there I was going to end up in the brig!"

"Well you might have done if it was not for that stroke of luck, me knowing Rostron," said the Professor.

"Right then! I wonder what the room service is like here! I don't know about the rest of you, but I could do with a drink, nearly dying really makes you thirsty!"

CHAPTER 71

Back in London, Ahmed Hawass hung back slightly allowing the photographer to take his picture. A large crowd had gathered outside the Oceanic House, the headquarters of White Star Line, all desperate for information. Ahmed's eye fell upon the subject of the photographer, a young boy, a paper seller with a bundle of papers tucked under one arm. In his hand he was holding a sheet sign with the large words printed upon it 'Titanic disaster – Great loss of life.'

A chill ran down Ahmed's spine, and a flurry of questions filled his mind. What had happened to the Von Brauns? What had happened to the Mummy? What of the items that the Von Brauns were aiming to retrieve – were they at the bottom of the Atlantic?

With the picture taken, Ahmed moved to the boy and bought his copy of The Evening News, then moved off to read it, but there was nothing in it that he did not already know from the other news and reports. So, thrusting the newspaper aside into the hands of an elderly gent, he moved over to the large double doors of Oceanic House itself, where a list of survivors had been placed. Fighting his way through the throng he managed to get a look at the names. It did not take him long to spot the distinctive format of the Von Brauns' name. Otto and Elisabeth were safe, but there were still many unanswered questions that would have to be addressed. Still, all would become clear in time. By now his New York counterpart would have realised too that the Von Brauns were safe, and would no doubt be putting his own plans into operation.

Then two more names on the list suddenly jumped out at him.

Montacute, J Miss

Montacute, C J Prof

He let out a genuine cry of surprise.

Charles and Jazmine Montacute were on the ship too!

This no doubt meant that they had been onto the Von Brauns from the start of the trip, and would not have left them unhindered. It seemed the journey to New York had turned out to be more eventful than he could possibly have envisaged.

Realising that nothing more could be gained, he moved off into the street and hailed a Hansom cab, for he had other things on his mind; the disposal of the body of Lord Rainsbury.

A modern version of the ancient Egyptian embalming had taken place on the corpse. The internal organs had been removed, and as a final insult, were disposed of by having them mashed into a bloody pulp, then fed to stray dogs. Then, using linen made in Egypt some three weeks ago, but specially treated to look, feel and smell old, the remains of the body of Lord Rainsbury had been carefully wrapped to create a Mummy. It was a far cry from the plans of a burial in the family vault which Sir Thomas had planned in anticipation of his eventual demise.

Ahmed had been more than pleased with the results of the Rainsbury Mummy. Even an expert would be fooled by the results, and this fact had already been proven with other such new creations. In the British Museum there was a Mummy on display on the fourth floor nearest the west entrance labelled: 'Unknown Egyptian Mummy 25th Dynasty', but Ahmed knew that it was one of his, created just four years before, the body of a British government official who had stumbled upon his operation, and had to be disposed of. The Rainsbury Mummy, however, had a much different fate ahead of it. Bizarrely there was always a strong market for Egyptian Mummies. Many ended up in museums, while some found their way to private collectors who were prepared to pay very large sums of money for them. Ahmed had been approached by two men who wanted to use the Mummy to exhibit in their 'Chamber of Forbidden Horrors', a tourist attraction on the south coast. The required checks had been made and it was decided that the two men were legitimate in their request, and so a meeting had been arranged.

Eventually the Hansom arrived at its destination, a small restaurant which was used by Ahmed as a 'safe' meeting

413

place away from the Embassy where various meetings and business deals could be carried out.

The restaurant was closed, but Ahmed rapped upon the door, and after a few moments the owner appeared and opened it greeting him warmly.

"Greetings, Ahmed."

"Greetings, Mustapha. Did the Mummy arrive alright?"

"Yes, it is in the back room ready for viewing."

"Good," said Ahmed. "Take me to him."

Mustapha nodded, then led Ahmed to the back room. The Rainsbury Mummy had been placed on a table and covered with a simple white sheet. Beside it, standing up on its end, but placed out of the way, was the long crate that had been used to transport the Mummy to its present location. Ahmed moved to the table and lifted the top half of the sheet and looked down at it.

It was a masterpiece, totally indistinguishable from the genuine article.

Ahmed smiled to himself, inwardly congratulating himself on the setup he had created. It was a flawless system, one that was so ironic, as not only did it create funds for the cause, but was the ultimate revenge on those people who had to be dealt with for their crimes against Egyptian heritage. The Rainsbury Mummy was to be the eleventh one that he had created and sold. His superiors in Cairo were going to be very pleased with his efforts.

"They are here," called a voice.

Ahmed and Mustapha turned to the doorway where a young man, a worker in the restaurant, was standing. "Do you want me to show them through?"

Ahmed replaced the sheet and nodded.

A short while later the man returned with the two visitors in tow, before disappearing back to his duties. The two men's attention was automatically drawn to the shrouded figure on the table.

"Is that it?" asked the larger man, almost in awe.

Ahmed nodded silently.

"Oh, you must forgive my rudeness!" the large man said. "I was just taken aback with actually being so close to the item that I've been after and thought beyond my reach. My name is Ben Wildman and this is my colleague and co-owner of my business, Harold Doyle."

Ahmed nodded in response. "A pleasure to meet you both. But, let us not waste any time with idle chit chat. Let us get down to the matter in hand." Ahmed then moved back to the Rainsbury Mummy and carefully took off the sheet, dropping it to one side.

Wildman and Doyle looked down at the Mummy in a mixture of surprise and awe, before Wildman finally was able to speak. "Amazing, just as I imagined it would be. Do you know who he was?"

"No," Ahmed lied, "the Mummy was found just outside Luxor, taken from an unmarked tomb. It is suspected that it was a lesser nobleman, but it is certainly from no earlier than the 28th Dynasty. However, for your purposes it will serve you well."

Wildman nodded. "The price is high though, a thousand pounds. Is there any room for negotiation?"

"None," said Ahmed firmly, "there is a degree of difficulty in acquiring such an item. Transportation costs have to be paid and officials have to be persuaded to look the other way at the right time." That of course was a lie, the Mummy had never been out of London since its creation, but his customers would not know that. Ahmed then reached into his pocket and produced a small bundle of papers which he held up. "The price also includes these."

"What are they?"

"Forged documents," was the reply, "including proof of legal ownership, and officially stamped licences allowing you to take the Mummy from Egypt." These documents were always included with a sale of a Mummy. Invariably, at some point in the future, someone will ask if the Mummy was acquired legally, and want to see the relevant paperwork. This also served as a method of deflecting attention away from himself.

Wildman turned to look at his friend who nodded. He then took out a large bundle of bank notes from his pocket. "Five hundred now and the rest once we have arranged for transport."

Ahmed nodded. This was the usual way the transaction proceeded. Reaching out he took the money, and with the other hand gave over the forged documents. "Gentlemen, may I congratulate you on such a good purchase. But I must ask you not to take too long in its removal."

"Oh we won't," said Wildman.

Then before Ahmed knew what was happening Wildman produced a small whistle, placed it to his lips and blew it hard. Moments later the door to the room flew open and in came five uniformed officers of the Metropolitan Police Force, who quickly grabbed the surprised Ahmed before he could react.

Wildman stepped forward. "Let me introduce myself properly. My name is Detective Inspector Benjamin Wilder, and I arrest you for the suspected murder of Lord Thomas Rainsbury."

"What!"

"I have strong reason to believe that you were involved in the murder of Lord Rainsbury and that you have just tried to sell me his body in the guise of an Egyptian Mummy."

"You cannot arrest me!" protested Ahmed. "I am a diplomat. I will claim diplomatic immunity."

416

"Thought you might say that," said Doyle reaching inside his pocket and producing a sealed letter, "but this solves that little issue. It is a telegram confirming the termination of your position with the Egyptian Embassy, authorised yesterday in Cairo. Seems that the authorities you work for are suddenly eager to sever all ties with you."

"No, no you are lying!"

Wilder smiled and looked over at the Mummy. "You have gotten yourself in a lot of trouble Mr Hawass and there is no-one for you to turn to."

Ahmed shook his head. "No, no, it was not me who killed Lord Rainsbury. It was......" his voice trailed off realising that he could not tell the truth.

Wilder stepped forward, and in a low voice that only Ahmed could hear. "I know the truth about you and the creature that you control. I received a lengthy telegram from my contact. It's not possible to have a resurrected Mummy stand trial, particularly one at the bottom of the Atlantic, so I will have to make do with you. I've got more than enough to see you swing for this."

"I will co-operate with you fully," said Ahmed, suddenly changing tack. "I will give you all the information I have about my activities. We can make a deal!"

"A wise choice," replied the Inspector, although he knew that it would make no real difference to Ahmed's fate. "And I advise you pay particular attention to your association with Otto and Elisabeth Von Braun."

Ahmed turned to look Wilder in the eye and smiled. "Who?"

Wilder held his gaze, realising that despite being betrayed by his own people, Ahmed, through reasons that he would never likely know, would not deliver the Von Brauns to him. "Right lads!" he said turning, "take him away, and let's get Lord Rainsbury here seen to."

417

CHAPTER 72

Back on the Carpathia, after careful consideration, Maggie Brown decided to get rid of her green statue, despite the fact it had saved her. She presented it to Captain Rostron as a personal thank you for rescuing, not only her, but the other survivors. Captain Rostron took it and had it locked in his personal safe. A statue of this kind, to a Captain, which could warn the owner of potential danger, would help to keep his ship and, by extension, its passengers safe.

For the remainder of the voyage to New York, there was no sign of the Von Brauns, with the spreading controversy of the way Otto had managed to gain access to a lifeboat and his behaviour towards Mallory, they kept themselves out of everyone's way. Opting to stay the entire journey in their cabin, only venturing out at night when sure that there was no-one around. This allowed the Professor, Jazmine and Mallory to actually spend some time together, to rest and in part get over their trip on Titanic. Mallory was even able to arrange a few weeks leave with Oldfield and Harper, who were more than happy to let him have the time off after all his hard work.

On Thursday, 18th April the Carpathia arrived back in New York. Its first stop was Pier 59, where it dropped off the Titanic's lifeboats, before heading the short distance to Pier 54, where it was to finally berth.

"My goodness!" commented Maggie, looking out at the waiting throng from the deck as they waited for the Carpathia to be tied off and the gangways lowered. "Look at them all!"

"The events of Titanic are causing massive shockwaves around the world," commented Jazmine. "I was speaking to Harold."

"The wireless man?" asked Maggie.

Jazmine nodded. "Yes, and he told me, from what he had heard via the wireless that it was in all the papers, and plans for an enquiry are already in motion."

"Hardly surprising," said the Professor. "There was a tremendous loss of life on a brand new ship that was not ever supposed to sink! I'm sure that this story is going to run and run, I would not be surprised if people are still talking about this in fifty years time!"

"But there have been other shipping disasters before," said Mallory. "And I hate to say it, but there will be more to come."

"Agreed," replied the Professor thoughtfully, "but I have a feeling that Titanic will be the one that will be remembered and talked about."

"Professor," said Mallory, "look over there, the Von Brauns."

Everyone looked to where Mallory had indicated, and there was Elisabeth and Otto, fighting their way back through the people that had gathered on the Carpathia's deck.

"Well we all know where they are heading," said the Professor. "Down to the gangway to get off the ship as soon as possible."

"Right then," said Mallory. "If we are going to catch up with them we best get moving."

"Father, look!" exclaimed Jazmine, suddenly pointing.

The Professor looked to see a number of uniformed men approaching, looking around intently for someone.

"I have a feeling that I am wanted!" said Jazmine.

"Yes," replied the Professor. "I heard that all members of Titanic's crew, or what was left of them are going to be kept separate, seems that the powers that be do not want them talking to the press, or anyone official come to that, regarding what happened."

419

"We'd better get moving then," said Mallory. "Jazmine, can your ankle cope with a bit of a run?"

She coyly smiled. "I think so, although I might need to lean on you a bit!"

Mallory nodded, trying to hide a blush.

"Come on!" urged the Professor, missing the exchange, "they're getting closer."

"Oh don't worry about that!" said Maggie, "I'll handle them." She then nodded goodbye to Jazmine and Mallory before turning to address the Professor directly. "Charles, it has been a pleasure, and do not forget your promise to take me and my husband for tea at the Ritz. I shall be in touch shortly!" Before he could respond she turned and headed over to the men, ready to make a scene to allow them all to get away.

With Maggie causing a distraction, the Professor, Mallory and Jazmine were able to slip away, heading off the main deck, to make their way to the main gangway which they quickly descended to find themselves on the New York dockside, surrounded by the world's press, and a throng of people who were waiting to see the survivors of the disaster.

"There they are!" said Mallory pointing to the Von Brauns who had disappeared into the terminal building.

"I see them!" cried the Professor. "Come on! Don't let them get away!"

A photographer moved forward to try and take a picture, blocking Mallory's way, but soon found himself pushed aside as the three moved past. By now the Von Brauns had virtually crossed the open space of the large terminal building, and were on the other side heading out to the street beyond.

"They are going to get away!" cried Mallory.

"Then move faster!" cried the Professor trying to put on an extra burst of speed, aiming towards the exit.

"I would if my ankle was not still hurting!" retorted Jazmine, doing her best to keep up.

The Professor burst out of the exit door onto the street beyond, with Mallory and Jazmine just behind; he looked around fearing that the Von Brauns would be gone, but instead they were just standing on the sidewalk, out of breath.

"Otto! Elisabeth!" roared the Professor as he caught up with them. "You cannot escape me!"

"Oh, I think that I can!" replied Otto sneering. Then immediately from around the corner there was a screech of tyres, and a blue Model T Ford, with black fenders, driven by a large mean looking man, came into view and pulled up sharply beside them. The back door of the car flew open and out emerged a tall, olive skinned man dressed in a dark suit and wearing a red fez. Down the side of his face was a long scar. "Ah, Professor Charles Montacute and his delightful, if not wilful, daughter Jazmine." He turned slightly. "And you must be Captain Richard Mallory, a pleasure. I have heard so much about you!"

"You have the advantage," replied Mallory to the newcomer.

"He is Abdul Taha," announced the Professor. "A rather unsavoury character, who has tried to kill me on no less than three occasions."

"Two," replied Abdul calmly. "Professional pride will not allow me to count that pot shot I took of you last summer in the Alps. Anyway, never mind that, there is no time to waste." He turned to the Von Brauns. "I have your papers all ready; your ship leaves in less than half an hour. You are heading back to England."

"What?" cried Elisabeth, "but we have our mission here in New York!"

"Not any more," replied Abdul. "Due to the events that have taken place, our masters have decided that you need to be recalled. Oh but don't worry, it's only for a short time. You'll soon be back on active service." He motioned to them to get in the car. Otto nodded and turned to the Professor, Mallory and Jazmine. He smiled, and clicked his feet together. "Until next time, my dear Professor." With that he, followed by Elisabeth, disappeared into the back of the car.

"Well I must bid you goodbye for now," said Abdul. "I hope that you have a safe, uneventful journey home." With that he climbed in the front passenger seat and the Ford began to move off at speed, the tyres screeching, and the smell of burning rubber filling the air.

Jazmine moved forward to the kerbside and lifted her arm, calling out for a cab, ready to continue the pursuit, but she felt her arm being grabbed by her father who shook his head. "I don't think we are in any condition to go chasing them back across the Atlantic." He laughed. "For one thing all our clothes, possessions and money went down with Titanic."

"But they are going to get away!" she protested.

"Oh, don't you worry yourself about that," said the Professor. "We'll catch up with the Von Brauns another time, only, not today."

"So what next?" asked Mallory.

"Back to the White Star offices," replied the Professor. "I'm sure that they will be able to offer us some help, or at least some money so we can sort ourselves out."

"You know," said Mallory, "I've always wanted to take a look around New York, perhaps we could take in some of the sights?" He looked over at Jazmine hopefully, who nodded slightly in response.

"Actually," said the Professor, stroking his beard thoughtfully, "I was thinking we could take the opportunity to take a trip and look up Dr Tumblety."

"A friend of yours?" asked Mallory.

422

The Professor shook his head. "No, never met the man, in fact he's dead."

"Ah," replied Mallory sympathetically.

"Oh no, don't get me wrong," said the Professor quickly, "my interest in him is purely an historical one."

"How so?" asked Mallory, starting to wonder if he was going to be dragged into some other adventure.

"Well you know the Whitechapel murders, Jack the Ripper and all that, which took place thirty years ago?"

"Yes, who doesn't?"

"Well, not many people know that he was actually a credible suspect. He fled here to America, and just afterwards the murders stopped, but no one has followed his trail and took it any further. I'm certain that there must be the chance of picking up some interesting information."

Richard Mallory found himself looking over at Jazmine, who was smiling excitedly at the thought, and before he realised it, found himself saying, "Sounds great, where do we start?"

EPILOGUE

Some time in the very near future..........

Victoria Mallory sat in the audience of the small television studio; her eyes firmly fixed on the stage in front of her. Overhead was a large screen showing the long abandoned Harland and Wolff drawing rooms, which now had been turned into a studio, and was the main location of this 24 hour 'Titanic Special' which was being broadcast live across the globe.

Below the suspended television, was TV presenter Gail Anne-Moore, who was looking over at her Floor Manager, waiting for the signal they were going live. The rest of the set had been kitted out to look like a hospital mortuary, complete with a dissection table on which was a covered body. It was this body which Victoria, or Vicky as she preferred to be called, was interested in.

Vicky had originally been invited to be in the main studio in Belfast, in her capacity as an Historian, and the fact her Grandfather Richard Mallory, her Grandmother Jazmine Mallory, nee Montacute and her Great Grandfather, Professor Charles Monacute had all been passengers on that fateful ship. However, realising the events which were going to take place in this small London studio, she declined, and insisted that she attend this 'break away' segment instead, which although going to be aired live, due to the nature of what was going to happen, was going to be an optional extra for the more 'hardy viewers'.

Vicky allowed her gaze to go back to the big overhanging screen, where the reporter, a man in a suit, with a picture of a large rigid airship, was finishing the current item before announcing the splitting of the programme. "......and so it seems that fate finally caught up with Otto and Elisabeth Von Braun; they may have been able to escape Titanic, but were not able to survive the R101."

Vicky smiled to herself – if only they knew the truth about what had gone on, on that airship! The adventure had seen her Grandfather and Great Grandfather again in pursuit of the Von Brauns, only this time it was to try and capture a secret map of the Paris catacombs which was said to lead to a secret treasure horde, left hidden by the Knights Templar. Mallory and the Professor survived the crash, and even managed to retrieve the map, only being thwarted by Templar descendants who ended up trapping them in a collapsed catacomb tunnel for days, while they themselves found and cleared out the hidden treasure.

With the link finished, explaining what was happening, the large overhead screen went blank and Gail Ann-Moore, with the signal from her Floor Manager, took over.

"Fascinating stuff! And welcome to all our viewers who are brave enough to tune in for this slightly gory, but none the less exciting, section of the show."

Gail stopped and turned to address a different camera.

"Now, immediately after the Titanic sank, thoughts turned to the recovery of the dead. Over the next six weeks 328 bodies were recovered. The rest were never found, their bodies, not having life jackets, were swallowed up by the sea and taken to a watery grave. Out of those bodies found, 119 of these were unrecognisable, and were buried at sea, while the remaining were brought back to Halifax where 59 were reclaimed by relatives, and repatriated to their own countries. The 150 remaining bodies were buried in three different cemeteries in Halifax."

She turned again, as the cameras switched.

"……and it is to the Fairview Lawn Cemetery that we now turn our attention. The final resting place for 121 victims of the disaster, and one body in particular. Now we are joined here by Dr Ray Walters, who headed the exciting work which brings us here today. Dr Walters, please tell us about your project at Fairview."

"Certainly," replied Dr Walters as, with a deep breath, he launched into his well-rehearsed response. "For many years there were a number of unconfirmed reports that there was one final unidentified Titanic body buried in the cemetery. This was verified a few years ago when a document was found giving further details. It stated that in late November 1912 an unidentified body was washed up in Halifax, caught up in wreckage that was clearly from Titanic. Now because of the poor condition of the corpse, it was clear that it was never going to be identified, so it was decided just to bury it at Fairview."

"The condition of the corpse, you mean from the time in the water?" asked Gail, pressing for the more accurate description they had gone through in rehearsal.

"No, not just that," replied Dr Walters, "the documents stated that the left hand, of what we ended up calling body 331, was missing, and it seems that the poor soul did not die from drowning or hyperthermia, but had perished as a result of fire, possibly being caught in an explosion. The document also said that the head was almost totally severed."

"Now tell us about the body's original burial."

"Well as you know, the Titanic bodies at Fairview were buried in one location. However, body 331 was not interred with the rest of them, but placed over in a separate grave. The reason for this is unknown, although the myth that grew up about the body was that it was cursed and had to be buried in a separate plot, a plot that was unmarked and soon became 'lost'. Now it was only with the finding of the document that we were able to find its exact location."

426

"And this has presented itself with an amazing opportunity hasn't it?" said Gail.

Dr Walters nodded, almost excitedly. "Yes, very much so. Some years ago, attempts were made to identify the body of an unknown baby. Part of this project involved digging up a number of the Titanic graves. In doing so it was discovered that many of the contents of the graves were no longer there, due to a rising water table below the ground which had basically destroyed what was there."

"But body number 331 was separate from this."

"Yes," confirmed Dr Walters, "it, like the surrounding graves, was totally untouched, being on higher ground. We gained permission for an exhumation, which was carried out just over a month ago."

"And what did you find?"

"More than we dared to expect. The simple wooden coffin was fully intact and when we looked inside, the body itself was still there and in a remarkable state of preserve. In fact from what we have documented, it is just the way it was when it was buried all those years ago."

Gail turned directly to the camera. "And that brings us up to the present day." She turned to look at the covered body, before turning back round to camera. "Other than a visual assessment of the body, and x-rays which were taken and promptly sealed in envelopes without examination, the mysterious body number 331 has not been tampered with or looked at in any real detail; until tonight, for live on television we are going to carry out, as much as we are able, an autopsy on body number 331 - the last body of the Titanic."

With that Dr Walters moved to the table, took hold of the sheet and dramatically pulled it back to reveal body No. 331, to the gasp of the audience.

Vicky stared transfixed at the sight of the body, which was lying with the right side towards the audience. She knew all

427

too well who this burnt, handless and nearly headless body was.

The adventure that her relatives had been through on the Titanic, all those years ago, had been told to her time and time again. First by Grandpa Richard and Grandma Jazmine as a child, and then after their passing, by her Mother and Father, who also knew all about the true history of the Titanic's maiden voyage to New York and the Von Brauns un-dead instrument - The Mummy. .

"Now Dr," Gail continued, "can you tell us what is about to happen?"

"Certainly. First we will make a visual inspection of the body before opening the sealed x-ray. This will give us an idea of where we shall start when we actually go into the body."

Vicky turned to the man beside her and whispered, "There, now you have the evidence in front of you, will you agree to act with me?"

The white haired man, in his late fifties, Professor David Upton, from the University of Liverpool, and lifelong friend to Vicky, paused and sucked air in through his teeth. "The body does match your story, but what you are asking of me puts me in an awkward position."

"Things are going to get a lot more 'awkward' if you don't let me act!" she replied.

"But are you totally sure what you say is true?"

"Professor Upton, you have read my Grandfather's private accounts and that of the hidden police files, both here in England and America, not to mention the surviving passenger statements."

He slowly nodded.

"It all fits!" She looked back at the stage. Dr Walters had in his hand one of the x-rays which was also being displayed on the screen.

"Well, what do you make of it?" asked Gail excitedly, leaning in towards Dr Walters.

"Well there does seem to be something there; here hold this." He passed her the x-ray before going back to look at the same spot on the body. "Looking closely I think that, yes, there does seem to be some kind of incision already made in the chest. I think the gap is big enough. Yes." With that he reached for what looked like a large pair of thin tweezers, before carefully inserting them into the hole. Then a few moments later he brought out the object which had been embedded deep in the chest and held it up for the cameras to see.

"This is absolutely amazing," said Gail. "It looks like a piece of jewellery, a scarab?"

"Look, the fingers!" whispered Vicky to the Professor with a real sense of urgency in her voice.

Professor Upton looked at the burnt fingers of the corpse. They were moving slightly, twitching, flexing. "By the gods Victoria, you are right!"

"Yes I know, with the black scarab removed, the creature is coming back to 'life'. Now hurry!"

Professor Upton reached into his pocket for the item which he had sneaked out of the Egyptian exhibit at the British Museum and handed it over. "At the very least, Victoria, get me the black scarab as a consolation!"

She nodded in response.

Suddenly from the stage there was a loud moan, seemingly from the corpse itself, causing Gail and Dr Walters to jump back in surprise, then, to the sheer horror of the audience, the corpse actually started to move, slowly trying to raise itself up onto its elbows.

By now Vicky Mallory was on her feet, carefully running down the steps, her eyes fixed firmly towards the stage. In her left hand she carried a double edged long dagger, which had been concealed in her sleeve, while in her right hand she held the object given to her a few moments earlier by Professor Upton – a gold chain, on the end of which was an ancient red scarab beetle...........